"Tony Hillerman calls M[...]
It is no wonder. [She] b[...]
frontier in a way that h[...]

"Now widely considered the most accomplished heir to Tony
Hillerman's legacy." —Scripps Howard News Service

"A great storyteller." —*The Daily Oklahoman*

"Filled with color and depth, authenticity and richness,
Coel's writing brings the reservation community alive."
—*Ventura County (CA) Star*

*Praise for Margaret Coel's
Wind River Reservation Mysteries*

THE GIRL WITH BRAIDED HAIR

"Margaret Coel continues her winning streak with *The
Girl with Braided Hair* . . . Her narrative grabs the reader
from the first page." —*The Denver Post*

"Engaging . . . Bringing her trademark Western flair to
nonstop action, Coel keeps danger hanging over Vicky's
head as she follows a trail of clues to their startling conclusion." —*Publishers Weekly*

"Coel continues to combine full-bodied characters, vivid
landscapes, and snappy dialogue, and she builds suspense
effectively . . . This series, with its expert use of Western
settings and Native American themes, remains among the
best read-alikes for Tony Hillerman fans." —*Booklist*

"There is a wealth of background on native customs, past
and present, and the descriptions are real and poignant . . .
Descriptions of the West and the Plains are vivid. The novel
is a welcome addition to the series. Highly recommended."
—*CrimeSpree Magazine*

"Another wonderfully evocative story of the struggles of
the Arapaho to retain their heritage while living in a white
man's world." —*Kirkus Reviews*

continued . . .

"What Tony Hillerman has done for the Navajo, Margaret Coel has done for the Arapaho."

—Futures Mystery Anthology Magazine

"Ms. Coel brings to life both modern-day and the turbulent '70s reservation life. Readers will be drawn to the plight of the Native Americans both then and now . . . *The Girl with Braided Hair* will stay with you long after reading the final line."

—Fresh Fiction

"The author shows her expertise yet again . . . Coel weaves a compelling tale with very human characters . . . [She] has an impressive background in native history as well as the talent to bring her characters to life . . . An engrossing read." *—BookLoons*

"Coel never ceases to enthrall readers in her captivating stories. Her latest is no exception as her rich, evocative characters solve a mystery that's more than thirty years old." *—Romantic Times*

THE DROWNING MAN

"An accomplished writer, Coel chronicles her terrain with fresh depictions . . . Best of all is the deep character development she embeds in the plot . . . Coel plays it out with a flair for deep-seated human drama. Think shades of Chekov on a Wyoming rez."

—The Santa Fe New Mexican

EYE OF THE WOLF
Winner of the Colorado Book Award for Popular Fiction

"A winning combination of interesting and complex characters, fascinating settings . . . and great atmosphere."

—The Denver Post

WIFE OF MOON
Winner of the Colorado Book Award for Popular Fiction

"The research and historical attributes are native to [Coel's] writing. Historical events here spawn fiction, and ever so naturally."

—The Denver Post

KILLING RAVEN

"Coel's fans will find this book satisfying."

—*Rocky Mountain News*

THE SHADOW DANCER

"Coel not only presents a vivid and authentic picture of the Native American, past and present, but also captures the rugged and majestic atmosphere of Wyoming." —*Publishers Weekly*

THE THUNDER KEEPER

"Coel has obvious respect for the land and people who populate it . . . She creates dense and compelling characters in complex stories to entertain her loyal fans." —*The Denver Post*

THE SPIRIT WOMAN

Winner of the Colorado Book Award for Popular Fiction

"Intriguing Arapaho and Shoshone history and realistic treatment of contemporary Native American issues . . . A winner."

—*Library Journal*

THE LOST BIRD

"Engrossing . . . Enjoyable characters and a super mystery."

—*The Literary Times*

THE STORY TELLER

"One of the best of the year." —*Booklist* (starred review)

THE DREAM STALKER

"Seamless storytelling by someone who's obviously been there."

—J. A. Jance

THE GHOST WALKER

"Coel is a vivid voice for the West." —*The Dallas Morning News*

THE EAGLE CATCHER

"She's a master." —Tony Hillerman

Berkley Prime Crime titles by Margaret Coel

BLOOD MEMORY

Wind River Reservation Mysteries

THE EAGLE CATCHER

THE GHOST WALKER

THE DREAM STALKER

THE STORY TELLER

THE LOST BIRD

THE SPIRIT WOMAN

THE THUNDER KEEPER

THE SHADOW DANCER

KILLING RAVEN

WIFE OF MOON

EYE OF THE WOLF

THE DROWNING MAN

THE GIRL WITH BRAIDED HAIR

THE
GIRL WITH
BRAIDED HAIR

MARGARET COEL

BERKLEY PRIME CRIME, NEW YORK

THE BERKLEY PUBLISHING GROUP
Published by the Penguin Group
Penguin Group (USA) Inc.
375 Hudson Street, New York, New York 10014, USA
Penguin Group (Canada), 90 Eglinton Avenue East, Suite 700, Toronto, Ontario M4P 2Y3, Canada
(a division of Pearson Penguin Canada Inc.)
Penguin Books Ltd., 80 Strand, London WC2R 0RL, England
Penguin Group Ireland, 25 St. Stephen's Green, Dublin 2, Ireland (a division of Penguin Books Ltd.)
Penguin Group (Australia), 250 Camberwell Road, Camberwell, Victoria 3124, Australia
(a division of Pearson Australia Group Pty. Ltd.)
Penguin Books India Pvt. Ltd., 11 Community Centre, Panchsheel Park, New Delhi—110 017, India
Penguin Group (NZ), 67 Apollo Drive, Rosedale, North Shore 0632, New Zealand
(a division of Pearson New Zealand Ltd.)
Penguin Books (South Africa) (Pty.) Ltd., 24 Sturdee Avenue, Rosebank, Johannesburg 2196,
South Africa

Penguin Books Ltd., Registered Offices: 80 Strand, London WC2R 0RL, England

THE GIRL WITH BRAIDED HAIR

A Berkley Prime Crime Book / published by arrangement with the author

PRINTING HISTORY
Berkley Prime Crime hardcover edition / September 2007
Berkley Prime Crime mass-market edition / September 2008

Copyright © 2007 by Margaret Coel.
Excerpt from *Blood Memory* copyright © 2008 by Margaret Coel.
Cover art by Tony Greco & Associates.
Cover design by Lesley Worrell.

ISBN: 978-0-425-22327-7

BERKLEY® PRIME CRIME
Berkley Prime Crime Books are published by The Berkley Publishing Group,
a division of Penguin Group (USA) Inc.,
375 Hudson Street, New York, New York 10014.
The name BERKLEY PRIME CRIME and the BERKLEY PRIME CRIME design
are trademarks belonging to Penguin Group (USA) Inc.

PRINTED IN THE UNITED STATES OF AMERICA

10 9 8 7 6 5 4 3 2 1

This is for Lillian Hope Harrison

Wó:ukohéi hó:kecóúhú hi´seihi´hi´

ACKNOWLEDGMENTS

This story owes much to many wonderful people on the Wind River Reservation and in Fremont County, Wyoming, whom I wish to thank for allowing me into their lives over the years and for their never-failing kindnesses and hospitality.

I especially want to thank Edward R. McAuslan, Fremont County coroner, and Edward L. Newell II, Fremont county and prosecuting attorney, for their willingness to answer my questions and set me straight on many procedural matters.

Thank you, also, to Robert Pickering, Ph.D., forensic anthropologist, deputy director, Buffalo Bill Historical Center, Cody, Wyoming, for enormously helpful information, suggestions, and advice.

A special thank you to the wonderful Missy Martin who generously shared with me her experiences of the Wind River Reservation in the 1970s. And to my baseball expert and nephew, John Dix, who is Father John's coach; to Michael Carrigan for guiding me through many aspects of criminal law; to Edie Stevens for helpful information on employment law.

As always, I am indebted to those trusted friends with keen instincts on what makes a piece of fiction sing and who were willing to read all or parts of this manuscript and make astoundingly good suggestions: Karen Gilleland and Beverly Carrigan, Boulder; Philip F. Myers, Fairlawn, Ohio; and Virginia

Sutter and Jim Sutter, members of the Arapaho tribe. I am also indebted to Father Anthony Short, S.J., for his friendship and never-flagging encouragement.

And to my husband, George, for so much of the above. *Ho'hou'!*

Ani'qu, *Our Father in Heaven!*
Now I am singing it—Hi'ni'ni!
I am singing it,
I am singing it,
That loudest song of all,
That resounding song—Hi'ni'ni!
—Arapaho song

. . . justice was outside in the hard light, and
injustice, too . . .
—Henry James, *The Ambassadors*

1

1973

SHE had to get off the rez.

The truth of it was so simple that Liz Plenty Horses started to laugh. Odd how the choked sound of her own laughter was lost in the noise of tires scraping the dirt and wind pumping the old Ford and whistling through the cracked windshield; it gave her the sense that things were almost normal. Everything would be fine. She kept her eyes focused on the cone of yellow headlights stretching into the darkness ahead. A misunderstanding, that was all. They'd gotten it all wrong—gotten *her* all wrong. Didn't they know her? She would never betray the American Indian Movement, never betray the others. AIM meant everything to her. Salvation. Life itself.

Liz gripped the steering wheel, aware of the sharp pain of her nails digging into the flesh of her palms and of the fear rushing over her, like a blackness closing in, as if the borders of the Wind River Reservation themselves were folding up around her, trapping her in a gulley and suffocating her.

The baby started to cry. Holding the wheel steady with one hand, Liz reached back, gripped the edge of the cardboard box that she'd padded with scraps of blankets and turned into a crib. She rocked the box slowly, gently, careful not to pull it off the seat, and started singing. "Baby mine, beautiful girl, the sun is gonna shine on you and me, and we're gonna be fine. We're gonna be fine." Her voice sounded cracked and tear strained, but she forced herself to keep singing. Songs were reassuring; they made you less afraid. If she could reassure Luna, hardly a month old—wasn't yesterday her birthday? My God, she'd forgotten her own child's first birthday, the passing of her first month. If this tiny girl wasn't afraid, then she wouldn't be afraid either.

But the black fear was there, like a presence seated beside her. She could feel the icy sharpness. She'd felt it the minute she'd stepped into the house. She'd gotten the message an hour earlier; one of the members had knocked on the door of the trailer. Meeting at the house on Yellow Calf Road. She'd better be there. She'd shown up late; the meeting had already started. The living room was jammed with members, perched on the sofa and chairs, slouched on the floor, legs stretched out, so that she saw the scuffed soles first, then the frayed blue jeans and the bright red, blue, and yellow shirts trimmed with ribbons, then the long black hair trailing over the shoulders and the red headbands stretched across the brown foreheads.

Oddly, the coldness had made her conscious of her own hair, long and thick and black. She'd pulled it back and worked it into a single braid—working all of the troubles and problems, all of the uncertainties into the braid that hung almost to her waist. Putting the troubles away for a while, she'd told herself. Yet it was the braid that made her stand out, look different, even though she'd worn a red headband, like the others. She should have left her hair hanging loose.

"Sorry, sorry," she'd heard herself saying, clutching the baby to her chest—and thank God, Luna was sleeping—as she'd stumbled over the stretched legs and dropped into a vacant spot on the floor, aware of the brown eyes following her like searchlights. She'd heard the voices when she'd stepped onto the front stoop, but the conversations had stopped when she'd walked inside. Smells of tobacco and sweat and stale coffee sucked the oxygen from the room.

She remembered looking around for Robert Running Wolf and Brave Bird, but neither of the leaders was there. Jake

Tallfeathers was there, though, he and two other Arapahos leaning shoulder to shoulder across the bar that separated the living room from the kitchen. It had been Jake and Ruth Yellow Bull and Liz, herself, Arapahos all of them, who had brought Lakotas to the Wind River Reservation after the standoff at Wounded Knee. They'd grown up on the rez; they knew where the Lakotas could hide out. They'd helped them blend in with the Arapahos. The Feds had chased all over Denver and Chicago and Minneapolis, sure that the AIM warriors had gone back to where they'd come from. They weren't looking on another rez. Lakotas had been here for months now, and no one had been arrested.

She'd searched Jake's face for some clue to the iciness in the room, but there was only the blankness of a stone.

"What is it?" she'd managed. Now, thinking about it, she could still feel Luna's lightness against her chest, the soft blanket falling over her arm, the almost imperceptible motion of the baby's breathing.

"Brave Bird got killed." A man's voice had cut toward her, and she'd turned her head, scanning the room. The other brown faces were set like Jake's, unreadable masks. She wasn't sure who had spoken.

"Killed?" She'd heard the disbelief in her own voice. Brave Bird was strong. He'd done so much since he came to the rez. Led the protests and demonstrations, organized the AIM warriors that listened in on the police calls, then raced to the crime scenes to make sure no one was beaten up or shot by the police, saw that food and firewood got to people who didn't have any, called on the members to be brave, to stand up for their rights as Indians. He was the heart of AIM, the soul of everything the movement stood for.

"Got shot couple hours ago." Another voice, from across the room. "Police shot him in Ethete."

"I didn't know," Liz had said into the quiet pressing around her. But in that instant she'd known everything. What it meant, what they had assumed. The Wind River police had stopped her last week, tried to pin a DUI on her, but she hadn't had anything to drink. Still they'd taken her to the jail in Ethete. Luna, too. Kept her in jail for twelve hours, sent Luna off with some social services woman Liz had never seen before, asked her a lot of questions. Where's Running Wolf? They'd wanted to know. Where's Brave Bird? How many Lakotas hiding here? Tell us where the safe houses are. You cooperate and we'll make things easy on you, drop the DUI charges. Nobody's gonna know. You don't talk, no telling what the judge is gonna throw at you. Put your kid in a foster home. Gonna be tough, Liz.

She'd told them she knew her rights, and she had the right to a phone call. She'd been shaking; her voice trembling. But she'd been a member of AIM for almost a year, and the most important thing AIM had taught her was that she had rights.

A policeman had finally led her to a phone in the corridor. It surprised her how easy it was. All she had to do was demand her rights and they were hers! She'd called Ruth Yellow Bull, knowing that Ruth would find Brave Bird or Robert. Within the hour, a lawyer had burst through the door to the room where they'd been questioning her. "DUI?" he'd said. "You got evidence, file a charge. Otherwise we're out of here." It hadn't been that simple. They'd kept her in jail until the court hearing in the morning.

Liz reached back and rocked the baby's box. They'd assumed—all the stone-hard faces crowded in the house— they'd all assumed she'd snitched, that she'd told the police where Brave Bird was staying in Ethete. It was a horrible mistake. Robert would straighten it out, just as she knew it had been Robert who had sent the lawyer and later had sent Ruth with the money to bail her out. She had to talk to Robert. Where was he? She had to get off the rez until she could find him. Give him time to talk to the other members, convince them of her loyalty. She couldn't just hang around, waiting, waiting, waiting . . .

She started singing again: "It's a long night coming. Train's rolling on into the darkness. Gonna get on that train, gonna roll on outta here. Roll on through the darkness and into the light, just you and me, baby, on that train."

She couldn't shake the image of Jake moving his head—a slow, methodical nod—as if she'd said exactly what he'd expected: I didn't know about Brave Bird. The other eyes had pulled away, darting about the room and staring down at their boots, but Jake had fixed her with a black, steady look. She'd had to look away. She'd pressed Luna's tiny body so tightly against her that it was as if the baby were part of her own body, a third breast she'd grown, wrapped in a faded pink blanket.

She had no idea, she'd said. The words sounded choked and hesitant. The stale tobacco smells filled her lungs. No idea whatsoever. "How did the police know where to find him?" she'd managed. He'd been using the name Daryl Redman. All the Lakotas used different names. "How had the police known?"

"Someone gave him up." There had been a steely coldness in Jake's voice.

"Nobody'd do that." She'd stumbled on, fear squeezing her throat like a rope. "Nobody on the rez would turn an Indian over to the police." And all the time she'd understood that they had already come to a conclusion and made a decision. The conversations she'd heard outside on the stoop were about her. *Liz Plenty Horses is the snitch.* Jake had looked at her as if he were staring into space, as if she were no longer there.

After a while, they'd started to leave—uncurling from the floor and getting out of the chairs. Liz had pushed to her feet, holding on to the baby plastered against her, and begun weaving her way past the sweat-soaked shirts and through the odors of cigarettes and hair oil. She got into the line filing out the door and started across the yard toward the Ford wedged behind two trucks, hurrying from the footsteps behind her. Engines stuttered, then roared into life. Headlights streaked across the bare dirt and cut through the darkness. Tires started skidding in the dirt.

The footsteps had come closer. Loreen Yellow Bull—Ruth's cousin; she recognized her in the flare of headlights—had walked past, then glanced back. "Watch yourself," she'd whispered.

Loreen had hurried ahead and climbed into a brown truck, headlights on, motor running, the truck shaking like a bull ready to burst out the gate. Jake was behind the wheel.

The other trucks and cars had turned left onto the road, but Liz had turned right, keeping an eye on the rearview mirror, the breath burning in her throat. She'd pressed down on the accelerator. They knew who she was. She'd thought they knew her.

The baby was still crying. Liz kept jiggling the cardboard

box, tears stinging her face. She was on Seventeen-Mile Road, the lights of Arapahoe blinking in the distance. What was she thinking? She couldn't go to the trailer where she'd been staying since she'd come back to the rez. Grandfather's trailer. When she was a kid, she'd explored every inch of the rooms that ran one into the other—kitchen, sitting room, bath, and finally the bedroom with windows that curved around the back just below the ceiling. Grandfather had died while she was at Pine Ridge, and the trailer was hers, all that she had. She'd found the key under the rock in front of the kitchen window.

They would be waiting for her there.

Luna was quiet now, which made it easier to think. Liz wiped at the moisture on her face. She had to pull herself together. She couldn't fall apart; she had a baby to think of. She slowed along the side of the road and waited for the oncoming headlights to sweep past. Then she swung the Ford in a U-turn and drove west. The gas needle bounced just above empty. She could make it to Ruth Yellow Bull's house and spend the night. Ruth hadn't been at the meeting; maybe she hadn't heard the news. She'd leave first thing in the morning. Ruth might even have gas she could siphon.

She swung left onto Plunkett Road, her gaze frozen to the pavement bending around the curves. After a couple of miles, she tapped at the brake pedal, turned right and bounced over the barrow ditch and across the dirt yard that spread in front of the small house. The white siding shone in the headlights. The windows were dark, and for a moment, she stayed in the car, trying to work out another plan if Ruth weren't home. Finally she got out, pulled the rear door open, and slid the cardboard box across the seat. She lifted it in both arms and, holding it close, made her way to the house. She kicked at the base of the wooden screened door.

There were no sounds apart from the wind flapping a towel against the pole of the clothesline that jutted from the side of the house. Liz kicked at the screened door again. "Be here, Ruth," she said out loud. "Please be here."

A light switched on inside, sending rectangles of light out onto the dirt. The inside door opened about two inches, and a thin slice of Ruth's face appeared in the crack. She stared at Liz with one eye. "What're you doing here?"

"I need a place for tonight. I thought . . ."

"You crazy? You can't stay here."

"It'd only be for a few hours," Liz said, trying to squeeze the desperation from her voice. "We'll be gone soon's it gets light."

"Don't you know what's going on?"

"I didn't have anything to do with Brave Bird gettin' shot."

"They're gonna put a snitch jacket on you."

"You know me, Ruth. You know it's not true. I'd never betray any of the members."

"You gotta go somewhere else. Jake hears you stayed here, he'll beat the shit outta me."

"Ruth, please . . ." The door slammed shut.

Liz stared past the screen at the dark wood for a long moment. It was as if a black wall had risen in front of her. The glow of lights disappeared from the windows. "Please, Ruth," she said again, but she was speaking to the wall.

Liz stumbled back through the darkness to the car. The baby began stirring in the box, emitting little chirping sounds, like those of a baby bird. She shoved the box onto the backseat and slid in behind the wheel. Maybe there was enough gas to get to Lander. She would head for Highway 287 and drive south, get as far away as she could before the gas gave out. A snitch jacket, Ruth had said. They wanted her dead.

2

THE air tasted of summer—of dust and dried sage and brittle grass. Cottonwoods straddled a dry creek bed, branches splayed against the blue sky, and the lumps of sagebrush scattered about shimmered like water in the sun. There was a reddish tint to the bluffs that rose out of the earth. A hot wind knocked against the Toyota pickup and whistled through the cab, nearly drowning out *The Magic Flute* that blared from the tape player on the front seat. It was the last Monday in July, the moon when the chokecherries begin to ripen, in the Arapaho Way of marking the passing time. Father John Aloysius O'Malley shifted into low gear and pointed the pickup down a slight decline. He could feel the rear tires slipping. Pebbles and dust spewed from beneath the wheels and laid a thin golden film over the rearview window. The slope flattened into the gulley that trailed the base of a bluff. He followed the tire tracks that ran across the brown earth.

"Might wanna head out to the Gas Hills," Thomas Whiteman had told him. The elder's voice had cracked on the telephone, and for a moment, Father John thought the call was breaking up. "Somebody buried in a gulley out in no-man's-land. Wild animal got to the bones." The old man sounded like himself again, the voice strong with indignation. "Ain't right, Father. Buried alone, nobody knows where you are, nobody prays for you, blesses your body."

Father John had written down the directions, trying to picture the location: Gas Hills Road, east of Highway 789, just beyond the border of the Wind River Reservation, nothing much out there. He'd been at St. Francis Mission on the reservation now for almost ten years, seven years as the pastor—longer than the Jesuits usually left a man in one place, for which he was grateful; he could find his way blindfolded down the asphalt roads and the narrow dirt tracks and across the vast emptiness by the feel of the wind, the sound of the old pickup's tires thumping on the hard-packed earth. He was familiar with the wild, remote areas around the reservation. So many times he'd hiked into the wilderness to think and pray and draw near to the silence. God was in the silence.

Whenever a body had been found in the wilderness—a rancher or a hiker spotting something protruding from the earth, something that didn't belong—the phone had rung at St. Francis. And on the line, the Fremont County sheriff, the local FBI agent, the Wind River police chief, or one of the Arapaho elders: "You might wanna come, Father."

"Coroner's out there now," Thomas Whiteman had said. "They're gonna be moving the bones pretty quick."

He'd told the elder he was on his way, then he'd walked down the wide corridor in the old administration building to the office of his assistant, Father Ian McCauley. He'd found the man curled over a stack of papers on a desk marked by the rings of countless coffee cups that had rested on the surface through the decades. The sun bursting through the window gave a yellow cast to the other priest's scalp beneath his thinning, sandy-colored hair. Father John told him he'd be out for a while.

"Emergency?" Father Ian hadn't looked up.

"Dead body out in the Gas Hills."

"Jesus." He'd looked up then and shook his head. "I'll hold down the fort," he'd said, which had struck Father John as ironic. His assistant would handle the phone calls from the Arapaho parishioners and visit with anybody who happened to drop by—"You busy, Father? Got a minute?" In the Old Time, white men had defended the forts—held them down—*against* the Indians.

Father John had made his way back down the corridor, past the framed black-and-white photos of the past Jesuits at St. Francis, dark eyes trained on him through wireless spectacles perched on prominent noses. He'd jogged across the mission grounds to the old pickup parked in front of the redbrick residence. Years before he'd come here, somebody had donated the pickup to the mission; for some time now, the odometer had been stuck at one hundred and twenty-two thousand miles. He'd driven around Circle Drive, tires squealing, past the old gray stone building that had once been a school and was now the Arapaho Museum, past the white stucco church with the stained glass windows in the geometric symbols of the Arapaho and the white steeple that seemed to sway with the cottonwood branches shading the roof, past the two-story yellow stucco administration building. He'd turned down the tunnel of cottonwoods and headed east for 789, a route he'd taken so often that he half suspected the pickup could find the way on its own.

Now he could see vehicles parked ahead in the gulley. Sheriff's deputies in tan uniforms were milling about with men in blue jeans and dark shirts, sleeves rolled to the elbows, wind plastering the shirts against their backs. Father John parked between a white SUV with Fremont County emblazoned on the sides and the gray pickup that Thomas Whiteman drove.

"Hey, Father." Gary Coughlin, detective in the sheriff's office, looked up from the carton he'd been rummaging through in the back of a van. He ducked his head through the strap of a black camera.

"What do you have?"

"Not much left but a skeleton." The detective beckoned with his head as he started around the van toward the group of officers in a half circle near the base of the bluff.

Standing inside the circle was the gaunt figure of Thomas Whiteman, a black cowboy hat shading the elder's wrinkled, brown face. With both hands, he slowly lifted a pan toward the sky. A thin wisp of smoke trailed out of the pan into the wind, leaving behind the faint odor of burning cedar.

Heito'eino'hoowuciixxokuno'. The old man's voice punctured the noise of the wind. *Woow heetneechoohun.* The Arapaho words seemed to hang in the air around the circle of officers standing with heads bowed. Father John understood some of the words; he could guess at the rest: Your relatives are nearby. Now you can go home.

The elder finished the prayer, then nodded at Father John. The half circle began to pull apart, the officers glancing back, waving him forward with their eyes. It was then that he saw the ocher-colored bones protruding through piles of brown dirt, as if they had been laid out. Except that he knew that wasn't true. Whoever had left the body had probably pushed it into a shallow, hastily-dug grave, and the piles of dirt were the remnants of that grave.

The officers pulled apart to make a space for him, and he stepped closer. A raven rose from the side of the bluff and flapped away. The bones were small in diameter, yet long. Long femur, long humerus. Knobs of the long spine emerged from the dirt. The thin arm bones had been pulled back. Frayed pieces of rope were tied around the wrist bones. He could see the breaks in the bones. The skeleton was face down, so that the back of the skull was visible, and on the left side was a small, round bullet hole. And something else: a long rope of braided hair still attached to a piece of dried scalp. The braid wound over the spine, disappearing into the earth, then protruding again. It was black hair, faded with the brown dust of the earth.

Father John swallowed hard against the horror that rose inside him, the bitterness of bile. He got down on one knee and made the sign of the cross over the bones. "God have mercy," he said out loud. "God, have mercy on this woman." That it was the skeleton of a woman, he was sure. The delicate bones, the long black braid, and some inexplicable sense that this had been the body of a woman. Indian men wore braids, but there was something about the hair. It looked fine; it might have been silky once.

It struck him then, not for the first time, that God was not limited by time—by minutes and hours and days that passed into years. That God was eternal, and all time was present to Him. "God be with this woman," he said again, praying for her *then*, when she had died this terrible death.

He noticed the debris scattered about, poking from beneath the bones—pieces of leather, faded scraps of calico and denim, the heel of a boot, pieces of metal that might have been buttons or snaps or rivets. The detritus of a life, he thought.

"Coroner agrees," Detective Coughlin said, moving next to Father John as he stood up. "Skeleton's most likely a woman."

"How long has she been here?"

Coughlin shrugged. One of the other officers was pointing a camera toward the scalp and adjusting the lens. A series of clicking noises cut through the buzz of conversation and the whoosh of the wind, and for the first time, Father John was aware of the wind gusting. It didn't surprise him; the Arapahos said the wind always blew when a body was disturbed.

"Forensics might be able to ballpark a date. Depends what they can get from the pieces of clothing and boot. Not much left. All we know for sure is that she was a homicide. Nobody ties his arms behind himself and shoots himself in the back of the head. Animals been digging here. Coyote or fox, maybe a wolf, dragged a femur about a hundred yards down the gulley. Couple of rock hunters come along this morning looking for rocks and arrowheads. One of 'em had a dog that got hold of the femur, and the men went looking for the source. Came upon the grave and called us."

That would be the two men in Levi's and black Stetsons, Father John was thinking, talking to another officer over by a green four-door pickup.

"She's Indian, that's for sure."

Father John turned around. He hadn't realized that Thomas Whiteman had come up behind them.

"It's possible," Coughlin said. He exchanged a glance with Father John. They both knew that the skeleton was probably that of an Indian woman.

"Yeah, she's Indian." The old man was nodding, confirming his own theory. "Black braid like that. You don't see no white people with that kinda hair. One of our own people," he went on, still nodding, "left out here by herself for a long time. Well, now we found her, and we're gonna get her buried proper so she can go to the ancestors in peace."

Father John didn't say anything. He could almost feel the detective swallowing his own comments. It would be a while before the coroner released the body—not until the investigation into the woman's death was complete, and with a death that probably occurred years ago, the investigation would take a while. Still, the Arapahos would be anxious to bury her in the traditional way, anxious that until they did, her soul would be walking the earth.

Coughlin said, "Just as soon as possible."

"We wanna know who she is."

"So do we."

The elder nodded at this and started to walk away. Then he turned back. "We're not gonna forget her," he said, before starting again for the gray pickup.

"Not gonna be an easy case to solve." The detective was shaking his head. "Could be an old homicide, which is gonna make it a very cold case. Witnesses die and move away. Evidence evaporates. Killer could be dead." He shrugged. "Sometimes they're impossible, cases like this."

"The Arapahos are going to want to know who she was and what happened to her."

"Lot of murders never get solved, Father. It's not a perfect world."

"When will you have the forensics report?"

"Oh, man. Bad enough the elders are going to be on my case. Am I gonna have to put up with you bugging me?"

"Simple question, Gary."

"Okay, simple answer. Could take a couple weeks before the coroner gets the full report."

Father John nodded. "I'll be in touch," he said. Then he made his way through the officers still milling about and headed toward the pickup.

"I'm sure you will," Detective Coughlin called after him.

3

VICKY Holden sipped at her coffee and let her gaze run over the handsome young man and beautiful young woman at her table, scarcely able to believe they were her children. Lucas, now twenty-seven, and so much like his father in the way he tossed his head, motioning for the waiter, that it made her heart turn over. The hum of traffic in downtown Denver hummed over the restaurant's patio. Light from the lamps at the periphery flickered in his black eyes, and that reminded her of Ben, too, the pinpricks of light in his dark eyes. And Susan was truly beautiful, or was it her imagination? The fond hope of any mother for her twenty-five-year-old daughter? And yet, when they'd followed the maitre d' through the dining room and out onto the patio, she'd seen the heads swiveling, the eyes following the slim, striking girl with the shiny black hair that swayed across her back.

And yet, Vicky couldn't shake the image of the skeleton discovered in the Gas Hills last week; a girl, maybe Susan's age, beaten and shot to death and left in a grave in a gulley. She'd read the articles in the *Gazette* before she'd left for a visit with the kids in Denver; the moccasin telegraph was loaded with gossip and rumors. Who was she? What had happened to her?

"What, Mom?" Susan said, turning slightly in her chair.

Vicky shook her head. "You look great, that's all," she said, trying to force back another image now: the small, brown faces at the screened door the day she'd left the children on the reservation with her mother, after she'd finally summoned the courage to leave Ben to try to make a better life for them. She supposed that Susan resembled her. Wasn't that what people always said? Susan was clean now. No more drugs and alcohol, and she'd lost the crowd she'd been hanging with. She was excited about a new job.

Vicky glanced across the table at Lucas. "You both look great," she said. She was nineteen when Lucas was born. Not much more than a child herself, she was thinking. Two years later, Susan was born. But there had been ten years of dancing around Ben; the smells of alcohol and lipstick and the skin and hair of other women on his clothes, the shotgun temper, the hard thrusts of his fists in her face and stomach.

"Same for you, Mom." Susan gave her a complicit smile, as if they'd been sharing secrets. Girl talk, huddled together over a water cooler. "So why don't you come clean about Adam?"

"You've been waiting all weekend to ask?" Vicky shook her head and gave a little laugh despite the barb of barely camouflaged hostility in Susan's question. There was always a sharpness in Susan, like the barbed wire you forgot about until it pricked you again. She didn't blame her. She'd taken the girl from her father. It wasn't something you explained to a child, and she would not explain it now and cloud the image that Susan held of her father.

There was the thump of hip-hop pouring out of a passing car, the ratcheting of a bus engine. The sounds seemed muted and far away, background noise to the memories that jostled one another. She'd tried to push the bad memories away. She didn't want them, yet they'd had a way of intruding all weekend. Always the images of the small, brown faces bobbing behind the screened door as she'd backed out of the yard.

Tomorrow morning Lucas would return to a cubicle somewhere in a Denver skyscraper and do whatever he did to keep the computers operating in his company. Susan would fly back to Los Angeles and a new job generating the computer magic of special effects for some movie, and she would drive back to the Wind River Reservation and her own life.

Lucas looked up from the credit card slip he'd just signed. "Lakota, right?" He slipped the card into his wallet, then leaned forward toward the flickering candle and pushed the wallet into a back pocket. His hair was black and shiny, trimmed short and brushed back from a high intelligent forehead. There was a little hump in his nose, the mark of the Arapaho. The candlelight gave his skin the tone of honey. His smile reminded her of when he was a little boy and had just come upon a new discovery. "Should we expect a wedding?"

Susan looked away at this, as if the knots of people strolling past the patio on the sidewalk had demanded her attention.

"Adam and I are law partners," Vicky said, wondering how they had managed to get through the zoo and the Museum of Nature and Science, the play at the performing arts center, and the hike into the foothills today without one of the kids bringing up the subject of Adam Lone Eagle.

Susan was still staring out over the sidewalk, and Lucas pressed on: "Come on, Mom, tell us what we don't know."

Vicky tried for a laugh. It sounded tight and forced. "If there were anything to tell, you would be the first to know."

"We already know." Susan's head snapped around. "Moccasin telegraph works in Denver and L.A., you know. We've heard all about you and Adam."

"He's a good lawyer. I admire him very much." Vicky wondered what other news the moccasin telegraph had delivered—that she and Adam were lovers? That Adam spent almost every night at her apartment?

"Maybe we should go to the rez and have a talk with him," Lucas said. "You know, what are your intentions toward our mother?"

"His intentions? For heaven's sakes, Lucas."

"His intentions are honorable, of course." Susan directed the comment toward her brother. "Isn't that what every man wants a woman to believe?"

"Come on, you two," Vicky said, reaching for a lighter

tone. "I'd love to have you visit." But not for a while, she was thinking. It wasn't Adam's intentions that she doubted; it was her own.

Vicky got to her feet and headed back through the restaurant, aware of the scraping sound of chairs on stone and the footsteps of Lucas and Susan behind her. The air was close and stuffy inside, unlike the warmth of the summer evening on the patio. She was aware of the way the few diners still lingering over coffee or dessert lifted their eyes as they walked by.

The nighttime streets of LoDo were busy. Sedans and SUVs crawling past the crowds that strolled the sidewalks and darted through the openings in the traffic. Lucas had to jam on the brakes to avoid two girls running across the street, waving and hollering at a knot of young people on the other side. Vicky felt her muscles tensing. She was no longer used to the congestion and traffic that had seemed normal when she'd lived in Denver. Then, after she'd gone home and started her law practice in Lander with the crazy idea that she could help her people, it was the open spaces that seemed normal. They had really never left her; they were part of her spirit. She was looking forward to the long drive tomorrow through the emptiness of Wyoming.

"We're out of here," Lucas said. The tires squealed into a left turn onto a side street. The hum of traffic receded as he drove on. There was only an occasional pedestrian hurrying along the sidewalk. A couple of more blocks, another turn, and they were back in a stream of traffic crossing the Platte River. Ahead, lights twinkled in the hills of Highland, the familiar neighborhood of century-old bungalows and Victorians where Vicky had once lived. Lucas had bought a house not far from the house she had rented.

On the other side of the viaduct, Lucas turned out of the traffic and into the side streets again. He drove slowly past the cars parked at the curbs and the dark tunnels of alleys. The headlights swept into the circles of light falling out of the street lamps.

"Whoa! What was that?" Lucas hit the brake pedal, and the car jerked to a stop. Vicky threw out one hand to brace herself against the dashboard; the seatbelt bit into her shoulder. Then they were rocketing backward.

"What're you doing?" Susan shrieked from behind. Vicky could feel Susan gripping the back of the seat.

"You see that?"

"See what?" Susan said.

The street was suffused in the soft moonlight. The houses were dark, except for a dim light in the second-floor window of a house farther down the street. The car came to a stop, then Lucas backed up a few more feet and made a sharp turn into an alley. He drove past a small group of people—three or four men, a couple of women hunched next to the fence of a back-yard. In the headlights bouncing ahead, Vicky could see two figures: the tall, thick-shouldered man in a white tee shirt and blue jeans; the girl crumbled against a garage. The man lifted a boot with a high heel and rounded toe and kicked the girl in the stomach. Then he grabbed a fistful of her long, black hair and yanked her upward against the garage door, his other arm pulled back, fist clenched.

Lucas was out of the car. He launched himself past the on-lookers and threw his weight into the man, who stumbled backward, grappling for purchase on the chipped concrete apron of the garage, the twisted features of his face bobbing in the head-lights, his mouth opened in a mixture of rage and surprise. Lucas grabbed the raised arm, but not before the man let go of the girl's hair and drove a fist into Lucas's middle. He twisted away, then reared back, head lowered. His fist caught the man's jaw, knocking him off balance for a half second before the man came back, both fists pounding Lucas.

Vicky managed to get the glove compartment open, then the console box, frantic to find a flashlight, anything she might use, barely registering the sound of Susan screaming behind her. "Call 911," Vicky yelled, throwing open the door and running her hand under the edge of the passenger seat as she slid out. Finally her fingers found a cool, hard plastic object. The scream-ing stopped. She could hear Susan shouting that they needed help as she gripped the flashlight and ran toward Lucas who had managed to back the man against the garage door. She was aware of the girl's soft cries of pain through the sounds of boots scraping the concrete, the hard thrusts of fists against muscles and bones, the quick gasps of breath. Lucas threw another fist toward the man's jaw, just as he dodged sideways and butted his head into Lucas's chest. In an instant it was Lucas backed against the garage door, the man gripping his throat with one hand, winding up for another punch into Lucas's stomach.

Vicky screamed and swung the flashlight into the side of the man's head. He whirled toward her. Lucas dived for him with more force and anger than she could have imagined was in her son. He started pounding on the man, not letting up, until the man doubled over, dropping onto one knee, then the other, and finally folding onto the concrete, arms outstretched, unconscious. Even then she wasn't sure that Lucas wouldn't jump on top of him and continue pounding.

"The girl, the girl," Vicky shouted.

Lucas took in a series of quick breaths, still standing over the prone figure, staring down at him. "Bastard," he said. He swiped the back of his hand across his mouth. "You filthy bastard."

Out of the corner of her eye, Vicky could see Susan moving through the headlights like a wisp of smoke. There was no one else in the alley; the little crowd had disappeared. Vicky knelt down beside the girl and wrapped her hand around the thin wrist, her fingertips probing for the sign of a pulse. She was unconscious, bruises welling on her face and arm, grip marks on her throat. The noise of a siren swelled in the distance, the only sound apart from the sharp in and out of Lucas's breathing.

"Is she dead?" Susan's voice was hushed, barely a whisper.

"No," Vicky said. She had the pulse now, faint and erratic. She was almost dead, she was thinking. If they hadn't gotten here, the girl would have been dead.

Lucas turned back to the man, and for a moment Vicky thought he might lift his foot and kick at the prone figure, but Lucas remained still, peering down at him, and she marveled at the restraint in her son, the control over himself, so unlike his father.

A cacophony of sirens filled the air. Vehicles were approaching from both ends of the alley, headlights flashing over fences and garages and power poles. Lights had switched on in the houses behind the fences and dark backyards. She could hear a dog barking, doors slamming. The vehicles ground to a halt: three police cars, an ambulance. Doors opened and slammed shut, and a group of officers in dark uniforms moved into a half circle around them.

"What's going on?" One of the officers tossed out the question. He glanced from Lucas to Vicky, his gaze passing over Susan.

"This girl needs help." Vicky was still crouching beside the unconscious girl. The shaking had started. She felt it moving through her arms and across her back, down her legs. She wasn't sure she could stand up, that her legs wouldn't give way beneath her.

A couple of medics broke through the half circle and went down on their knees beside the girl. Vicky tried to scoot away to give them room, steadying herself with one hand against the ridged wood of the garage door.

"What about him?" The officer stepped over to the man stretched out on the asphalt, still unconscious. Another medic knelt beside him and probed at his neck a moment before his fingers came to a rest. He glanced at his watch.

"He was beating the hell out of her," Lucas said.

"And you took care of that?"

Vicky pulled herself upright along the door. She found the handle and leaned onto it. "My name is Vicky Holden and I'm an attorney," she told the officer. "My son, Lucas. My daughter, Susan." She gave a nod in the direction of each of her children. "We were on our way to Lucas's house when we passed the alley and saw that man beating up on this girl. We drove into the alley to help her. There were other people here, just watching. They've left."

"Okay." The officer took in a long breath, then let it out slowly, as if he were letting go of a different scenario he'd been constructing in his mind: alley fight between Indians and whites. It happened in this neighborhood, except that it would have been more usual if the fight were between Mexicans and whites.

"We need your names, addresses, brief statements." Another officer had pulled out a small notepad and was flipping through the pages with the tip of a pen. The medics still hovered over the girl and the man. Two medics were dragging stretchers out of the back of the ambulance.

"We'll also need complete statements at police headquarters downtown tomorrow," the officer said.

Vicky started to say that she was leaving for Wyoming tomorrow, that her daughter had to return to L.A. She stopped, aware of the medics sliding the girl onto a stretcher. She looked so small. So helpless. "We'll be there first thing," she said.

"Any idea who the bystanders were?"

Vicky shook her head.

"We'll talk to the neighbors, see if we can find them."

"The bastard should be charged with attempted murder and first-degree assault," Lucas said.

"Thanks for the advice."

"We can testify that we saw him beating the girl," Vicky said. She was still shaking, and she could hear the shaking in her voice. She glanced at Susan, who had moved next to Lucas. Lucas had his arm around her. The color had drained from her face. "We all saw what happened."

After they had given their names, addresses, and telephone numbers, after they'd told the officers again what they had seen, they got into the car and Lucas started backing out of the alley. The ambulance had already pulled away with both the girl and the man inside. Only one of the police cars was left, the two officers walking up and down the alley, shining flashlights across the concrete and along the bottom rim of the fences.

"God . . ."

"Don't say it, Mom," Lucas said, but Vicky knew by the silence in which they drove on that both Lucas and Susan knew what she was thinking. It might have been Susan, alone in an alley in L.A., with some drug dealer or rotten boyfriend deciding to teach her a lesson. It was probably what had happened to the girl who was no more than a skeleton in the Gas Hills. It could have happened to Susan, and she could have ended up dead.

But they didn't know the rest of her thoughts: It might have been her. In their own home. At the hands of their own father.

4

WILLIE Nelson blared from the radio—"Blue Eyes Crying in the Rain." A river of asphalt flowed ahead as far as Vicky could see, sunlight flashing on the bumper of a semi in the distance. On either side of the highway, the plains rolled and pitched and melted into a sky as clear as blue glass. Here and there a ranch house lifted itself out of the brown earth, but the only continuous signs of life were the antelope that had been racing alongside the highway for miles. She passed Sweetwater Station, a rest stop with picnic tables and a scattering of vehicles parked in front of the low brick building that housed the restrooms. Ahead were Cedar Draw, Sheep Mountain, Blue Ridge. And in the northeast, the Gas Hills, where the skeleton had been found.

She'd been awake most of last night, drifting into a half sleep until the images of the unconscious girl curled in the alley and the bones of a young woman in the Gas Hills had collided in a nightmare that startled her into wakefulness. She'd stared into the darkness, knowing that Susan and Lucas were also awake, the images from the alley looping through their minds. When they were children, she'd always known if they were awake, lying quietly in their beds, and it was as if they were still connected to her by an invisible umbilical cord. She could almost see the images that must have played in Susan's mind, the nightmare terrors spliced with pictures of the man kicking and punching the girl.

And Lucas, staring into the darkness of the den downstairs, worrying about the girl. Oh, how well she knew him. Always worrying, just like when he was a child, the little spy in the house who knew everything, but was too small to do anything about it. The memory of Ben Holden was not as sacred to his son as it was to his daughter.

They had been at the police headquarters at eight o'clock this morning, she and Lucas and Susan, ushered into individual cubicles, giving statements of what they'd seen, what they had done. The girl was in serious condition; not that Detective Hopkins, who seemed to be in charge, had said so, exactly. It was what Vicky had heard in the undercurrent of conversation. Her name was Julie Reynolds. Julie Reynolds, nineteen years old, in intensive care at Denver Health Sciences, on a respirator. Her attacker was Theo Gosman, twenty-five and a member of a prominent Denver family. Already lawyered up, the detective had said, with the firm of Owens and Lattimore, known for obtaining acquittals of criminal charges against well-heeled clients.

The sound of her cell ringing cut through her thoughts. Vicky fumbled in her bag on the passenger seat and extracted the small, plastic phone. "This is Vicky Holden," she said, clamping the phone to her ear, her eyes still fastened on the silvery asphalt unfurling itself. Two golden-tail hawks swooped over the highway before rising into a long, flat glide, their shadows flickering on the plains.

"Where are you, Vicky Holden?" It was Adam, and she knew by the lightness in his tone that he was glad to reach her.

"Just passed Sweetwater."

Adam was quiet a moment. "Another hour," he said. "How'd everything go? Kids okay?"

They were fine, Vicky told him. She'd tell him later about the girl in the alley.

"A group of women are wanting to see you."

"What? Who are they?"

"From the rez. Annie knows them."

Annie Bosey knew everybody on the Wind River Reservation, Vicky was thinking, which was one of the reasons she'd insisted on bringing her secretary to the new firm that she and Adam had formed. "We need somebody more professional, more polished," Adam had said. Someone more fitting with the type of firm they intended to build, the important cases they would handle on natural resources, land management, issues of tribal sovereignty. "Annie knows everybody," Vicky had said. "And she needs the job." Still in her twenties, divorced and on her own with two kids. It never left Vicky's mind that she herself had been like that, struggling to look after Lucas and Susan in between the waitressing job and her classes at the University of Colorado in Denver. It had defeated her, and one day she'd driven the kids back to her mother's on the reservation, promising she'd be back for them. But by the time she'd come back, with a law degree and a job at a Seventeenth Street firm, the kids were grown. They didn't need her anymore. Adam had understood all that, she knew, and he'd agreed to let Annie stay on.

"What do they want?" Vicky said.

"I suspect Annie knows, but she's not saying. They want to talk to you, that's all. You planning to come to the office?"

"I guess I am now," Vicky said. She'd been planning to go straight to her apartment, unpack, and get caught up on the files she'd taken to Denver and never found the time to open.

"I'll have Annie let them know. Oh, and Vicky?"

She'd been about to break off the call, the tip of her index finger brushing the end key. She waited.

"It'll be good to have you home."

"See you soon," she said. She pushed the key and tossed the phone onto the bag crumpled on the seat. She was beginning to think that every time she left his sight, Adam Lone Eagle half expected that she wouldn't return.

THE brown faces swiveled toward her as Vicky stepped into the reception area. Diana Morningstar and Mary Blue Heart leaned against the closed door to her office. Six other women were scattered about the room. Vicky searched for names: Elsie Barret and Rona Blackman on the folding chairs that Annie must have pulled from the closet. Nan somebody—what was the woman's name? Janice Silver, Mickey Littleshield, Shana Graybull. They were quiet and reserved—it was the normal way—black hair flowing about their shoulders, hands clasped in their laps, brown eyes fixed on her.

It was Annie, jumping up from the desk across the office, who said, "They've been waiting most of the afternoon."

Vicky tried for a smile that was part acknowledgment and part apology. "Better come in," she said, starting for her office. The two women against the door stepped aside, and Vicky pushed the door open and walked to her desk, aware of the shuffling noises of the women starting after her. She hooked the strap of her bag over her chair and waited while they filed inside and bunched together along the back wall. Except for Diana Morningstar and Mary Blue Heart who dropped into the chairs in front of the desk. The appointed spokeswomen, Vicky thought.

"Sorry to put you to any trouble," Diana said. She was a slight woman in her late forties, a couple of years older than Vicky, with threads of gray glistening in her long, black hair. She'd been in the grade ahead at St. Francis Mission school, the prettiest girl in school, lit with energy and laughter. Vicky remembered wanting to be like her, the way Diana walked across the mission grounds, the little bounce in her step, tossing back the long, shiny black hair, and all of the boys watching. Now she was struck by the prominence of Diana's nose, protruding from the thin face and sunken cheeks, like one of those flimsy noses kids wore on Halloween. Deep wrinkles spread from the corners of her eyes and creased her long neck. Her arms were thin, hanging from the sleeves of the white tee shirt with *Blue Sky People* written in blue across the front. Her legs might have been sticks inside her blue jeans.

"You're the only one we could think to come to." This from Mary Blue Heart, nearly as thin as Diana. She was younger, still in her thirties, Vicky guessed, with a mass of curly, light brown hair inherited from a white ancestor and a complexion that changed from light to dark as she moved her head under the fluorescent ceiling lights. She wore a blouse that folded over the top of khaki slacks and revealed the little bulge of a still-new pregnancy.

"You read about the skeleton out in the Gas Hills?" Diana asked.

Vicky nodded. A front-page article in the *Gazette*. "Rock Hunters Find Human Skeleton." A homicide. The victim had been shot to death. A bullet hole in the back of the skull. Not until almost the last sentence did the article mention that the coroner believed the skeleton was that of a young woman. There had been two other articles, asking for information on any young women missing from the 1970s. Contact the sheriff's department. And Annie had brought up the skeleton several times before Vicky had left for Denver. "Heard anything?" she'd asked. "Lots of us are wanting to know who she was." Which had let Vicky know that the moccasin telegraph was buzzing with speculation and theories.

And here they were, women from the reservation drawn to an anonymous young woman, shot to death and left in the wilderness of the Gas Hills.

"Mind if Annie joins us?" Vicky said.

Diana and Mary nodded in unison, as if they'd wanted to ask, but hadn't been sure of how to bring up the matter without being impolite.

Vicky lifted the receiver and pressed a button. It was a moment before Annie picked up, and Vicky suspected she'd had to dart back to the desk from outside the office door where she'd probably been listening. She asked her to come in, then waited while Annie dragged a folding chair across the carpet, opened it at the corner of the desk and sat down.

"I been telling everybody you'd help us," she said.

Diana nodded. "She died out there all alone."

"Except for the murderer," Annie said.

"That's what's got us upset," Diana went on. "The bastard shot her and got away with it. Tied her arms back. Took her to that godforsaken place, put a twenty-two bullet in her head, and that was after he'd beaten her half to death."

"Tied her arms back?" Vicky said. The article hadn't mentioned anything about that. It was the kind of information investigators liked to keep quiet, the kind only the killer might know.

"My sister, she's a clerk in the sheriff's office," Mary said. "That's what she heard from some of the guys that went to the site. It was pretty bad, she says. Bones dragged out of the grave by animals, scattered around. She says they're not doing much of an investigation. Just skipping over the fact that somebody murdered her, like she wasn't important."

"She deserves more than that, right?" Diana tossed a glance over her shoulder at the women leaning against the back wall, arms folded across their waists. Two of the women started nodding. "Least she deserves is her own name. What does it matter that it happened a long time ago? She was alive once. I mean, she was like us, wasn't she? Walking around, going about her business. Then some sonofabitch thought it was okay to kill her, punish her, most likely, for something she did that made him mad."

They were all nodding at this, and Vicky felt the knot start to tighten in her stomach. The dead woman could have been any of them. The girl in the alley. Susan. Herself. My God, what were the statistics? So horrible that she'd wanted to block them from her mind, regretting the fact that she'd come upon them. Homicide, the number one cause of death for Native American women.

"I tol' 'em you know Detective Coughlin," Annie said. "You can tell him the women on the rez want answers, tell him no way should the killer be walking around free after what he done, tell him that woman needs to be back with her family, buried properlike along with people that loved her. You can tell him that."

"It's a murder case," Vicky said, threading her way through the logical, legal explanations forming in her mind. "There's no statute of limitations on murder. Coughlin will investigate the death. That's his job."

"Then why haven't we heard anything else?" Diana leaned forward and clasped her hands around her bony knees. "Couple articles, that's all. You know anybody missing, you should contact the sheriff's office. I'd say, anybody that's gone missing, the sheriff and the police oughtta already know about it. We hear that nobody at the sheriff's office is talking about the skeleton anymore. It's like that girl's forgotten, left on a shelf out in the coroner's property room."

Vicky started to say that the forensics tests probably hadn't come back yet, then thought better of it. Behind the dark eyes trained on her, she could see the resolution and the fear. There was something about the girl, shot to death and left in the middle of nowhere, stripped to nothing but her bones, that held the women in its grip. At the least, the girl should have her name back.

She said, "I'll have a talk with Detective Coughlin."

"I said Vicky'd help," Annie said.

Diana Morningstar was the first to break into a smile, but it was slow in coming, like the gradual cracking of a clay mask, as if it had taken a moment for the news to become real. "Thanks," she said. The others were nodding and smiling, pushing away from the back wall, starting for the door.

Diana and Mary got to their feet and started after the others. Then Diana whirled back: "You'll call?"

"As soon as I learn anything," Vicky said.

Annie was on her feet, folding the chair. She waited until Diana had closed the door, then she said, "Adam's been waiting to see you."

It always took her by surprise when she saw Adam Lone Eagle, as if she were seeing him again for the first time: the handsome, imposing look about him, the black hair flecked with gray and the dark eyes that shone with light, the blue shirt opened at the neck, the sleeves rolled over his brown, muscular forearms. Even when they'd spent the night together, then had gone different ways—she to court, perhaps; Adam to a meeting with tribal officials in Ethete—she always felt the little prick of surprise when she saw him again at the office—so like a warrior in the Old Time, a chief, walking toward her, the way he was now, crossing his office, arms outstretched, face relaxed in a smile that made him even more handsome.

"Man, am I glad you're back," Adam said, gathering her to him. He held her close and laced his fingers through the back of her hair. The fabric of his shirt was soft against her face, and the faint odor of aftershave washed over her. She heard his heart beating. She was thinking that she must try to love him.

"It's been a long weekend," he said. His breath was warm on her forehead. After a moment he let her go, except for her right hand, which he kept in his. "What's with all the women?"

She explained that they wanted assurance that the sheriff's detective hadn't forgotten the skeleton in the Gas Hills.

"Why would they forget?" Adam let go of her hand, walked around the desk and sank into his chair. He combed his fingers through his hair. "Don't tell me you're going to waste a couple of hours over at the sheriff's office so you can tell the women everything's following its natural course."

"What if it isn't?" Vicky perched on the edge of the chair in front of the desk. "What if the women are right and the investigation has been pushed to the lowest priority? It's not like the woman was shot to death yesterday. It probably happened a long time ago."

"Okay. Then what?"

"That's what I intend to find out."

"Oh, Vicky." Adam shook his head and lifted his eyes to the ceiling a moment. "Send Roger over to have a talk with the detective in charge." Roger Hurst was the young lawyer, just three years out of law school, that they'd hired several months ago to handle the mundane cases—DUIs and divorces and leases—that walked through the door almost every day, the residue of her one-woman law practice, before Holden and Lone Eagle. She and Adam would concentrate on the important cases that made a difference. Indian lawyers practicing Indian law.

"We've been over this," Vicky said. "Sometimes there are going to be . . ."

Adam lifted one hand, palm out. "I know, I know. Those cases that you can't resist, you feel compelled . . ."

"I promised them I'd be the one to talk to Detective Coughlin."

"Why, Vicky? Why does it matter so much? The woman, whoever she was, has been dead a long time. Maybe her family doesn't know what happened to her, but surely they've come to the conclusion that she isn't coming home. Maybe she'll never be identified, and nobody will ever know what happened to her."

It was then that she told him about the girl in the alley, how Lucas had driven past the little crowd—standing there, watching. How he'd jumped out of the car and gone to the girl's defense. How he'd stopped the beating. "It could happen to any of us," she said, but what was still raw—a wound ready to break open—was the realization that it could have happened to Susan. "Nobody should get away with murder."

"So you're gonna camp out at the sheriff's office . . ."

"And ask a few questions," Vicky said, getting to her feet. "Are you free for dinner tonight?"

"I was hoping you'd propose more than dinner," Adam said.

5

THE beige stone building, bathed golden by the morning light, resembled the bluffs that rose unexpectedly out of the earth around Lander. Most of the building housed the detention center—the county jail—but the rear section was given over to the sheriff's office. Vicky drove around the building and parked in a space marked Visitors. She walked across the asphalt that yawned like an alley between the rows of vehicles and the glass door next to the red Coco-Cola dispenser shoved against the wall. Black letters on the glass said: Fremont County Sheriff's Office. Vicky let herself inside.

The entry was small, an afterthought carved out of a corner when the mighty purposes of the building had been constructed. Squinting at the computer screen on the desk across from the door was a woman about thirty with shoulder-length blond hair brushed behind her ears and pinkish skin marked by a band of dark freckles across her nose and cheeks. It was a moment before she looked up. She didn't say anything.

"Vicky Holden," Vicky said, snapping a business card on the desk. She'd probably been here a hundred times, but she'd never seen the woman. "Here to see Detective Coughlin."

The woman took another moment—the light gray eyes glancing at the card—before she said, "You got an appointment?"

"I'd appreciate it if you would let him know I'm here."

The woman tossed her head to one side, as if she could toss away the disruption, and picked up the phone. The gray eyes fastened again on the screen. "You got a visitor, a Ms. Holden," she said. Then she dropped the receiver and, still looking at the screen, said, "He'll come and get you."

Vicky stepped away from the desk and looked around. Nothing but a pair of doors flanking the desk and cement-brick walls muffling the activity on the other side: the faint sounds of voices, doors shutting, people moving about.

One of the doors swung open. Gary Coughlin, a big man dressed in blue jeans and a dark, plaid shirt, leaned into the entry. "Vicky? Follow me," he said, waving the folder in his other hand.

Vicky brushed past him and waited until he'd closed the door and ushered her down a corridor with doors on either side. "Thanks for seeing me," she said as he fell into step beside her.

"Must say, I was surprised to get your call." He veered sideways and handed the folder to a short, heavyset man who'd just emerged from behind one of the doors. "This what you're looking for," he said. The other man nodded and backed through the doorway.

Coughlin stopped at the opened door across the corridor. He dipped his head a little so that the fluorescent ceiling light shone on the quarter-size scalp in the back of his dark hair.

Vicky stepped into an office about the size of the entry. A wedge of sunlight bursting past the narrow window lay over the folders and papers stacked on the desk, taking most of the space. A computer occupied a small table between the desk and a metal file cabinet. Pinned to the wall above was a map of Fremont County, crisscrossed with red and blue lines that marked off the boundaries of the reservation and the towns of Lander, Riverton, and Dubois from the vast spaces of the county itself—the jurisdiction of the sheriff's department. On both sides of the map were framed photographs: Coughlin posing with a petite blond woman and two small, towheaded boys; Coughlin in a fisherman's vest and waders, grinning and holding up a trout that might have measured two feet; the two boys in swim trunks and orange inflated vests running through the water at the edge of a lake; the blond woman in a long, white wedding dress.

"So I been asking myself, which one of the Indians we picked up this week are you here about?" The detective had to turn sideways to work his way to the swivel chair behind the desk. "Got two or three DUIs, and Les Willows in again for loitering and public drunkenness. My opinion, old Les likes to pay us a visit from time to time and get sobered up. So who's your client? I thought Hurst was taking on the small potatoes cases."

Vicky took the chair next to the door. "I'm here about the woman found murdered in the Gas Hills," she said.

The detective pulled a blank face. He let a couple of beats pass before he said, "You mean the skeleton. Under investigation, Vicky. You know I can't discuss an ongoing investigation."

"That's what I'm here about," she said. "The investigation. People on the reservation want to know that the woman's murder is being investigated."

"Well, what the hell do they think we're doing here? Playing Monopoly?"

"Two articles in the paper, Gary. One asking for information on any woman who might be missing."

"It's not like my phone's been ringing off the hook with responses."

Vicky sat back in the chair, taking a moment before she said, "That's it? Two weeks since the bones were found, and that's it?" But that wasn't it, Vicky realized. Coughlin was looking at the corner of the ceiling, avoiding her eyes, running the palm of his hand across his mouth.

"Come on, Gary," Vicky said. "There must be something you're working on. I'd like to go back to the reservation and tell the women . . ."

"Women?"

"They're very upset. They identify with that woman murdered in the Gas Hills. They think it could have been them or someone close, maybe a daughter." *It could have been Susan.* "And the thing is, it doesn't look like the sheriff's office is placing a lot of importance on the murder."

The man waved a hand between them, fingers outstretched. "We both know that's a damn lie. It doesn't matter when the murder took place. We're investigating it the same as if it happened yesterday."

"Then give me something to take back. Anything yet from forensics?"

Coughlin leaned back and, lacing his fingers over his shirt, swiveled from side to side a moment. Finally, he said, "We got the report a couple of days ago. These things take time. It's not like the lab had a lot to go on. Skeleton wasn't even intact. Some bones were missing."

"What else?" Vicky felt the small office begin to blur around her. There was more! All of her attention narrowed on the man seated on the other side of the desk. When the detective didn't respond, she said, "It's a public record, you know."

"It's an ongoing investigation, Vicky." Coughlin took a moment, then he swiveled around, got to his feet and yanked open the top drawer of the file cabinet. He ran his fingers over the files crammed inside, extracted a thin folder, and slammed the drawer shut. Dropping back onto his chair, he slapped the folder onto the desk. "She was shot in the back of the head. Twenty-two slug found inside the skull." He went on, eyes fixed on the top page. "Beaten before death. Several teeth missing; evidence of bleeding into the jaw bones. We gave all that to the *Gazette*. I'm not gonna give you anything that we won't be releasing in the course of the investigation. Nothing that only the killer knows. You know the drill."

"What can you give me?" Vicky said.

He shrugged, opened the file folder and started thumbing through the white sheets. "Trouble is, what we know so far is just enough to get people all agitated, bring up a lot of stuff from the past, and none of it's gonna help our investigation. Just the opposite. Could throw up obstacles that'll keep us from identifying the dead woman and figuring out what happened to her.

"What are you talking about?"

"Date of death." He pulled out a sheet and stared at the lines of black type. "Pieces of clothing found under the bones were pretty well disintegrated, but the lab managed to get some identifiable manufacturing marks. Heel on what was left of a boot was manufactured from the late '60s to 1972. Metal studs on pieces of blue jeans turned out to be Levi's made in the same period. Obviously murder couldn't have taken place prior to the late '60s. Based on the condition of the bones and the physical evidence, forensics ballparks the murder about 1973. Most likely in the warm months because the killer would've had a real hard time digging a grave in frozen ground." He stared at the typed sheet a moment, then snapped the folder shut. "You know what was going on then?"

"AIM," Vicky said.

"You got it. American Indian Movement, Indians passing through from all over the country, protesting and raising hell, demanding Indian rights, hiding out from the law. Nothing but trouble and violence. Every law enforcement agency in the county was working overtime trying to keep Indians from killing one another, whites from killing Indians and vice versa."

"Part of the civil rights movement," Vicky said. She had been in her teens then, trying to catch the eye of the basketball captain, studying for exams, riding her horse in the pasture. She could remember the whispered conversations between her parents in the kitchen, the protest marches in Fort Washakie, and her father saying, "We're staying home. It's not our business what those Indians are doing." It wasn't until later that she'd realized it had been their business—Indian rights were their business. She had started dreaming about becoming a lawyer then, to help ensure that her people had rights. But that was before she'd met Ben Holden, just out of the army, home from Germany, and more handsome and confident than any high school boy she'd ever dated. It wasn't until ten years later, after she'd broken away, that she'd remembered her dream.

"Was she Indian?" Vicky said.

"Yeah, she was Indian. Report says the flat shape of the face, projecting cheekbones and shovel-shaped incisors are consistent with Native American heritage. She was around twenty years old."

The women were right, Vicky was thinking. The girl was Indian and she was young. She kept her gaze on the detective, his head bent over the opened folder, eyes skimming another sheet. Then he started flipping through the other pages, taking a couple of seconds to digest each one before he shuffled them back into place. "Postpartum pits on the inside surface of the pelvic bones," he said finally. "She'd given birth."

Vicky had to close her eyes against this piece of information. It was a moment before she opened them again. She stared into the blur of sunlight drifting over the papers on the desk, inching toward the folder. It was worse than she'd thought. It was not only the murdered girl. There had been a child.

She said, "What about any young women reported missing at that time?"

Coughlin gave her an exasperated smile. "Sixteen to be exact, between 1970 and 1975. Every one accounted for, either dead or alive. There's nobody missing from this county at that time that we don't know about. You know what that means? She came from somewhere else. Woman from another reservation, moving around." He leaned across the desk. "There was a little piece of red cloth under the skeleton. I talked to some of my neighbors, old-timers who were around then. They tell me you could spot AIM Indians by the black hats or the red bands they'd wear around their hair. Looks to me like she was one of them. Came through here and met her fate. Bottom line, Vicky. Chances of ever identifying her are slim to nonexistent."

"Then whoever killed her got away with it."

"You know how many killers are walking around free? We're not living in a perfect world. People commit murder and get away with it. Police do the investigations and, most of the time, they finger the murderer, but sometimes the evidence is missing—the hard proof they need to get the murderer convicted. So, case remains unsolved until . . ."

"Someone comes forward. A witness or accomplice willing to testify."

"You got it. We're looking at a murder that took place more than thirty years ago. Witnesses and accomplices could have moved on, could be anywhere. Could be dead, for that matter. So we got an old homicide with a victim most likely not from the area and nobody around who knows what happened."

"But if you could get her DNA," Vicky said. She could see the faces of the women in her office, the dark eyes shadowed with fear and worry. Another woman murdered. No one held accountable.

"Yeah, and what good's that gonna do? What are we gonna compare it to? Same with a dental workup. We'll get one done, and maybe we'll get lucky and find her dental records. Don't count on it."

"What about a facial reconstruction? You could distribute her photo to newspapers in the region, distribute it to all the reservations . . ."

"We're working on it now. Soon's we get the reconstruction, we'll distribute the photos everywhere, but I gotta remind you, this is a cold, cold case. This is a block of ice at the bottom of a frozen lake. Like I said, everything changes in thirty years. We have to be realistic about our chances."

"Is that what you want me to tell the women on the rez?"

"Tell them we're as concerned as they are. We want to find the SOB who did it. We're never gonna close the case. But unless we catch a break, unless somebody knows something or heard something, unless we get something to go on . . ."

He shrugged.

"I'll be in touch," Vicky said, getting to her feet. She worked her way around the cramped space to the door. The detective was already there, holding it open and nodding her into the corridor.

"I'll see you out," he said.

VICKY spotted the white paper on the dashboard inside her Jeep as she crossed the asphalt lot. She reached the Jeep and stopped. Past the sunlight dancing in the windshield, she could make out her name printed in black on the front of an envelope. She glanced at the doors. The Jeep was still locked, just as she'd left it.

She looked around. There was no one else in the parking lot, nothing but a row of parked sedans and pickups with the white vehicles of the sheriff's department at the far end. The sound of a lawn mower whirred in the distance. The wind blowing over the asphalt was hot and sweet-smelling with the odor of newly-mown grass. A dump truck lumbered down the street, turned right, and disappeared behind the bungalows across the street.

Vicky glanced back at the massive, beige stone building.

Sunlight winked in the blank-looking windows. Nothing moved; there was no sign of life. The building might have been vacant. She fished her key out of her bag and pressed the open button on the remote. The lock buttons jumped up, and Vicky slid onto the seat and reached for the envelope. The air inside was so hot, she could hardly breathe. Leaving the door open, she ran a finger under the envelope's flap and pulled out the sheet of paper folded in three. In the center of the paper, were thick, black capital letters: STOP.

Vicky got out, slammed the door shut and hurried back to the building. In the entry, she told the blond receptionist that she had to see Coughlin again.

"He might've left," the woman said. "I think he was going out."

"Call him for me, please," Vicky said. The man hadn't left. There was no one in the parking lot.

The receptionist had the receiver pressed to one ear. "That lawyer again. Says she has to see you." She dropped the receiver. "He's on the way. He has appointments, you know, so I hope you won't be taking too much more of his . . ."

The door on the left swung open. "What'd you forget?"

Vicky stepped into the corridor and waited until he'd closed the door. She had no intention of providing the receptionist with any gossip to pass around. "This was on my dashboard," she said, thrusting the envelope into the detective's hand. "Whoever left it got into a locked car."

Coughlin worked the folded sheet past the flap, then stared at the word a moment. "You sure?" he said.

"It was locked, Gary. But somebody put that inside. It's part of the message. Whoever did it can do anything, get in anywhere. Somebody knows who she was," Vicky hurried on. "Somebody here and now knows what happened thirty years ago."

The detective was shaking his head. "What else are you working on?" He waved the sheet of paper between them. "This could refer to anything."

"It refers to the skeleton." Vicky could feel the truth of it. "The women came to see me yesterday. Somebody must have found out that I'd agreed to talk to you." She shrugged. "I'd agreed to put some pressure on you, let you know the women want this case solved. Whoever it is was waiting for me to show up here. He wants me to back off. He must be hoping that if nobody on the rez says anything, you'll dump the case in the unsolved files."

"Okay, okay," Coughlin said, and she realized she'd raised her voice. "I'll check the outside security cameras, see what they picked up. I also intend to talk to people on the rez and shake things up a little. Somebody's bound to want to talk about thirty years ago."

Vicky stared at the man for a long moment. That was not going to happen. People on the rez were not going to open up to a white man.

She thanked him and made her way back across the entry and the hot asphalt to the Jeep, glancing around as she went, half expecting someone to materialize out of the haze of heat and the wind. There was no one.

6

1973

THE lights of Lander glowed in the black sky ahead. The Ford's headlights flowed down the highway a short distance before being swallowed into the darkness. Liz felt suspended in space, plunging through a dark void, the only people left in the world, she and Luna. The baby had started to stir in the backseat, and Liz could hear the faint thrusts of tiny fists against the sides of the cardboard box. The baby would be awake in a minute, awake and hungry, and, oh God, she was out of formula. She'd given Luna the last can a couple of hours ago, just before she'd gone to the meeting.

Liz hunched over the wheel, trying to keep her own breathing quiet, hoping that the hum of the engine and the rhythmic sweep of the tires on the asphalt would lull the baby back to sleep. In the dim light of the dashboard she could see the needle bouncing on empty. She tried to think how much money she had. A couple of dollars in her wallet. Some change in the bottom of her purse. There might be a few quarters in the jockey box, what whites called the glove compartment, some dimes or nickels on the floor. If she could get to Lander . . .

She gripped the wheel hard, willing the car to keep going,

conscious of the darkness rolling like clouds outside the windows. The baby was starting to make little wake-up noises. How well she knew everything about Luna, the sounds she made when she was hungry or needed a change, or wanted company. It was odd to know so much about someone that, just a month ago, she hadn't known at all. Except that even before Luna was born, she'd felt the light kicks inside her and known her baby wanted something. Maybe for her to turn over or sit in a different position or go for a walk. Little by little she'd come to know her baby.

The baby would want to eat. She had to get more formula, and that wouldn't leave much for gas. Not enough to get anywhere, Liz was thinking. Not enough to get out of Lander, but Ardyth was in Lander, and in some part of her, Liz realized that, for the last thirty minutes, ever since she'd left Ruth's, she'd been heading south toward Ardyth's place. There was no other place to go.

Ardyth LeConte had been living in Lander for almost a year, ever since she'd walked away from AIM last fall. "I don't need any more of this shit," she'd said. They were still in Washington, D.C., organizing cars for people to get back to the rez after the Trail of Broken Treaties, that had started with so much hope, had ended with so much pain. Liz had no idea how Ardyth had gotten back across the country. She hadn't returned to Pine Ridge, and it wasn't until Liz had moved back to the Wind River Reservation that she heard Ardyth was living in Lander. Got herself training as a nurse's aide and a job in a nursing home. Become like *them*, that's what Robert and Brave Bird, Loreen and Ruth and all the others said. Ardyth was whiteized.

They'd come to see her once, Loreen and Ruth and Liz. They'd wanted to see how she was making out, for old times' sake, Ruth had said. After all, they'd been through a lot together, and what sense was there in letting it all go because Ardyth decided to become white? They could stop by, say hello, see what it was like in the white world. And who knew? Maybe Ardyth was ready to come back.

It was the beginning of June, Liz remembered, already hot, the wind blowing like a fan turned on high and the baby heavy inside her. Ardyth hadn't been at home, so they'd hung around the yard awhile, sitting in the pickup with the doors open, feet dangling over the running board, eating the sandwiches and drinking the Coke they'd lifted off the convenience store, and waited. They were sure she'd show up, but now that Liz thought about it, Ardyth had probably been at work, because that's what she did. She went to work every day, like a white woman in the white world.

Luna started making gurgling noises that Liz knew would progress from whimpering into full, panicked cries of hunger. The lights ahead were more distinct, like torches burning on the horizon. The gas needle lay flat on empty, but a minute ago she'd caught it jumping below, and there was something about the engine, the kind of hesitancy that meant it was about to stop. She could feel her heart thumping against her ribs. Just a little farther.

She drove around the bend into the edge of town. Streetlights flooded the pavement in front of the gas station and convenience store across the highway. Luna was crying, and the high, piercing wails almost masked the sound of the sputtering engine. Liz could feel the floorboard jerk beneath her. She shifted into neutral, coasted across the oncoming lane and rolled down the paved ramp to the parking lot in front of the store. When she shifted back into drive, the Ford jumped forward a few feet, which was enough to line up with the gas pump.

She opened the jockey box and ran her hand under the papers until her fingers brushed the cool pieces of metal. She scooped out three quarters, then leaned over and swept her hand under the seat. About sixty cents worth of dimes, nickels, and pennies. She checked the bottom of her purse, found another quarter, and pulled the dollar bills out of her wallet. Stuffing the wad of money into her jeans pocket, she got out. She lifted Luna out of her box, put the baby against her shoulder, and, patting the small back, headed into the store. "It's okay," she kept saying, trying to ignore the weight dropping like iron in her stomach. "Get All Your Supplies Here" flashed in red and yellow lights inside the plate glass window.

"Help you?" The man behind the counter laid a thick arm on top of the cash register, leaned sideways over the counter, and fixed her with watery blue eyes that looked as if he were weeping. He had hair that resembled yellow plastic, the way it stood out around his fleshy, red face. There were marble-sized pockmarks in his cheeks and across his forehead.

"You got baby formula?" Liz had to shout over the baby crying.

"Second aisle. I'll walk you," he said, swinging around the counter.

Liz started after him along shelves stacked with candy bars and breath mints and chips. He had thick buttocks that swayed from side to side, and he kept glancing back at her, making sure she wasn't helping herself to any candy bars, as if she wanted any of his stinking candy. She stroked the round back of Luna's head; the damp black hair clung to her palm, like corn silk.

"Here you go," the man said, waving one hand over a shelf of baby formula.

Liz stared at the price tag fixed below the cans and jiggled the baby in an effort to calm her. She could buy two cans and still get a few gallons of gas. She picked up the first, stuffed it in the crook of her arm next to the baby, and grabbed the second. "That's all I need," she said, the falseness of it clanging in her ears.

"Okeydokey," he said, ushering her ahead, not about to repeat the mistake he'd made when he let her walk behind.

"What're you doin' in these parts anyway?" He swung his bulk around the end of the counter and waited for Liz to set down the cans, which he picked up one by one as he pressed the keys on the register.

"What?" Luna was wailing now, tossing her head back, blinking up into the fluorescent lights. "Buying stuff. I need gas."

"What, the convenience store on the rez run dry?"

"I'm visiting a friend," she managed. Her throat felt dry and tight, her cheeks warm with anger. Why was she slipping into the role he expected of her? Indian girl with no rights— no rights to exist.

"How much?"

"What?" she said again.

"You got somethin' wrong with your hearing? How much gas you gonna put on your bill? You owe me a dollar fifty for the formula."

Liz pulled the coins and crumpled bills out of her jeans pocket and spread them on the counter with one hand. She pushed a bill and two quarters toward the register. That left two dollars and some change. She pushed the bills toward the others.

"Two dollars," she said, patting Luna's back. She dropped her face and kissed the top of the baby's head. "It's okay, okay," she whispered.

"Your friend better be close by." The white man jabbed at the keys. The register made a series of clanking noises before the drawer popped open. He stuffed the money into the narrow compartments, slammed the drawer shut and tore off the white receipt that had popped out of the top.

"You got two bucks on number two," he said, nodding toward the red and yellow lights blinking in the plate glass window. "You know how to pump gas?" His fingers were working the receipt into a ball. "Don't want nothing busted up out there."

Liz picked up the cans of formula and, pressing them against her, pushed the glass door open with her foot and hurried back to the car. She set the baby into the cardboard box and crawled in alongside. It took a moment to locate the baby bottle wrapped in the diapers in her bag, pull the tab on one of the cans, and fill the bottle. All the while, Luna was screaming, arms and legs flailing. Liz picked her up and squeezed a drop of milk out of the nipple onto the baby's pink tongue. A look of surprise came into Luna's black eyes, then she latched onto the nipple, making loud slurping noises.

Liz settled against the backseat watching the shadows and light move across the tiny face and the hungry way the little pink mouth worked at the nipple. For a moment, the fear and worry gave way to a sense of hope. "Baby, baby," she sang. "We're on the train to happiness now. See the light shining ahead for us. You got that light in your eyes, baby. I see it shining there for us, just for us . . ."

She shut her own eyes and there was Jake Tallfeathers, watching her from across the room at the meeting, his fist knocking the countertop—tap, tap, tap. Her eyes snapped open. The white man was leaning down, tapping on the window.

"Get your gas and move on," he yelled. "Can't have no loitering around here."

Liz pulled the bottle away and laid Luna back in the box. The baby was gulping screams as Liz got out. She opened the gas tank, jammed in the nozzle and stared at the black numbers jumping in the white box on top of the pump, conscious of the muffled sound of Luna's crying, the white man watching her from the other side of the car. It was never like this when they were together—Arapaho, Sioux, Crow, Blackfeet, Ojibwa, and a lot of tribes she'd never heard of, gathered together, standing up to the white man.

The hose bucked to a stop in her hand. She put it back into place, closed the gas cap, and got in behind the wheel. The white man loomed in the side mirror as she drove past the pump. She pulled into the vacant lot next to the station, and crawled into the backseat. She gave the bottle to Luna again and made herself sing, trying to focus on the song she'd written when she'd learned she was pregnant. Her voice was trembling; she couldn't keep it calm: "Baby, baby, it's a long way to go. The road is hard, I'm telling you now. I love you so. Pick up your pack and keep on going. Keep on going. Keep on going."

She thought Luna's eyes were drooping, but she couldn't be sure in the darkness pressing around the car. Beyond the darkness, across the vacant lot, the gas station stood in a well of light, red and yellow neon lights flashing through. The sucking noise stopped, leaving only the trace of her own voice humming the song. She was singing at the bar in Rapid City when Jimmie Iron had walked in. Another song she'd written—*Mama said, you get in the car, girl. We're gonna ride outta here, ride into a new life and everything's gonna be fine. I promise you, promise you. Mama lied. Girl, there's a new man gonna take care of us and everything's gonna be fine. He's got eyes like diamonds and gold in his pockets. I promise you, promise you. Mama lied.*

She could see Jimmie smiling as he lowered himself onto the bar stool. He spoke out of the side of his mouth when the bartender walked over, because he hadn't taken his eyes from her. Pretty soon he was drinking a bottle of beer, but she could tell he wasn't paying attention to the beer. And that had made her want to laugh right in the middle of the song. She'd strummed a wrong note on the guitar, thinking that the bartender could have handed Jimmie any kind of drink and he wouldn't have even noticed.

She switched to another one of her songs, one she usually didn't feel like singing, but that night, with Jimmie watching her, it had just come out, almost on its own. *Indian girl, you're a long way from home, that's what they told me. Indian girl, you'd better get along. I didn't listen, no I didn't listen, 'cause there were dreams I had, dreams waitin' for me. Oh, I had dreams waitin' for me.*

It was good then. *Ni isini.* She'd felt warm all over, like summer sunshine coming over her after the long, freezing winter. When she'd finished the set, he'd walked over. "What's an Indian girl doing here?"

"Singing. Didn't you hear?"

"Yeah, I like what I hear," he'd said. "Like what I see, too. Like that long braid you got down your back."

"You from around here?" She'd never seen the likes of Jimmie Iron at Pine Ridge. He wasn't exactly handsome, but strong looking with dark eyes that looked straight at her and a feeling of power in the way he held his head and walked, like he owned a piece of the world. He was from Minneapolis, he'd said. Moved onto the rez for a while to get things organized. She ever heard of the civil rights business going on? Happening for everybody 'cept Indians. Now things were gonna be changing, did she know that? We're gonna get what's ours, get our rights. White folks don't think we got any rights. We gotta teach 'em otherwise. It's gonna be a good ride. You wanna come along?

And she'd said, yeah, sure. Why not? Rights? What was he talking about? White folks didn't think Indians had any rights, well neither did Indians. Not any she knew. They'd been living in a two-room shack on Pine Ridge after her mother decided to leave the Wind River Reservation and go find Ray, the Lakota she'd met barely two months after her father had been killed in that car wreck. She'd pushed Liz into the back of an old Pontiac with torn seats and trash littering the floor and said, "We're gonna get us a new life." Liz remembered singing to herself all the way to Pine Ridge, to keep from crying because Mom didn't like crying. She always said, "You gotta be tough to be an Indian girl." Liz had made herself concentrate on Grandfather and the trailer where they'd been living, and for a long time after Mom had taken her away, she'd put the images of Grandfather and the trailer in her mind at night so she could sleep when Mom and Ray were drinking and fighting.

"Meeting tomorrow night," Jimmie had said. He described the house off the road that ran south out of Wounded Knee. "You'll see the cars parked out in front. There's gonna be a lot of us. We're goin' to Washington, caravans of Indians from all over the country. Gonna pay a visit on our Great White Father." He'd laughed at that, a deep rumbling noise that had bubbled out of his throat.

Liz had laughed with him. She understood even then that there was no Great White Father.

"You wanna come to the meeting? Might wanna join up?"

"Why not?" she'd told him again.

Something was moving at the edge of her vision now. Liz glanced over at the convenience store. The white man had come outside and was looking her way. He swung around, yanked open the door and strode inside. She saw him moving toward the cash register, dragging the phone along the counter, clamping the receiver to his ear.

God. She had to get out of here. The white man would have the police here in a couple of minutes. They'd arrest her for loitering or trespassing or being Indian. She settled Luna back in the box, got behind the wheel and drove out of the lot, tires squealing as she pulled onto the asphalt. She headed onto Main Street, trying to remember the street they'd turned on when she and Ruth and Loreen had come to see Ardyth. The brick buildings looked eerie in the yellowish wash of the streetlights. Black plate glass windows looked like the entrances to dark tunnels.

She took a right and drove into the darkness of a residential neighborhood, searching for some landmark, something to point the way. There was nothing.

7

THE sun blazed overhead by the time Father John drove into the mission, "Der Vogelfänger bin ich ja" blaring from the tape player on the seat next to him. He'd spent the morning visiting parishioners at Riverton Memorial—Molly Boggles and her new baby girl, Esther White Horse, still in intensive care after the automobile accident. He'd given the sacrament of the last rites to James Fox, eighty-one years old, body ravaged by diabetes and kidney failure, an old man waiting to die, and at peace about it. He'd thanked Father John for the sacrament. It made him feel better, he'd said, as if Father John were the one who needed to be comforted.

The mission buildings around Circle Drive stood out in relief against the brightness: the administration building and the church, the museum, the two-story, redbrick residence. He parked the Toyota pickup in front of the residence, alongside the blue sedan that his assistant, Father Ian McCauley, drove, turned off the tape and got out.

Walks-On, the golden retriever he'd found in the ditch after he'd been hit by a car several years ago, lay stretched on the lawn in a patch of shade, head framed by his front paws.

The vet in Riverton where Father John had taken him had managed to save his life, but not his hind leg, something the dog hadn't seemed to notice, or had considered not worth noticing compared to the fact that he was still alive. Father John had brought him to the mission and named him Walks-On-Three-Legs—a tribute to the dog's courage, he thought. He, himself, was still shaky at the time—well, that hadn't changed—with moments coming out of nowhere, like a brick wall dropping in front of him, when all he wanted in the world was a glass of whiskey. Oddly enough, watching Walks-On lope across the mission grounds on three legs, well, it still gave him a sense of courage.

The minute Father John got out of the pickup, the dog ran toward him, then pivoted on his hind leg and sprinted for the house. Father John ran up the sidewalk after him. It was a game they played—who could get onto the front stoop first. Walks-On usually won, leaping over the two concrete steps and positioning himself wide legged on the stoop, tail flapping against the door. Father John had to nudge him aside to let them both inside.

The aroma of fresh coffee rolled down the hallway and gathered in the entry like invisible fog. He set his cowboy hat on the bench and followed Walks-On into the kitchen. Father Ian sat at the round table in the center of the room, working at what looked like a bologna sandwich. He gave Father John a little nod. Elena was at the sink, hands plunged into soapy water. The suds crawled up her brown arms almost to her elbows.

"Sandwich's in the fridge, whenever you're ready," she said, glancing over one shoulder, swishing a plate through the water. A breed, people hereabouts called people like her—half Arapaho and half something else. In Elena's case, the other half was Cheyenne, which showed in her rounded, flat face and squared build. She had the high forehead and hooked nose of the Arapaho, and the black eyes that, when she trained them on him, had a way of penetrating into his soul, much the way his mother used to look at him when he was a kid. Elena had been taking care of the priests at St. Francis for at least three decades, Father John figured, although she claimed not to remember how long she'd been the housekeeper. "Long enough," she'd told him once, "to know the peculiar ways of you Jesuits."

"I was hurrying to get back for lunch," he said, making his way past her and the corner of the stove to the cabinet. He found the dog food and poured some into the dish on the floor. Then he found his sandwich on a plate in the refrigerator and took it over to the table. Ian, who always seemed to be on time, had already eaten his sandwich. A good priest, Father John had to give him that, the kind of assistant he'd been praying for, one who would make the effort to fit in, get to know the people, like the place.

"I heard that before." Elena turned halfway around and gave him another knowing look.

"Provincial called this morning," Father Ian said. He was about forty, younger than Father John by eight or nine years, with thinning sandy-colored hair and bushy brown eyebrows that climbed toward his forehead, and a determination that flowed into everything he did, from counseling parishioners and keeping track of the mission's finances, or lack thereof, to saying Mass and staying sober. He'd arrived six months ago, straight out of rehab, eager for a job, eager to prove himself, hurrying up the sidewalk lugging an old suitcase and a box of books, the hint of alcoholic flush still in his cheeks. My God, Father John had felt as though he were watching the rerun of an old movie in which he'd starred, and the pastor waiting in the doorway was Father Peter, willing to give him a chance when nobody else would take the risk.

"Any message?" Father John was aware of the sound of dishes clinking together and water swirling down the drain. He took a bite of his sandwich.

"Said to call as soon as you got in."

He could feel his heart speeding up now. There was always the possibility that this was the call, the one that would send him away from St. Francis. He'd already been here three years longer than the Jesuits usually left a man in place. Too many entanglements, relationships, involvements—it was always a danger. Better that the priest remained always free to go on. *Here I am, Lord. Send me.* But the provincial had let him stay while he'd cast about for a replacement, sending one assistant after another, a bit like throwing darts against the wall, hoping that sooner or later one would stick.

And now there was Father Ian McCauley.

"Any other messages?" Father John asked, feeling a conscious urge to change the subject.

"I got one." Elena dried her hands on a towel, poured some coffee into a mug and set it in front of him. "You didn't get your coffee," she said.

"Pour some for yourself," he told her. It was a routine they'd developed over the years. Whenever Elena wanted to sit down and talk to him, she always made a big point of pouring him some coffee or refilling his mug.

She filled another mug and dropped heavily onto the chair between him and Ian—Ian watching the scene play out, Father John realized, as if he were taking mental notes. Father John could almost read the thought behind the other priest's eyes: So this is how it goes.

Elena sipped at her coffee, taking a moment before she said, "How come nobody knows that poor dead woman's name?"

"You're talking about the skeleton?" Father John said. "Is that the message?"

"Yeah, that's what we want to know."

"We?" Father Ian said.

"Women hereabouts." Elena gave Ian a quick look, before bringing her eyes back to Father John's. "They told me, ask Father John how come nobody cares who she was or what happened to her."

"I don't think that's the case," Father John said.

"How come nothing's happened? They're gonna leave her bones on a shelf in that county building out by the airport, like she was nobody."

"The sheriff's detective—"

"Hasn't done squat. Two weeks it's been now since you went out to Gas Hills and blessed her bones. Couple of articles in the newspaper. Anybody know a woman gone missing? You heard anything?"

Father John shook his head. He took a drink of his own coffee.

"It doesn't mean—" Ian said.

"It means they're gonna forget about her. Only we can't forget. The younger women, they're really upset, 'cause you know what they're thinking? Something happens to one of 'em, you know what I mean? Boyfriend starts pounding on 'em, and they could end up out in the Gas Hills like that girl, and nobody cares. Well, some of 'em got together and went to see Vicky. You and Vicky, you're the ones that gotta let that sheriff know we're watching him. There's not an Indian woman on the rez gonna vote for him next election if he don't find out what happened to that girl."

"Investigations take time," Father John said. Still, he'd been thinking about the skeleton himself, wondering why there hadn't been any new developments. Now he wondered if Elena and the women didn't have a point, if the sheriff's office hadn't moved the investigation to a back burner. It was probably an old murder. It wasn't going to be easy to solve.

"I'll give Detective Coughlin a call," he said. "See if he's found anything."

"Tell him—"

"I'll tell him," Father John said.

AFTER lunch Father John headed to his office across the field of dry grass enclosed by Circle Drive. The sun beat on his arms, and a hot wind whipped at his shirt. He would call Coughlin first, he decided. Then he would return any other messages on the machine. He'd take a stab at the work on his desk—letters to answer, bills to pay, classes to arrange for the fall—then he would call the provincial. He'd wait as long as possible to get the news. He'd already waited a long time, hoping it wouldn't come, starting every day with the same prayer: Let it not be today, Lord.

He could hear the phone ringing as he crossed the drive. He took the cement steps in front of the administration building two at a time and hurried across the wide corridor to his office on the right. A ringing phone had its own insistence, its own sense of emergency. There was always the possibility that whoever was calling needed a priest. He crossed the office and lunged for the phone on his desk.

"Father John," he said. He could hear the out-of-breath note in his voice.

"Ah, you're back." It was the voice of Father Bill Rutherford, the provincial of the Wisconsin Province, which, through a decision by the powers-that-be, had come to include Wyoming. "Something has come up. I trust you have a moment?"

Father John stepped around the desk and dropped into the old leather chair with the depressions and ridges that conformed to his own body. Yes, he had a moment. His senses were sharpened; his voice sounded loud in his own ears. He could hear a truck rumbling past on Seventeen-Mile Road. A chair scraped the floor down the corridor in Ian's office.

"What is it?" he said.

"What would you think of a sabbatical?"

"A sabbatical?"

"It's been nine years since you've had a break," Father Rutherford said. There was a pause, and Father John could hear the unspoken words clanging like a bell over the line: your last break was the year you spent in rehab at Grace House. "Everyone needs a break now and then." The provincial hurried past the awkward silence. "How does Rome sound?"

Father John stared across his office out into the corridor at the photo of a past Jesuit at St. Francis and wondered if Ian would fit his photo somewhere in the lineup with the other Jesuits who *used* to be here. "I'm not ready for a sabbatical," he said, trying to keep the conversation on the topic. He didn't want to leave St. Francis, that was the point. Everything else was meaningless.

"What a great time we had in Rome," Rutherford went on. "You remember? Walking all over the city with those heavy backpacks. Must've walked ten miles every day. Took in everything. Vatican. Forum. Coliseum. Pantheon. Piazza Navona. Trevi Fountain. What'd we miss? Not much, I'd say. Ate a lot of great Italian food, and never gained a pound, we did so much walking. You remember?"

"Look, Bill," Father John began. The truth was, he didn't remember much about that summer. They were still scholastics. He and Bill Rutherford and three other classmates—he'd be hard-pressed to come up with their names now, it seemed so long ago—had gone to Rome to do some research in the Vatican Library on the early church. Aside from his books, everything he owned was on his back. He'd looked forward to the trip. He'd been drinking more and more, but the trip was supposed to be the end of it, his own rehabilitation program in the archives. He had a vague memory of sipping wine in piazzas, throwing back whiskeys in bars, and once, drinking foot-high tumblers of beer in a closet-sized restaurant across the street from San Giovanni in Laterano. Or was it some other church? They'd done the same, Bill and the others. Odd, he'd thought then, how they could always stop.

"Somebody else probably needs a sabbatical," he pushed on. "Send him."

"I'm not *sending* you, John. This isn't an order. It's an opportunity. You'd stay at St. Ignatius, help with parish work. There's a lot of dialogue in the Society now on bringing the Christian message to indigenous peoples around the world. With your experience on the reservation, you could make a valuable contribution. Six months. How does that sound?"

"What's this all about?"

"Truth, John?"

"I'm waiting." He heard a vehicle slowing on Seventeen-Mile Road, then turning into the mission grounds.

"Okay. The truth is, you love St. Francis Mission. A sabbatical in Rome would maybe make a transition easier."

"Transition to . . ."

"I've got a man eager to do mission work. Father Paul Newton, you heard of him?" When Father John didn't say anything, the provincial went on: "Real scholar, John. Expert on the history of American Indian law. He'd like to spend time on a reservation, interview the elders and the educated people, get their reactions to the various laws. He's drawn to the Wind River Reservation. Seems to think the people have a keen sense of the past and the way various legislation has affected tribal societies. With Father Ian in place—he's doing fine, right?—it's a good time to make the change."

Father John pressed his fist against his forehead. He could hear the sound of Bill Rutherford's breathing at the other end of the line. So this was the call he'd been expecting for the last three years. It was bound to come. *And what're you gonna do, son?* His father's voice sounded in his head. He could see the old man slumped over the kitchen table, nursing a cup of coffee—half coffee, half whiskey, the mixture of odors permeating the air. *That's gonna be the hardest, that vow of obe-*

dience you're gonna have to make. You'd better think about it. Think about it. Think about it.

He'd thought about it. Sure, it would be tough, but it would all be tough—celibacy, poverty, obedience. But he would be a priest, and he would do it.

"He is doing fine, isn't he?" Bill Rutherford said.

"Yes, Ian's fine." He could manage St. Francis Mission just fine. Maybe do a better job than Father John had done. The man was more practical, more organized. He had a better handle on finances. The mission would be fine.

"I'm not ready to leave," he heard himself saying. He was the one who would not be fine. From outside came the noise of a vehicle stopping in front of the administration building.

"Be honest, John. When would you ever be ready? You've been there nine years. You know the rules . . ."

"Six years as superior," Father John said. He'd been the assistant for three years until Father Peter's heart had started to give out and the provincial had sent him to a retirement home. Even then, Father Peter hadn't wanted to leave. "The place gets to you," he'd said. "Gets under your skin, eats at you, takes chunks out of you, so when you leave, part of you stays here." He was shaking his head, and Father John remembered the way the light from the desk lamp had shone through his thick white hair. "I'm afraid it will feel like I'm missing an arm or a leg," he'd said.

"Either way you look at it," Bill Rutherford said, "I believe it's time . . ."

"You're ordering me to Rome." There was the click of footsteps on the concrete steps outside, the whoosh of air as the front door opened.

"No, no. A suggestion that you might want to take advantage of a new opportunity. I leave it to you, John, to consider. Consult with Ian, see if you think he's ready to take over as pastor. Take a little time . . ."

There was the clack of heels on the wood floor in the corridor, then Vicky stood in the doorway. Father John locked eyes with her. "I'll get back to you," he said into the receiver.

8

FATHER John got to his feet and motioned Vicky forward with the receiver before he set it into the cradle.

"You have to leave?" she asked, still planted in the doorway, her eyes fastened on his.

Leave! He smiled and shook his head. It was as if she'd been listening in on the conversation, except that he understood she was asking if he'd been summoned by one of his parishioners, somebody in the hospital or in some kind of trouble.

"Not now," he said. It would be later that he would have to leave, he was thinking. He motioned her to one of the chairs propped against the wall and started around the desk. "Coffee's hot. Care for some?"

She waved away the suggestion, then walked past him to the oblong window with sunshine flaring in the glass. She was dressed in what she called her lawyer clothes—blue blouse, dark skirt, and silver earrings that dangled and glistened through her black hair. She stared outside a moment—gathering her thoughts, he knew. He always knew when something was bothering her. He perched on the edge of the desk and waited until she swung around and faced him. Her eyes shone with intensity.

"What was it like," she began, "out in the Gas Hills where the girl was killed?"

Father John waited a couple of beats before he said, "You know the place, Vicky. Desolate. Sagebrush and arroyos. Thomas Whiteman was there. We both blessed the remains . . ."

"You mean the skeleton," she cut in. "All that was left of her, a bunch of bones that the coroner says were broken, a skull with a slug inside and some of the teeth knocked out. She was Indian, and she wore a long braid. Strange, isn't it, the way every part of her was smashed and left to disintegrate, but her braid, where she'd tied up all her worries and fears, all her problems, and tried to put them away—her braid was still there."

"What's this all about?" Father John said. How well he knew her. They'd worked together on a lot of cases. Lawyer and priest, a good team, he'd always thought. She never came to the mission unless something was troubling her.

It hit him then. She'd located the girl's family, been drawn into their grief and outrage, and now she wanted to help them and she wanted *his* help. "You know who she was?" he said.

Vicky tossed her head in a gesture somewhere between defiance and despair. She gathered a piece of hair in her fingers and pushed it back from her face. Tiny beads of perspiration dotted her nose. "Nobody knows who she was," she said. "Except the monster that killed her." She stepped back from the window and started circling the room—the chairs, the door, the window. She thought on her feet, he knew, and he could imagine her in the courtroom, circling from the defense table to the jury box to the judge's desk, arguing all the time, connecting the lines, making the point.

"I just came from Detective Coughlin's office," she said, stopping in the middle of the room and crossing her arms. She tapped her fingers against her forearms as if she were playing the scales on a keyboard. "She was twenty years old. She'd given birth."

Father John pinched the top of his nose between his thumb and forefinger. This was something new. There was a child involved.

Vicky went on: "Forensics places her murder in 1973. Sometime in spring or summer or early fall, in the warm weather."

"That's a long time ago," he said.

"You sound like Coughlin." She started pacing again, still tapping her fingers. "A cold, cold case, he told me." She stopped at the window and turned around, a small, dark figure backlit by the brightness outside, her face in shadow. The sun glistened in her hair. "There won't be a burial until she's identified, and she may never be identified."

Father John waited, and after a moment, she went on: "Several women from the rez came to see me. They don't want her forgotten, John. I don't want her forgotten. She could be any of us, any Indian woman beaten up, shot, left in the wilderness."

Then she was pacing again, telling him about being in Denver with Lucas and Susan, coming across a man beating a girl in a downtown alley, jumping out of the car and running to stop the beating. "She would have been killed," Vicky said. "She might still die. I spoke with the prosecutor in Denver on my way over here. He's waiting to add murder to the assault charges. All I could think of in that alley was that it could have been Susan. It could have been me. It could have been"—she swept one arm toward the window—"any woman out there. Left to die alone in an alley, like the girl in the Gas Hills. She deserves a name, John. Her killer shouldn't get away with it."

"Almost thirty-five years, Vicky. He could be dead."

She gave a quick, dismissive nod. "He's walking around. He got into the Jeep somehow, left a message on my dashboard. One word: stop."

Father John felt his fists clench. He didn't want to think of her in danger. He couldn't stand the thought of anyone hurting her. "Did you tell Coughlin?"

She waved a hand between them. "I gave him the message."

"There must be security cameras . . ."

"Coughlin's checking on what they may have caught. But anybody clever enough or . . ." She paused. "Experienced enough to get inside my car would know about the cameras. He would have made sure that his face wasn't exposed."

"You have to be careful."

"At least the message lets Coughlin know the killer is still around," she hurried on. "He thinks he's still safe, that nobody's ever going to know who he is, that he will never have to answer for taking that girl's life. What am I supposed to tell the women? That her murder may never be solved?" She waited a couple of beats. "Coughlin says he's accounted for all the women reported missing at that time. In other words, they were found. Some were found dead."

"She might have come from somewhere else, another reservation."

Vicky pursed her lips at this, as if he hadn't told her anything she didn't already know. "It doesn't mean no one on the rez knew her. Even if she was from somewhere else, she must have had contacts here. Otherwise, why was she here?"

Father John realized he was nodding. It was logical, the path she was taking. "There are people on the rez who were here in the 1970s," he said. "It's possible someone knew her. If Coughlin had something to go on, it would help the investigation. He could ask around . . ."

"He could also run through a canyon with a stone wall at the end. Come on, John. Nobody's going to talk to a white detective about the seventies. It was a violent time. AIM was on the reservation. Indians from all over. City Indians, my father called them, trying to take over the rez, stirring up trouble. People were divided. My own family was divided. Dad broke with one of his cousins because he'd joined AIM. My parents were progressives, the kind of Indians that AIM called 'whiteized' because they sent their daughter to the mission school. Dad went to work on the highways every day, a hundred degrees in the summer and ten below in the winter, it didn't matter. We had running water and an indoor toilet, the things that AIM scoffed at. Such things weren't Indian, they said, but Dad said they wanted to take us back to the buffalo days, the Old Time, and those days were gone."

Father John walked around the desk and perched on his chair. "What makes you think they'd talk to a white priest," he said.

"They'll talk to you," Vicky said. "They might talk to me. We have to try, John, before the investigation is forgotten."

"I told some of the elders I'd drop by the senior citizens center this afternoon," he said.

The tension that had lined her face dissolved in the smile she gave him. "Call me if you learn anything," she said. "Anything at all." She picked up the bag she'd dropped on a chair, headed toward the door, then turned back. "This is important to me," she said.

"I understand," Father John said. She'd told him about Ben, sitting here in his office, weeping into a tissue, saying how she'd never told anyone, how no one would have believed her. Ben Holden, one of the leading men on the reservation, foreman at the Arapaho Ranch. Everybody knew him; everybody respected him, and she had respected that, not wanting him to be diminished. But she'd said something else, he remembered, that made even more sense now. She'd told him that she couldn't forgive herself—forgive herself!—for protecting him, because it wouldn't have made any difference. She had protected him for no reason at all. None of his friends would have thought less of a man who considered it okay to beat his wife, because so many of them did the same.

"I knew you'd help," she said, and then she was gone, her heels clicking in the corridor. There was the slightest disturbance in the air as the door opened and shut.

T H E senior citizens center was a low-slung building under a mansard roof covered with wood shingles that sloped almost to the ground. A few trucks parked at odd angles stood in front. Beyond the building, the brown earth ran unobstructed into the far distances and melted into the pale blue sky. Father John parked next to a white truck. A hot wind beat at his back as he hurried up the graveled sidewalk and yanked open the door.

There was a vacant feeling inside, despite the elders seated at the table in front of the window across the large hall. Other tables and chairs were scattered over the scrubbed-tile floor. Over against the side wall was a table that held a metal coffeepot and stacks of foam cups. From the kitchen beyond the closed door on the right came the rattle of dishes and the clank of metal against metal. The odors of fresh bacon grease mingled with the aroma of fresh coffee.

Father John was halfway across the hall when Thomas

Whiteman threw up one hand, like a traffic cop, and nodded toward the table with the coffeepot. "Help yourself," he shouted. His voice reverberated around the empty hall.

Father John went to the side table and poured some coffee. He stirred powdered milk into the black liquid until it turned the color of caramel, then carried the cup past three vacant tables and sat down on the chair that Thomas had nudged away from the table with his boot.

"Glad you could stop by," Thomas said. He had on a light blue Western-style shirt with silver snaps in front and brown broncos on the yokes. His white hair was caught in two braids that hung down the front of his shirt. His brown face was mapped with squint lines and laugh lines and worry lines. He sat sideways, one arm resting on the table, and squinted past the light that glowed in the window.

The other elder sipped at the coffee in a foam cup and nodded. Hugh Bad Elk was close to seventy, a big man with the muscular shoulders and the broad chest of a man half his age. He was always at the ten o'clock Sunday Mass, sitting at the end of the second pew on the right, like a door blocking the exit, his wife, Lucy, and grandkids filling up the rest of the pew.

"Sermon you gave last Sunday was okay." He set the cup on the table. His hair was still black, streaked in gray and pulled back from his pockmarked face into a ponytail. "How the Creator don't want us staying where we are, how He keeps pushing us forward. Wants us to keep growin', that what you said?"

"That's what I said." Father John shook his head and smiled at the irony. Was that really what he'd said? Two days before the provincial had called? He took a sip of the hot coffee that dropped through his chest like a strand of liquid metal.

Thomas cleared his throat and said the weather'd been so hot, the fields were burning up, and it wouldn't surprise him if the wind blew the reservation all the way to Nebraska. Hugh added there was so much dust blowing outside his house, he thought he was gonna have to take a shovel to dig out his truck this morning. "Everything okay at the mission?"

Father John said that everything was okay. Then, sensing that the polite preliminaries were over and the time was right to launch into the subject on his mind, he said, "Some of the women on the rez are upset about the murdered girl in the Gas Hills. The autopsy confirms that she was Indian."

"Took all them tests to come up with that?" Thomas shook his head. "Her hair was braided, wasn't it? That's why one of them sheriff's detectives thought he'd better give me a call. Save himself some trouble later if folks found out she was Indian and there was nobody there to bless her. Called you for the same reason, right?"

Father John nodded. It was a lonely place, sad. He had a hunch that calling one of the Arapaho holy men and the mission priest to the site might have been more for the sheriff's deputies and the coroner than for what was left of the girl buried in the gulley.

"It looks like she was killed in 1973," he said.

The elders stared at him with blank faces, waiting for him to go on. It struck him they'd already discussed the matter and had reached the same conclusion.

"Early seventies," Hugh said finally. "That's what we figured. AIM people."

The hall went quiet. Hugh went back to drinking his coffee and Thomas turned toward the window. Outside, clouds of dust whipped across the plains. "Sonofabitch never got caught," he said, shifting around and squaring himself to the table. He bowed his head and ran his forearm across his brow. Little tracks of perspiration blossomed on the sleeve of his blue shirt.

"The women want to know what happened to her," Father John said. "They want her murder solved."

"Tell 'em we're gonna give the girl a proper burial, see that she goes to the ancestors. Her ghost's not gonna be walking around anymore looking for the way to the sky world. We're gonna take care of her, soon's we get the bones from the coroner."

"The coroner's going to need help identifying her. Detective Coughlin's going to need help. Somebody on the rez might remember her."

Thomas exchanged a quick glance with the other elder, then cleared his throat. He set his hands on the table and laced his fingers together into a tight grip. White knuckles rose like miniature mountain peaks out of the brown skin. "Nobody's gonna want to talk about that old time. It's over and done with, and I say good riddance. You gotta tell them investigators that we need to bury her."

"She has to be identified first, Grandfather," Father John said. His voice was soft. He waited a moment, then he said, "She had a child. The child would be grown now, in the thirties probably. It's possible her child is here."

Hugh cleared his throat, as if he were about to say something. He shot a glance at Thomas—the elder one, the holy man—then sat back, dropped his head, and studied the front of his yellow shirt.

Thomas said, "They came from all over, them AIM people. Lakota, Blackfeet, Crow, Ojibwa, Cheyenne. Most of 'em city Indians trying to figure out who the hell they were. Didn't know nothing about our culture and ways. Never went to the elders and asked permission to come on the rez. They just came. Thought they was gonna take over, run the rez their way. Held demonstrations, marched around with the flag upside down, that was their way. Shouting for Indian rights. Demanding treaty rights, saying the government's got to give back all the land that was ours in the treaties. One day, they left. Took some of our people with 'em, some of the young warriors just back from Vietnam and having a tough time. AIM give 'em the kind of battle they wanted to fight. I heard there was miles of trucks and vans full of Indians from all over that went to Washington to see the Great White Father just like in the old days."

He gave a bark of laughter, threw his head back and stared at the ceiling, as if he were watching the images of the caravans converging on the Capitol. "Took over the BIA building. Could've gotten a lot of people killed, with them soldiers surrounding 'em, like in the Old Time. Couple warriors did get killed, if I remember right. Went to Pine Ridge and took over Wounded Knee. From what I heard on the moccasin telegraph, Feds came rolling in with assault weapons and armored trucks, like it was Vietnam. Whole town was destroyed. Lot of people got wounded. After it was over, the Feds went after those Indians real hard. Some of 'em came here, looking to hide. There was people here that helped 'em. It was a bad time. Feds crawling all over the place, and there was gossip all the time that AIM was gonna occupy some place on the rez next."

Hugh sipped at his coffee. When Thomas didn't continue, he said, "Folks like us were working, raising kids back then. Hell, we didn't have time for demonstrations and marches. They had a big demonstration in Fort Washakie. I was real worried they'd take over the tribal offices, 'cause I had a job in accounting. How was I gonna get paid if I couldn't work? They hated those of us in the younger generation, AIM did. Said the mission school turned us into white men. People that went AIM's way were the young vets and the old traditionals living out on their ranches like in the Old Time. They thought AIM was gonna bring back the old ways."

"No good's gonna come from going into all that," Thomas said. He was shaking his head, the white braids swayed across his chest. "Lot of people got hurt. AIM pushed folks into separate camps. You was for 'em, or you was against 'em. Either way, you might get killed."

"There was lots of murders in that time." Hugh pushed his empty foam cup into the center of the table. It spun like a top, then tipped over, spilling out little drops of black coffee. "Two or three hundred all over Indian country, I heard. Maybe more. Most of 'em never solved. Just bodies that turned up in ditches and graves out on the prairie. Police shrugged 'em off. Indians killing Indians, is what they thought. There wasn't any justice for those dead Indians."

"There wasn't any justice for the dead girl, either," Father John said. "It's an old case," he hurried on, "and Coughlin may not make any headway in the investigation unless we can come up with something that might help."

Thomas drew himself upright along the back of his chair and squared his shoulders. "You go asking questions, Father—I don't mean no disrespect—but people ain't gonna like it. There was a lot of violence on the rez back then. There's people that might be what they call 'accessories.' If that old stuff gets dragged up, they're gonna think they could get in trouble. They're gonna be scared."

"Police shot one of them AIM people over in Ethete, if I remember right," Hugh said, crossing his arms and pushing against the back of his chair.

"Do you have a name?" This was something, Father John was thinking. There would be records, police reports.

Hugh gave him a half-second blank stare before turning toward the man next to him. "Remember that AIM guy got himself shot?"

Thomas was shaking his head. "Nobody from around here. Lakota, I think, from Pine Ridge, hiding out here. Police got on to him, went to talk to him, and there was a big shoot-out. My little brother happened along when it was all coming down. He says a bullet parted his hair, and he took off running across the plains. Ran in a big circle around Ethete until he got home."

Father John picked up his cowboy hat and got to his feet. He reached across the table, shook the weathered hands, and thanked the old men. Then he set his hat on his head and started back across the vacant hall.

"Hold on, Father." Thomas's voice behind him.

Father John turned back.

"We can put the word out, see if somebody might be willing to talk to you about that time, but could be dangerous. You gotta be careful. People that got secrets ain't gonna want you or any detective pryin' into 'em. Girl's been dead a long time. We don't need any more murders, you understand?"

He said that he understood, thanked them again, and hurried toward the door. Outside he clamped his hat down in the wind and let himself into the pickup. A red-tailed hawk circled over the senior citizens center, then dipped toward the dirt parking lot before flapping its wings and rising high overhead. The fear that had gripped the reservation thirty years ago was still holding on, he realized. Even Thomas and Hugh were affected. They hadn't given him names. It might be dangerous, not only to him but to them. But they would put out the word on the moccasin telegraph. Even that could be dangerous.

But he had something: the police had killed an AIM member in Ethete.

9

VICKY drove onto the wood planks that crossed the barrow ditch. The small white house set back from the road looked deserted—curtains half drawn in the windows, a skinny black dog sniffing at the wooden stoop in front. Her cell started ringing, and she dragged it out of her bag as she guided the Jeep across the dirt yard and parked at the stoop. The dog loped off, a wild thing, like a coyote. An Indian dog, whites would say. She recognized Adam's number on the screen and pressed the cell to her ear.

"Hi," she said. This morning, she'd told Adam she'd be back by midafternoon. She stole a glance at her watch. Four thirty. In the rearview mirror, Aunt Rose's old green sedan with the bent front fender was bouncing across the planks.

"Where are you?" Adam said.

"I stopped by to see Aunt Rose."

There was a long moment of silence. "I thought we were going to take off early, go for a hike in Sinks Canyon, have a picnic."

She was still in her lawyer clothes, the blue skirt and light blouse she'd picked out this morning. Her feet felt achy in her pumps. Vicky waved at the old woman in the sedan pulling in alongside her and told Adam that she'd be at her apartment by six.

That seemed to be acceptable, because he said, "How is she?"

Vicky got out of the Jeep, still gripping the cell. She pulled her bag across the console and the driver's seat and slammed the door. Aunt Rose was coming around the front of the sedan, pumping both arms as if she couldn't wait to get them around her. "She seems fine," Vicky said.

"See you at six." The cell cut out. Vicky was trying to stuff it back into her bag when she felt herself enclosed in Aunt Rose's arms, pulled against her soft bosom. She had the fleeting sense of being a child again, safe in her mother's arms. Aunt Rose was her mother's sister, which, in the Arapaho Way, meant that she was also her mother.

"Been a while since you come by." Aunt Rose let her go and stepped back, looking her over and leaving Vicky feeling a little wobbly, stuck somewhere between childhood and adulthood.

Finally, she said, "Better come inside. Get some iced tea. Hot enough to roast a rock out here."

Vicky followed her up the stoop and waited while she fumbled with the knob and pushed the door open. It wasn't locked. No one locked doors on the reservation. It wasn't until she'd moved to Denver that Vicky had started locking her door. Even then, it had been hard to remember.

The living room was surprisingly cool. A little fan stood in one corner, the metal head moving back and forth like the head of a robot, riffling the edges of the magazine on the coffee table. Vicky could feel the cool air on her legs.

"You sit down," Aunt Rose said, nodding toward the sofa with a star quilt folded across the top.

"Let me help . . ."

"Sit," she said.

Vicky dropped onto the sofa and leaned back into the cushions. It was like coming home. The house looked the same as when she was a kid: the same worn brown sofa and wood chair with the blue cushions and the blue ottoman with the white cover. Past the doorway to the kitchen, she could see the wood table and chairs, sun flowing over the tabletop. There was the sound of running water and metal clanking against glass, comfortable sounds.

After a moment, Aunt Rose was back, carrying two glasses of iced tea. Vicky took the glass she handed her. It felt cold and moist against her palm. She waited while Aunt Rose settled herself in the blue chair, lifted her feet onto the ottoman, then let out a long sigh and took a drink of her own tea.

There were a few moments of catching up, synchronizing the rhythms of their lives: How you been? Staying busy. Sure been hot, and then Aunt Rose said, "How's that man of yours?"

"Adam's fine," Vicky said.

"You like him, huh? A Lakota. Arapahos in the Old Time stayed as far away from them as they could. They were fighters, those Lakotas. Take over the entire plains, if they could've figured a way."

"He's a good man."

"Made you forget about that priest?"

"Auntie, please. There was never anything . . ."

Aunt Rose threw up one hand. "You don't have to tell me. Didn't stop you from having feelings."

"We're friends. We work a lot together. Cases come up—" Vicky shrugged. Her heart was thumping. Why was she going on like this? She could feel Aunt Rose watching her, peering through her skin to what was going on inside.

She said, "I wanted to talk to you about the nineteen seventies."

The old woman's eyes widened into large, black stones that turned opaque, as if she were now staring at her from behind a curtain. "This about that girl with the bullet in her skull out in the canyon?"

Vicky nodded.

"Skeleton's all that was left of her, the newspaper said. She'd been there a long time. I figured she might've gotten killed back then. Lots of trouble with those AIM people."

"Diana Morningstar and some of the other women came to see me. They'd like to see the girl get justice."

Aunt Rose nodded and sipped at her tea. A moment passed before she said, "Everywhere I go on the rez, gas station, convenience store, senior center, women are talking. Girl oughtta be buried with her own name. Killer oughtta be caught. They asked me if you'd make sure that detective in charge keeps looking for the killer. I tol' em not to bother you. Not your business. Sounds like some of 'em bothered you anyway."

"I want to see her get justice, too, Auntie."

The old woman nodded. "What good's our wanting it gonna do?"

"I've talked to Detective Coughlin. He's working the investigation, but she was murdered more than thirty years ago. If we can give him names of people who might be willing to talk about that time, he'd have something concrete to go on. If we can . . ."

"We?"

"I've asked Father John to talk to people who were on the rez then. People trust him." Vicky ignored the knowing look that froze in the old woman's face. "It's possible some of the women will talk to me. Even the smallest piece of information might help the investigation."

"You shouldn't get involved." Aunt Rose finished off her tea, then shifted sideways and set the glass down hard on the little table next to the chair.

"I'm hoping you can help me, Auntie."

"Your mother and me, we stayed away from AIM and their demonstrations and marches. Closed down the curtains, kept to ourselves. You were just a kid, going to school. Your mother worried all the time things were gonna blow up on the rez, like they did at Pine Ridge where those Indians took over a whole town. Held on to it, too, for a couple months. Little kids in that town with their folks, and the Feds were shooting at all of 'em. It was bad, and we were scared they was gonna do the same here. Worst part is, some folks went along. Said AIM was gonna get our rights. They was looking out for the people, running Indian culture schools." She gave a snort of laughter and rolled her eyes upward until only the whites showed in her brown face. "City Indians never been on a rez before, and they was teaching people about being Indian!"

"Who went along?"

"What?"

"Any women, that you remember?"

"Vicky . . ."

"Please, Auntie." Vicky stopped herself from telling her about the girl in the alley in Denver. It would only worry her. She'd lie awake nights thinking about what might have happened if there had been a weapon and the man had turned on Lucas or Susan or her. "It's important," she said.

"It's always important when you get yourself into dangerous stuff you oughtta stay out of. Practice your law. Take care of your man. Take care of yourself."

"It's part of that," Vicky said. It was part of taking care of herself; as if in finding justice for the girl, she could, in some strange way, find justice for herself and the years with Ben. She hurried on: "It's part of practicing law. The killer shouldn't be able to hide any longer. He should be brought to justice."

"What if he's dead?"

Vicky swallowed the hard lump forming in her throat. The killer wasn't dead. He'd left a warning on her dashboard. She said, "The murdered girl had a child, Auntie." She could hear the pleading note in her voice.

Aunt Rose threaded her fingers together and looked at her hard. "They use to beat up people that didn't go along with 'em."

"It was a long time ago." Vicky tried to blink away the image of the word floating in front of her: STOP. A warning, that was all. He hoped to scare her, call her off. Let the case fade from everyone's memory. And yet, he was still in the area. He had killed a girl once, and now he was watching her.

"Way I look at it, they were mean then, they're gonna be mean now." Aunt Rose shifted about and clasped her hands in her lap. Finally she settled back. "Promise you'll be careful."

Vicky nodded and tried for a reassuring smile. She could feel the muscles twitching in her cheeks.

"You might wanna talk to Donita White Hawk over on Boulder Flats Road. Those White Hawks always made it their business to know what everybody was doin'."

VICKY tapped out the numbers for directory assistance when she got into the Jeep. She asked for White Hawk on Boulder Flats Road, then shifted into reverse and backed into the yard while the operator searched for the number. Another moment, and she was across the planks, driving down Blue Sky High-way, a phone across the reservation buzzing in her ears.

"Yeah, hello." A man had picked up. Vicky asked for Donita White Hawk.

She wasn't home—the voice was laced with irritation and a hint of sleepiness—and who wanted her, anyway?

Vicky gave her name and was about to say that she was an attorney.

"I know who you are," the voice interrupted. "What d'ya want with Donita?"

"I'm hoping she can help me with a case."

"Donita don't hang around with the kind of low-life Indians you lawyers hang with."

"Of course not," Vicky said. "When might I reach her?"

The man seemed to be considering, and after a moment, a loud sigh, like a cough, sputtered down the line. "You might catch up with her at work tomorrow. Early shift at the Sunrise Café in Riverton."

Vicky thanked him, pressed the end button, and was about to slip the cell into her bag when it started ringing. She knew it was Adam, even before she glimpsed the readout.

"I'm on the way," she said. The dashboard clock was blinking 6:02. It would be another thirty minutes before she got to the apartment. The asphalt blurred through the stretch of plains ahead, and the sun burst off the hood of the Jeep.

Adam said he'd wait.

IT was cool in the mountains, and peaceful. The faintest sounds—an engine backfiring, a dog barking—drifted on the air from somewhere below. Halfway up the dirt road that wound above them, they'd found a vacant picnic table over-looking a creek that plunged through a stand of evergreens. They'd set the cooler Adam had brought on the table, then hiked up the narrow dirt path next to the creek, dodging the branches that slapped at them. Adam went ahead, picking the way around the boulders that jutted out of the dirt, holding back the branches until Vicky stepped past, then letting them slap into place before he raced ahead.

Long gray shadows lay over the path that had gotten steeper.

The last daylight glowed through the trees. Vicky had the sense that they were climbing away from everything familiar—the sound of traffic sputtering past the office on Main Street, the bungalow-lined streets of Lander, the open spaces of the reservation. They might have been in the Old Time, she thought, watching Adam climb up the boulders as if they were stair steps. Warriors always walked in front of women to make sure the path was safe, to protect them from the danger lurking ahead. There could be wild animals, the enemy.

Adam stood on top of a boulder and looked out across the chasm of space. He seemed preoccupied, weighted down with something. Vicky lifted herself from one boulder to the next until she was beside him. The wind gusted around them. Below were the rooftops of Lander, lights flickering on in the shadows. "What is it?" she said.

He was quiet a moment before he said, "I got a call this afternoon. My uncle died in Pine Ridge."

"I'm sorry, Adam," Vicky said.

"The funeral's in three days. I have to go."

"Yes, of course." Adam's relatives would all be there, she knew.

"It'll be dark soon," he said. He took hold of her hand and pulled her close. His lips were warm on hers. "We should head back," he said after a moment. Still he waited a little longer before starting down through the boulders. Vicky started after him, then veered off on another path that looked less steep.

Adam was waiting when she got down, and they started walking along the trail to the picnic area. He was talking about tomorrow's meeting with Charles Crow at the tribal offices, how the director of economic development on the rez had insisted on a meeting as soon as possible. They'd already discussed this on the drive to Sinks Canyon, and she realized now that all the time he'd been talking about Charles Crow, he'd probably been thinking about his uncle, waiting for the time to tell her, to speak the words that would make his uncle's death real and irrevocable.

Instead, he'd told her that Crow had mentioned a civil lawsuit, something about Indian rights. It was important. Were they interested?

Naturally they were interested, Adam had told him. They'd formed the law firm—Holden and Lone Eagle—to handle the kind of cases that protected the rights of Indian people. They were getting busier all the time, more and more cases coming their way from both the Arapahos and the Shoshones on the reservation. Tribes from other reservations had started to call. Adam had spent last week in Montana talking with Crows about a lawsuit against the state over a large tract of disputed land. The cases—the DUIs and divorces and wills—went to Roger. They were practicing the kind of law they both wanted to practice, Vicky reminded herself, although there were times, when a grandmother or an elder had shuffled into Roger's office, that she'd felt a pang of guilt that she wasn't the one to help them.

"Meeting at nine o'clock," Adam said. "That work for you?"

They came out into the flat, grassy meadow that ran into the bare dirt of the picnic area. Adam had turned around and was waiting for her to catch up. "There's a woman I have to talk to tomorrow morning," Vicky said. She was thinking that she could get to the café early enough to talk to Donita and still get to Ethete by nine.

Adam didn't move. He stood at the edge of the dark blue shadows falling over the meadow, his eyes lit with annoyance in the half light. "What's going on?" he said.

"We'd better eat before it gets dark." Vicky walked past him. She opened the cooler, pulled out a checkered cloth and spread it over the end of the picnic table. Then she laid out the paper plates, the soda and sandwiches they'd picked up at the grocery store.

Adam threw one leg over the bench and dropped down, still waiting, she knew, for a response. Finally she sat down across from him and told him about her talk with Detective Coughlin. When he didn't say anything, she pushed on: Coughlin was bound to run into blank walls; sooner or later, the thirty-five-year-old case of a murdered Indian girl would be forgotten.

"Why didn't the women take it up with Coughlin?" Adam said. "They didn't have to drag you into it." He seemed to realize that wasn't true—the women wouldn't go to the sheriff's office by themselves—because he started unwrapping a sandwich, giving the task his full attention. Then he reached into the cooler, extracted a bag of chips and tore it open. Finally he said, "Roger can follow up with Coughlin, apply a little pressure, make sure he understands the Indian people expect a full investigation."

"He needs something to go on."

"Roger can explain to the women."

"I mean, Coughlin needs names of people who were on the rez then. Somebody might remember the girl."

"Look, Vicky . . ." Adam laid his hands flat on either side of the paper plate.

She cut in. "He beat her up before he shot her." God, why was she telling him this? Shadows had crept across the picnic area, and the sky was thick with dark clouds. It would be pitch dark soon, the kind of darkness that fell in the mountains on overcast nights. "He knocked out some of her teeth."

Adam was staring at her. He'd set the rest of his sandwich onto the plate, popped the tab on the soda and left it in place. Behind his eyes, she could see that he was putting it together. "You're assuming the killer was native," he said. "Not all Indian men beat up women, Vicky."

She took a bite of her sandwich. After a moment, she said, "He could still be around. There was no reason for him to leave. He committed the perfect murder. The skeleton was buried for more than thirty years. It never would have been found if animals hadn't dug it up."

"Did you hear me, Vicky?" he said. "Not all Indian men beat up women."

"I know," she said. Adam had never lifted a hand to her, and she knew—it had taken a long time, she realized now— before she had allowed herself to *know* that he never would.

Adam took a moment before he said, "What if they weren't from here? The killer or the victim? They could have been passing through. Lots of AIM people were moving around reservations back then. We had a couple hundred come to Pine Ridge."

"What was it like at Wounded Knee?"

"I was twelve years old, Vicky."

"You were there."

"We lived fifty miles away." Adam took a drink of soda, drew his fingers across his mouth, and looked up at the sky. "My cousin Jerry was there," he said finally. "Took a bullet in the leg. He still walks with a limp." He shook his head—a slow moving back and forth. "They wanted justice, that was all. An Indian had been stabbed to death. The white man responsible bragged about bagging himself another Indian, but nothing was done about it, so the family turned to AIM for justice. When the authorities refused to arrest the killer, AIM decided to go to Wounded Knee. It was where the soldiers had slaughtered Big Foot's band in 1890. It was a symbolic gesture, Vicky, a way of saying to the government, give us justice or kill us the way you killed us back then. They nearly did get killed. FBI agents and federal marshals surrounded the town. I mean, they brought in armored vehicles, automatic weapons. My cousin said there was an army general there. It was like Vietnam. They were shooting day and night at Indians holed up inside town, living on canned food from the trading post. Went on for more than two months. When it was all over, after they thought they'd negotiated some kind of agreement, the Indians came walking out with their hands up, and you know what the Feds did? Slapped on handcuffs, took them to jail, charged a lot of Indians with assault, arson, theft, interfering with federal officers, trespassing, and everything else they could throw at them. People were indicted. Some went to prison."

"What about those who got away and went into hiding? They could have come here. Maybe the girl came with them." Vicky paused. "You'll be in Pine Ridge this week. You could ask your cousin . . ."

"Ask him what? Were you indicted, Jerry? Been lying low ever since? Hoping everybody's forgotten about the whole mess?"

"He might know of a girl who came to the Wind River Reservation."

Adam finished the last of his sandwich and started rolling up the paper it had been wrapped in. He creased the package of paper with his fist, then tossed it into the cooler. "You don't understand, Vicky. Wounded Knee isn't something people talk

about. They don't want to remember because, you know what?
It was all for nothing. There wasn't any justice that came out
of it, just more of the same. Same discrimination, same signs
up in the store windows in Rapid City—No Indians Wanted.
People just wanted to go home to their families and go on, you
know. Just live."

It was almost dark. Another ten minutes, and they'd have a
hard time making their way the short distance to Adam's
truck. And Vicky had the strong urge to leave this place, as if
the gathering darkness itself were pushing her away. "We'd
better go," she said. She picked up the plates and soda cans
and put them in the cooler.

Adam hoisted the cooler into the truck bed, then walked
over to her. She felt his arms wrap around her and pull her
close. She could hear the steady, certain beating of his heart.
"Let it go," he said. "Let Coughlin handle the investigation."

"It's still about justice," she said. "Aren't we still looking
for justice?"

"We have to pick our battles, Vicky. We have to win the
battles we pick. Getting the sheriff to conduct a major investigation into a thirty-five-year-old murder? That isn't a battle
we're going to win."

"What will I tell Diana Morningstar and the others?"

"The truth."

Vicky pulled away. She opened the passenger door, slid onto
the seat, and pulled the door shut behind her. Adam was right,
of course. So what if she came up with the name of someone
who might have been a member of AIM back in the seventies?
Coughlin would pay that person a visit, ask a few questions, get
a lot of evasive answers. Nobody wanted to talk about that time.
Coughlin would file the homicide in what was probably a big
drawer crammed with a lot of other cold cases that would never
be solved. She could tell Diana and the others that she'd spoken
to the detective. She'd done all she could. It was enough.

VICKY sat up in bed. The sheets clinging against her skin
were warm and moist. Her hair felt matted. She blinked into
the darkness and tried to get her bearings. Faint pencils of

light from outside glowed around the edges of the curtains. She was aware of the steady in and out of Adam's breathing and the warmth of his body beside her. She was in her own bedroom, she told herself. She was safe. Her heart was crashing against her ribs.

She'd heard a soft crying. She realized she'd been dreaming of the girl. She'd been following her through a labyrinth of some kind, the girl's long, black braid swinging across her back like a rope as she moved ahead. Vicky ran after her, struggling to keep her in sight, afraid she would dissolve into the shadows. Then the labyrinth had started changing shape. It was a dark alley hemmed in by fences and garages, black shadows falling down brick walls. Then a narrow gulley with dark slopes rising on either side. The girl disappeared into the shadows, and Vicky had cried out. "Who are you?" She was frantic; her heart was thumping. "Tell me who you are, so I can find you." The only sound had been the crying.

Vicky felt her leg brush against Adam's. He started moving about. He flung out an arm, as if he were searching for her, and patted her hand. He was still asleep. The rhythm of his breathing hadn't changed. Outside, a car was idling, and she realized that it wasn't only a dream that had awakened her. It was the sound of an idling car in the middle of the night. She folded back the sheet, slipped out of bed and walked over to the window. She fingered the edge of the curtain and pushed it aside. The street lamp flared in her eyes a moment. Then she saw the silver sedan parked at the curb across the street. It looked like a man behind the wheel—the short, dark hair, the big shoulders. She moved to the side of the window, waited a couple of seconds, then looked back. The engine growled, as if he'd stomped on the gas pedal with the gears in neutral. Then the sedan pulled away from the curb and shot down the street, two red taillights blurring in the darkness.

"Vicky? What is it?" Adam's voice was filled with sleep.

"Nothing," she said.

"Come back to bed."

Vicky crawled in beside him, grateful for the warmth of his body and the strength of his arms around her. After they had made love again and Adam had fallen back asleep, she lay still, staring into the darkness. She would have to find the girl, she knew. No matter what Coughlin did, no matter how hopeless the idea of searching for a girl murdered a long time ago seemed, she was going to have to find her.

10

ELENA lifted herself into the passenger seat and settled her large woven bag onto her lap. "Sorry to put you out, Father," she said.

"No problem." Father John closed the door and hurried around the pickup, giving a little wave to Elena's husband, Gus, as he went. The old man stood in the door of the small brown house, shifting between the door frame and the walking stick gripped in his hand.

Elena was saying something as he got in behind the steering wheel, as if she'd begun talking to him through the windshield and was continuing. He started the engine and backed out of the yard, trying to catch up. "I think he's gone back to drinking," she said.

It was a beat before Father John realized she was talking about her grandson, Jeffrey, who drove her to the mission every morning. She'd given up driving herself after a drunken sixteen-year-old had sideswiped her car out on Seventeen-Mile Road. She had no intention, she'd informed him, of going out of this world mangled and crushed. Gus had stopped driving sometime before the accident, when diabetes dimmed his eyesight. Which left them dependent—two old people, although Elena had never told him her age; old enough, was all she'd say—on the kids and grandkids. Twenty minutes ago, the phone had rung in the residence. Jeffrey hadn't shown up this morning. Would he mind . . .

Father John had told her he'd be right over. He'd wanted a moment to talk to her alone, anyway. It was hard at the residence; she was always busy—cooking, dusting, doing the laundry. He'd given up urging her to rest, take a little time for herself, sit down. She seemed to take it as an insult, as if he thought she wasn't up to the job anymore, which wasn't the case. He couldn't imagine the residence without her.

"Is Jeffrey still going to work?" he asked. He drove south on Left Hand Ditch Road, the early morning sunshine splintering in the window, already hot on his arm. Jeffrey had a college degree. He was an accountant at the Riverton office of the state highway department.

"Far as I know."

That was a good sign, he told her. He was thinking how things hadn't really gotten bad for him until he'd started missing classes at the prep school where he'd taught American history, because, the truth was, he was unable to get out of the chair where he'd drunk himself into a stupor the night before. It was then that his superior had given him the choice: a back office in which to drink himself to death, if that was what he wanted, or rehab. He'd chosen rehab, but not right away. A substitute teacher had taken over his classes, while he'd stayed drunk for days in the overstuffed chair—both comfortable and familiar, the chair and the whiskey. He remembered trying to pray, the prayers knotted in his throat. Then, by the grace of the God he couldn't even pray to anymore, he'd managed to lift himself out of the chair, stumble down the corridor to the superior's office, and say he was ready.

"Sooner or later, they're gonna let him go," Elena said.

Out of the corner of his eye, Father John could see the frozen look of defeat in her face. "We'll be hearing all about Indian rights and how white people hate us and are always looking to fire us, 'cause that'll be easier than stopping the drinking. Could you talk to him, Father?"

"Of course." Maybe he could persuade Jeffrey to come to

the AA meetings at the mission—he'd come before, and he'd stayed sober for a while. "There's always hope," he said.

A long moment passed. Finally he brought up the subject of the skeleton. They were heading down Seventeen-Mile Road, the sun bursting through the rear window now and the blue, printed words, St. Francis Mission, blinking on the white sign ahead. He told her about the autopsy report. "She was murdered in 1973," he said.

Out of the corner of his eye, he saw Elena shaking her head. White strands glistened in the gray hair curled around her face. The frozen expression started to crack as her thoughts shifted from Jeffrey to the skeleton. It was like watching the slow shifting of tectonic plates.

"Everybody figured that was when she got killed."

Father John glanced over at her. This place was full of surprises. The moccasin telegraph had probably been busy with different theories and had hit on the right one.

Elena sat straight backed, staring through the windshield. Finally she said, "Nothing left of that poor girl but bones. Didn't take a lot of tests to figure it must've happened a long time ago. There was lots of trouble back in the seventies. Seventy-three was the worst. She was probably one of them AIM people. They were violent."

"Some of them could still be on the rez," he said. "Somebody might know who she was."

"Well, nobody's gonna talk, if that's what you're getting at."

"It's the only way Detective Coughlin can solve the case."

She seemed to consider this a moment. Then she said, "You can take a rope and throw it down the middle of the rez. Half the people on one side didn't want anything to do with AIM. Tried to ignore all the goings-on, didn't want trouble for their families. Other half was what I'd call interested, maybe even liked what AIM was saying, all that talk about how the government oughtta treat us like sovereign nations, 'cause that's what the old treaties said. Demanding Indian rights." She gave a little laugh, as if she were clearing her throat. "Thirty years ago, we didn't know we had rights. Just did what white people said, 'cause they were in charge. Maybe we started looking at things different, after AIM was here."

"Any Arapahos join them?" He was pushing, he knew. If

she'd wanted to give him names, she would have done so by now. And yet, in the softening of her expression, he knew that she'd do what she could to get justice for the murdered girl.

"AIM people came from all over the place," she said. "Lots of 'em was city Indians, never set foot on a reservation before. Some Arapahos might've joined in their protests, but that didn't mean they joined AIM. Just meant they were interested. Nobody knew for sure who belonged, and people didn't ask questions, know what I mean? Lots of folks were scared. There was a big demonstration over at Fort Washakie, and somebody blew up a bridge, I remember that. And some sheep got shot out on a ranch. Feds said that was AIM's doings, but moccasin telegraph said it was just some Indians feuding and they put the blame on AIM. Problem was, nobody knew for sure. FBI was swarming all over the rez; I never seen so many Feds. We didn't know what was gonna happen next, but we knew something was gonna happen. AIM might take over Fort Washakie or Ethete, like they took over Wounded Knee. We were real scared they might take over the mission."

"Take over the mission?"

"AIM hated the mission," Elena said. "Said it made us like white people."

Father John turned past the sign and drove into the tunnel of cottonwoods. *Hated the mission?* St. Francis was a safe place, a place of refuge for more than a century. His own refuge. Through the trees, he could see the windows of his office in the corner of the administration building—the office would be Ian's when he left—and on the other side of the drive, the old house that was more like home than any other place he'd ever lived. He felt an immense sadness at the thought of leaving. A few pickups and cars stood in front of the church. Father Ian had taken the early Mass. It would be over soon.

"Said Indian people needed to keep to our own ways," Elena was saying. "Our own religion. Oh, we made plans for when they came."

"What are you saying?"

"To take us over, occupy the mission like they did Wounded Knee. Father Mike said we'd have to leave as fast as possible. We were gonna run to the creek, wade across, and keep going."

"Everybody?"

"Except for Father Mike. He was gonna stay."

Father John smiled. In the corridor of the administration building, there was a photo of Father Michael Leary among the other photos. A bantam weight, narrow shoulders, thinning hair, and intense eyes peering out of glasses perched a little way down his prominent nose. Father John knew the type: short, wiry Irishman, tough as nails. He'd heard the man had died in a retirement home last year.

"One night we thought AIM had come," Elena said.

Father John slowed around Circle Drive, past the vehicles of people attending the early Mass, and parked in front of the residence. He turned off the engine and turned toward the old woman, who was staring straight ahead. She might have been watching images flash across the windshield—the mission as it was then, the people who had been here.

"What happened?"

"It was about a week after July Fourth, I remember," she said. "We had a picnic here for the summer school kids, and some of the women stayed late to clean up. We was in the kitchen when we heard the gunshots. Father Mike came running down the hall, shouting, 'Go, go!' The guns kept firing. Father Mike grabbed the phone off the hall table and called the police. 'They're here,' I remember him yelling. Didn't even say *who* was here, 'cause everybody knew. He shouted again for us to run out back, but he was running for the front door. I couldn't believe he was going right to the gunshots. We went after him. I think there was three of us women. None of us was gonna leave the mission to AIM, not if Father Mike was staying. He crossed Circle Drive and ran through the field, and oh, did he run fast. I remember thinking I didn't know he could run like that. He went past the church and down the alley, straight for Eagle Hall, 'cause that's where the gunshots were comin' from.

"We followed him. We were furious. We wasn't thinking, just running, mad as hell. What right they got to come *here*? I guess we thought we was gonna tell 'em off or something. We was gonna back up Father Mike, that's for sure. By the time we got over to Eagle Hall, the sirens were blaring. Father Mike crashed right through the front door. I don't think he stopped to open it first. And then we saw that they were shooting out the windows."

Elena laid her head back and started laughing. "Firecrackers, Father. They was nothing but firecrackers. Next thing we knew police cars was everywhere. The police and the Feds surrounded Eagle Hall, and one of them shouted for everybody to come out with hands up. Then Father Mike walks out with two men looked about twenty years old." She was still laughing, swiping the back of her hand against her cheeks. "You know what was really funny? They was white! Couple of white hippies hanging around the rez, thinking if they got close enough to Indians some Indian might rub off on them. They was bored, so they stirred up a little trouble. Well, they got trouble, all right. Feds threw them on the ground, handcuffed 'em, and took 'em away. I heard they got a suspended sentence, long as they left the rez and never came back."

An engine coughed into life across Circle Drive. In the rearview mirror, Father John saw people coming out of the church and working their way down the stone steps toward the parked cars and pickups.

Elena wiped at her eyes a moment, then opened her door. "I gotta get the oatmeal cooked," she said.

"Elena, wait." Father John set his hand on her arm. "Somebody left a note on Vicky's car warning her not to get involved in the investigation."

She blinked at him several times, as if she were trying to comprehend.

He pushed on: "The girl's killer could still be here."

"They was dangerous," she said. "All them AIM people. They talked good, but you crossed 'em, you'd be in trouble. Everybody was scared of 'em, and they liked it that way. Kept people scared. They was violent, Father. Lots of things they did got swept away, 'cause people got sick and tired of trouble and just wanted to forget about it. Any AIM people still on the rez, you bet they're not gonna want old stuff dragged up again. You ask me, they're still violent." She paused for a moment, her brown eyes narrowing into slits of worry. "Better tell Vicky to stay away from 'em. If they killed that poor girl back in the seventies, they'd kill again to keep it quiet."

Elena was already out of the pickup before Father John could get around the front to help her. She brushed past him and hurried up the sidewalk, shoulders squared with determination. She'd done what she could, said her piece—he could almost hear her telling him so—and now it was up to him to warn Vicky to stay away from AIM.

"Hey, John. Wait up!"

Father John swung around. Ian was hurrying across the field enclosed by Circle Drive, taking long strides, arms bent and head thrust forward as if he were about to break into a run. Father John started across the drive toward him. The wild grasses in the field shimmered gold in the sunshine. "What's going on?" he said.

"Some guy . . ." Ian said. He was out of breath, gulping in air. "Wants to see you right away. Says it's important."

"Who is he?" There was a black pickup parked near the church.

"Didn't say. Indian, maybe Arapaho. I'm not sure." He shrugged. Ian had been at St. Francis six months. It was at least that long, Father John was thinking, before he'd been able to distinguish Arapahos from other Indians. "Said something about the elders looking for . . ."

Father John cut in. "Where is he?"

"Waiting in the last pew."

Father John started across the field. This was what he'd been hoping for. The elders had gotten the word out on the moccasin telegraph that he wanted to talk to AIM people and the man waiting in the church had come to find him. One of the grandmothers came out of the church and headed for the pickup.

"John!" Ian's boots pounded behind him.

Father John swung around. The other priest was closing the gap between them.

"You might like some company," Ian said. "The guy's drunk. You never know . . ."

Father John put up one hand. He could finish the thought himself—you never know what a drunk might do. "It'll be okay," he said, starting back across the field. He'd faced drunks before. He knew drunks. He'd been one.

He bounded up the concrete steps in front of the church and let himself through the double doors. He could hear the pickup crunching the gravel on Circle Drive. A column of bright light ran down the aisle, then disappeared as he pulled the door shut behind him. The faint odor of alcohol wafted through the small vestibule. He stepped into the back of the church. There was no one in the pews. "Hello!" he called. The sound of his own voice vibrated through the emptiness.

He started down the aisle, glancing at the pews. Somebody had dropped a black coin purse and someone else had left behind a pink scarf. He slid along the kneelers, picked up the items and continued down the aisle. No sign of anyone, yet the black pickup was still out in front when he came in. A sense of uneasiness came over him. He could feel his muscles begin to tense. The man had sent Ian for him, hoping that he'd come alone. He'd wanted to meet him alone, but where was he?

A shushing noise, like that of a boot slipping on tile—the unsteady footstep of a drunk—came from the sacristy. Father John crossed between the tabernacle that resembled a miniature tipi and the drum that served as an altar. The door leading to the back hall and the sacristy stood open, even though Ian would have closed it, he was certain.

Father John stepped into the hallway. The outside door at the end also stood open, like the door to the sacristy itself, and the smell of alcohol was so strong that he held his breath, trying not to breathe it in, yet wanting to at the same time. He stepped into the sacristy, the odor filling the air like incense. Everything neat and tidy, just as Ian had left it, except that one of the cabinet doors was slightly open, as if someone had attempted to shut it in a hurry. He looked inside the cabinet. A single stack of white altar linens, the pottery bowl and chalice that he used for the Communion bread and wine. There was nothing valuable in the sacristy, but the man—whoever he was—hadn't known that.

He put the items he'd found in the church into the cabinet and stepped into the hall. He closed and locked the outside door, then walked back into the church, moving slowly now, deliberately. The pickup was still outside, which meant the man was somewhere, waiting for him.

11

FATHER John made his way slowly down the aisle, watching the side aisles, the vestibule for any sign of movement, of shadows shifting. Quiet permeated the church, like the quiet of a vault punctuated by the fall of his own footsteps on the thin carpet. He had the sense of someone watching him.

"I know you're here," he said. The sound of his voice reverberated around him. "Come out."

He was almost at the last pew when the figure of a man slid from behind the pillar that braced the right side of the vestibule. He planted himself in front of the door, swaying forward and backward in an obvious effort to get his balance. The smell of whiskey rolled off him in waves. He was slightly built with stooped shoulders, a baseball cap pushed back on his head, strands of black hair hanging about his face. He wore blue jeans, a dark shirt, and a black leather vest that even in the shadows looked worn and scuffed. Father John tried to place him. In the congregation at Sunday Mass? At a powwow or celebration or meeting? It was no good. He'd never seen the Indian before.

"Who are you?" He stopped at the entrance to the vestibule,

a few feet from the man, struggling to ignore the invisible presence of alcohol in the space between them.

The Indian shrugged. "Hear you're lookin' for information."

"You were on the rez in the seventies?"

Another shrug. "I ain't had nothing to eat in a while."

"Let's go to the residence." Father John took a step into the vestibule. "You can have some breakfast."

The Indian shook his head. He shifted his weight against the door, then stood still, as if he were grateful for the support. "You got some cash?"

Father John didn't take his eyes from the man. It wasn't food he wanted. He'd gone into the sacristy, trailing an odor of whiskey, looking for something he could pawn, something that might be worth enough cash for a bottle. Today's bottle, and tomorrow he'd figure out how to get another bottle. He knew who the Indian was then. One of the park rangers—the drunken Indians that hung around the park in Riverton, living from bottle to bottle, like the fort Indians who had hung around the forts in the Old Time, addicted to the soldiers' whiskey, willing to sell anything—blankets and horses and women—for a bottle of whiskey. Somehow the moccasin telegraph had reached the Riverton park, and the Indian had seen the way to get some cash.

Father John's instincts were to tell him to leave, that he could come back when he wanted to go into rehab, when he'd had enough, when he wanted help. And yet, the Indian could have been involved with AIM thirty years ago.

"It depends," he said. "What do you know?"

The Indian's dark eyes darted about the vestibule. He pressed himself against the door. "Her name," he said.

"Are we talking about the skeleton found in the Gas Hills?"

The Indian gave a half nod.

"How do you know her?"

"Back then—" He hesitated, then plunged on. "I get home from Vietnam, everything's going to hell on the rez, just like before. No jobs, nothin' to do, no place to go. Signs everywhere: No Indians Wanted. Indian gets killed, nobody cares, and there was guys getting beat up and run over, and the cops sayin', ah, go ahead, kill yourselves off. Then AIM Indians show up and say, why we livin' like animals? We're not animals. They say, show respect, get some respect. They say, we got rights, and we gotta make the whites give us what's ours." The Indian started rubbing his forehead with the knobs of his fingers, as if he'd hit a blank wall in his mind and wanted to jog his thoughts back into place.

"Did you join them?" Father John said.

"You got somethin' to drink?"

Father John shook his head. So that was what the Indian had been looking for in the sacristy—the wine that he and Ian consecrated at Mass. He wondered if the Indian had seen the bottle of grape juice that the pair of recovering alcoholic priests at St. Francis Mission sipped at the consecration. "Maybe you oughtta try to eat something . . ."

The Indian was shaking his head so hard that his shoulders also shook, as if he were in a spasm. "I gotta get some cash," he said. "You got money around here? You take up collections, right? You gotta have some money."

"Tell me about the girl," Father John said. "Was she part of AIM? Is that how you knew her?"

"They was mad at her."

"What do you mean? Who was mad at her?"

"Everybody. Jesus, Father, you gonna let me have some money or not? I gotta get a drink. I'm sick, see." He thrust out his hands. They were quivering. "I'm real sick."

"I can help you get help," Father John said.

"I need a drink, okay? I'll tell you about the girl, and you give me some money, okay?"

"What about her? What had she done?"

"Shot off her mouth to the police, told 'em where one of the big shots was hiding out, got him killed, that's what she did."

"Do you mean the AIM member killed at Ethete?"

"Look." The Indian put his hands out again. They were shaking harder. "I'm telling you what I know, okay? It wasn't like I was one of 'em, the big shots. They come from other places, and they was givin' the orders around here. I marched in some demonstrations, carried signs around, and I got a few bucks. It was like a job or something. Then they had all that trouble up on Pine Ridge—them AIM Indians took over the town, and that was something. I mean, who would've thought a bunch of Indians could take over a town, and this being in the 1970s, I mean, not a hundred years ago! Afterward some of the big shots came here, that's what I heard. Hiding right here under the Feds' noses, and they never found 'em until the girl opened her mouth."

"Who was she?"

The Indian didn't say anything. He was staring down one leg of his blue jeans at the floor.

"Come on," Father John said. "You know who she was."

"You gonna give me the cash?"

"We'll talk about it later. Who was she?"

"Arapaho, that's what I know. I heard she was livin' up at Pine Ridge, and that's how she got mixed up with AIM. I heard she was a singer, always singing, like she had plans to be a big star, make recordings and all that, like she wanted to be somebody."

"You said you knew her name," Father John said.

"I only seen her one time after the big shot got killed. There was a meeting, and a lot of people come out for it, and everybody was mad as hell, I remember that. Well, she comes to the meeting. We was all shocked. I mean, she'd been in jail! She'd talked to the police! It was like she wanted to die or something. Why didn't she get outta here, go hide someplace else? Instead, she comes walking in like she didn't know what was goin' on. She was holding a baby, I remember that. I started feeling sorta sorry for her, 'cause she had a baby and wasn't nobody there gonna help her. She was small, you know, and real pretty, and she had her hair all braided up, like she'd braided up all her troubles and they wasn't gonna bother her no more. That braid hung all the way down her back. I remember her walkin' in the room, climbing around people, stepping over everybody's feet, and the guy sittin' next to me says, 'What the hell's Liz doin' here?'"

"Liz." Father John repeated the name slowly, letting the sound of it burrow into his mind. The skeleton in the Gas Hills was a girl named Liz. "What was her last name?"

"I only seen her that one time. How would I know? She's Arapaho. I remember 'em saying, how come a Rap talked to the cops? Jesus, Father, I'm in bad shape."

"You need help, man. I can take you to detox at the hospital."

"I need a drink, okay? What d'ya know about it?"

"I know a lot."

The Indian let out a strangled laugh. "You don't know shit."

"I'm an alcoholic like you."

The Indian tried to stare at him, blinking several times as if he wanted to bring the alcoholic mission priest into focus, and finally looking past him into the church. "I gotta get a drink," he said.

"What happened to her?"

The Indian was staring at the floor. "Heard she took off, got away."

"What makes you think she's the skeleton?"

"'Cause they was so mad at her for snitchin'. Got me to thinkin', maybe she didn't get away. Maybe they put a snitch jacket on her and she got killed."

"Who are we talking about? Who was mad at her?"

"Everybody. We hated snitches."

"Who are you? What's your name?"

"I don't got a name now. Used to, maybe, I don't remember."

"What do they call you in the park?"

"Joe. They call me Joe. We got a deal, right? I give you her name, you give me some money."

Father John dug the crumbled bills out of his jeans pocket and flattened them against his palm. Six one-dollar bills. He set them in the brown hand stretched toward him, shaking and eager.

"Come back when you're ready to quit," he said. "I'll help you." If I'm still here, he thought. Then another thought: Ian would help the man. It didn't matter if he was here; the mission would go on.

The Indian clutched the money a long moment before he began stuffing it into his vest pocket, as if he were reluctant to let it out of his hand. Then he turned to the door and, shifting from one foot to the other to get a firmer purchase on the floor, gripped the door knob and started to pull, floundering backward as he did so. Father John reached out to steady him, then took hold of the edge of the door and swung it open. He stayed with him down the steps and out to Circle Drive. The black pickup was no longer there, and he realized it must have belonged to the woman coming out of the church. The Indian kept going, planting one foot in front of the other, weaving a little with each step before taking another plunge ahead. Father John watched the man until he'd reached the tunnel of cottonwoods and blended into the shadows that striped the road. He'd wanted the cash, that was all, but he'd known something. The girl's name was Liz.

"God help you," he said out loud, as if the Indian were still standing there. Or maybe it was the girl he was praying for, he wasn't sure. "God help them both," he said.

A row of pickups stood in front of the Sunrise Café, bumpers nudged against the curb. Parked on the far side of the parking lot were three semis. Through the plate glass windows, Vicky could see the cowboy hats and baseball caps bobbing over the tables as she pulled in between two of the pickups. The minute she opened the door, aromas of coffee, hot grease, and cinnamon floated toward her on the low-pitched sounds of men's voices. She walked over to the end of the counter, conscious of the heads turning along the counter, the eyes staring at her across rounded, thick-set shoulders. She kept her own eyes on the white woman with hair bleached the color of a yellow crayon and a white apron tied around her wide waist, jaws working a piece of gum as she poured coffee into a cup halfway down the counter. After a moment, the woman set the metal pot onto a burner and started toward Vicky. "What can I get ya?" she said.

"Is Donita in?"

"Donita?" She tossed her head toward the swinging metal door with a window at the top that framed a small view of the kitchen. "She's cookin'. Who should I say wants to see her?"

"Vicky Holden," she said.

"You that Indian lawyer I heard about?"

Vicky ignored the question. It hit her that it might make things uncomfortable at the café for Donita if the owner thought she was in some kind of trouble with the law. "Would you mind telling her I'd like to see her for just a moment?" she said.

The woman chewed on the gum for a half second, considering. Then she turned and disappeared through the metal door that swung behind her, squealing on the hinges. Through the window, Vicky watched her sidle next to a tall woman with black hair caught in a donut-shaped bun who was flipping pancakes at a grill. Another moment passed before the waitress pushed back through the metal door. "You're gonna have to wait. Donita's busy now. Want some coffee?"

Vicky said that would be fine and settled onto the stool still warm from the buttocks of the trucker who had just gotten up and was ambling over to the cash register by the door. She sipped at the coffee when it came and kept one eye on the metal door. The coffee was almost gone when the door finally swung outward. The woman walking over was probably in her sixties, with slim shoulders, honey-colored skin, and black hair gone to gray and pulled back so tightly that it gave her face a strained look. She resembled other members of the White Hawk family, Vicky thought. Donita's brother had been a couple of years ahead of Vicky at the mission school.

"You tryin' to get me fired?" she said. "Boss don't like personal business on his time."

"Sorry," Vicky said. "I don't want to cause you any trouble. Is there someplace else we could meet? I'd like to talk to you."

"About what?"

"The seventies on the reservation." Vicky paused a moment, then she said, "AIM."

Donita White Hawk's jaws clamped together. A long hiss sounded through her teeth. "About that skeleton," she said, her voice so low that Vicky had to lean across the counter to catch the words. And yet, it wasn't a dismissal. The woman's shoulders curled forward with a kind of inevitability. "Ten minutes, out in back," she said. "I'll take a break."

Vicky nodded, but Donita had already flung herself against the metal door. She was swallowed up behind it, the door rattling back and forth, her slim figure bobbing behind the window.

Vicky retraced her steps across the small café and let herself out the front door. A warm gust of wind whipped her skirt against her legs as she walked past the Breakfast Specials and Best Coffee in Town signs plastered against the plate glass, cowboy hats swiveling over the tables inside. She could feel the eyes boring into her as she passed.

In the graveled alley behind the café was a collection of pickups and cars—a couple of which looked abandoned—parked alongside twin Dumpsters with cartons that spilled over the top. It was chilly in the shade of the cottonwood that towered over the wood fence on the other side of the alley. Hugging herself, Vicky walked into the rectangle of sunshine on the far side of the Dumpsters. The screened door at the back of the café hung partly open, emitting small squeals in the warm breeze. The main door looked sealed. Hot, greasy odors wafted out of a vent and mingled with the smells of trash. For a half second, she thought that the ringing phone came from inside the café, then realized it was her cell.

"This is Vicky Holden," she said, after she'd found the cell in her bag.

"I've talked to someone who remembers the girl." It was John O'Malley's voice, and it was comforting despite the note of caution.

"Who is it?" *Someone who remembered.*

"One of the park rangers. Calls himself Joe. I don't know how reliable his information is. He might have invented the whole thing. He needed a drink badly."

"Tell me what he said." Vicky was aware that she was holding her breath. She had the sense that they were reaching out for the girl, that they could almost touch her.

"He said she was an Arapaho, her name was Liz."

"Liz? That's all he said? There could have been dozens of Liz's on the reservation."

"He said she'd been at Wounded Knee. She came back to the reservation, and AIM blamed her for the fact that the police had shot a member in Ethete."

"So they killed her." It was making sense now. Beat her up, knocked out her teeth, shot her in the head and left her to rot in the Gas Hills. Vicky could feel her heart jumping.

"That's one of the things that's odd, Vicky. He said he'd always thought she'd gotten away, left the reservation."

"What's the other thing?" Vicky glanced at the back door of the café, thinking she'd heard the knob rattle. The door still looked sealed, as if it had been painted in place.

"He says she had a baby."

Vicky took a moment. Her heart was still pounding. "It has

to be the same girl. She didn't get away." They were getting close—she could feel the truth of it—almost touching her, and yet the girl was slipping like smoke through their fingers.

The café door cracked open, then jiggered backward, scraping the floor. Donita stepped down onto the gravel and reached around to pull the door shut behind her. Then she shook a cigarette out of a half pack.

"I'll call you later," Vicky said. She pressed the end button and walked back through the shade toward Donita, who was cupping her hand over the cigarette and flicking at a lighter that stuttered in the breeze.

12

"WHAT'D you come here for?" Donita said. She kept her gaze on the red glow at the end of the cigarette.

Vicky walked across the gravel between the front of a pickup and the Dumpster. "I'm hoping you can help me."

"I don't know about that skeleton, if that's what you're gettin' at. What d'ya want?"

"It's a cold case, Donita. If I can give the sheriff some names . . ."

"You working for the sheriff?" For the first time, Donita looked up. There was a shadow of hostility in her eyes.

"Working . . . ?" Vicky hesitated, aware of the blunder. If Donita thought she was connected to the sheriff's department, she wouldn't tell her anything. And neither would anyone else on the rez when the news went out on the moccasin telegraph.

"You some kind of informer?"

"No," Vicky said. "I'm trying to get information for Detective Coughlin that will help the investigation. The girl was murdered in 1973. Her killer might still be around." She paused. "He is around," she said. "I'm sure of it. He should be brought to justice, don't you agree?"

Donita took a long drag on the cigarette, then dropped her hand alongside her blue jeans and flipped off the cone of ashes. She was squinting into the sunshine, as if there were a message printed on the front of her eyeballs. "I don't know anything about it."

"I heard," Vicky began, selecting the words—it was like trying to pick her way across the rocks in a creek; one slip and she would be in the water—"that you might have known people involved with AIM."

"So what? Lots of people got involved with AIM. It wasn't all bad, you know, the way people talk today. They ran schools. Did you know that? Culture schools so kids could learn their own Indian culture. Learn their own language. They kept watch on the police so they didn't beat up on Indians and throw 'em in jail for no reason. They were always fighting for our rights."

Vicky waited a beat before she said, "I think the girl's name was Liz. She was Arapaho and she was part of AIM. She might've been at Pine Ridge for a while. Did you know anyone like that?"

"What d'ya think?" Donita's eyes widened in surprise. "That I was one of the big shots? One of the leaders? The only time I saw them, they were driving by in some pickup. Most of them came from other places. They gave the orders. Show up at Fort Washakie and demonstrate in front of the BIA offices or the jail. Drive over to Seventeen-Mile Road 'cause we're gonna close it down. My boyfriend—God, what a jerk—wanted to be a big shot like the AIM guys, so he says, come on, we're gonna march, we're gonna demonstrate, we're gonna kiss their asses 'cause I'm gonna be one of 'em. So I did what he said, and you know what?"

She took another long drag on the cigarette before tossing it down and rubbing it into the gravel with the toe of her shoe. "I loved it, all that marching and shouting. I loved it, 'cause it was like saying 'We're Indian, and we're proud. We're proud.' I never felt so great about anything since. We made people take notice. They couldn't ignore us like they were used to doing, like we weren't even there, weren't even alive."

"There must've been other Arapaho girls marching. Try to think, Donita. It's important. Was there anyone named Liz?"

"You hear what I'm telling you? If she went to Pine Ridge, she was on the inside. Riding around in one of the pickups, how do I know? I never saw any Liz marching out in the hot sun."

"What about your boyfriend. He might have met . . ."

"Yeah, he might've, only one night about twenty years ago he drank a bottle of vodka and smashed up his truck. Killed himself. Couldn't happen to a nicer guy, you ask me. I gotta get back to work." Donita pivoted about and flung open the screened door.

"Is there anyone else who might have known Liz?" Vicky said, stepping behind her, grabbing the edge of the screened door as Donita shoved the other door into the café. The clank of dishes and hum of conversation drifted outside. "Someone closer to the insiders." She was talking to the woman's back. "Liz had a child. Her child would be grown up now. He'd want justice for his mother. Or maybe it was a girl. She'd want . . ."

Donita turned around. She kept her arms at her side, like a soldier at attention, and stared past Vicky's shoulder into the alley, her lips moving around inaudible words. Finally she said, "I had a friend, Loreen. She got mixed up with one of them."

"Loreen? Where can I find her?"

"Try the cemetery over at Ethete. He shot her."

"My God," Vicky said.

"Got off on some kind of technicality, like it wasn't important, you know? Some Indian girl dead. Who cares?"

"Who was he?"

"Lakota, called himself Jake. Jake Walker. Wasn't his real name, just what he was using around here. Real name was Jake Tallfeathers. Hung around here after they let him out of jail, like it was no big deal, Loreen's death. Then I heard he got hit by a truck." Donita's voice was so low that Vicky had to lean closer to catch what she was saying. "You think you're gonna get justice? Forget it. Nobody's gonna care about some Indian girl that got killed back in the seventies. All that marching and demonstrating and shouting didn't mean anything. We still don't have rights. You want to know the worst part?" She bent forward, pulling the door with her. The café noises were muffled. "Lot of Indians got killed back then by their own people. And what did the white authorities do? Nothing. You gonna get justice for all of them?"

"We can't give up," Vicky heard herself saying. It was the courtroom voice, and the confidence in it surprised her. "We can try to get justice for Liz."

Donita went back to staring into the alley. Tiny spots of moisture bubbled at the outside corners of her eyes. Finally she said, "Loreen and her sister were both real tight with AIM. I heard they both went to Wounded Knee. I see her sister around the rez sometimes. Her name's Ruth Yellow Bull. You know her?"

Vicky shook her head. She supposed she might recognize the woman if she saw her. A familiar face at the powwows or one of the celebrations, but not anyone she knew. "Where can I find her?"

"Far as I know she's still living out on Mill Creek Road, same brown house Loreen lived in. Only thing, she won't want to talk to you."

"I'll take my chances."

"Do me a favor," Donita said, throwing a glance over her shoulder into the café. "Don't tell her I was the one that sent you, okay? I don't want any trouble with AIM."

"What are you saying? They're still on the rez?"

"You don't get it, do you! There's people around that knew what was going on back then. They knew about some of the killings. Maybe they're the ones who got orders to shoot people, and maybe that's what they did. You think they'll want you snooping around into that old stuff? I'd watch my back, if I was you." Donita flung herself past the opened door and kicked the door shut.

Vicky walked down the alley and around the corner of the café. She slid into the Jeep, ignoring the pairs of eyes following her on the other side of the plate glass window as she backed into the parking lot. Then she shifted into forward. The right tire climbed over the edge of the curb, and she bumped out into the traffic on Federal, struggling to bring into focus this altered sense of reality. Donita might have been talking about somewhere else, not the reservation Vicky had always known. A different place, a place where killers went about everyday lives, gassing pickups at the pumps, stopping in the convenience store for sodas and chips, dancing in the powwows, going to the Sun Dance.

And one of them could have killed a girl named Liz.

ADAM was in front of the tribal offices as Vicky drove into the parking lot—pacing back and forth, glancing at his watch. The sun shone on his white shirt. He must have heard the noise of her tires cutting across the bare dirt because he swung around and watched until she'd parked a few feet away. Then he bounded over to the Jeep and flung open the door.

"Where've you been?" he said, annoyance and impatience beating in his voice. "Our appointment was ten minutes ago."

"You could have started." Vicky slid out and headed for the entrance. The door slammed behind her.

"It's an important meeting." Adam's footsteps sounded behind her. "We both have to be there from the beginning." He reached around and yanked open the glass door.

Vicky was aware of him beside her, their footsteps beating a rhythm down the corridor past the doors opened onto different offices of the Arapaho Nation: Natural Resources, Tribal Registration, Blue Sky Education. She turned into the office next to the sign that said, Tribal Economic Development, aware of Adam's annoyance nipping at her with the razor sharp teeth of a puppy.

A woman, probably in her thirties, with long black hair and dark, serious eyes, looked up from behind the counter that separated the narrow waiting·area from another corridor of offices in back. "Hey," she said, rolling back in her chair and fixing them with a calm, deliberative stare. "Charlie'll be with you in a minute."

Vicky avoided Adam's eyes. Indian time, she was thinking. The meeting would start when everyone had arrived, but she and Adam—she had to be honest—they were both on white man's time, old habits from law school and practicing law in the outside world—three years in a Seventeenth Street law firm in Denver for her, and a good seven or eight years, first in L.A., then in Casper, for Adam.

She was about to take one of the plastic seats pushed against the wall next to the door when Charlie Crow emerged from the corridor behind the counter. He handed the black-haired girl a folder stuffed with papers, then leaned over her shoulder and jabbed at the folder with a ballpoint, speaking in a voice that was almost a whisper. Finally he looked up. "Adam!" he said. "Good to see you, man. Come on in." He waved toward the opening between the end of the corridor and the wall.

"You know my partner, Vicky Holden." Adam stepped back and ushered her ahead.

"Don't believe I've had the pleasure," Charlie Crow said, sticking out his hand. His grip was hard, Vicky thought, the palm roughened with old blisters. He was an Ojibwa, somewhere in his sixties, she guessed, but with the energy and easy motion of a younger man. His hair was still black, and he had narrow eyes wedged between the canyon of his forehead and his prominent cheekbones. His face was pockmarked, the leftover of some childhood disease, she guessed. He might have been slim once—he had that look about him—but now he carried pillows of fat around his middle.

She watched him shake Adam's hand—patting him on the back, as if they were the oldest of friends, and tried to recall the article about Charles Crow in the *Gazette*. The tribes had hired an economic development director to bring new jobs to the reservation, encourage companies in the area to hire Indians, initiate job training programs. He'd held the same position on other reservations. He was an expert, like other experts her people brought in when they needed them. He'd been on the rez for about six months. It occurred to Vicky that maybe that was why Crow had called her and Adam—Adam was also an outsider. He was Lakota.

"First door on the right," he said, waving toward the corridor. "I'll be there in a minute."

Vicky could hear the low exchange between Crow and the girl at the counter as she and Adam stepped into a small office with papers and photographs tacked to a corkboard on the wall behind the desk, a computer taking up most of a side table, and books stacked in a bookcase. She took one of the two chairs in front of the desk. Adam remained standing a moment, then dropped down in the other.

"Sorry," he said. "I didn't mean to snap at you. It's just that tribal business . . ."

She looked away from the intensity in his eyes.

"We're top on the list of law firms the tribes use now, Vicky. We're getting the reputation for being the Arapaho and Shoshone law firm. We can't blow it. Lawyers are lining up behind us waiting for us to stumble so they can get a crack at the tribal business. So where were you, if you don't mind my asking?"

Vicky told him about talking to Donita White Hawk at the café in Riverton, ignoring the way Adam started shaking his head the minute she mentioned that Donita had taken part in some of the AIM demonstrations in the seventies.

"What are the chances somebody's going to know the murdered girl? Look . . ." He hesitated, as if the ground he'd found himself crossing had started to shake. "We have more important things . . ."

Vicky shifted toward him. "More important than justice for a murdered girl?"

"Sounds very serious." Charlie Crow walked into the office. Behind him was another Indian, also in his sixties, but with the look of an old man—thinning gray hair pulled back into a ponytail from a narrow brown face etched with lines. His mouth seemed set in a downward curve. He wore jeans and a red plaid shirt that clung loosely to his concave chest. "Meet Mister," Charlie said.

"Mister?" Adam got to his feet and reached past the corner of the desk to shake his hand.

"Real name's Bennet, Lyle Bennet," the Indian said. "Picked up the nickname along the road somewhere. Most folks call me Mister."

"Have a seat." Charlie snapped open a wooden folding chair that had been leaning against the side of the filing cabinet. "Mister's the reason we're having this little meeting," he said, making his way around the desk. He sat down in the swivel chair, opened a file folder and started spreading out the papers, taking his time, studying each one as he set it into place. Then, directing his gaze at Adam, he said, "Mister's been working out in the oil fields now for—" He turned toward the other man. "How long's it been? Ten, twenty years?"

"Eighteen next month."

"Eighteen long years working for the Mammoth Oil Company, handling equipment, working the heavy machines."

"Guess I just about done it all." Mister was nodding, eyes fixed on the ceiling.

"About five years ago, Mammoth instituted a new policy. Random drug checking for employees."

"Ain't a bad policy," Mister said. "Some of them young bucks come out to work pretty stoned. Mess you up real bad, they get their hands on some of that equipment."

"Right," Charlie said. "They get arrested on possession and sent to drug court. Long as they comply with the rules, tribe helps them get clean and go back to being productive members of society. We're not protesting the company's policy. They have the right to test employees. Only they don't have the right to practice racism and discriminate."

"What do you mean?" Vicky said.

Charlie's gaze was still on Adam, as if he were the only lawyer in the office. "Don't have the right to discriminate against Indians," he said again.

Mister cleared his throat, making a low, growling noise. "Only employees have to take the drug test are Indians."

"How do you know that?" Adam turned toward the thin man perched on the end of the wooden chair, hands clasped between bony knees that poked through his jeans.

"Got let go," Mister said. "Said my test was positive, 'cause I was takin' that drug the doctor give me for my heart. I seen that other guys got let go was Indians like me. Started askin' around, talkin' to some of the boys I worked with. Lotta white boys, and they tol' me they never got no tests. They said, 'What the hell you talkin' about? Drug tests?' "

"Looks to me like we've got a major action against the Mammoth Oil Company for discrimination," Charlie said. He'd made double fists over the papers fanned in front of him.

"If what you say is true . . ." Vicky said.

"Oh, it's true," Charlie said. "Every Indian working for the company tells the same story. No white guys out in the fields getting tested. I talked to other Indians who were terminated. Mister's been a big help getting the names. We got the go ahead from the tribal council to bring an action against the company. We can't let them get away with this kind of stuff. You interested?"

"We'll look into it," Adam said. "See if there are grounds."

"What d'ya mean if? I told you . . ."

"We'll need the names of Indians employed at the company. We'll have to interview them about their experiences. We can file a complaint under the Civil Rights Act with the Equal Employment Opportunity Commission. But before we do that, we'll send a letter to Mammoth and ask for a response in order to forestall lengthy proceedings before the commission. We may be able to work things out. We'll let them know that we expect Mister and any other Indian employees unjustly terminated to be reinstated with full back pay. We also expect all discriminatory practices to end. If Mammoth digs in their heels, we'll go ahead with the complaint. Another option would be to bring a civil lawsuit."

Mister reached out, grabbed the corner of the desk and pulled himself to his feet. "Count me in," he said. "I'll testify against them no-good sonsabitches. Just tell me where to show up. That's all you're wanting now?" He leaned over the desk, still gripping the edge.

"Appreciate your coming by," Charlie said.

The man pivoted on the heels of his boots and started for the door, planting one foot after the other as if he were crossing a ditch on a log.

"Let him go with no retirement," Charlie said after Mister had disappeared through the door. The slow, steady thud of his footsteps sounded in the corridor. "Eighteen years and all he got was a boot out the door."

Vicky scooted forward in her chair. "He shouldn't have been terminated for taking a prescription drug." He was old, she was thinking, trying to hold on to a job until he could collect enough retirement to keep a roof over his head and food on the table.

"Tell that to Mammoth Oil. They have the lab tests—their own lab, of course—that say Mister tested positive for cocaine, an out-and-out lie. Mister never used coke, never was arrested. He didn't know what to do, so he came to see me. Figured I might know how to help him." He shook his head. "Issue here is that the only employees getting tested are Indi-

ans. That's what this is all about. Indian rights, you understand?"

Charlie swiveled the chair from side to side before jumping to his feet. "We have to fight for our rights every day," he
said, as if his thoughts had gotten caught in a loop.

Vicky waited a moment before she said, "Were you at Pine
Ridge in the early seventies?" Out of the corner of her eye,
she saw Adam's head snap toward her. She could feel the
warning in his expression.

"Vicky, not now," he said.

"Excuse me?" Charlie said.

"I was wondering if you knew any of the AIM members
who were fighting for Indian rights back then?" Vicky said.

Charlie stared at her a moment, his eyes narrowing into pinpricks of black light. "Yeah, I knew a lot of them. My brother
went to Pine Ridge. Got shot at Wounded Knee. I had cousins
and buddies getting shot at by the Feds back then. Me? I was in
Nam getting shot at by the gooks, so I missed all the fireworks
at home. But they had guts, AIM people. They stood up for Indian rights, just like we have to do. Here's a list of some of the
Indians employed at Mammoth." He handed a thick file folder
across the desk. "I'll get a complete list of Indians terminated
for failing drug tests that nobody else had to take."

Adam picked up the folder and said they'd get on it right
away. Vicky felt his other hand tighten around her arm as he
guided her toward the door. Then he was rushing her down the
corridor and through the reception area toward the entrance.

"What's it going to be, Vicky?" he said when they were
outside, crossing the parking lot, gravel crunching under their
shoes. "We gonna practice law, or are you going off on wild
goose chases?"

"Her name was Liz," Vicky said.

"What?"

"Liz! She had a name, Adam. She was Arapaho and she
had a child. She probably went to Pine Ridge. There was a
chance Charlie Crow might have been there. Indians from all
over the West were there. He might have known who she was."

"Okay. Okay." Adam let go of her arm and ran the palm of
his hand across the little beads of sweat on his forehead. "How
do you know this?"

"John and I . . ."

"Father O'Malley? What's he got to do with it?"

"We've been talking to people. There are people on the rez who know what happened back then. Someone knows what happened to Liz."

"Are you listening to yourself?" A couple of women emerged from the building and started toward them. Adam took Vicky's arm again and steered her closer to the Jeep. "The girl out in the Gas Hills was shot to death, Vicky. Anybody who knows about it has kept quiet for more than thirty years. They're going to do everything they can to keep you from finding out. For godssakes, let Coughlin handle it."

Vicky got behind the wheel of the Jeep and started to pull the door shut, but Adam was holding on, leaning into the opening. "I'm trying to tell you that bringing up the past could be dangerous. You shouldn't get involved."

"I'm already involved." Vicky turned the ignition. She hadn't told him about the message on her dashboard: STOP. It would only give him more ammunition. "I'll see you at the office," she said. The engine growled into life, and she slipped the gear into drive. God, she wished John O'Malley were here. He understood; she didn't have to explain everything. The Jeep was moving as the door slammed. She could see Adam framed in the side mirror, hands jammed into the pockets of his khakis, waves of frustration and worry moving through his expression.

She turned onto Blue Sky Highway and headed south for Mill Creek Road.

13

THE computer blinked and sputtered into life. Images formed and reformed until finally text and photographs filled the screen. Father John typed in American Indian Movement and waited while the machine went through another set of silent gyrations that displaced the initial images with a list of websites, American Indian Movement and AIM in bold, black print. He scanned the list. It would take all morning to read through them. He clicked on one that looked promising and sat back, the machine taking longer this time.

It was the quiet time of morning, the brief interval after Mass had ended, the half dozen pickups crawling around Circle Drive out onto Seventeen-Mile, and the day got under way, with other pickups driving onto the mission grounds. He always looked forward to this time to work on next Sunday's homily, pay bills, catch up on a little reading. He was halfway through *Sitting Bull's Pipe*, a new biography of Sitting Bull. It lay open on the desk next to the stack of bills he'd taken a stab at paying, arranging them chronologically, paying the oldest bills first, always hoping that the donations—the little miracles—would tumble into the mailbox in time to pay the others before they went to the collection agency.

He was about to return to the list of websites when the one he'd clicked on came up, thick paragraphs of black type under an inch-high headline, "On the Trail of Broken Treaties: Remembering Our Fight for Indian Rights."

He skimmed through the text, a discussion of the march to Washington, D.C., by a panel of Indians at a conference on Indian-government relations in Rapid City. The four-mile-long caravans led by the American Indian Movement had reached the capital on November 3, 1972. AIM demanded that the government recognize the sovereignty of tribes and deal with tribes according to treaties made in the nineteenth century. Indians occupied the BIA building on Constitution Avenue for five days. Troops surrounded the building, guns trained on the windows and doors.

"Like we were still fighting the war on the plains," said one panelist. "Troops versus Indians."

"What did it get us?" asked another.

"Got us a lot of publicity. Maybe people sat up and started taking notice of us."

"Well the government rejected all our demands. Handed out sixty-six thousand dollars to pay the cost of getting people back home. I'd say they bought us off real cheap."

"Put the leaders on the FBI's list of dangerous extremists."

"FBI was just waiting for the chance to throw them into prison."

"You think anything happened since then?"

"Wounded Knee happened."

"I'm talking about racism, discrimination. You think that's changed?"

"Maybe it's never gonna change."

Father John studied the postage-size photos of the panelists. They looked like college students with dark, intense eyes staring into a future already set into place, like concrete poured into a form. He felt a spasm of sadness. *Maybe it's never gonna change.*

He went back to the list and clicked on a site with Wounded Knee jumping out of the description. The site, when it came up, was composed of newspaper articles written during the siege itself. He skimmed through the articles, looking for something new, something different, something that might explain how a young woman ended up shot to death.

There were the explanations of events that led to the takeover at Wounded Knee: AIM demands that officials in Gordon, Nebraska, prosecute the white men who beat up a Lakota and paraded him around town half-naked before the man died; Indians riot in Custer, seeking justice for the murdered Lakota; Indians burn chamber of commerce building to the ground; AIM leads march on the BIA building in Pine Ridge protesting the low rents that the BIA collects on tribal lands; and finally, AIM leads the takeover of Wounded Knee.

There were other articles on the siege itself; Indians held the town for five weeks, with FBI agents, federal marshals, BIA police, and sheriff's deputies surrounding the town.

Here was something new: an interview with one of the AIM spokesmen. "We have old men with us," said Ernest Laughing Dog. "They are *with* us! They are the ones that have kept the memories of when our people lived free on the plains and ran our own lives, when there were no rules laid down by the Great White Father, no boundaries on our lands, when we were a great nation, a proud people with rights.

"We got lots of young people, too," the interview continued. "We got Vietnam vets that come back to nothing. No jobs, no hope. Nothing but signs up at stores saying No Indians Wanted. They're with us at Wounded Knee, them vets, and they know how to shoot. We got women here, too. They're cooking and washing clothes and looking after the little ones. Wouldn't be here if it weren't for the women. They were the ones that said we gotta move forward and demand our rights. One of 'em said, let's go to Wounded Knee, 'cause it was here where the people got slaughtered a hundred years ago. Might be we get slaughtered again, just like then, but we got no choice. We gotta stand up for what's right."

Father John read through the final article on the end of the siege. A lot of people had already left the town, sneaking past the FBI lines, fading into ravines and dry ditches and eventually making their way back to their homes on Pine Ridge. When the last holdouts came out, hands over their heads, they were thrown to the ground, handcuffed, and hauled away.

Within weeks, five hundred Indians were indicted on charges of arson, theft, assault, and interfering with federal officers. Almost two hundred went to prison. Those who eluded capture left Pine Ridge and sought refuge on other reservations.

Father John moved back through the articles, studying the photos of Wounded Knee taken with telescopic lenses. Some Indian men, standing guard, holding shotguns and rifles. Another photo of three women stooped over a campfire, preparing food, much like the photos he'd seen of women in the villages in the Old Time. There was even a photo of a woman carrying a baby on her back. He studied the faces, but the photos were blurred and grainy; they could be photos of anyone.

"Were you there, Liz?" he said out loud into the building's quiet. He sat back, half expecting the sound of Ian's boots clambering down the corridor to see who might have come in, then he went back to the website. He clicked through three pages before he spotted another article that looked promising: "AIM Member Shot."

It was what he'd been looking for. The *Gazette*. August 13, 1973. *A Lakota man who went by the name of Brave Bird was fatally wounded by a Wind River police officer in a shoot-out in Ethete last night. According to a police spokesman, Brave Bird's real name was Daryl Redman, whose last known address was Pine Ridge, South Dakota.*

The local FBI office confirms that Redman was a member of AIM wanted by the FBI on charges related to the takeover of Wounded Knee last February. The FBI had believed he was hiding on the Wind River Reservation, but had been unable to locate him. The Wind River police received a tip about his possible whereabouts and had gone to a house in Ethete to check it out. "He came out firing," said the police spokesman. The officer who shot Redman was identified as Jesse Moon.

"We think other AIM fugitives may be hiding on the reservation," said a spokesman for the local FBI. "Like Redman, they adopt pseudonyms and try to blend in to the local population. They are armed and dangerous. People should not approach them, but should notify the police or the FBI." The spokesman also cautioned that harboring such fugitives is a federal offense. "Anyone who helps them could be sent to prison with them," he said.

"Got a minute?" Ian's voice cut through the quiet.

Father John looked up from the computer screen. He hadn't heard his assistant in the corridor, but now he was standing in the doorway, head thrust forward like a pony poised to lurch into the room.

"Take a seat." He nodded toward one of the side chairs pushed against the wall, then clicked on exit and watched the site vaporize on the screen.

"Made up your mind yet?" Ian said. He folded his lanky frame onto the edge of the chair.

Father John shifted his gaze across the top of the screen to the other priest. He stopped himself from asking, "About what?" He knew Ian was talking about Rome. Forget about the sabbatical, he'd been telling himself, hoping the provincial would also forget, and everything would go on, the way it had for the last nine years. Who was he kidding? It had never left his mind; it had only been hiding in a shadowy place where he'd refused to look, and it had jumped out, flashing and screaming, before Ian had even finished his question.

He got up and walked over to the window. The cottonwood branches moved sideways in the breeze; little furrows of wind ran through the grasses. Walks-On sprawled next to the steps at the residence, intent on the bone wedged between his front paws. The sky was a dome of clear blue glass, and in the distance the peaks of the Wind River range shimmered in the sunshine. This was home. He turned back. "I'm not ready for a sabbatical," he said.

Something like a shadow crossed Ian's face. He swallowed and seemed to make an effort to assemble an expression that appeared neutral and unconcerned, but the effort left Father John with the sense that Ian was disappointed, that he was waiting for the chance to run the mission.

"I spent a wonderful month in Rome a few years ago," Ian said.

"Did you?" Father John tried to keep his own expression neutral. He braced himself for a recitation of the interesting, historical, beautiful places in Rome meant to nudge him into taking the sabbatical.

"Wouldn't mind going back."

Father John held the other man's gaze a moment, then he

walked around the desk and dropped back onto his seat. This was new, a curveball when he'd been expecting a straight pitch. "You'd like to take the sabbatical?"

"What would you think?" Ian hurried on. "I've been reading up on the deliberations in Rome about ways the Christian message might be manifested in non-Western cultures. I haven't been here as long as you . . ." He raised both hands as if to ward off an objection. "But I've been here long enough to contribute to the conversation."

Father John swallowed back the impulse to laugh. An obvious solution, and it hadn't even occurred to him. The provincial wanted someone in Rome with experience on a reservation, someone with insight on bringing Christianity to indigenous people around the world. And he had another Jesuit eager to come to St. Francis who could take Ian's place.

"I'll talk to the provincial," he said.

"I'd like to come back, John. You know, after the sabbatical . . ."

"No guarantee," Father John said. That was the thing that had made him ignore the whole idea. He could feel it now, like a hard knot in his stomach. If he left St. Francis, there was no guarantee that he would ever return. The same was true for Ian. Another Jesuit would come; everything would change, and the future would form and reform into shapes that would be different from anything either of them might imagine.

"I wouldn't want to go unless I could be assured of a position here when I return." A hard note of stubbornness sounded in Ian's voice. He wouldn't have to go at all, Father John was thinking. *He* was the one the provincial wanted to take the sabbatical. He could almost hear Bill Rutherford's laugh when he told him that Ian wanted the sabbatical, but only on condition . . .

Ian got to his feet and started for the door. He set a hand on the frame and looked back. "I guess I shouldn't pack my bags just yet," he said, giving a half nod, as if he were reluctant to let go of the possibility.

Father John stared at the phone and listened to the sound of Ian's footsteps receding in the corridor. Finally he lifted the receiver and pressed the keys for Bill Rutherford's office. The voice on the other end sounded lethargic and bleary with the heat of the Milwaukee summer. "Sorry, Father O'Malley, the provincial isn't available at the moment. What is this about?"

"He knows what it's about," Father John said. "Ask him to call me." He could hear the relief in his voice. He wouldn't have to speak to Rutherford right away, listen to the urgency pulsing down the line: "You're the one I had in mind, John." It was a brief, blessed reprieve from the inevitable. He still had time.

He hit the off button, then started over again, this time pressing the keys for the Wind River Police Department. "This is Father O'Malley," he told the woman who'd picked up. "Let me talk to Chief Banner." Art Banner had been the police chief on the reservation as long as Father John had been at the mission. He couldn't imagine the police department without Banner, but then, in a reverse way that made him stifle a laugh, he couldn't imagine himself without the mission.

"Sorry, Father." The woman's voice was friendly, as if she were chatting with him across the desk. He tried to picture the operator who sat behind the glass window, answered the phone, and buzzed in visitors: a little overweight, short black hair, always smiling. "Chief's in a meeting," she said. "Probably be tied up another hour or so. Want me to have him call you?"

Father John glanced at his watch. Almost nine o'clock. He'd planned on stopping by the senior center this morning for coffee with some of the elders and he had promised Irma Dancer when she was about to be released from the hospital last week that he'd visit her at home, which should put him in Fort Washakie by eleven. "Tell Banner I'll stop by later," he said.

He set the receiver in the cradle and waited, half expecting the ringing to begin. Bill Rutherford would expect him to take the sabbatical, and he wouldn't allow much time for him to change his mind.

Father John closed the book on Sitting Bull and made a small attempt at straightening the desk. Then he crossed the office and lifted his cowboy hat off the rack. He walked down the corridor and told Ian he'd be gone the rest of the morning, then retraced his steps and let himself out the front door, hurrying, he realized, before the phone started to ring.

14

THE brown house had a vacant look about it—no vehicles parked in the dirt yard, no towels or blue jeans flapping on the lines strung along one side. Still, it was the only brown house she'd passed on Mill Creek Road. She slowed down for a right turn and bounced across the barrow ditch. Fresh tire tracks crisscrossed the dirt. A vehicle had been here not long before. She stopped near the wooden stoop at the front door and turned off the ignition. If Ruth Yellow Bull was home, she would have heard the Jeep. If she wanted visitors, she'd come outside. It wasn't polite to step onto the stoop and bang on the door.

Vicky waited for a couple of minutes before she got out. She slammed the door hard. The warm breeze whipped her skirt around her legs, and she could feel the sun burning past her hair into the back of her neck. She gave it another minute, then walked up the wooden steps and knocked on the door, trying to ignore the idea jabbing at her like a spear. Maybe she had become whiteized, like the grandmothers said. All those years in Denver going to school, working in a large, white firm—she, the token Indian—and what had she really been doing? Trying to be white? Trying to forget who she was, where she'd come from? Becoming a *ho:xu'wu:nen*? A lawyer living by the white man's rules, and all the time, losing some part of herself.

I came home! She'd wanted to say to the grandmothers when they'd turned away from her at the powwows or the tribal meetings and whispered among themselves, loud enough so that she could hear. *Well, look at her. Don't she think she's something? Made herself real big, like a chief. Don't she know, women don't have no business being chiefs?* It was Ben Holden who had been like a chief, a leading man on the reservation, and she had left him, just driven off one day. It amazed her when she thought about it. Had she really believed she could make it on her own? Woman Alone, the grandmothers called her—*Hi sei ci nihi*—because it was true. And yet it was strange, about the name. It had given her strength and courage, and she knew that even when the grandmothers had turned away, they had still blessed her with the name.

And here she was banging on the front door of a house on the rez, like a white woman. There was no sound inside, no scrape of footsteps or clack of a door. Nothing except the faint reverberation of her own pounding. She stepped back and glanced around. A dark pickup was coming down the road, the bed swaying as if it might break away from the cab, little clouds of dust swirling around the tires. The pickup slowed a little, then dived to the right, jumped across the barrow ditch and plunged toward the Jeep. It slid to a stop, both doors swinging open. A heavyset woman with gray hair that hung in clumps around the shoulders of her denim shirt and a round face marked by deeply set lines and what might have been old scars got out of the pickup. Two little boys, maybe eight or nine, piled out on the passenger side and started pushing and pummeling each other until one of them was down on the ground, the other kicking at his legs. "Knock it off," the woman shouted as she came around the hood of the Jeep.

"Ruth Yellow Bull?" Vicky had to shout, too. One boy was crying, the other yelling. She stepped off the stoop.

"Who wants to know?"

"I'm Vicky Holden."

"Oh, yeah. You're that lawyer lady." Without moving her feet, Ruth Yellow Bull rolled herself sideways toward the two boys, still jabbing and yelling at each other. "Shut up, you hear me? I have to come over there and kick your butts?" She rolled back. "What d'ya want?"

"I'd like to talk to you about a girl named Liz. She was active in AIM back in the seventies."

Ruth Yellow Bull didn't say anything at first, but her eyes narrowed, as if she were trying to bring something into focus, something forgotten. "Why'd you come here?" she said finally.

"I understand you were part of AIM back then."

"So what? Lots of people joined up." She turned back to the boys, this time stomping her feet in a half circle. "Get them bags of groceries into the house," she shouted. Vicky noticed the three brown bags in the bed of the pickup, propped against the rear of the cab. It was a moment before the kids stopped wrestling and sauntered over to the pickup. The taller boy lifted out two bags and smashed them into the chest of the other boy, who staggered off, fighting to keep the bags upright. Then the other kid dragged the last bag across the bed and over the side of the pickup and headed for the house.

"Grandkids," Ruth said. "Who needs 'em?"

Vicky tried to catch the younger boy's eyes, then the older boy's, but they kept their eyes averted and plodded on, brushing past her. "Is their mother at work?" Vicky heard herself asking. Gray dust streaked the small brown faces and clung to the plaid shirts and blue jeans. The boys' hair, black and knotted, seemed stuck to the wrinkled collars of their shirts, and she wondered if this was how her own children had looked, unwashed and uncared for, after she had left them. She blinked back the idea; her mother had loved them and taken good care of them, that was the truth, just as her mother had loved and taken good care of her.

"Work? Yeah, she's at work all right, at some meth house. Look, I don't know nothin' about AIM. Whoever sent you here is a damn liar if they said I did."

"What about Liz? She was an Arapaho who went to Pine Ridge. It's possible she was at Wounded Knee before she came back here. You might have run into her, or heard about her."

"What the hell's this all about?" Ruth crooked both elbows and set her hands on her waist, fingers spread apart across her ballooning abdomen. She bent her head forward, like a bull ready to charge.

"It's possible she was murdered," Vicky said. "It could be her skeleton that was found out in the Gas Hills."

The woman dropped her hands and went over to the stoop. Gripping the railing with one hand, she swung her thick legs onto the first step, then the second, and finally planted herself in front of the door, which hung open into the shadows of the living room. Past the edge of a sofa, Vicky could see the two boys jostling in the kitchen. The sounds of paper crackling and something hard bouncing across the floor drifted outside.

Still holding on to the railing, Ruth looked down. "Don't got nothing to do with me."

Vicky tipped her head back and locked eyes with the woman. "I heard you were at Wounded Knee," she said.

"Who the hell you been talkin' to?"

"It doesn't matter. I understand there were other Arapahos at Pine Ridge," Vicky said, not taking her eyes away. "Could I come in? I'd like to talk to you for a moment. It's possible you might remember."

"Maybe I don't want to remember. Maybe it don't matter anymore, 'cause it's over and done with. It's the past, and ain't you heard, the past is deader than a skinned rabbit. What's it to you, anyway?"

"It's a cold case," Vicky said. "I'm trying to find something that will keep her murder from being buried in a file with a lot of other unsolved murders. I'd like to see her given a proper burial, with her own name. Whoever killed her has gotten away with it for more than thirty years. I'd like to see him brought to justice."

"I don't know nothing about it. I don't know nobody by that name." The woman hesitated, her lips working around soundless words. Then she said, "Besides, maybe she deserved what she got."

In the narrowed eyes and the set of the woman's jaw, Vicky realized that she was lying. She waited a moment, allowing the lie to grow between them, like an expanding bubble that couldn't be ignored. "Why, Ruth?" she said. "Because she'd talked to the police, and the police killed one of the AIM members? Is that why she deserved to die?"

The woman leaned forward until the railing cut into her fleshy middle. "I don't know what you're talking about. I don't know nothin' about that time. Maybe I was stoned, so I don't know what came down." She lifted her head and gazed for a long moment across the road and beyond, to the empty plains. Finally she pushed off the railing, swung around and stepped into the house. "Forget about it." She threw the words over one shoulder. "Nobody cares what happened then."

"You know what he did to her, Ruth." Vicky called out to the woman's back, hoping she wouldn't slam the door shut. She had to hold her hair back against the gust of wind that swept across the yard, blowing up billows of dust. "He beat her up first, broke most of her bones, knocked out her teeth. He took her to a desolate gulley and put a bullet in the back of her head. He's a monster, Ruth, and I think he's still on the rez."

Ruth turned back, her eyes like black lines slashed across the flesh of her face. Her lips were moving, forming and re-forming around silent words as she negotiated some track in her head. Vicky held her breath and waited. Then something new came into the woman's expression, some acute look of fear that turned her features into an icy sculpture. She grabbed the edge of the door and, stepping backward, slammed the door shut.

Vicky waited a moment, half hoping that the door would open again, that the woman would say, "Come in; I'll tell you all about her." Because she was certain now that Ruth Yellow Bull knew a girl named Liz. She *knew.*

The door stayed closed. From inside the house came the muffled noise of the boys yelling and the sharp, staccato notes of Ruth's voice punctuating theirs.

Vicky went back to the Jeep and crawled inside. She felt limp with frustration. She was so close, so close. She'd found someone who knew about that time, knew about a girl named Liz. But she wouldn't tell what she knew. She'd closed the door on that time just as she'd slammed the front door on her and Father John. It was over. All over, she'd said. It was dead.

Vicky turned the ignition and backed around the yard. She drove forward, dipping down into the barrow ditch before crawling up the other side, then turned onto the road. Holding the wheel steady with one hand, she rummaged in her bag on the passenger seat with the other and pulled out her cell. She started to punch in the number for the sheriff's department.

She had something now. She and John O'Malley had come up with a name: Liz. And she'd found a woman who'd been at Wounded Knee, and that woman, she was sure, knew what had happened to Liz.

She pressed the end key. Ruth Yellow Bull would not talk to Detective Coughlin. She would deny she'd ever gone to Wounded Knee, and who could prove otherwise? She would keep her secrets because . . .

Because she was afraid. Vicky tried to swallow, but her mouth had gone dry, her tongue felt like a bloated twig flapping against the back of her teeth. Ruth Yellow Bull was afraid because the killer was still around and if she talked, if she told anyone what she knew, he would kill her.

The noise of the cell ringing broke into her thoughts. She turned onto Plunkett Road and pressed the cell against her ear. "Vicky Holden," she said.

"Oh, Vicky." Annie was shouting, as if Vicky were across the street. "I've been trying to get ahold of you," she hurried on, and Vicky realized she hadn't checked the messages. "Adam wants to know when you'll be in. He wants to get started on that discrimination case."

"Tell him I'm on the way," Vicky said, surprised at the ripples of irritation running through her. It would be a big case, with either a major complaint with the Equal Employment Opportunity Commission or a major lawsuit, unless Mammoth Oil agreed to settlement and stopped discriminating against Indians. There would be a lot of work; people to talk to, statements to obtain. They'd have to prepare an initial letter to Mammoth's legal department. It was the beginning of a long and complex process, and she was also eager to get started. Of course she was. Wasn't this why she'd come home, to help her people get their rights?

She'd call Coughlin, tell him what she'd learned, and leave the case of a girl murdered years ago to the proper investigators, just as Adam had said. This wasn't her fight.

Then she realized that Annie was talking about a call that had come from a law firm in Denver.

"What was the message?" she asked. She knew the firm—high-profile criminal defense attorneys for wealthy clients. She could guess the message, even as Annie launched into the explanation. They were defending someone named Theo Gosman charged with assaulting a woman in an alley. Would she be willing to be interviewed?

Vicky didn't say anything for a moment. There was no reason for her to consent to an interview with the defense attorneys for the man who had beaten the girl in the alley. But she knew the way the game was played. If she or Lucas or Susan refused an interview, it would be used against them in Gosman's trial. The defense would try to make it look as if they were biased or trying to hide something.

"Anything else?" she said. Her thoughts were spiraling like a gyroscope toward a single point: The girl in the alley would have been dead if Lucas hadn't taken the side street. She could have been like Liz, beaten and shot in an empty canyon where there was no one about, no one to take a different turn and help her.

And Liz's killer was still around.

"Diana Morningstar called," Annie said.

"The women want to talk again?" This was a good sign, she was thinking. Someone in the group might have learned something. They were all upset, on edge. A skeleton with no name might be any of them. Except that, now, the skeleton had a first name.

"She says they've been putting flyers around the rez about the skeleton. Wants to see you alone. Tonight, she said. Wants you to meet her in the park by the river. There was something . . ."

"What do you mean?"

"I don't know. Something about her voice. She sounded kinda scared. My guess, she doesn't want anybody to see her talking to you."

Vicky said she'd be at the office in about thirty minutes. She pressed the end key, turned south onto Highway 287, and drove toward Lander.

15

1973

MAIN Street was almost empty, a couple of cars parked at the curbs, light glowing in the second-floor windows of a building. Circles of streetlights splashed down through the darkness and, half a block ahead, the stoplight melted from yellow into red. Liz gripped the steering wheel and tried to think. Loreen had driven the day they'd come to Lander to see Ardyth—Liz squeezed in the middle of the front seat of a pickup, Ruth leaning out the passenger window, banging on the side as they'd sped down Main Street, whooping and hollering like an Indian, she'd boasted later. Givin' white folks what they expect.

They'd driven down Main Street and turned—where?

At the stoplight, Liz remembered, because they'd had to wait behind a white-haired old lady in a big pink car with big chrome fantails. And why the hell could she remember *that* when she couldn't remember how to get to Ardyth's?

They'd turned right.

She had the rest of it now. She made the turn and drove into a residential neighborhood with bungalows and old trees drooping into the darkness over the lawns and cars along the curbs. A field of stars blazed in the black sky, and moonlight washed over the street. There had been a big white house on the corner, she remembered, like an old farmhouse. Ardyth lived in the little brown house in back. There were a couple of other buildings scattered about, too, probably left over from the farm. All she had to do was find the big white house on the corner.

"The river is flowing." Liz sang quietly as she drove toward an intersection. The sound of her own voice floated about her. She could hear Luna let out a long sigh in the back. "Gently it goes, taking the pain. Soon we'll be going. Didn't I tell you so? Everything's gonna be real nice. Didn't I tell you so?"

She was going on instinct now, a feeling of bravery coming over her, like an invisible companion next to her in the front seat. It had to be here somewhere, the big white house. She drove toward the outskirts of town and took a parallel street back, stopping at every intersection, peering left and right. She'd gone three blocks when the façade of a two-story white house loomed out of the moonlight on the next block. The Ford lurched as she pressed down on the gas pedal. She reached back to keep Luna's box from sliding onto the floor, then turned into the gravel driveway next to the house and drove to the small brown house in back that looked like a little rich girl's playhouse, with its peaked roof and flower boxes with wilted flowers at the windows. Lights shone in the kitchen window. There were no curtains, and she could see the row of cabinets and a framed picture of mountains slanting sideways on the wall. Ardyth walked into the kitchen, head bent toward something on the counter. Her head snapped up. She turned toward the window and peered out.

Liz started across the strip of bare dirt between the car and the house, holding Luna's box close, one arm looped over the top. Ardyth was already standing in the open door.

"My God, Liz," she shouted. "What're you doin' here?"

It started to come out then, the fear and panic she'd been pushing down and trying to cover up with songs. Liz felt as if she were floating away from herself, looking down on the dark figure standing in a puddle of light at the opened door, clutching a cardboard box, weeping and shaking. Another figure stepped toward her.

Then she was back in her body, Ardyth's hand cool on her arm as she stumbled into the house.

"This about AIM?" Ardyth said.

Liz blinked into the bright kitchen light. "The cops killed Brave Bird," she said, the words tumbling out, distorted and slurred. "They think I gave him up. I gotta find Robert. He's the only one that can fix it."

"Shit. They'll come after you."

"I need a place to stay until . . ." Liz stopped. The expression on Ardyth's face started to harden like clay baking in the sun. She was glancing at the window, as if she expected another car to come down the driveway. Then she looked at the cardboard box.

"Jesus, Liz," she whispered. "You've got the baby with you."

"Just a little while, until I get ahold of Robert."

"Loreen and Ruth know where I live." Ardyth hadn't taken her eyes from the box. "They'll tell them, whoever's after you."

"Robert'll know what to do."

"You sure have a way of getting into trouble, Liz. Better hide the car in the shed out back." Ardyth pivoted toward the counter and began rummaging in a drawer. "Lock the doors," she said, freeing a padlock from beneath the clutter of knives and measuring spoons and other kitchen utensils.

Liz set Luna's box on the table, took the padlock, and hurried back outside. A gust of warm wind rounded the corner of the house and whipped at her as she sank into the car. She drove to the shed, then got out and yanked at the double wood doors that squealed on their hinges like trapped animals. She got back into the car and rocked across the threshold onto the soft dirt floor, the walls of the shed closing around her. She had to squeeze herself out the door and inch alongside the car, wincing at the rough wood walls that bit at her arms. She shoved the doors hard into the wind, snapped on the padlock, and ran back to the house.

The cardboard box was gone. The table was clear, nothing but the faint gleam of light reflecting in the surface. "Luna," she screamed. "My baby!" Liz plunged through the doorway into the living room behind the kitchen. "Luna! Luna!" she shouted. A column of light from the kitchen lay across the tan rug on the floor. The sofa and chair looked like shadows on the wall.

"Be quiet." Ardyth appeared in the doorway on the right— a moving shadow coming toward her. She leaned over and turned on the lamp next to the sofa. "You'll wake her up," she said, tossing her head toward the doorway. "You can stay in the bedroom. I'll sleep on the sofa."

Liz clamped a fist against her mouth and tried to swallow back the scream that had formed in her throat. "She's all I have," she managed. "She's everything."

She darted for the bedroom, feeling the heat of Ardyth's eyes boring into her back. The bedroom was small. Moonlight filtered across the cardboard box on the chest. Liz bent over and straightened the blanket around the tiny body, then she looked around. Clothes hung on a rack along the wall. A narrow bed jutted into the room, taking up most of the space. She stared at the star quilt thrown over the bed. Most of her life she'd slept under the star quilt her grandmother had made. There was a clanking noise in the kitchen, followed by the sound of the refrigerator door opening and closing. She pressed her fist against her mouth to keep from sobbing and went back into the kitchen.

Ardyth stood at the counter pulling the tab on a Coke can, and Liz was struck by the way in which her friend had changed in the last few weeks. She seemed taller and thinner, all angles and edges. Her black hair was pulled back into a ponytail, which gave her face a stretched look, like that of brown hide pulled across the top of a drum.

"You better eat," she said, glancing at Liz out of eyes narrowed into slits. She set the Coke on the table next to a plate with a sandwich cut in half.

"I need to call Robert first," Liz said. She walked across the kitchen, picked up the phone on the counter, and dialed Robert's number. She closed her eyes and listened to the buzzing noise, her hand numb around the receiver. Her legs were like water. There was no answer, just the buzzing going on and on.

She hung up and dropped onto the chair in front of the plate, aware for the first time of the emptiness expanding inside her. She wasn't sure when she'd last eaten. Sometime this morning, she guessed, before she'd taken Luna to the clinic for her checkup. Afterward she'd stopped at Loreen's to pick up the box of flyers on Saturday's general council meeting that she'd promised to fold and deliver around the reservation. *People gotta get involved.* She could hear Robert's voice in her head. *Gotta get their asses over to the council meeting.*

Take part in what the Arapaho and Shoshone business councils are planning for them.

Where are you, Robert?

"Crazy," Ardyth said, sitting down across from her. "They must've gone crazy. It was you that found the place for Brave Bird to stay. Helped him get to know the ropes, blend in with people on the rez. What was his real name?"

"Daryl Redman," Liz said. She bit off a piece of the sandwich, then took another bite and swallowed hard. The food seemed to drop into a vast, hollow canyon.

"Yeah, I heard on the radio that Daryl Redman got shot at Ethete. I didn't know who they were talking about until they said he went by the name of Brave Bird, wanted by the FBI in South Dakota for trespassing, robbery, assault on federal officers. Now the Feds know one of the leaders was hiding out here, they're gonna be all over the rez looking for Robert and Jake and the others. They're gonna be looking for you. They're gonna want to talk to you, see what you know . . ."

"I never told the police anything."

Ardyth threw up a hand, palm out, fingers spread. "That doesn't mean the Feds won't arrest you for harboring a fugitive or something. You can bet they know you were at Pine Ridge. They're gonna suspect you. Loreen and Ruth, too. You're all gonna have to watch it. No way will Robert want you picked up again. He'll find you someplace to hide out." She crossed her arms on the table and leaned over. "You should get out, like I did. Why didn't you get out last fall in Washington after Jimmie got killed?"

Liz didn't say anything. She took another bite of sandwich and washed it down with a drink of Coke, and tried to push back the images flashing in her head, as if Ardyth had slapped a series of photographs on the table. She didn't want them.

"We were going to make a difference," Liz said, trying to shift the conversation from the direction it was heading. She could hear the hesitancy in her voice.

"We both know that's crap," Ardyth said. "Sure there were convoys of Indians arriving every day from all over the country. Thousands of Indians, and we thought that would be enough to make the president notice us. What a laugh! They promised us good places for the tribal leaders and the holy men to stay in, remember that? What did they get? Same as the rest of us got, rat-infested basements in old churches. Jesus, the toilets didn't even work. Everything smelled like shit. You remember the rats? Big as cats, running over the cots they said we should sleep on. Like anybody got any sleep. Jimmie and Robert went around to all the churches, said we'd go to the Bureau of Indian Affairs, every damn Indian in the city, and demand our rights. You remember?"

Liz nodded, and Ardyth went on about how she didn't mind for herself and the rest of the ordinary Indians, but it wasn't right to put the tribal leaders in rat-infested church basements. And the holy men, the spiritual leaders of the people! It just wasn't right, not when any tribal chief from Timbuktu or someplace you never heard of that came to see the president got to stay in some nice hotel . . .

Liz sat back and stared at the black and gray images fixed in her head. Ardyth's voice rumbled on like a washing machine in the background. Jimmie looked so handsome in his white leather jacket as he walked through the people jammed in the basement. He jumped up on a table, waved his arms. You could have heard a pin drop. Everybody was looking at him, not at Robert, standing behind the table, holding it steady. People trusted Jimmie. For just a moment, his eyes had turned toward her. She'd patted her stomach and he'd smiled at the secret they shared. Then he'd shouted that first thing tomorrow, everyone should go to the BIA. "They're not getting away with the same shit," he'd shouted. "We're here together. We are the people!"

The crowd took up the chant as Jimmie and Robert strode back across the basement and disappeared up the steps. *We are the people. We are the people.* Even now, Liz could hear the sound drumming in her ears.

After they had left, she'd gone with some of the others to get bread and cans of soup. The kids had started crying, they were so hungry, so someone had taken up a donation. She could see herself walking down the dark sidewalk, part of a group of Indians with a purpose. Thinking about it now, she felt the same stab of pride that she'd felt then, the way a song brings back an old feeling. It didn't matter about the basements. The Indian people were together, and that was all that mattered.

She'd had to wait at the store while the clerk ran into the back for change. The others had gone on ahead. She was walking alone, juggling two bags of groceries, when she heard the loud thud and the sound of groans as she passed the alley behind the church.

She whirled about and looked down the alley at the dark figure of a man bobbing in and out of the shadows. He stooped over and picked up something—it looked like a piece of metal that might have fallen off a car. He lifted his arm, and it was then, as he started swinging the metal club, that Liz saw the white jacket on the man sprawled on the asphalt. She dropped the grocery bags and ran into the alley, the sound of cans clanking on the pavement behind her mingled with the thud of metal against flesh and bones.

"Stop! Stop!" She threw herself toward Jimmie's body, but she was moving in slow motion, suspended in space, trying to cover his body with her own, barely conscious of the pain that flashed down her arm.

She felt herself spinning around, crashing against the brick wall. Jake's hand was on her throat. His other hand lifted the metal over her head. "You want what he got?"

"You killed Jimmie!"

"Shut up! I oughtta kill you, whore." He threw a look down the alley toward the street. A truck lumbered by. Then a white police car.

Jake pressed his hand over her mouth. "Shut up," he said, a whisper this time. "You're gonna walk outta here, go back to the basement. Understand?" The police car must have turned around, because it passed the alley again. "You open your mouth, I'll kill you."

She'd tried to nod, she remembered, but he was pushing her head back against the brick. She stared past his hand at Jimmie, lying so still, folds of the white jacket turning black with his blood.

"Get outta here," Jake said, releasing her.

Liz slumped against the wall a moment. Her body had turned to rubber; she wanted to throw up.

"Go!" Jake pulled her off the wall and shoved her toward the street.

She remembered looking back at Jimmie as she'd stumbled

forward, the alley and the dark brick walls, even Jimmie, blurred with her tears. She tripped over a can of soup, and hit the pavement. Red hot pain seared her shoulder. She lay in the alley, gravel biting into her face, and sobbed out loud, barely conscious of Jake moving around her, picking up cans, stuffing them into a brown bag.

Then she felt herself being yanked upward, and she scrabbled to get a hold on the pavement. Jake shoved the grocery bag at her. "I should've killed you," he said. "Get back to the basement before I change my mind."

"Liz?" It was Ardyth's voice cutting through her thoughts. "You okay?"

"Yeah." She tried for a reassuring smile. "Just thinking about Washington."

"Whole thing was stupid, when you think about it." Ardyth shifted in her chair and stared at some point across the kitchen. "We show up at the BIA building. All we want is to talk to the commissioner, demand decent hotels for the tribal leaders, get an appointment to present our grievances to the president. Thing was, we had a snitch with us."

"What? You sure?"

Ardyth shrugged, as if it didn't matter. "Of course, I'm sure. Why do you think there were armed riot troops that showed up at the BIA? Soon's we got there, we were surrounded by troops. Jesus, just like the Old Time with the soldiers surrounding the villages. We didn't have any choice except to take over the whole damn building. Called it the Native American Embassy, for godssake. Robert got everybody organized. I had to work in the stinking so-called laundry, washing out dirty underwear in sinks, hanging 'em on ropes we strung around the basement. We were so busy we didn't even hear about Jimmie getting mugged and beat to death for a couple days."

Liz closed her eyes a moment. "I was working in the kitchen when I heard."

"Yeah, I felt really bad for you since you were gonna have his kid and all. You said, soon as the occupation was over, you were gonna leave AIM. Only you didn't leave. Why not?"

"I just changed my mind, is all," Liz said. She'd been cleaning up the kitchen after supper when Jake had burst through the door. He was drunk, and she'd wondered where in hell he'd gotten alcohol. Leave me alone, she'd said, but he'd started circling her, keeping his eyes on her, and she'd thought he might kill her then. She could hear the muffled noise of music coming from a radio somewhere, and the sounds of voices floating down the corridor beyond the door, but if she screamed, no one would hear her.

"What do you want?" she'd asked.

He'd grabbed hold of her braid then and pulled her across the room into the closet they'd turned into a pantry. He'd kicked the door shut, so there was just the two of them in the darkness, with only a rim of light at the bottom of the door. The air was thick with the smell of whiskey; his breath was hot on her face.

"You know I could kill you," he said.

"You're not going to kill me here. The cops won't let anybody leave until they find out who did it."

He was quiet a long moment before he said, "Don't even think about taking off."

"You don't need me," she'd said.

"Oh, you're wrong. I need you right by my side so I can watch you every goddamn minute. You're gonna stay around, got it? You're gonna forget what happened. Jimmie and me, we had a beef, that's all. Not your business, so forget about it. You leave, and I'll hunt you down. Wherever you go, I'll find you." He'd gripped her throat then and began squeezing. "I'll break your neck." Finally he'd let go and stumbled out of the closet. She'd listened to him crashing around the kitchen before she heard the door open and shut. Still, she'd waited several minutes before she'd left the kitchen and gone up to the room she was sharing with Loreen and Ruth and Ardyth.

"So why didn't you?" Ardyth said.

"What?"

"Get out after the occupation? We could've been killed there, you know, if the soldiers had stormed the place. We were just damn lucky Nixon didn't want Indian blood on his hands right before the election, so he called off the army."

Liz shrugged, thinking how she'd gone to Robert, told him everything, and how Robert had said it was AIM business, not any business of the cops, and he'd handle Jake. He'd see that

AIM took care of her, too, with the baby coming. She shouldn't worry; and that was it—wasn't it?—the fact that she had nowhere else to go. She hadn't seen her mother in almost two years. She didn't even know where her mother was now. All she had was AIM. "I just decided to stay on for a while," she said.

"You really believed all the crap, didn't you? AIM could make a difference, and everything was going to change."

"Something like that."

"Yeah." Ardyth was shaking her head. "Now look at the fix you're in. You better get ahold of Robert tomorrow, 'cause you'll have to leave here."

16

"BEI Mannern, welche Liebe fuhlen" rose over the sound of the wind rushing through the opened windows. Father John slowed through Fort Washakie, past the tribal office building, the sun glinting on the bronze sculpture of Chief Washakie in front. He saw the heads turning in the passing pickups, the surprise registered in people's faces. He was used to the attention his operas drew as he drove across the reservation. "We know where you are," an elder once told him. "We hear you coming." There was the kid who stopped him in the hall the day he'd been invited to speak about the Plains Indian wars at Wind River High School. "What's so great about opera?" the kid had asked. "Live with it awhile," he'd told him. "Then you tell me." He'd loaned him his tape of *Madame Butterfly*. "Start with Puccini," he'd said.

He parked in the lot adjoining the squat redbrick building with the sign that said Wind River Law Enforcement. The front door was as heavy as steel. He let himself into a small cubicle with a tiled floor, concrete walls, and an antiseptic odor. Behind the window above the counter on the right, two officers in gray uniforms were hunched over a stack of papers on a side table. The heavyset one looked up, then walked over and bent toward the metal communicator. "Hey, Father," he said. "How can we help you?"

One of the Connellys, Father John thought. Arapahos with an Irish ancestor who came to Mass from time to time, usually at Christmas and Easter. "Chief Banner in?" he said.

"Hold on. I'll get him." The officer moved sideways toward a telephone and picked up the receiver. "Father John's here." His voice sounded muffled away from the communicator. He stepped back. "Be out in a minute. How's everything at the mission?"

Everything was fine, Father John said, which seemed to satisfy the officer because he gave a nod, stepped back to the side table, and started thumbing through the stack of papers the other officer had set aside. Father John crossed his arms and leaned against the concrete wall. He'd been here more times than he could count. Beyond the inside door was a corridor with offices on either side. Another corridor led to the tribal jail at the back of the building. There was a visiting room off that corridor—the concrete walls, the narrow view through the window of the exercise yard with concertina wire wrapped around the top of the walls. He'd talked to dozens of inmates in that room. They usually began with, I didn't do it, Father, and moved on to, I didn't mean to do it.

He wondered about the girl named Liz. Why had AIM believed she'd talked to the police? Had she been arrested? Brought to the jail? And in the visitor's room, a detective, sitting across the table, promising her—what? That charges against her would be dropped? All she had to do was provide the names of AIM leaders hiding on the reservation.

The door next to him swung open, and Chief Art Banner leaned forward. He was on the far side of middle age, a good six feet tall, with a wide chest that strained his gray uniform shirt and a large head balanced on a thick neck. He had short-cut black hair sprinkled with gray and dark eyes that had an opaque look, crowded with too many sights. Father John shook hands with the man, then followed him down a corridor and through an open door on the left.

"How you been?" the chief said, nodding to the plastic chair in front of the desk. He worked his way between the

metal file cabinet and the edge of the desk and sank into a
swivel chair. Behind him, the window framed a view of a pine
tree and the street beyond.

"Okay," Father John said. He sat down and hooked his cowboy hat on one knee. The polite preliminaries had to be ob-
served, he was thinking, even in the police chief's office. It took
a few minutes to discuss the Eagles' game last Saturday. The
Eagles had ended the Lander team's unbeaten record: 6 to 5.

"Heard you called this morning," Banner said, finally guiding the discussion to the point of the meeting. "Figure it must
be important for you to come over here."

Father John told him it was about the skeleton in the Gas
Hills.

Banner pulled a file folder out of the stack pushed to one
side of the desk and set it down in front of him. "Got a copy of
the forensics report," he said. "Indian girl, maybe Arapaho,
around twenty years old, killed in 1973. Hard case, this one.
Skeleton might as well be prehistoric. We got about the same
chance of finding out who killed her. Sheriff's jurisdiction,
Detective Coughlin's problem. My guess is, he'll lose it in the
files." He set both elbows on the folder and clasped his hands
in front of his mouth. "You heard something?"

"Her name was Liz," Father John said. "She was Arapaho."

"And your source would be . . ."

"A park ranger. Indian called himself Joe."

Banner leaned back against his chair, hands still clasped,
elbows dug into the armrests. "Let me ask you, John. You give
him any money?"

"A few bucks. I know where you're going."

"He'll tell you her name was Tinker Bell and she came
from Neptune, if he thinks that's what you want to hear."

"Not this time," Father John said. He'd heard so many lies
in the confessional and in counseling sessions, he could almost hear them coming before the other person had uttered
the words. It was like having an invisible antenna attached to
his skin. "He said she was part of AIM."

Banner unclasped his hands, shifted forward, and brought
his fists down onto the desk. "You know the beehive this could
stir up? AIM had anything to do with that killing, it'll tear the
reservation apart. Half the folks out there"—he tossed his

head back toward the window—"think AIM walked on water, could do no wrong, certainly wouldn't kill some girl. Doesn't mean they were members, necessarily. Lot of folks were fellow travelers, hanging back and cheering AIM on. Other half thinks AIM was a bunch of thugs that wanted to take over the reservation. Hated their guts. AIM tore the reservation apart. I doubt the sheriff's office is gonna want to stir up those feelings based on the ramblings of some park ranger named Joe."

"The killer could still be on the reservation. Somebody left a message on Vicky's dashboard. It said, 'Stop.' "

Banner nodded. "Coughlin sent over the report. Thought we ought to know an Arapaho might be in danger. Security cameras picked up a nondescript male opening the door of the Jeep. Cowboy hat pulled so low, his face was hidden. Didn't look like anything unusual. The guy is a pro, whoever he is. Made it look like he was using a key, instead of jimmying the lock. Message he left could mean that either he or somebody else doesn't want anybody probing into what went on back in the seventies. Let the past be. People that supported AIM, lot of 'em changed their minds as time went on. Maybe somebody doesn't want to remind folks that he was involved with AIM. Look at it this way, if you used to be a Communist, you want to remind folks about it?"

"Look, Banner." Father John leaned forward. "An AIM leader named Daryl Redman—went by the name of Brave Bird—was shot in Ethete by a police officer. It's possible that Liz gave him up, and that's why she was killed."

"According to Joe."

"It's possible."

Banner leaned back again, letting his fleshy hands fall from the armrests. "Nineteen seventy-three," he said. He pulled in his lower lip a moment and stared into the corner of the room. "I just got back from Vietnam. Trying to get on the police force, stay out of trouble, stay out of the way of AIM and all their marches and demonstrations that, far as I could see, weren't doing anything but causing trouble and making people anxious. I remember when that shooting went down in Ethete. Man, I thought there was gonna be a revolution. There were two camps; you were either on one side or the other. Either that Lakota was a saint, or he was the devil deserved to get shot. Only good came out of it, I heard, was that the other AIM leaders hiding here took off. I guess they figured if one had been given up, maybe others had, too."

"How can I contact the officer, Jesse Moon? If the girl was the source, he might remember who she was."

"Jesse Moon," Banner said, staring at the ceiling now. "Haven't thought about him for a long time. 'Bout ruined the man, that shooting. It's not easy to take a human life, John. It marks you, opens up a raw place in your gut that never heals over. Not an experience I ever want to have, but if some dude comes out firing, I'm gonna shoot him and hope I get him before he gets me. That's my job. Jesse said he didn't want any more of it. Left the force. Come to think of it, I got hired on right afterward, so I guess he opened up a slot for me. Tell you the truth, I don't know what became of him." He took a second before he said, "You're not going to let this go, are you?"

"We'd like to see the girl get justice," Father John said.

"We?"

"Vicky and I."

The chief made a tipi with his hands and smiled at him over the tips of his fingers. "You and Vicky, crusaders for justice," he said.

Father John had to glance away from the knowingness in the chief's eyes: Dear Lord, did everyone on the reservation *know* about his feelings for this woman? Was it so obvious? Was he so obvious that people could read him like a book? He had to force himself to look back at the man across from him. "Someone out there," he said, nodding toward the window and backing away from the topic of Vicky, "knows what happened to the girl. We're trying to locate that person, give Coughlin something to go on. We don't want to see the case filed away. Neither do the elders," he added. "They want to see her buried properly, with her own name."

Banner blew out a stream of air and lifted himself to his feet. "I'll see what I can get on Jesse and get back to you."

"One more thing." Father John stood up. "It's possible the girl had been arrested prior to the shooting."

Banner seemed to consider this a moment before he said, "I'll pull the records." He shifted his weight and went on. "One condition, John. You get any names of the girl's associates, you come to me or go to Coughlin. Some of those AIM people might still be dangerous. No way are you to approach them. Understood?"

"Understood," Father John said.

"Goes for Vicky, too."

"I'll tell her."

H E would tell her now, he thought, pulling the cell out of the glove compartment when he reached the pickup. He started to press the keys for her number, then hit the end key. He'd call her later, after Banner got back to him and he had something to tell her. He dropped the cell onto the passenger seat, turned on the tape player—"Dies Bildnis ist bezaubernd schön"—and turned up the volume. The engine sputtered like a drumroll into the music. He drove out of the parking lot and down the street toward the highway, the aria almost drowning out the sounds of the clanking engine and whirring tires. Tamino sets out to find the girl abducted by the evil Sarastro. How fitting, he thought.

I T amazed Vicky, how thorough Adam was. Meticulous and thoughtful in everything he did. It was the Indian Way. The Arapaho Way. "Be thoughtful in all things," Grandfather had told her. She'd never forgotten his words, yet it was strange how she'd sometimes forgotten to be thoughtful. By the time she'd gotten back to the office, Adam had already mapped out the steps they would take to file a complaint with the EEOC, should Mammoth refuse to settle with Mister and the others. They'd spent the afternoon in the conference room—she on one side of the table, Adam and Roger on the other, papers piling up in the middle. Roger would handle the initial phase of chasing down the other Indian employees and arranging interviews. Grunt work, everybody knew, but no one called it that.

Then, while Adam went to his uncle's funeral, she would get the rest of the names from Charlie Crow and begin interviewing people and documenting the elements of a complaint—dates of the forced drug tests, results. It was almost six o'clock before they'd gathered up the papers and slipped them into file folders. Roger had left fifteen minutes earlier, claiming an appointment, and Vicky and Adam had exchanged glances: an appointment with Annie. Another romance in the office, but like their own romance, Vicky thought, nobody discussed it.

"Where do you want to go for dinner?" Adam said, scooping up the file folders.

"I can't tonight." Vicky glanced at her watch. She had ten minutes to meet Diana at the park.

"Oh?" Adam walked around the table and held the door for her, disappointment and expectation playing across his face. She knew that he planned to leave early tomorrow for Pine Ridge.

"I agreed to see someone," she said, brushing past. She started down the corridor, his footsteps behind her. She crossed the reception toward her office, then turned. Adam had stopped in the middle of the room, folders clasped under one arm, hands stuck in the pockets of his khakis. She had the sense that she was seeing him for the first time—the black hair tousled from the hours of work, the tiny scar beneath his cheekbone, the flash of pain in his dark eyes. His shirtsleeves were folded halfway up his brown forearms; his khakis were wrinkled. They should be together, she thought, in accord. She should agree with him. Wasn't that what couples did?

Images of the girl in the alley flashed in her mind, like the frames of a black-and-white movie that she couldn't stop watching. The man's fist hitting and hitting, and Lucas rushing at him, and she behind Lucas, gripping the flashlight. The images always dissolved into those of a girl named Liz, alone in the Gas Hills with her killer.

She said, "Diana Morningstar wants to talk to me again. Probably about the skeleton. I can't let it go, Adam. I'm sorry."

"Okay." He shrugged, as if it didn't matter, and took a diagonal path past her to his office. She felt the vibrations running across the floor as the door slammed shut.

She went into her own office, pulled her bag out of the lower drawer in her desk, and retraced her steps, hurrying across the reception room, out into the corridor and down the stairs. She crossed the entry and let herself through the glass door into the lingering afternoon heat that had accumulated over Main

Street. Sun glittered on the windshields of passing vehicles, and exhaust belched from a truck, leaving a foul odor in the air. She walked around the corner of the building and threaded her way through the pickups and sedans parked in the lot.

She spotted the windshield across the hood of a pickup when she was still twenty feet away. The sight stopped her cold. For a moment, she felt as if she couldn't breathe. She had the sense that she'd stepped into a river, water rushing about her legs, the sandy riverbed receding beneath her feet. She had to lean against the pickup to get her balance. Then she started for the Jeep, not taking her eyes from the windshield—the large hole on the passenger side, the black lines fanning across the glass, the shards littering the hood and sparkling in the sun.

A wooden bat lay next to the front tire, and a white piece of paper fluttered from the twisted wiper. She reached across the glass shards, slipped the paper free and unfolded it. One word scrawled in black: STOP. Her hand was shaking. She forced herself to tighten her hold on the paper to keep it from scattering away in the breeze. There was no one else in the parking lot, nothing but the collection of sedans and pickups parked in improvised rows. And yet she had the sense of being watched. She turned slowly, taking in the surroundings: one, two, three—eleven empty vehicles. Bordering the lot, the blond brick façade of her office building; the oblong window that framed part of the staircase. The alley on the right, weeds poking through the asphalt. Across the alley, the small buildings stacked against one another. The street on the left, traffic blurring past. There was the steady thrum of engines, the squealing of a brake.

Then, moving into her peripheral vision: a figure on the sidewalk. She swung about and watched a young woman with an infant on her back disappear past the corner of the building.

She made herself take a deep breath, turned back to the Jeep, and dug her cell out of her bag, her gaze moving between the shattered windshield and the bat. He'd left the bat as a warning. For an instant, she felt that her legs would buckle beneath her.

She started jabbing at the numbers for Detective Coughlin's office. Her finger slid across the keys, and she had to start over, forcing herself to focus on the first number, then the next.

"What the hell . . . ?"

She nearly dropped the cell even as she registered that it was Adam's voice behind her, Adam's hand gripping her shoulder. She turned toward him and he pulled her close, enclosing her in his arms. She felt his heart hammering. "My God, Vicky," he said. "Who did this?"

"The killer." She blurted out the word. "It has to be the killer."

"I'm calling the police." Adam took his arms away and pried the cell out of her hand.

"Detective Coughlin." She gave him the number as he punched the keys.

A moment passed. Adam studied the windshield, then his eyes fixed on the bat. She could read the thought moving across his face. The killer had used a bat to break the girl's bones.

17

THE park was busy. Kids kicking soccer balls across the grass, families lingering over picnics at the tables, the sun arching in the western sky, the air still warm. Vicky glanced around, trying to spot Diana Morningstar sitting alone somewhere, maybe on a blanket, maybe on a bench at one of the tables.

It was almost seven; Diana had probably waited for a while, then left, thinking she wasn't coming. Vicky took in a couple of gulps of air. She was still out of breath. She'd walked the four blocks to the park—brushing aside Adam's offer to drive her, and that was after she'd brushed aside his pleas to drop the matter and leave the investigation to Coughlin.

The detective had agreed with Adam—walking around the Jeep, studying the smashed windshield, scribbling notes in a pad cupped in his hand. "You've done enough," he'd said, picking up the bat and setting it in the back of his SUV. He placed the piece of white paper in a plastic bag and set it next to the bat. "Two messages. I'd say whoever it is, he's serious."

"What do you mean?" Adam said. She hadn't told him

about the first note left on her dashboard in front of Coughlin's office. She hadn't wanted to listen to the arguments that she should stay out of the investigation.

"Didn't she tell you?" Coughlin stared at Adam—two men discussing her, as if she weren't even there. "Same message two days ago. Arrogant sonofabitch put it inside the Jeep parked outside my office."

"Vicky, listen to me . . ."Adam said. A mixture of worry and fury blazed in his eyes.

"I'm handling the investigation," Coughlin cut in.

Something changed behind Adam's eyes then. The fury dissolved, but the concern remained. They both knew that no one on the rez was about to talk to Coughlin about AIM. After a few futile efforts, he'd have no choice but to file away the case.

After Coughlin had finally driven out of the lot, she'd left Adam standing by the Jeep, pressing the keys on his cell for someone to replace the windshield. He would wait until the job was finished, he'd told her. Then he'd wait for her at her apartment.

She walked across the grass, dodging a soccer ball, scanning the area for someone sitting against a tree or perched on a rock by the river. Children's noises—laughing and shouting—filled the air. A guffaw went up from the little crowd around a picnic table. It hit Vicky that Diana might not have come. *She doesn't want anybody to see her talking to you.* Something might have caused her to change her mind.

Vicky started back across the grass. The soccer ball was rolling toward the river, five or six kids chasing it. Quiet descended over the crowd at the picnic table as she walked past. She was about to turn onto the sidewalk when someone called her name. A quick shout, a hushed yell: "Vicky!"

She swung around. Diana Morningstar emerged from the clump of pine trees on the far side of the grass, head bent forward, hands thrust in the pockets of a sweat jacket. Vicky hurried toward her. "I didn't think you were coming," Diana said. Her hair was pulled back into a ponytail, gray strands tucked among the black. Light shone in her dark eyes as she glanced between the street and the park.

"Sorry," Vicky said. "Something came up." She had no intention of telling her about the smashed windshield, the bat, and the message.

"Let's talk over here." Diana pivoted about and headed back through the trees. Vicky stayed in her footsteps, ducking around the sharp-faced trunks, bending under a couple of branches.

Parked on an apron of bare dirt was a brown pickup. Vicky could make out the tire marks where the pickup had bumped over the curb, driven around the trees and made a series of maneuvers until it faced the direction in which it had come. She could hear an engine gearing down, but the street was out of sight.

Diana threw open the driver's door and crawled in behind the wheel. She waited until Vicky had walked around the front and gotten into the passenger side before she pulled the door shut. The windows were up, and the instant that Vicky shut her own door, the cab filled with stale air that smelled of cigarette smoke.

"What is it?" Vicky said.

Diana held on to the steering wheel with both hands. She stared through the windshield, her gaze scraping over the dirt and trees. Little beads of perspiration blossomed at her temples. Finally she looked over. "I'm scared," she said.

"What happened?" Vicky tried to push away the image of the bat. She swallowed hard, willing her own fear back into the shadows of her mind.

"I heard the news on the radio, how the girl was killed in 1973, how she was Indian. And I'm thinking, somebody around here must know about her, and we can help the sheriff . . ."

She broke off, and Vicky gave her an encouraging nod. She said that she'd thought the same thing.

"So I called the girls and we decided to print up some flyers, put 'em around the rez. You know, nothing special. Just a headline about the girl's skeleton in Gas Hills, asking anybody with information to call me. Anonymous, you know. I put my number on the flyers."

And this, Vicky understood, was the reason Diana was scared. "Who called?" she said.

"First thing this morning—I wasn't even out of bed—the phone started to ring. It was a man."

"Did you recognize the voice?"

"Could've been anybody. I don't know who he was, but the next time . . ."

"The next time?"

"He called three times, always the same voice. First time, he said, 'This is a warning. Take down your flyers. Stay out of it,' and he hung up. Thirty minutes later, he called again. 'You get the message?' Before I could say anything, he hung up again. I kept waiting for him to call again. I was late to work, 'cause I drove around and pulled down the flyers. He called me at work! I'd just sat down at my desk when the phone started ringing and I knew, Vicky, I swear I knew it was him again. I was shaking. He knows where I work! He must know where I live! I picked up the phone and said, 'Who the hell are you?' I was almost glad it was him. I mean, what if I'd said that to a customer? He said, 'Good girl. Maybe you'll stay alive.'"

"Oh, God." Vicky glanced away from the raw fear in Diana's eyes. Someone was coming through the trees, and she felt the sharp prick of panic until she saw it was a kid after the ball. He scooped it up and headed back toward the grass.

"I called the others," Diana said. "I told them the detective was hard at work on the case and we didn't need to worry. I don't think they believed me, but we have to back off, Vicky. Don't you think?"

Vicky nodded. "It's too dangerous," she said, giving her the same advice she'd been given. She hoped Diana and the other women would take it.

"I don't know who he is, but he knows *me*! That's all I could think of. I didn't want to take a chance on him seeing me with you. He'd think I was still trying to find the murderer." She drew in a sharp breath. "It could be him."

"You did the right thing."

Diana was glancing about and nodding. She'd let go of the steering wheel and started pulling at her fingers, as if she might wring out the dread and fear. She locked eyes with Vicky. "You're gonna keep going, aren't you?"

"I've gotten some information," Vicky said. "Her name was Liz. She was part of AIM. She'd been at Wounded Knee."

"Jeez!" Diana slapped the edge of the steering wheel. "You better stay out of it."

"I think I'm getting close to something, otherwise we wouldn't have heard from him."

"He called you?"

"He sent the same message." Vicky tried for a reassuring tone. "Tell the others not to do anything more."

Diana hunched forward and dropped her face into her hands. The noise of her breathing—great hauls of air, in and out—punctuated the voices of the kids shouting beyond the trees. Vicky realized that Diana was crying. A moment passed before she flattened her palms against her cheeks and smeared at the moisture. Leaning against the door, she stared at some point beyond Vicky. "I feel so guilty," she said.

"There's no reason."

"Nobody cares what happened to her, what she went through. What right did he have to end her life? He should pay, but he's just gonna keep living his miserable life, laughing at everybody 'cause he got away with it." She let out a shuddering breath. "I been having these dreams. I hear her crying, just crying and crying, only nobody's there to help her."

Vicky laid her hand over Diana's. "Listen to me," she said. "We know more than when we started. We know her name."

"First name, is all." A halfhearted shrug. "What's that gonna do?"

"She was Arapaho. She went to Pine Ridge. She sang songs. She had a child."

Diana squared herself against the steering wheel. The muscles along her jaw tightened; the blue vein in her neck was throbbing. She kept her eyes straight ahead. "He'll come after us." She snapped her shoulders around. "I can feel him watching me. He's gonna be watching you, too."

"I've talked to Detective Coughlin," Vicky said, hurrying past the truth. Whoever he was—the killer, someone protecting the killer—was already watching her. He'd already delivered his message. "He's working hard on the case."

"What's that mean? What's that really mean?"

"He's contacting people on the rez."

"Jesus, Vicky. That's not gonna do anything."

"The point is, he's not dropping it." Vicky took a moment. "So it's okay, Diana. It's okay for you to back away. I'll tell Coughlin about the call."

"No! You can't do that! He'll find out. He'll think I'm a snitch, and he'll kill me for sure."

"Okay, okay. I won't bring you into it," she said. Coughlin already knew that someone wanted to head off an investigation. He'd seen her windshield. He had the messages.

"What about you?"

"Don't worry. I'll be fine."

"He's not gonna give up. Soon's he finds out some detective is nosing around the rez . . ."

"Diana . . ." Vicky began, then swallowed back the sensible advice she was about to deliver. You'll be okay. Everything will be fine. Don't worry. What a bunch of lies. The man had left the bat behind. It was part of the message. He could smash her the way he'd smashed the windshield.

In Diana's eyes, Vicky saw that she was waiting for the sensible advice, ready to scoff and turn away. Any thread of trust she'd managed to cling to, any belief she still had in Vicky, would snap like the dried strands of a rope. "Maybe you should go somewhere else for a few days," Vicky said. "Give Coughlin a chance to see what he can come up with."

"Go somewhere else? What about my job?" Diana turned toward the windshield again, and for a moment, Vicky felt as if the thread had snapped. Outside was nothing but the patch of bare dirt bordered by the trees and, beyond, the normal sounds of traffic trawling Main Street, as if everything were normal. As if a killer wasn't walking around. "I got some vacation coming," she said finally. "I guess I can go to my sister's in Rawlins."

Vicky said that would be a good idea, trying for a sense of lightness, as if that would solve everything. A few days, she was thinking. What did a few days matter? The killer had gotten away with murder for more than thirty years!

She pushed down on the door handle and was about to get out when Diana said, "He keeps calling!"

"What do you mean?"

"Three, four times, all hang ups. No messages, thank God. But I know it's him. I can feel it. He's not gonna stop."

"Maybe you should go to your sister's tonight," Vicky said. Diana was nodding. She'd already reached the same conclusion. "Don't tell anyone else where you're going." Still nodding, gulping sob-breaths, as if just the acknowledgment that she should leave made the danger more real and immediate.

Vicky got out and waited until the pickup had turned past the trees, churning up little puffs of dust and leaving ridges of tire marks in the dirt. Then she made her way back across the park and started walking fast toward her apartment, hoping the fear might drain away in the movement of her arms and legs.

SHE lay very still. Her eyes roamed through the darkness in the bedroom. Looming against the walls, the chest of drawers, the vanity, two chairs piled with clothes—great hunks of black shadows. Slats of dim light worked past the window blinds and fell like spilled paint over the carpet. The apartment was quiet, apart from the soft, rhythmic sounds of Adam's breathing. His arm lay curved along her hip; she could feel his pulse, steady and strong. But there was something else, she realized. Something that had awakened her. Something that was wrong.

Vicky inched away from Adam's arm, and when she did, his arm started moving, sliding back and forth. His fingers searched the crumpled sheet for her. She lifted herself onto one elbow and peered around the room—muscles tensed, her own hands clenched into fists—and waited for the shadows to re-form—into what? Into an intruder? Into the killer?

But there was no one else in the room. Everything was the same as last night when they'd fallen into bed together, she and Adam, after she'd reassured him that, yes, it was best to leave the investigation to Coughlin—she and Diana had agreed— and surely Coughlin, staring at her smashed windshield, had gotten the message that the killer was still around. And no, she really didn't want anything to eat—the odor of Chinese in the brown paper bags on the counter had made her stomach lurch because the truth was, she'd felt slightly sick hurrying back along Main Street, past the office and the vacant parking lot with tiny specks of glass glistening on the pavement where the Jeep had been parked—or had she only imagined the glass still there, a reminder that he was watching?

He was watching. She'd stayed on Main Street, passing the occasional couple strolling along, her own reflection darting in and out of the storefront windows, the stores themselves shuttered in darkness. Surely he wouldn't come after her on Main. Then she'd had to turn into her neighborhood and walk the three long blocks through the fading light and the blue shadows, with vehicles parked at the curbs and lights coming on in the front windows of bungalows, and people in the safe world inside moving past the windows.

She'd run up the two flights to her apartment, not wanting to enclose herself in the elevator, and had been grateful that Adam was waiting. Yes, she'd agreed. It was best to back off. While he was at Pine Ridge for his uncle's funeral, she'd concentrate on lining up statements from the other drug-tested Indians, as well as from the few white employees at Mammoth Oil that Mister had said would testify that they'd operated the same equipment as the Indians, yet had never had to take the tests. She'd send the initial letter to Mammoth Oil demanding compensation for the Indian employees discriminated against, and the battle would be on. The kind of battle they'd wanted to fight, the reason they'd both become attorneys, the reason they'd formed the law firm—Holden and Lone Eagle—attorneys for Indian rights.

She'd been dreaming about the girl again, she realized. It was the dream that had awakened her. Maybe it had been the soft crying, the same crying Diana had heard in her dreams. But she wasn't sure if it was a girl with long, braided hair on the prairie years ago, or the girl in the alley. They were merging, she realized, like shadows moving together.

But it wasn't only the dream. Something present and real and dangerous was close, like a sudden chill in the air. We could always feel when the enemy was near, Grandmother said. Vicky could hear the familiar voice, as if Grandmother were seated on the chair across the room, Vicky's and Adam's clothes piled around her, telling stories of the Old Time that she'd heard from her own grandmother, about how the women always knew.

The enemy would come at night, sneak up on the village when the warriors were asleep. But we would wake up. We'd feel the chill in the air and hear the quiet that was too quiet, and we'd know they were coming. The ponies would start snorting and pawing in the corral. We'd wake the men. All the tipis in the village, the same: Wake up, wake up. They're coming. And the warriors, drowsy and confused at first—let me sleep, woman—would throw off the buffalo robes and grab the weapons stored by the flap—rifles and bows and arrows— and run out into the night—run naked 'cause there was no time to dress. And the women would gather the children, hold them close, and try to calm them—shush, shush, it'll be fine—and wait, listening to the sound of the rifles firing, the swift parting of air as the arrows whizzed past the tipis.

It was the women who knew.

Vicky slipped out of bed, careful not to pull the sheet or blanket. Adam was quiet now, lapsed into some safe and peaceful place. She found her robe on the chair and managed to pull it around her as she went down the short hallway. This wasn't the Old Time, she told herself. This was now, and she'd had a bad dream, that was all. The night was warm, and yet she felt chilled. Something wasn't right.

She stopped at the end of the hallway and surveyed the space that opened into the shadows ahead: the closet-sized kitchen where she and Adam were always bumping into each other when they tried to fix a meal; what passed for a dining room on the other side of the counter. Across the space was the living room with everything normal—the sofa and chairs, the TV and side tables, the wrought iron lamps like black sticks against the walls. Light from outside flared in the windows and deposited wells of light around the counter, on one of the chairs, on the carpet in front of the sofa.

God, what was wrong with her? She had to get ahold of herself. She had to stop obsessing about a girl murdered thirty years ago! *The past is not ours to change.* Grandmother's voice again. *We must go on. Always remember that. We will go on.*

And the girl in the alley, and all the other vulnerable women, and Susan and herself and . . .

God. God. God. Adam was right. They would do what they could do now for their people. They couldn't undo what was done. They couldn't prevent . . .

And that was it, she realized. That was the invisible curtain always hanging between them. He accepted reality—we will do what we can—and she wanted to prevent the horror, as if that were possible. As if finding a killer who'd escaped justice for thirty years would somehow prevent the murder of any other woman. It was ludicrous, ludicrous, and yet, it was the women, Grandmother said, who tried to prevent the attacks.

She was about to retrace her steps down the hallway when the coldness crept over her again. She could feel the goose pimples erupting on her arms, as if she'd ventured out of doors into a blizzard. She moved past the kitchen and into the dining room, conscious of her bare feet padding over the vinyl, then the carpet. She held her robe closed with one hand; the fingers of her other hand walked across the counter. She surveyed the whole area, satisfying herself that no one was there. There was nothing unusual. God, she had to shake this feeling.

She was aware of moving toward the door, pulled by some invisible force, as if the enemy were there, outside the village. She peered through the peephole, looking up and down the corridor as far as the tiny concave glass allowed. It might have been a corridor in an abandoned building, with all the inhabitants gone, doors closed behind them, and nothing but the carpet worn gray in the middle by the tread of their footsteps and the light bulbs burning dimly from the ceiling, and the bulb near the elevator blinking on and off. Directly across the corridor was the closed door to Mrs. Burton's apartment. It took an act of will to imagine that the elderly woman was beyond the door, sleeping in her bed. That anyone was beyond the closed doors, and that the doors themselves, like the door at the end of the corridor, next to Mrs. Burton's, didn't lead to empty stairs winding between the floors of an abandoned building.

There was no one there.

She started again for the hallway, then reversed direction

and made her way through the well of light on the far side of the table to the window. She came at it sideways, aware of the iciness clamping on to her like a vise. She looked down onto the street. The streetlamp threw a circle of yellow light over the asphalt and sidewalk two stories below. She could see Adam's green pickup parked at the curb.

Across the street was a sedan, gray looking under the over-hanging branches.

Vicky moved closer to the edge of the window. Someone was behind the steering wheel. A man, and she was sure of that, despite the knit cap that might have covered a woman's hair. He sat low in the seat, head turned toward the street, watching over the top of the windowsill.

Watching Adam's pickup, she realized, as if he expected Adam to emerge from the building entrance below and drive off, leaving him—the killer in the gray sedan—the only one there.

Vicky stepped back along the table, making a wide circle to the counter, so that he couldn't see her. She picked up the phone, pressed 911, and moved back to the edge of the window, waiting for the buzzing noise to give way to a human voice. And when it came, she said, "There's a strange man waiting outside my apartment. Please send a car."

"Has he done anything . . ."

"He's wanted by the sheriff," Vicky said. It was the truth. "He smashed my windshield with a baseball bat this after-noon."

"Vicky? What is it?" It was Adam's voice in the hallway, his footsteps pounding the carpet. "What's going on?" He swung past the kitchen and came toward her.

"Get back," she shouted, seized with a new fear. The man could have a gun, and then she knew with a certainty as sure and cold as a block of ice that he'd been waiting—waiting at the curb with a clear view of her apartment—waiting for her to move into a window.

But Adam was still coming toward her, and he was the one framed in the window.

"You all right?" The disembodied voice on the phone, a million miles away, was drowned out by the sound of her own screams—"Get down! Get down!"—as Vicky threw herself against Adam, knocking him off step, the two of them bumping against the table. The gunshot sounded like the explosive pop of a firecracker, and Vicky was barely aware of the noise of shattering glass and the sound of shards of glass falling out of the frame like icicles dropping off a frozen roof.

18

FATHER John found Jesse Moon at a seedy garage punched out of the rear of a strip mall on Federal. Walking toward him through the noise of hip-hop blaring from a radio somewhere was a paunchy-looking Indian, medium height with wide shoulders and muscular brown forearms that hung beneath the short sleeves of grease-smeared coveralls. He might have been still in his fifties, black hair trimmed short over his ears, exposing half circles of pink flesh. His eyes were black slits cut into a round, fleshy face.

"Lookin' for somebody?" he shouted over the radio noise without moving his lips. Behind him, a younger-looking version of the man, somewhere in his late teens, stared up into the innards of a black sedan balanced on a metal pole close to the ceiling. Mixed odors of grease, stale coffee, and chemicals floated in the air.

"Father O'Malley, St. Francis Mission," Father John said, extending his hand.

Jesse Moon grabbed on to his fingers and squeezed hard. "Eric, turn that blasted thing down," he shouted over one shoulder, then looked back. No change in his expression.

"Banner called thirty minutes ago. Said you'd be stopping by." The radio faded into the background. There was the sound of metal banging metal. "I'm telling you right now, I don't know nothing about that skeleton. Don't know how it got there. Don't how who she was, and tell you something else, don't care. Not my business. Police work, I gave it up. Leave it to the other chumps."

"Do you have a few minutes?"

"Pretty busy here." He threw his head back toward the sedan on the pole and his teenaged look-alike bouncing a wrench against the palm of one hand, staring at them.

"My pickup could use an oil change." Father John held out the keys.

Jesse Moon's expression changed at this, a slow crack of understanding that stopped short of a smile. He took the keys and tossed them across the garage in the direction of the teenager who scrambled to pull them out of the air. "We gotta take care of Father John here. Change the oil."

The kid gave a shrug of annoyance at the inexplicable vagaries of the adult world, then ducked around the rear of the sedan and started drumming on the buttons at a panel on the far wall. There was a humming noise interrupted by a series of staccato squeals as the pole started dropping, the sedan quivering on top.

"Over here," Jesse said, starting for the front corner of the garage behind an L-shaped wall of brown, plastic panels. He swung around the opening and dropped onto a chair at a card table piled with the kind of papers, Father John thought, that resembled the bills covering his own desk.

He took the only other chair, sliding it sideways to fit his legs in the cramped space until he was at a right angle to the Indian who seemed to be waiting, working over something in his head. Beyond the rectangular window cut into the paneled wall, the kid had started backing the sedan out of the garage.

"Don't like going back there," Jesse said. "Not something I like thinking about."

"I understand," Father John said. "We're hoping to chase down the girl's identity . . ."

"We?" the Indian cut in.

"The elders," Father John said. "And some of the women

on the rez. We'd like to see her properly buried, her killer brought to justice. Her first name was Liz."

Jesse nodded and began staring at his hands clasped over the table. "What's this got to do with me?"

"It's possible she was killed because somebody in AIM thought she'd given up Daryl Redman's hiding place."

"You know what it's like to kill somebody?"

Father John took a moment. A kind of quiet dropped over the small space, the muffled beat of hip-hop and clank of metal receding into the distance. They were moving into new territory. "You were a police officer doing your duty," he said, finding his counseling voice.

"You one of them shrinks? I had enough of them after it happened." Jesse lifted his eyes to a vacant spot on the paneled wall. "Allen and me was partners for three years, went through hell together, trusted each other, know what I mean? I trusted him with my life. He'd say the same about me. We went over to the house in Ethete. Had a delivery truck, like we was making a delivery in the area. Doin' initial surveillance for the Feds, was all. I wasn't planning on killing anybody."

Father John waited for the man to go on—a story he didn't want to tell, and yet had to tell. There had been so many counseling sessions, so many confessions that opened with "Don't wanna talk about it," and always the initial shrugs and nods, and then the person would be plunging into the vastness of it— plunging across the plains, unable to turn back.

"It was the Feds' deal anyway. Should've been them checking on the house. Would've been except they'd been all over the rez lookin' for AIM leaders hiding out here. Sure, people hereabouts were helping 'em out. They seen AIM was trying to help Indians. Trouble was, the Feds were coming in like gangbusters. Surrounding the houses, shouting in bullhorns, 'Come out, hands up,' guns trained on the doors. Out came elders and grandmothers leaning on walking sticks, and pregnant women dragging a bunch of kids after 'em, and everybody shaking and throwing up they're so scared. Tribes got mad at all that harassment. So we worked out an arrangement. We do the initial surveillance, see if there's anything goin' on, any strangers hanging around, before the Feds came swooping in. So I ended up killin' a man."

"That's gotta be tough," Father John said.

"Yeah, tough." Jesse brought his eyes to Father John's. "I'm outside a delivery truck, hood up, looking inside. Allen's behind the steering wheel, like, you know, we're making a delivery of packages and the frigging truck broke down about fifty feet up the road. Good spot to watch the house. Allen whips out his binoculars from time to time. Looks through the windows and tries to see who's moving around inside. Looking for visitors, anybody comin' and goin'. Nobody. We're thinking it's a dead-end deal. Maybe the most wanted is inside, but we can't be sure. Right behind the house is this day-care place, and about the time I'm thinking we oughtta pack up and turn the whole thing over to the Feds, I hear the kids yelling and laughing and I think, no fricking way. We're sitting here till hell freezes over or somebody comes outta that house, whatever comes first. Then he come out. The most wanted.

"Allen gives him a wave out the window. 'Got a tow coming,' he shouts. And how was we gonna get a tow? Not like there was cell phones back then, but that's what he yells. And Redman figured it out. He turns around like he's bought the story and he's going back into the house. Allen and me, we look at each other and we know, that's the guy the Feds got on the wanted posters. Next thing I know, Redman reels around. He's got a revolver and he's blasting the truck, aiming for Allen, and Allen goes down—just drops behind the windshield. Then Redman swings toward me and looks at me for half a second. That was all I needed, that half second. I shot him. Got him twice. Heart, gut. I seen that look on his face, like he knows he's made a big mistake, hesitating."

Father John waited a moment. The sounds of the radio and a car door slamming grew into the quiet. Then he said, "What did you do afterward?"

Jesse blinked once, twice, as if he were trying to fit the question into some recognizable pattern. "Went running to Allen, see if he was okay. Bullet grazed his shoulder. God, the poor bastard couldn't even shoot straight. That made it worse, you know what I mean, 'cause I started thinking, no way he could've hit me. I could've walked over and knocked the gun out of his hand . . ."

"He could've gotten lucky."

"You sound like the shrinks, all right. They didn't see his face. He was scared. Some poor Indian—Lakota from Pine Ridge, is what he was—going to the barricades to get rights for all of us. So he was part of AIM that took over the BIA in Washington. Took over Wounded Knee. Trespassing, damaging property. Jesus, so what?"

"I meant, what did you do when it was all over."

Jesse Moon waved one hand toward the paneled walls and the garage behind them. There was the grinding noise of an engine turning over. The pickup's engine. Father John would recognize it anywhere. "Quit the force, got a loan, and bought this place. Been fixing cars ever since, and you know what? I like it that way. Fixing things, finding ways to make them work. Same for my kid. That's what he's learning to do. Fix things."

"The police might have picked up the girl for something. Is she the one who tipped off the police?"

"Like I told you. I don't know nothing about the girl. What'd she get picked up for?"

"Banner's checking the records."

"Tip didn't come from any arrest," Jesse said. "Feds got a phone call. Anonymous tip, they said, but everybody knew the Feds had snitches talkin' to 'em. So the local agent asked for our cooperation. You know, like we're all cooperating, all great friends goin' after the bad guys. Like I said, last time the Feds got a tip from one of their so-called anonymous sources, they come close to killing some innocent people. Thing about Indians, they know the Feds are on the prowl, they might call in a tip about a cousin they got a beef with, just to make his life miserable. God, I never stop thinking, how come it wasn't just some guy mad at his cousin?"

Jesse struggled to his feet, knocking against the edge of the table, scattering some of the papers. "Eric oughtta have your job done," he said, "else I didn't teach him nothin'." He started past the table, then stopped. "One more thing," he said. "Wasn't a girl that made that phone call."

"You sure?" Father John said. Things weren't making sense; the pattern that had started to emerge began to scramble.

"I remember it real good." Jesse gave a succession of nods, each nod hammering the memories into place. "The chief says to me and Allen, go check out the house, 'cause some guy called in a tip to the Feds."

"Guy? You sure he said guy?"

Jesse nodded. "I'd remember if it was a woman."

Father John took this in for a moment before he said, "Who do you think it was?"

"You think I haven't had a lot of years of thinking on this? Way I got it worked out, some FBI snitch knew the cops would show up at the house and Daryl was gonna put up a fight. I figure somebody set him up—murder by police officer." Jesse was shaking his head, a slow back and forth of sadness and resignation. "It happens."

"Somebody in AIM?"

"That's how I got it figured. Only AIM leader ever got caught on the rez was Daryl Redman. Rest of 'em hid out here long as they wanted. People looking after 'em, moving 'em around, keeping 'em safe. Must've been one of his AIM buddies wanted Daryl out of the picture. Otherwise we never would've found him."

"What happened to the others?"

Jesse gave a shrug. "Moved out, most of 'em. New lives, new names."

"There might be some still around."

The man took a moment before he said, "Wouldn't surprise me none. Might've gotten themselves new names and started fitting into the rez, like ordinary folks."

A phone started ringing. Jesse dropped his head and scanned the piles of papers tumbling over the table, eyebrows moving together in a puzzled line at the fact that there was no phone visible. It was then that Father John realized the ringing came from the cell clipped on his belt. He reached around, pulled it free, and gave a little nod in the direction of Jesse's back as the man headed out of the cubicle.

"Father John here," he said. He could hear the clip-clop of Jesse's boots across the concrete floor on the other side of the paneled partition.

"Found the records you were asking about." Banner's voice boomed through the cell as if he were yelling across the reservation. "Turns out a couple of women named Elizabeth were arrested in the summer of 1973. Elizabeth Toldwell, fifty-two years old, public drunkenness, record as long as my arm for drunk and disorderly. Not the Elizabeth we're looking for. It's the other one. Twenty-one years old. Stopped for speeding on Seventeen-Mile Road and brought in on a bench warrant August 4, on a citation from two months earlier. Cited for public disturbance at a protest outside tribal offices in Fort Washakie and for refusing lawful orders to disperse. No-show on court date. Not surprising. From what I hear, there was a lot of that in those days. People cited for marching without a permit, blocking public buildings, generally turning the rez into a circus. Not many showed up for court."

"What was her name?"

"Elizabeth Plenty Horses."

Elizabeth Plenty Horses. Father John let the name roll around in his head a moment. The skeleton—the fragile, cracked bones and the thick, dusty black braid—now had a name. Elizabeth Plenty Horses.

"Address was a mobile home over on Seventeen-Mile Road," Banner was saying. "Government houses there now. Mobile homes all cleared out."

"How long was she in custody?"

"Overnight. Went before the tribal judge the next morning. Fined her three hundred dollars and let her go. She didn't have any money on her. Here's the list of contents in her bag: Lifesavers, pack of cigarettes, matchbook, small notepad with something like poetry scribbled on the pages, pencil, tissue, lipstick, six-cents worth of pennies."

"How'd she pay the fine?"

"She didn't. Somebody paid it for her. Name of Ruth Yellow Bull. Know her?"

"It's possible," Father John said. He might recognize her if he saw her. There were so many faces filling albums in his mind, and not all of them had names attached. Still he felt as if he knew them—the powwows, the rodeos, the celebrations and meetings, even Mass on Easter and Christmas when, it seemed, everyone on the rez came. All the brown faces passing by, all of them familiar now.

"She's still around. Lives over on Mill Creek Road. Something else," Banner hurried on. "Records say Elizabeth Plenty

Horses had an infant daughter about a month old in the car when she was picked up. Baby went to social services while she was in custody."

"Thanks, Banner," Father John said.

"I'm sending this over to Coughlin. It's his case."

"Right."

"What I'm telling you is that you and Vicky got what you wanted. Most likely you ID'd the skeleton. Soon as the coroner releases her, the elders can see about a burial. Far as you're concerned, it's over."

"Who killed her?"

"What? We don't know that."

"Then I'd say it's not over."

"Coughlin can check dental records, make a positive ID. Might be some relatives still around. We can help locate them, if they're on the rez. I'm serious about you and Vicky backing off after what happened at her apartment last night."

"What are you talking about?" The thrum of Jesse's voice out in the garage was nearly lost in the blur of hip-hop noise, all of it far away. He was on his feet, unaware of how he'd gotten there, the blood pounding in his head. "What about Vicky?"

"Somebody shot out a window in her apartment," Banner said. He added quickly, "She's okay, John. Nobody hurt. Coughlin thinks somebody's trying to call her off this case. Sent a couple of warning messages."

She hadn't told him! Why hadn't she told him? He would have said the same thing Coughlin probably said: Don't do anything else. Stay out of it. And she would have ignored him. She would have pushed on. He knew her.

He thanked the chief for the information and pressed the end button, conscious of Jesse standing in the doorway, wondering how long he'd been there.

"What do I owe you?" he said, pulling a thin wad of bills from his jeans pocket and dealing them onto the table, a ten, two fives, some ones. It was all he had.

"On the house."

"Maybe your son can use it." Father John pushed the money toward the stack of papers. He thanked the man again before he could raise any protest, and started forward. Jesse moved aside, and Father John hurried through the wall of hip-hop noise crashing over the garage, pressing in the number to Vicky's office as he went.

The phone was still ringing when he got into the pickup. Finally the answering machine kicked in: "Law offices of Holden and Lone Eagle. Please leave your name and phone number. Someone will return your call as soon as possible."

He hit the end key and called her apartment.

"Be there," he said out loud over the electronic buzzing in his ear. It was a long moment—four, five rings—before she said, "Hello." He had to take a half second for the wave of gratitude to wash over him—that she was alive, that she was safe, that she was at the other end.

"It's John," he said. "Are you okay?"

"I'm fine."

That wasn't true. He could hear the tension in her voice, the raw fear.

"How'd you know?" Vicky said. Then, "Never mind. It's probably all over the moccasin telegraph. It'll be on the radio sooner or later."

"Listen, Vicky," he began . . .

"Not you, too," she said. Anger in her voice now. "Don't tell me to back away from this."

"I was going to tell you the girl's name. It was Elizabeth Plenty Horses."

Vicky was quiet for so long that he wondered if the call had been dropped. "How did you find out?" she said finally.

He told her about the police records, how the girl had been arrested on a bench warrant and held in jail overnight. How social services had taken care of her baby daughter.

"A daughter," Vicky said, her voice low, as if she were speaking to herself.

He told her that a woman named Ruth Yellow Bull had paid the three-hundred-dollar fine. "She lives on Mill Creek Road. I think I'll stop by and see what she might have to say."

"I've already talked to her," Vicky said. "She'll say she never heard of Liz Plenty Horses. She'll lie through her teeth." She paused. "Give me forty minutes. I'll meet you there."

19

VICKY spotted the red Toyota pickup parked up ahead on Mill Creek Road. She slowed as she passed, gave Father John O'Malley a quick wave, then shot forward, watching the pickup jerk into gear in the rearview mirror and start after her. Little clouds of dust and gravel spit from beneath the tires.

They were the only vehicles in sight. The road ran straight ahead, cutting through the brown, open plains flattened in the heat of the midday sun. In the distance, the horizon melted into a blue gray haze. It had been close to seven this morning before she'd crawled back into bed, limp with fatigue and fear and anger and the sense that she was alone—*Hi sei ci nihi*. After the Lander police and Detective Coughlin had left the apartment, pages in handheld notepads covered with black scribbling, Adam had attached a flattened cardboard box to the gaping space in the window, and they had swept up the pieces of glass and the shards, which oddly had made her think of the brokenness of the girl's body. It was then that she'd started to cry.

"I'm not going to South Dakota," Adam had told her. *"I'm not leaving you alone."*

"It's your uncle's funeral. It's your family. You must go."

"You come with me."

They both knew that didn't make sense. There was the discrimination case to work on, people to interview. She had to stop by Charlie Crow's office today to get the names of other Indians who might join the case. And Adam would be back as soon as he could get here. No more than a couple of days, he promised. She shouldn't do anything else about the skeleton. Coughlin would handle everything from now on, and she'd agreed—out of the exhaustion and shock, she'd agreed to everything. Adam shouldn't worry.

And then Father John O'Malley had called and told her the girl's name: Liz Plenty Horses.

Vicky came over a rise that surprised her, camouflaged as it was in the vast sameness of the landscape. Ahead on the right, the brown house appeared like an alien growth that had dropped onto the plains. She slowed down as she came off the rise, then turned into the dirt clearing that passed for a driveway and drove across the barrow ditch. She parked in front of the house close to the wooden stoop and got out.

The door of the pickup slammed behind her; Father John O'Malley's footsteps scraped the dirt in rhythm with her own. They took the wooden steps on the stoop together. There was no time for the polite waiting in the yard, on the chance that Ruth Yellow Bull would open the door. She wouldn't want to see them.

Father John knocked hard on the frame of the screened door with squares of black wire jutting from the sides. He gave another hard knock, then looked at Vicky. The blurred noise of TV voices came from inside. Then the door was opening—a slow, hesitant slide. The sound of canned TV laughter mingled with the sweet smell of marijuana that wafted outside.

"What do you want?" The woman peered around the edge of the door.

"We have some information you might be interested in," Vicky said, gesturing with her head toward the tall man beside her. "You know Father John from the mission?"

"Nothing you got interests me. Get outta here and leave me alone, or I'm gonna sic the dog on you." The door started to close.

"We know about your friend, Liz Plenty Horses," Father John said.

The door snapped back. Ruth Yellow Bull stood in the opening, still gripping the edge of the door with one hand. Her other hand dangled at the side of her blue jeans, shaking. A German Shepherd stuck his nose through a broken square in the screen and emitted a low growl that seemed to work its way up from deep inside his entrails. The smell of pot was so strong that Vicky had to turn away to get a clean breath of air.

"I don't know any Liz Plenty Horses."

"You paid her fine at the tribal court in August of 1973," Father John said. His voice was low and calm, the voice of the counselor, Vicky thought.

"Three hundred dollars," he went on. "A lot of money then."

"That's a lie. You come here with your filthy lies, both of you. I want you outta here." She kept her hand on the door and took a step backward, as if she meant to fling the door closed.

"The Wind River Police have the records," he said. "We'd like to talk to you. May we come in?"

Ruth Yellow Bull didn't move for a moment. Then she came forward and kicked at the screened door. Father John took hold of the handle as the dog lunged forward, slamming his large body against the screen. The frame shuddered, and for an instant, Vicky expected the screen to pop out. The TV voice inside let out a howl of laughter.

"Stay!" Father John put his hand, palm up, in front of the dog's muzzle. The dog jerked backward, his rear legs scrambling for a hold on the vinyl floor. Ruth had a grip on his collar then, pulling him back until they both blended into the shadows inside. There was a sharp bark, followed by the clap of a door shutting somewhere in the back of the house.

Father John opened the door. Vicky stepped inside first, moving through a rectangle of light from the television screen—game show sounds of clapping and shouting: "Take it! Take it!" Daylight tunneled around the edges of blue curtains that drooped across the front window. The front door was still open, and sunlight shot across the vinyl floor into the dimness of the kitchen in back.

Ruth came padding down a short hallway. She leaned over

and turned off the television, then she slammed the door, leaving only the dim glow of light from the kitchen. "I told you, I don't know nothin' about her." She was shaking her head, a quick, almost spastic movement back and forth. A piece of gray hair fell over her forehead, and she shoved it back into place.

"Then why did you pay her fine?"

"So I paid a fine, so what?" she said. "We got lots of people outta jail. Paid the fines, got 'em bail, whatever they needed. That's what AIM did, helped Indians."

"You're saying AIM gave you the money?" Vicky said.

"Maybe. I told you, I don't remember. Maybe I was just the messenger. Somebody says, get over to the tribal court and give 'em some money so somebody can get out of jail, so I did. We done here?"

"Who sent you?" Vicky said.

The woman shrugged.

"I think that whoever sent you didn't want Liz Plenty Horses in jail," Father John said, still the low, coaxing voice and the tone with the underlying message: You can talk to me. It's okay. "She was probably killed not long afterward. Is that why he wanted her out, so that he could blame her for being a snitch?"

"I don't know who you're talking about."

"Someone who wanted her dead," Vicky said. They were on the same track, she was thinking, she and Father John O'Malley, and for the first time today, she felt less alone.

"Detective Coughlin will want to ask you the same questions," she said. "He'll come here." Vicky swept a hand around the room, gathering in the invisible odor of pot. "If you talk to us, I'll try to arrange for you to give a statement at his office."

Vicky let the suggestion and the implied threat—God, as obvious as the blue curtains on the window—hang in the room between them. She might have been in an interview room, she was thinking, with a client accused of a crime, claiming he was innocent—wasn't him that sold that pot, stole that truck, beat his girlfriend—and she had just said: I can't help you if you don't level with me.

Ruth Yellow Bull was working it over. She lowered her eyes

to half-mast, as if she were focusing on some argument in her head. It was at least two minutes before she said, "What do you want from me?"

"Tell us about Liz," Vicky said.

The woman walked over and sank onto the edge of the sofa. She gathered her hands in her lap and stared across the room. Vicky exchanged a glance with Father John; neither one said anything. This was a decision that Ruth had made, a frail, tenuous decision that could snap at the wrong word, the inappropriate encouragement.

"Those bones can't be Liz. She left the rez," Ruth said finally. "Never liked being Indian. Always wanted to be white, so she went and got herself whiteized, my opinion. Wanted to be some big country singer, always singing songs, dreaming of the big time. Went to L.A. or Nashville or someplace."

"What makes you so sure?" Vicky said.

Ruth's gaze swiveled from Vicky to Father John, then back again. "I heard it," she said. "I heard she took off, and we should forget about her." She seemed to reconsider this, kneading her hands together. "I seen her the night she left, okay? I never told anybody, wasn't nobody's business. She came to the house, nine, ten o'clock. Said she was in trouble, needed a place to stay for a while."

"What was she talking about?"

Ruth took a moment before she said, "She was a singer, all right, couldn't keep her mouth shut. Told the police where one of the leaders was hiding. Daryl Redman was his name, came from Pine Ridge. Police went out and shot him. We had to do a lot of scrambling after that to find new safe houses before the police and Feds took out the other leaders. Wasn't something AIM was gonna let go, her snitching. 'Course Liz said she didn't have nothing to do with it, and she was gonna straighten it out. Wanted to stay here, her and the kid, but I told her, Jesus, Liz, Jake hears you're here, he'll beat the crap outta me."

"Jake Tallfeathers?" Vicky said.

Ruth nodded. "Sonofabitch, ended up killing my sister, Loreen. Got off on some technicality. I heard he got himself shot in a bar up in Rapid City four or five years ago. Somebody sent me the newspaper clipping, said 'AIM Leader Killed.' Like I cared what the hell happened to him."

"What happened to Liz?" Father John said. "Where did she go?"

Ruth closed her eyes a moment, as if she were pulling the memory out of the shadows of her mind. "She was running out of gas, so I gave her some money. I heard she went to Lander, stayed with a friend for a while before she left the area for good."

"A friend?" Father John said.

"Ardyth LeConte was her name." Ruth gave a little shrug, as if the name weren't important. "She was in AIM 'til she moved to Lander and got herself whiteized. Became some kind of nurse. We went to see her a couple of times, some of us girls—Liz, too—and tried to talk sense into her. 'What the whites gonna do for you?' we asked her. 'Think they give a damn about Indians? Think they're gonna give you a job in their white hospitals? Maybe cleaning the toilets?' Didn't get nowhere."

"Ardyth LeConte," Vicky said. The name didn't ring any bells. "Where is she now?"

"Down the toilet, for all I know. Haven't heard of her in years."

"Liz must have had family here." Father John said. "Why did she go to friends?"

"She wasn't from here," Ruth said, her tone matter-of-fact, as if this was an obvious fact everyone knew, the same way that everyone knew that Liz Plenty Horses had left the area. "Maybe she lived here when she was a kid. Her grandfather gave her a trailer over where the government built them houses a couple years later. But she was livin' in Pine Ridge so long, she was like a Lakota. First time I ever seen her was in Washington. You ever hear of the Trail of Broken Treaties?"

Vicky nodded.

"Liz gets outta an old truck—man, there must've been a dozen Lakotas in that truck—drove all the way from South Dakota. She's got herself a guy she's hanging on to like he was life itself. That's how she got her baby, only the baby didn't get born 'til we got to Pine Ridge, after Wounded Knee was all over. Some of us Arapahos were hanging around, trying to stay away from the Feds. It was the leaders the Feds really wanted. They wanted to fry their hides. So we came here and found some places for the leaders to hide. Liz came, too."

"What about the father of her baby?" Father John asked, and in the question, Vicky could hear the clash of other questions: Why didn't he protect her? Was he the one who killed her?

"Jimmie, somebody," Ruth said. "Supposed to be one of the big shots from Pine Ridge. Well, the big-shot Indian warrior got himself mugged in an alley a few days after we got to Washington. Newspapers said he was beat to death. That's why Liz didn't have any business turning against AIM. They was the ones took care of her, seen she was okay with the baby. Never could figure out what she was thinking, snitching on Daryl like that."

"She wasn't the one who tipped the police," Father John said.

Ruth started laughing under her breath. Laughing and shaking her head. "Sounds just like her. 'Isn't me, Ruth. I swear. Never snitched in my life.' It was her, all right. She told the cops what they wanted to know so she could get her court hearing and get outta there. All she was thinking about was her baby, 'cause social services had her, and she was scared they wasn't gonna give her back. So she opened her mouth and started singing. Everybody knew it was her."

"Who's everybody?" Vicky said. There were other people on the rez, she was thinking, other AIM members. And one of them *knew* Liz's murderer.

"Leaders, big shots. I told you, I was a gofer. I was nobody, thinkin' I was gonna be somebody. The leaders, they went back to wherever they come from—Pine Ridge, Chicago, Minneapolis, Denver. They came from everywhere and nowhere, and they went back to nowhere. Most of 'em, probably dead like Jake. So who cares? The snitch got away."

"It was a man who called in the tip," Father John said.

Ruth opened her mouth, as if she might take in a deep breath and let out a yell. Instead she clamped her lips into a dark line and leaned forward. "Liar," she said.

"I spoke with the officer who shot Daryl Redman. The tip came from an anonymous caller. It's possible the caller was the snitch. It was a man's voice."

The woman gripped her hands together and brought them to her mouth a moment. Then she flung out an arm, took hold of the armrest, and pushed herself off the sofa. In a couple of steps she was at the door, flinging it open. "Get out!" she screamed, tossing her head toward the outdoors. "Get out!"

Vicky walked across the room and, stepping past the woman, went outside. She stepped off the stoop and started across the yard, conscious that Father John O'Malley was close behind her. She heard him thanking the woman.

"Lies!" Ruth shouted. "All lies, everything."

Vicky swung around. Father John O'Malley had stopped a few feet behind her. They were both staring at the woman on the stoop, shouting that everything she'd said was a lie, her hands flailing the air. She took a gulp of air and went on: "That detective comes around, I'll tell him how you threatened me, said you was gonna tell the cops a bunch of lies about me smokin' pot. So I tol' you a bunch of made-up lies, like you wanted."

She backed into the house, yanking the screened door shut behind her, and started fiddling with a latch that didn't seem to work. Her jaw was clamped tight. A loud hissing noise escaped through her teeth. "You," she said, jamming a finger against the screen at Vicky, "oughtta stay out of what's none of your business."

Vicky turned around and got into the Jeep. She started the engine, backed around Father John O'Malley's pickup, and drove across the barrow ditch. Out on the road, she shifted gears and pressed hard on the accelerator. Not until she was over the rise and out of sight of the house did she pull over. It was then she realized she was trembling. She had the sense that Ruth Yellow Bull *knew* someone had shot out her window last night. She *knew* that someone wanted her dead.

The red pickup pulled in behind her. In the side mirror, she watched Father John O'Malley walking up alongside the Jeep. She pressed the button and waited for the window to drop. "What just happened back there?" she said, fighting the trembling that threatened to hijack her voice.

"She faced the truth," he said. His eyes were searching the emptiness of the plains that rolled away from them. "I think she's been hiding from it for over thirty years."

"She knows what happened to Liz. She knows the killer," Vicky said. She could feel the truth of it, as if the truth had materialized next to them. And there was something else: "She's scared. She wants us to think that nothing she told us is true."

"She just didn't tell us all of it," Father John said, bringing his eyes to hers. "But she might have told us more than she realized. She said Liz was low on gas, so she gave her a little money. It's possible Liz got the gas in Lander."

"The old guy that runs the convenience store just as you come into town has been there forever. It's a long shot." And yet, Father John O'Malley was right. Ruth had given them more than she realized. "I can try to find Ardyth LeConte," she said.

"Let Coughlin trace her."

"And if he finds her? What then? Do you really think she'll talk to him? Do you think Ruth Yellow Bull's going to tell him anything?"

"You have to be careful," he said. "Is Adam around?"

She shook her head and told him about the funeral in Pine Ridge.

"You'd better stay at the mission for a while."

Vicky heard the sound of her own breathing, the shush of expelled air. "I'm not running away," she said. "I have work to do. I have an office and an apartment. I have a life, and Ruth Yellow Bull and the killer, whoever he is, are not going to take that away." She squeezed her eyes shut a moment, trying to push away the images in her head—the girl in the alley, the girl out on the prairie. "They're not going to run me off the way they ran off Liz."

"Listen, Vicky," and his hand was covering hers. She could feel her hand shaking inside his palm. "Call me when you get home tonight. Call me if anything seems unusual, if you see anyone . . ."

She was about to say, "I'll be fine," then pushed the words away, unable to muster the false bravado that was necessary. She let her hand stay inside his a moment before she made herself pull it free. "Annie tells me there's news about you on the moccasin telegraph," she said. "Rumor is that you're going to be leaving. Going to Rome. Is it true?"

Father John looked back at the prairie a moment. Then he said, "It's a rumor, Vicky."

"You'd tell me if you were leaving?"

"You'd be the first to know."

She gave him a little wave that was meant to assure herself, she realized, and started pulling forward, slowly at first, until he'd stepped back. Then she turned onto the road and pressed down on the accelerator, catching a glimpse of him in the mirror, watching after her. Nothing would be the same, she was thinking, without him.

20

"HERE we go."

Charlie Crow ushered Vicky down the corridor and into his office. She'd just stepped inside the tribal building when he emerged from an office on the left, crossed the foyer, and, without breaking stride, beckoned her to fall in beside him.

"We got Mammoth Oil on the ropes," he said, walking around the oak desk with a couple of stacks of papers on one side and a yellow pad open in the center, black marks, like doodles, scribbled halfway down the page. He slapped the file folder he was carrying onto the pad, pulled the swivel chair in from the wall where it had been pushed, and sat down.

"On the ropes?" Vicky took the metal chair across the desk. She found the notepad and pen in her bag and wrote the date and the name—Charlie Crow—on the top line.

"Look at this." Charlie thumbed through a file folder, extracted a sheet and, leaning so close to the desk that the edge cut into his fleshy middle, handed her the paper.

Vicky glanced at the letterhead: Mammoth Oil Company. She skimmed the two short paragraphs, then went back and read through them. The black printed words, slander, libel, defamation of character, harassment, cease and desist, jumped off the page. Should Charles Crow and Lyle Bennet, also known as Mister, continue to defame the reputation and character of Mammoth Oil Company, the company will have no choice but to take appropriate legal action.

She set the sheet on the desk and waited for the explanation that the man was about to provide. Swiveling side to side, fixing his gaze on some point past her shoulder, forming the words, the sentences in his head, coming up with some excuse—she could sense it—for whatever he'd done to precipitate the letter.

The swiveling stopped. "I called the legal department," he said. "Told them we had a problem."

"Are you handling the matter yourself? You no longer need Adam and me?"

"This was a couple weeks ago, after Mister come to me, said he got laid off for no reason. Told me about the drug testing that was going on. Little rule for Indians only. Hey, you Indian, take this cup and go pee. Made me so damn mad, I picked up the phone, called the head guy—course, he was too busy to talk to an Indian—so I got his secretary, Mr. Keating's assistant, she said, and I told her what they were going to do: stop discriminating against Indians. Real simple. You think some white guy in the CEO's office oughtta get it."

"Anything else you haven't told us?"

"Said I wanted Mister reinstated, or I'd go to the newspapers about their discriminatory practices."

Vicky could fill in the steps from the CEO's office to the legal department to the letter on the desk. The phone call would be construed as a threat. It was the last thing that she and Adam had intended. They had intended to send a letter *asking* the company for negotiations before any further action was taken. Now Mammoth Oil would be geared up for a fight. She and Adam would have to file a complaint with the EEOC. They were looking at long, drawn-out proceedings before Mister and the others saw any justice.

"They refused to reinstate Mister," Charlie was saying, "so I went to the tribal council. They okayed filing a complaint or even a lawsuit, and I called you and Adam. Where is he, by the way?" He cocked one ear toward the door as if he expected to pick up Adam's footsteps in the hallway.

"He had to go to Pine Ridge for his uncle's funeral," Vicky said.

"I'm still thinking about bringing in the press." Charlie passed over the news as if the death of Adam's uncle meant nothing, as if she hadn't even told him.

She raised her hand, palm outward. "Don't do anything else."

"What we have is a helluva lawsuit. Got the names here of more Arapahos and Shoshones employed by Mammoth." He went back to thumbing through the stack and pulled out another sheet. "Eight men, all victims of discrimination."

"Still employed?" Vicky said. "There may not be any damages."

"Rights violated every couple of weeks. I call that damages." Charlie Crow stared at her. "We got a lawsuit here, we're going after those bastards, and they're going to have to pay. Adam'll agree. When the hell's he getting back?"

Vicky snapped the notepad closed and stood up. "We'll file a complaint first," she said. "Another thing, when you call our firm, you get both Adam and me. If you don't like that, I suggest you take your problem to another firm."

"I just might do that." Charlie started to get up—a slow unfolding over the desk, hands on the edge pulling himself forward, then upward. "Far as Mammoth knows, Holden and Lone Eagle's the firm we retained. I can always tell 'em different."

"You've informed them that Mister has retained legal counsel?" This whole interview was rushing past like a fast-moving river. She felt herself paddling to stay afloat. The company was already aware of a possible complaint before the EEOC or a civil lawsuit. They were readying their defense; they'd fired the first shot, and she and Adam were still trying to figure out whether they even had a legitimate complaint. They hadn't interviewed the other Indian employees. And Mister? All they had was his word about what had happened.

"Wouldn't surprise me if Mammoth sent somebody over to your place last night, left you a little message."

"What?" Vicky said. "How do you know about that?"

"Somebody firing shots at your window?" He gave a low laugh that rumbled in his throat. "Anybody on the rez hasn't heard by now? Police chief himself was here first thing this morning, had a sheriff's detective in tow, somebody named Coughlin, asking people up and down the hall about AIM. AIM thirty-some years ago!" He picked up the notepad and let it drop from a height of a couple of feet. It skittered across the desk. "They think the skeleton they dug up out in the Gas Hills is some woman mixed up with AIM. Wasting a lot of time and money on ancient history. What the hell's the matter with them? We have Indians getting rights violated every day. Mammoth Oil treating Indians like dogs, and what're they doing about that? You ask me, Mammoth heard we're working with lawyers and they went after the lawyers. Dangerous business you're in, counselor. People don't like lawyers poking into their business."

Vicky started for the door.

"Maybe you should stop," he said.

She swung around and faced him, the word reverberating in her head. Two messages left on her windshield, one word: STOP. She studied the man, the dark skin, the squint wrinkles across his forehead, the eyes like black, opaque stones, the slicked black hair trimmed in an arc above the ears with the gray edges at the temples. Now his voice, drumming in her head: Seventy-three? I was in Nam, getting shot at by the gooks.

He gave her a quizzical look, then his expression rearranged itself into a half smile, the thin lips barely turning up. "All I'm saying is, maybe you ought to watch your step."

Vicky turned back and started down the hallway. Charlie's voice rumbled after her: "Have Adam give me a call."

She crossed the foyer, yanked open the door, and went outside. Mammoth Oil, sending a goon to shoot out her window when the two messages hadn't stopped her? The idea was ludicrous. And yet, Charlie had called the company before the first scrap of paper appeared on her dashboard. She and Adam had met with Charlie and agreed to look into filing a complaint. Then, the bashed in windshield, the second note. STOP. And last night, the gunshot that might have come at any time, but hadn't happened until Adam walked toward the window. She'd assumed the notes, the gunshot—all of it—were about the murdered girl, trying to frighten her, call her off. But it could have been Adam who was targeted last night.

It was possible—and this was a new idea—that somebody

meant to frighten both her and Adam away from—what? Filing a complaint against Mammoth Oil Company? Bringing a major lawsuit?

She let herself into the Jeep, turned the ignition and sat for a moment, listening to the engine purr into its regular rhythm, feeling an odd sense of relief. The messages, the warnings, maybe they didn't have anything to do with the murder of Liz Plenty Horses. Maybe no one was trying to stop her from finding out what had happened, maybe nobody cared anymore.

But every part of her knew that wasn't true. The elders cared. Women on the rez cared. And it wasn't Mammoth Oil Company trying to warn off Diana Morningstar.

She shifted into reverse, backed the Jeep into the lot, then drove out onto Ethete Road. She stopped for the red light at the intersection, pulled her cell out of her bag and pressed in the keys for the office.

Annie picked up: "Holden and . . ."

"It's me," Vicky said. The light turned green, and she started through the intersection. "Any calls?"

"Diana Morningstar called about thirty minutes ago."

"Did she leave a number?"

"Didn't want to. Said she'd call you later. Adam left a message before I got in this morning, said neither one of you would be in today. You okay? I heard about the shooting."

Vicky said she was okay. Then she told the secretary she'd be at the office in thirty minutes.

THE parking lot at Ray's gas and convenience store was vacant, except for the green pickup next to one of the pumps, a cowboy in a tan Stetson working the wet squeegee over the windshield. Father John slowed past the pickup and nosed into the curb in front of the entrance. An old man with gray hair and small, rimless glasses riding down his nose was stooped over the cash register, peering at him through the plate glass.

Sleigh bells rang into the convenience store as Father John let himself through the door and stepped over to the counter. "Lookin' for something special?" the man asked.

"I'm Father O'Malley from St. Francis," Father John said. "You have a minute?"

The man's face was pockmarked with freckles and old scars. The vertical wrinkles between his eyes looked as though they'd been drawn by brown pencils, and now they were drawing together in one deep line. "You planning on buyin' something, or just jawing?"

Father John pulled a dollar bill out of his jeans pocket and flattened it on the counter. "I'll help myself to a cup of coffee," he said. He walked over to the coffee servers against the wall, filled a foam cup of black liquid that had probably been sitting in the container all morning, poured in a couple of envelopes of powdered cream, and walked back.

"What's this about?" the old man said. He was drumming bony fingers on top of the register, throwing glances at the pickup still next to the pumps.

"You heard about the skeleton found in the Gas Hills?"

"What about it?" he said, still drumming.

"It might be the skeleton of a young Indian woman who stopped here for gas in the summer of 1973."

The old man looked at him over the top of the glasses, as if he were expecting him to go on, and Father John said: "You were here then, right?"

"Nineteen seventy-three? What, you think I look like some kind of computer? You think I remember every Indian gal ever come in here?"

"I was hoping you might remember her. She had an infant with her."

"Yeah, like that's something new." He pulled his hands off the top of the register and folded his arms over a thin chest, as if he were hugging himself in the cold. He began plucking at the sleeves of his yellow shirt.

"She came for gas, and she might have gotten something for the baby. Maybe some formula." Then he remembered something else: "She wore her hair in a long, black braid."

"Used to rob me blind," he said.

"What?"

"Yeah, some of them AIM girls back then. Driving down Main Street, raising hell, shouting all about their rights. Well, I got rights, too. Never was no call for them to come in here and clear out my shelves, way they did. Oh, they didn't think I saw 'em, but I saw 'em all right. Trouble was, I tell the cops, and next thing I know, somebody's gonna throw a firebomb through my window. So I shut up, is what I did. Tried to keep an eye on 'em best I could."

"You know the girl I'm asking about? She was one of them?"

"Black braid hanging all the way down her back. Yeah, yeah, she was one of them." He lifted one hand and clapped his upper arm. "Seen her with her baby lots of times. Come in here with the others, stuff their pockets, all of 'em. No call to do that, like I said." He stopped, tilted his head back and appraised Father John, as if he were seeing him for the first time. "You that Indian priest, right?"

Father John said that was right. It was how white people in Lander and Riverton thought of him, he knew. The Indian priest.

"Well, I want you to know something. I always treat Indians real fair, always have. Felt sorry for her the night she come in alone, just her and the baby. Offered to give her some formula, if I recall. Yeah, I think I gave her four or five cans of formula. Offered to pump her gas for her, even let her have a little more. "

"Any idea of who the others might have been?"

"Never got no names. I wasn't lookin' to fraternize with Indian girls, you know what I mean? They got their ways, we got ours. Always say, stick to your own."

"Did she mention where she was going?" Father John took a sip of the coffee. It was stale and bitter.

"Thirty-five years ago? You expect me to remember what she might've jawed about?"

"It's important. She might have been killed after she left here."

"Hey, wait just one frigging minute." The old man's hands shot up into the air, as if somebody had pulled a gun on him. "You sayin' I had something to do . . . ?"

"Hold on, that's not what I'm saying," Father John said. He took a moment to take another draw of the coffee, giving the man a chance to settle down. "She went to a friend's in Lander. Did she ever come in with a girl who was in nurses' training? Her name was Ardyth LeConte."

The old man had dropped both hands and was breathing hard, his chest pounding beneath the yellow shirt. "Told you, I don't got any names. Might be there was another gal with 'em at times. Once in a while she come in by herself. Far as I know, she wasn't lifting stuff, but I couldn't watch her every second. Seemed okay. Told me once she was in some kind of training program, gonna be a nurse. Well, ain't this unusual, I remember thinking. One of them's doin' something useful, instead of marching around and shouting. Yeah, I think she might've come in here one time wearing a white dress. Looked real white with her brown skin."

"Any idea of where she might have lived?" Lander was small, he was thinking. If he could even get a neighborhood, he might be able to trace her.

"How would I know that?" the old man shouted.

Father John took another sip, then dropped the nearly full cup into a trash receptacle. The interview was over. "Thanks for your help," he said, starting for the door.

"I tol' you, I never fraternized with 'em. Didn't want nothing to do with 'em. But I treated 'em good. Still treat Indians good. You tell 'em back on the rez for me, okay? They're gonna get a fair deal, they come to Ray's."

Father John gave the man a two-finger salute and let himself through the door. There was a low whine of traffic out on the highway, and little spurs of dust lifted over the concrete apron in front of the store. The green pickup was pulling out, emitting black tails of exhaust.

He slid behind the wheel of the pickup, started the engine and followed the exhaust out of the lot and onto the highway, trying to sort through the pieces, arrange them in order, tease out the meaning. A woman in Lander, a friend, an Arapaho named Ardyth LeConte. Someone in nurses' training, doing something, as the old man had said, not marching and shouting. Someone Liz Plenty Horses had trusted.

He drove through town, glancing down the side streets—the rows of bungalows and patches of lawn and tree branches swaying in the breeze, and the sun flaring over all of it—wondering which street Liz Plenty Horses had turned down.

Then he was on the road leaving town. He slowed through Hudson for the turn onto Rendezvous Road, feeling the frustration build inside him, brick upon brick. The murdered girl had a name, but where was the justice? One night she'd driven to Lander, scared and alone, with a baby in her car. She'd stopped at Ray's gas and convenience store, then driven into the night and disappeared.

Disappeared for thirty-five years. And what had he and Vicky come up with? An old man who may or may not remember Liz Plenty Horses, a woman who'd told part of the story and would never tell the rest. The truth about what had happened to the girl was as impenetrable and unknowable as the vastness of the plains opening around him.

And yet, there was someone else: a park ranger, reeking of alcohol, who had known Liz Plenty Horses and who might remember Ardyth LeConte. This afternoon he had two counseling sessions with parishioners, and there was the Eagles' practice. After all of that and before the liturgy meeting tonight, he'd take a drive over to the park in Riverton and see if Joe was hanging around.

21

"WE'RE gonna make a great baby," Jimmie said. They were lying in a sleeping bag outside somewhere. The ground beneath them wasn't hard at all. It wasn't even there. They were floating together in the field of stars blazing in the black sky. Then loud thuds filled the air, as if the stars themselves had started to explode, and she and Jimmie were falling, falling . . .

Liz sat up in the narrow bed. Someone was pounding on a door. She could feel the air moving around her. She blinked into the dimness and tried to get her bearings. Her skin felt cold and clammy, as if she'd been caught in the rain. Her tee shirt clung to her, and she realized she was lying on the star quilt in Ardyth's bedroom, still dressed in her jeans and tee shirt, ready to bolt out of there. She could hear Luna moving about in the cardboard box on top of the chest.

The pounding was harder. "Open up, Ardyth."

Jake's voice. Liz jumped off the bed and peered around the edge of the curtain. The rear of a dark pickup jutted past the corner of the house. She stumbled to the door, cracked it open about an inch, and searched through the shadows of the living room and kitchen. Headlights shone through the little pane of glass in the kitchen door.

Ardyth padded past and flipped the switch. Light flooded over the counters and vinyl floor. Liz could see the door bowing with each thud. Grabbing at the ends of the belt to a pink robe, pulling the belt around her waist, Ardyth leaned into the door. "Who is it?"

God, Ardyth knew who it was, Liz was thinking. Jake had come after her, just as they'd both known he would. Why had she thought she and Luna would be safe tonight?

The baby started to whimper. Liz moved to the cardboard box, picked her up and held her close. "Shhh," she whispered. "It's okay. It's okay." She could feel her own heart pounding against the warm bundle. If Jake heard the baby cry, he'd know she was here.

"Open the goddamn door, Ardyth," Jake shouted.

Liz stayed by the chest and peered past the edge of the bedroom door. Don't let him in, she whispered to herself in the darkness. But Ardyth had her hand on the knob and the door was opening. Jake pushed into the kitchen and took hold of Ardyth's shoulders. "Where is she?" he shouted.

Luna jumped in her arms, and Liz bent her head to blow on the baby's hair, her eyes fastened on the man in the kitchen, pushing Ardyth aside, stumbling toward the table. He picked up the Coke can and squeezed it in his fist. It made a loud popping noise.

"What are you talking about?" Ardyth said.

"Don't give me that shit."

"You come bursting in here in the middle of the night full of whiskey, looking for somebody. I don't know what the hell you're goin' on about. I don't know what you're up to. I got a job I gotta go to in the morning."

"Liz Plenty Horses come running here," Jake said.

"Liz? That's a laugh. Why would she come here? She thinks I turned white."

"Where'd you hide her?"

"You see anybody here? " Ardyth was shouting now, shouting and flinging her arms about. "Look for yourself. You see anybody?"

Liz pressed the baby against her chest and leaned against the wall, out of the line of vision. She could barely draw a breath. The shadows swerved about her, the kitchen light bobbed in the crack at the door. She squeezed her eyes shut, aware of the rough stucco biting into her skin, afraid that she was going to pass out.

The voices had gone quiet. There was the scuff of boots on the floor, the sound of something hard—one of the chairs—crashing against the table. Grandfather, Grandfather, she prayed silently, help me.

"She shows up," Jake shouted into the quiet, "you keep her here. You understand?" Another crash punctuated his voice.

"Dirty traitor," Jake said. His voice sounded farther away, as if he'd stepped outside. Liz eased herself forward and looked through the crack. Jake was in the doorway, one boot still planted in the kitchen, eyes darting about, debating with himself. She felt the hard knot of her breath in her throat, waiting for him to crash into the house again and check the bedroom.

He stepped outside. "Makes you a traitor, you help her. You'll get what she's gonna get."

Ardyth took hold of the door and slammed it shut, sending shockwaves rippling through the floor. Liz could feel the vibrations in her bare feet. She made herself take in a long breath as Ardyth pushed the lock into place. Outside an engine roared into life, headlights flashed through the kitchen window. There were the sounds of fists thumping on the sides of the pickup, voices yelling and shouting—"Whoopee! Whoopee!"—just like the caravans coming into Washington, Liz thought, Indians banging and shouting, like they were gonna get what they wanted, like they were in charge.

Ardyth was peering around the edge of the little window in the door, motioning with one hand for Liz to stay where she was. It didn't make any difference because Liz felt as if she had turned to stone, her feet riveted to the floor. She had no power to walk into the kitchen. Her chest was numb against the warm bundle of Luna's body. She kept listening for the sounds of the pickup driving out of the yard, but the sounds were coming closer—engine shifting down, tires digging into dirt. For a moment, the headlights glowed in the curtain at the window over the bed, then faded. The kitchen light went out, the bedroom sank into shadows. She could hear the pickup driving alongside the house toward the shed.

"Be quiet," Ardyth whispered into the crack. "They're not done yet."

They! Liz forced herself to move across the small space to the window. Jake wasn't alone. There was someone else in the pickup. By pressing the side of her face against the wall, she could see through the gap between the window frame and the edge of the curtain. The pickup stood in front of the shed, shimmying from side to side, headlights playing over the doors. Two men were in the front seat: dark shoulders and cowboy hats backlit by the headlights. Then the passenger door swung open. Jake got out and started pacing between the pickup and the shed. Finally, cupping both hands around his eyes, he leaned into the crack between the wood doors, then he took hold of the padlock and banged it against the wood. Finally he crawled back into the pickup and slammed the door. The pickup jumped like a bronco and lunged backward, veering so far to the left that Liz braced herself for a crash into the corner of the bedroom. Then it straightened and shot past. She heard the brakes squealing out front.

Doors slammed, and the pounding started again. Liz moved back to her position next to the chest. It seemed that Ardyth was taking her time, shuffling into the kitchen, flipping on the light again. She leaned into the door. "Go away," she shouted.

"Open the damn door, Ardyth." Jake's voice again. "Do I have to break it down?"

Ardyth pushed back the bolt. The door cracked open a little way before it slammed back against the wall and Jake strode inside. "You hidin' her in the shed?"

"The shed?" Ardyth looked small next to the man. She had to lift her head to look up at him. "You're drunk."

Jake held out the palm of his hand. "Gimme the keys."

Liz leaned against the wall again and closed her eyes. She had to think. The instant Jake went back to the shed, she would run out the front door. She'd find a place for her and Luna to hide, maybe a ditch somewhere.

"Get 'em from the landlord."

"What?" Jake hunched over Ardyth, one hand gripping her shoulder. Liz could see the fury and strength popping in his brown hand. She closed her eyes and tried to breathe.

"It's his shed," Ardyth said. "Go wake him up at fucking three o'clock in the morning and get the damn key."

Liz opened her eyes and struggled to bring the slice of the kitchen into focus. Jake was blinking down at Ardyth, as if she'd been speaking a foreign language he didn't understand.

"White house on the corner," Ardyth said. "He'll be real glad to have you pounding on his door. Probably call the cops."

Jake grabbed Ardyth by the throat and jammed her against the counter. Her head lolled sideways, like the head of a rag doll. Liz held on to the baby with one hand and pressed the other over her mouth to keep from screaming. She could feel Jake's hands tightening around her own throat that night in the kitchen of the BIA building. She struggled to stay conscious, the way she'd struggled then, when everything had gone black.

"I find out you're lying," Jake said, "I'm comin' back." He shoved her aside, spun around, and headed out the door, pulling it shut behind him.

Ardyth was slumped over the counter, rubbing at her neck. The roar of the pickup's engine filled the house. The noise became softer, receding into the distance. Ardyth took hold of the counter edge and pulled herself upright. Like an old woman, she gripped her way across the kitchen, the top of the chair, the table. Lunging for the door, she slammed the lock into place.

"They're gone," she said, burying her face against the door. Her voice was muffled and blurred.

Liz could feel the tension begin to leak out of her muscles, like water draining out of a faucet. She put Luna down in the cardboard box, found her sneakers under the folds of the quilt, and put them on. Then she grabbed the cardboard box and the diaper bag and went into the kitchen.

Ardyth was still at the door, her forehead propped against the edge of the window. She worked her fingers into her neck below her ears.

"I've got to get out of here," Liz said.

Ardyth turned around slowly. Tears glistened like a spray of crystals across her cheekbones. "You're as crazy as he is."

"I'm sorry he hurt you."

"It's nothin' compared to what he's gonna do to you. What the hell have you done?"

"I told you. Nothing."

"Nothing? Nothing? Jake's out to kill you for nothing?"

Liz swallowed hard. Luna was starting to wake up, and she thought that if the baby cried she didn't know what she would do. She didn't know how she could hold on. "Look, Ardyth," she managed to say, "I really appreciate your helping me out. Just give me the padlock key so we can get outta here."

"God, Liz. You really are nuts. How far do you think you'll get before they spot you? You think Jake and the other guy are the only ones lookin' for you? You wouldn't last five minutes. Go back to bed. Let 'em drive all over. Soon's they get tired enough or drunk enough, they'll give up and go back to the rez. Tomorrow morning first thing, you and the baby are outta here . . ."

Liz waited for the rest of it.

"Don't come back, Liz. I don't need this stuff. I left it all behind." She pushed herself off the door and started past. The pink robe hung open over a white tee shirt that stopped at her knees, the belt dangled at her sides. She glanced down at the baby. "God," she said. "You got the baby in this, too."

"I have to talk to Robert," Liz said. She was thinking about what Ardyth had said. There had been a snitch in Washington. Whoever it was could be on the rez. It was the snitch who had given up Brave Bird's hiding place, not her. She had to tell Robert. "He'll know what to do," she said.

"What? What's he gonna tell you? Jump in your car and go back to the rez? Go back to AIM? Keep marching and demonstrating? Find some caravan of Indians going God knows where, lookin' for the old buffalo days, thinking the Great White Father's gonna give 'em back? Wake up! The buffalo days are gone, all the AIM members in the world can't bring 'em back. You got to forget about Robert and get away from here, get yourself a job, take care of your baby. Yeah . . ." She drew her lips into a tight line; a red mark spread across her neck like a rash. "Be a white woman. What the hell difference does it make? Stay alive, Liz. That's all that matters."

She started for the door, then placed her hands against the

jamb and shoved herself backward. She turned around. "We'll talk in the morning, okay?" she said, a softer tone.

Liz waited until the footsteps had padded across the living room and she heard Ardyth settling onto the cushions of the sofa. Then she went over to the phone. She lifted the receiver and set it on the counter. Cradling Luna in one arm, she leaned close to the phone to muffle the noise of the keys and dialed Robert's number. She listened to the buzzing in her ear, shivering, the chill running into her bones. She let it ring a dozen times before she hung up.

22

VICKY found herself watching for the silver sedan. Driving south on Highway 287, down Main Street, through the intersections. Glancing at the side streets wondering if it were there, parked at a curb, waiting for her Jeep to pass. She pulled into the parking lot next to the office building and got out, still looking around—a habit now, she supposed. She couldn't shake the feeling that the silver sedan was somewhere close. *Listen to the danger,* Grandmother had said. *It will tell you when it approaches. Listen and be ready.*

She took the stairs that rose alongside the window that framed part of the parking lot and part of the street with pickups and SUVs crawling past. The outer office was vacant when she stepped inside. The minute she shut the door, Annie emerged from Roger's office, holding a thin stack of file folders.

"Phone's been ringing all morning," she said, waving the folders toward the desk. "I been here alone. Roger's over at the jail. Two Raps picked up on disorderly and disturbance in Riverton last night, but Roger says he'll have 'em out today. Couple of whites also involved. Funny thing, nobody arrested them." Annie walked over and stared down at the phone, as if it might ring again and she wanted to be ready. "Had to let some calls go to voicemail. Word's spread about the shooting last night. People want to know if you're okay. You'd better call your Aunt Rose. You sure you're okay?" She hurried on before Vicky could do anything more than give a quick nod. "Oh, and you got a call from that law office in Denver." She handed Vicky a small sheet of paper with a name and telephone number written on it.

Vicky glanced at the name of the prominent criminal attorney in Denver: Marshall Owens of Owens and Lattimore. This was about the assault in the alley again. The man wasn't wasting any time mounting a strong defense for his client. She folded the sheet and stuffed it into her pocket. "What about Diana?" she said.

Annie shook her head. "I'm sure she'll call back, except . . ."

"Except what?"

"She sounded kind of scared, I guess. Didn't want to leave her number, and the caller ID was blocked. Like she doesn't want anybody knowing the number, even you."

Diana was scared, all right, Vicky thought. She walked over to the door on the right, let herself into her private office, and sat down at her desk. Anonymous, threatening calls in the middle of the night. Of course Diana was scared. She wouldn't blame her if she never came back to the rez.

And what would that be? Another woman intimidated, running away.

She tapped at the keys on the computer until the morning's phone calls appeared on the screen. She scrolled through the list: Aunt Rose—she would have to call her right away, reassure her; two members of the tribal council; two elders, two grandmothers, a couple of people she hardly knew—family friends, people she'd gone to school with. All of them worried about her. She stared at the names. Odd how black type on a computer screen, words as flimsy as air, could have such an effect, make her eyes brim with tears until the words themselves melted before her. This was home; this was where she belonged. No one could make her run away.

She picked up the phone and called Aunt Rose, clearing her throat before she could speak when she heard the old woman's voice. "I'm fine," she managed. "Please don't worry about me."

Then, before Aunt Rose could issue the usual warnings, she said, "We know the girl's name. Liz Plenty Horses. She was Arapaho, but she'd lived at Pine Ridge. Did you ever know the family?"

"Plenty Horses." The name seemed to roll around Aunt Rose's tongue. "Old man by that name, lived in a trailer. Had a daughter named Mona, kinda wild, you ask me. Drinkin' and runnin' around, not taking care of her kid. Little girl, I recall. Then one day, the daughter and her kid were up and gone. Ran off with a Lakota that come through here. Darn near broke the old man's heart, 'cause they were all the family he had. Died a few years later. I heard he left the trailer to the kid."

The kid was Liz, Vicky was thinking, and she'd come home with her own baby, because she had a place where she could live. "What do you know about the kid?" she said, realizing Aunt Rose was waiting at the other end.

"Don't know I ever heard what became of her. Guess I always figured she stayed at Pine Ridge. Vicky, you be careful. Hear me?"

Vicky said she heard and hung up. Then she dialed the number for Owens and Lattimore and waited through the ringing, the receptionist, the secretary. She asked to speak to Marshall Owens. Finally, a male voice booming down the line: "Howdy, Ms. Holden," he said. "I'm representing Theo Gosman, the man you believe assaulted a young woman last week. We'd like to interview you and the other witnesses about what you think you saw. We'll be talking to your son, Lucas, tomorrow. We can send a lawyer to Lander, if you prefer."

What she preferred, Vicky was thinking, was that Theo Gosman was brought to trial, convicted, and sent to prison as soon as possible. "I'll come to Denver," she heard herself saying, and it hit her that maybe she was running, too. Away from the silver sedan, from the half-truths and silence, from the sound of crying in her dreams. She would spend a couple of days with Lucas. And she wanted to see how the girl in the alley was doing. She told him she'd drive to Denver tomorrow.

"Wonderful!" Owens said, as if he'd been prepared for a struggle. "We'll expect you at our office at ten o'clock the day after tomorrow."

"How is the girl?" Vicky said.

"Excuse me?"

"The victim. I believe her name is Julie Reynolds."

"I don't believe that's relevant . . ."

"Oh, it's relevant, all right."

"I see. I'm afraid I don't have that information," Owens said. Then he was thanking her for her cooperation, the usual niceties before the call ended, leaving a deadened buzz, a background noise to the phone ringing in the outer office.

She pressed the off key, still gripping the receiver, not taking her eyes from the closed door. It was a couple of seconds after the ringing stopped that the door cracked open and Annie's head poked around the edge. "It's Diana," she said, almost a whisper.

Now the phone key: "Diana? Are you okay?"

"I'm at my sister's." The words came in a rush, breathless and shaky. "Don't tell anybody, okay?"

Vicky told her not to worry.

"I been checking my messages at home," Diana went on. "There's gotta be a dozen calls. Most hang ups, but some of them . . ."

"A man's voice?"

"Same as before. Warning me off. God, Vicky, what if there's a chance he's the same guy that killed that poor girl?"

There was every chance, Vicky was thinking. She was about to tell Diana to stay at her sister's as long as possible, when Diana said, "I got another message from some woman. She saw one of the flyers we put up around the county, had my telephone number on 'em. Said she knew Liz. Didn't leave a name, but she left her number."

Vicky was already pulling a notepad out of the desk drawer, searching for a pen. She jotted down the number Diana gave her.

"I'm scared to call her," Diana was saying. "What if she's not for real? What if she and the guy leaving the messages are working together and she just wants to lure me into some kind of trap?"

"I'll call her," Vicky said, but she could feel a sharp prick of uncertainty. Diana could be right. The call might be nothing more than a trap set by the man in the silver sedan for two women—her and the woman on the other end of the line— determined to get justice for a girl murdered a long time ago.

She told Diana to stay at her sister's and hung up. Then she dialed the number she'd printed out on the notepad. Four, five rings. She waited for an answering machine to kick in, but it was a woman's voice, tentative and questioning, that came on the line. "Hello?"

Vicky gave her name, and said she was a lawyer in Lander and that she was returning the call about the flyer. "Did you know Liz Plenty Horses?" she said.

"I'm not coming to the rez." A familiar note had worked its way into the woman's voice—the shrill note of fear.

"Where are you?" Vicky said. "I can come to you."

"Casper."

Vicky glanced at her watch. Almost two o'clock. "I can be there about four," she said.

The woman gave her an address, apartment eleven, she said. Vicky scribbled the numbers onto the pad. "Who am I looking for?"

"Mary." She stopped, as if she were considering whether to give the rest of it. A tapping noise—a pencil or pen drumming against a hard surface—sounded at the other end. "Hennings," she said. "I used to live in Lander."

T H E apartment building was a two-story blond affair, with a brick façade and black-trimmed windows that gaped onto the quiet street running past. Vicky left the Jeep near the entrance and found the name Hennings and the number 11 above one of the mail slots in the foyer. There was a glass door that opened when Vicky pulled on the knob. She walked down the carpeted corridor that had a smell of newness—new carpet, new paint—glancing at the black metal numbers on the doors as she passed; 9, 10. She was about to knock on the door with a number 1 and a faint space where the other numeral belonged when the door inched backward.

"You Vicky?"

It surprised Vicky. She'd expected a white woman with the name of Mary Hennings, but the woman was Arapaho, sixty-ish, thin with bony cheeks and long, bony fingers laid against the door frame. She had a beaked nose, dark, squinting eyes, and a long neck that rose out of the collar of a blue dress. Her hair was gray and thinning. Vicky could see the white traces of scalp. "I heard you coming," she said, swinging the door into a small, tidy living room.

Vicky stepped inside. "Thanks for calling," she said. "Women on the rez want to see Liz's killer held accountable. The elders feel the same."

"What makes you think they're still around?"

"They?"

The woman nodded. "There were two of them. I just made some coffee."

Vicky said a cup of coffee sounded good, and the woman made her way around the sofa and small table with a place setting for one, positioned in front of the television, and went into the kitchen. She looked even more angular from the back: sharp, squared shoulders, shoulder blade lines that protruded through the blue fabric of her dress, flat, sticklike legs. There was the clap of a door shutting, the clink of glass. She came back carrying two mugs with steam curling over the rims. "Go ahead and sit down," she said, the scolding tone of a teacher—or a nurse—and placed the mugs next to a stack of magazines on the table in front of the sofa. She headed back into the kitchen.

Vicky took the end cushion and reached for one of the mugs. It had been a long drive, or maybe she was just tired from the lack of sleep last night. The coffee tasted like hazelnuts, and Vicky realized the only thing she'd eaten today was a breakfast bar she had munched on this morning as she'd driven to Ruth's.

The woman was back, rearranging the magazines to make room for a plate of cookies. "Help yourself," she said, dropping down onto the chair across from the table. She was breathing hard, as if the whole exercise had been strenuous.

"What do you mean, there were two of them?" Vicky said.

"They came to my house." She lifted her mug and sipped at the coffee. "I went by Ardyth then," she said. "Ardyth LeConte. After I got married, I started using my middle name, Mary. It seemed like a good idea to . . ." She took another drink, then traced the tip of the mug with a finger, considering. "Disappear."

"You were Liz's friend," Vicky said.

"I always thought she got away." The woman was shaking her head, a slow, sorrowful motion. "I guess I was hoping she got away. It was what I wanted, but in my gut . . ." She hesitated and took in a gulp of air. "I always knew they'd get her. I just put it out of my mind. I had to go on, you see. Got married. Got a new name. I wanted to put it all behind me."

"She came to you the night she was leaving?"

Mary Hennings nodded. "How'd you know?"

"Ruth Yellow Bull."

She gave a snort of laughter. "Surprises me Ruth told you anything. She was in thick with all the AIM people. We were friends for a while." She leaned forward and set her mug on the table. "If you want to know the truth, I was part of the movement myself. Went to Washington on the march. What a farce. After we got out of the BIA building alive, I said that was enough for me. I was going to follow the white road, learn to do something, get myself a job. I came back to the rez. Liz, Ruth, Loreen, the rest of them went on to Pine Ridge. 'Course, I didn't blame Liz. She had a baby coming, and what was she supposed to do? The guy she was with, Jimmie Iron—now he was a real good leader. Everybody trusted Jimmie. He got killed in an alley. Liz didn't have any family. Robert promised to take care of her."

"Robert?"

"Running Wolf. Another Lakota, if I remember right. One of the leaders of our bunch, along with Jimmie. A lot of 'em considered themselves leaders. You know, all chiefs, no Indians. Another one of 'em, Brave Bird, got shot in Ethete, and that pretty much left Robert and two or three others. Always acted like he was in charge anyway, Robert did. Didn't like anybody else trying to run things. He was always doing the organizing—go here, march there, protest over there."

"Where can I find this Robert Running Wolf?"

"I heard he left the rez that summer and went to Minneapolis, and I haven't heard of him since. Could be dead, for all I know. Lot of 'em are dead now."

Vicky took another sip of coffee, then bit into one of the cookies. After a moment, she said, "What happened the night she came to your house?"

"She was pounding on my door. She was crying. Had her baby, Luna, all wrapped up and in a cardboard box, holding on for dear life."

"Luna," Vicky said, letting the name stay on her tongue a moment. The baby's name was Luna.

"You gotta help me, she says," the woman went on. "To tell you the truth, I wasn't real glad to see her, 'cause I'd left that life behind. I was training for my LPN. They'd come over to my place a few times, Liz and Ruth and some of the other girls, trying to get me to reconsider. 'What're whites ever gonna do for you?' they'd say. 'AIM's helping people.' And maybe there was some truth in it, I used to think. Maybe I never would've got into the training course if it wasn't for the fact that the hospital didn't want AIM demonstrating out in front. I let Liz in, of course. But I told her she had to leave in the morning. I'm not proud of it, but I was scared. Some of the AIM people were mean, and they were violent. I saw enough in D.C. If she was in trouble, I didn't want them coming after me."

"They thought she'd snitched on Brave Bird and gotten him killed, but they were wrong," Vicky said. Then she told her about the anonymous phone call to the Feds that had been made by a man.

Mary was nodding, as if she'd already worked it out that it wasn't Liz who had snitched. "Whole thing was a big misunderstanding, just like she said. That's why she was trying to get ahold of Robert. Kept calling and calling, but he didn't answer. She said Robert would straighten everything out. But they came to the house for her."

"Who came?" Vicky said. For the first time, she felt herself getting closer to the girl, as if she might reach out and touch her hand.

"Jake Tallfeathers, you heard of him? Called himself Jake Walker when he come to the rez. Always throwing his weight around, acting like a big shot. Couldn't lead an old mare to water. He was mean, though. Never understood what Loreen saw in him. Used to beat the hell outta her. Jesus, why'd she stay with him? I saw in the paper that he got run over by a truck in Rapid City. I didn't think there'd be anybody crying over that."

"You said there were two of them who came after Liz."

"Other guy stayed in the truck. Never saw his face; didn't want to look, tell you the truth. Didn't want to know. Liz and the baby stayed in the bedroom. I thought I was going to throw up, I was so scared the baby'd start crying or Jake'd take it upon himself to search my little place. But he stomped out. He was drunk. The whole place smelled like whiskey after he left. I knew after he sobered up he'd be back. So did Liz. She wanted to leave then, but I convinced her to wait 'til dawn, cause they were probably cruising the streets looking for her car. She stayed, kept trying to get ahold of Robert, and that's what happened. He finally answered the phone, told her AIM was looking all over for her. She was crying, I remember, saying that she hadn't done anything. He told her it was going to take him a while to convince the others. She should go to the safe house in Denver. I gave her thirty bucks. It was all I had, and she and the baby left in the morning. I always thought she made it to Denver, stayed in the safe house awhile, then got away. Really got away. I used to imagine her in L.A. with a big singing career. She could really sing, that girl. Or maybe Nashville. She would've been good there. Raising her kid, marrying some nice guy that would look after her."

She bent herself forward and dropped her face into her palms. "I knew that didn't happen when I read the articles in the newspaper about the skeleton in the Gas Hills and saw the flyers."

"Jake found her," Vicky said. A dead murderer, she was thinking. But someone else had also been looking for her, someone who had stayed in the truck.

"You ask me, Jake Tallfeathers couldn't've found his head if it wasn't stuck on his neck. He was stupid, stupid and drunk. You ask me, the other guy was calling the shots, giving the orders. He's the one that would've figured that Liz got as far away from the rez as she could and went to a safe house in Denver. There were other AIM members that hid out in Denver."

"Where was the house?"

Mary shook her head. "Could've been anywhere. I heard AIM had more than one."

Vicky drained the mug of coffee and took another bite of the cookie. Her stomach was starting to feel queasy—the combination of hazelnut and chocolate and the image of Liz Plenty Horses clutching her baby, running for her life.

"Why didn't you call—"

Ardyth started shaking her head, as if she were anticipating the question. ". . . the sheriff with this information? I don't want to talk to the cops." Her head was shaking in quick spasms. "I saw the flyer. It had Diana Morningstar's number. I decided that might be safe. They killed Liz because they thought she talked to the cops. They're still out there."

"Where? Help me find the men who did this. Robert Running Wolf sent her to a safe house, but somebody made the decision that she should die. Who was it? Who gave the order?"

Mary scooted her thin frame to the front of the cushion and, leaning forward, got out of the chair. "I'm sorry," she said. "I really don't know. I've told you everything. You'd better go now."

"But you might take a guess." Vicky got to her feet. She could feel the woman backing away. It was like watching a door closing.

"They're everywhere, the so-called AIM big shots. Maybe they took different names, got on with their lives. But they don't want the past dragged up. They don't want to face their crimes, what they did to people. They'll do anything to keep it hidden." She threw a scattered look around the room, like a wild animal looking for a way out of a trap. "I probably shouldn't have gotten involved in this. It's really not my business. My husband's been dead for three years. I'm alone here, you see."

Vicky tried for a little smile, half sympathy and half the reassurance that she wished she felt. They were everywhere, the woman had said. The leaders and the killers. And one—or maybe more? How many might there be?—had shot out her window last night and left threatening messages on Diana's phone.

"Thank you," she said, reaching for the woman's hand, but Mary kept her arms folded close to her sides and crossed over her waist. Her face had gone as blank as a sheet of paper, her lips a tight line, as if she'd already regretted what she'd said and were mentally pulling it back.

Vicky stepped past the sofa and let herself into the corridor. Outside in the Jeep, she dialed Father John's number. When he answered, she told him all of it: How she'd found Ardyth LeConte who was now Mary Hennings; how Liz had fled to Ardyth's house; how Jake Tallfeathers and another man had come looking for her; and how she'd finally left for a safe house in Denver that one of the leaders, Robert Running Wolf, had sent her to. How Jake Tallfeathers must have found her in Denver and killed her. How Jake was probably taking orders from somebody else.

He'd taken it all in without interrupting, and she realized she'd been running on, hardly taking a breath. When she'd finished, he told her that he intended to go to the park in Riverton later and have another talk with the man called Joe. He'd let her know if Joe remembered anything else, he said, and she'd pressed the end key and tossed the cell onto the top of her bag on the passenger seat.

The drive back to Lander seemed shorter, the open spaces rolling past as everything that Mary Hennings said rolled through her mind. She let the thoughts rewind and start again. Liz had fled to a house in Denver, but where? *AIM had more than one*. Jake Tallfeathers and another man had come to Lander looking for Liz. But Robert Running Wolf was the one who organized things, and Liz had trusted him. Jake. Robert. Jimmie Iron. Brave Bird. They all had something in common— it looked like they were all Lakota.

Vicky kept one hand on the wheel as the Jeep plunged down the empty highway, the rear of a semi shimmering in the distance ahead, and picked up the cell. She tapped the key for Adam's number and pressed the cool plastic against her ear. For a long moment, there was silence. He was probably in a dead space in South Dakota, or maybe she'd driven into a dead space. She felt a jolt of surprise when the buzzing started.

Two rings, then the sound of Adam's voice floating inside the car, disembodied yet close. "Hi, there," he said.

"Listen, Adam," Vicky began. "I need your help."

"I'm on my way to my uncle's wake, Vicky," he said. "I'll call you later."

"Wait, Adam," she said, but she was speaking into a void. She glanced at the screen: Disconnected.

She pushed down on the accelerator, the wild grasses and stalks of the plains sweeping past, and drove for the back of the semi ahead.

23

KENNY Little Owl was a natural, the kind of hitter every coach dreamed about, the guy in the lineup who, with one swing, could change the game. Everybody in the league knew it. Father John rubbed the ball and tried to locate the pitch's spot, the way he used to focus when he was pitching for Boston College twenty-five years ago. Odd, the way the diamond he'd marked off behind the residence took him back to that time, the way in which, for a few moments, there was no one but him and the batter and nothing other than a little spot marked by the catcher's mitt. He watched Kenny settle into his stance, weight back, staring intently at him and where his release might be.

The kid was like a pro. Seeing the ball come at him, he shifted his weight through his hips. Head back, hands out, he connected and drove through. The ball arced overhead toward the yard behind the residence, the kids in the field chasing under it. Kenny and the kids waiting a turn to bat were jumping up and down and shouting, all of them exchanging high fives.

What he had to do for a win over Riverton on Saturday was put Kenny in the lineup after a couple of other hitters good enough to get on base. Kenny would bat them in; he could be counted on to clear the bases. Problem was, Riverton had a hotshot pitcher with an overpowering fastball that could strike out the other hitters before Kenny got to bat, which was why, this afternoon, they'd been concentrating on using the back of the batter's box, quick hands, and making contact. He'd been delivering some hard pitches to keep them focused on just making contact. Let's get on base, he'd told them, and they understood. Brown faces and big grins with white teeth too big for the rest of them, the kids wanted to win and prove to the other teams they were somebody, maybe prove to themselves.

He pitched more balls until every kid had another chance to bat, wondering if baseball might save them the way it had saved him, given him something to hold on to, something outside of himself and the second-story flat over Commonwealth Avenue and the ever-present reek of whiskey that floated up from his uncle's bar on the street level and joined the whiskey smells in the kitchen where his father spent the evenings slumped at the table, bottle at hand, the level of whiskey dropping.

By the time he and the kids had hauled the bags of equipment across Circle Drive and down the alley to the storage shed behind the administration building, a line of pickups and sedans was pulling into the mission. He waited until the parents and aunties and grandmothers had collected the kids and the line of vehicles began snaking around the drive and out toward Seventeen-Mile Road before he headed for his office.

There were no messages waiting, no urgent calls to return, no emergencies. He could hear Ian on the phone in the back office. Whoever had called while he was at practice, Ian had handled it. A good man, he thought. The mission would be in good hands.

He grabbed his cowboy hat from the rack and retraced his steps outdoors. Ten minutes later he parked the pickup on a side street next to the Riverton park and walked across the grass toward a group of Indians clustered around a picnic table, black braids and ponytails drooping across the stooped backs of ragged shirts, blue jeans hanging around thin hips. A hot breeze rustled the branches of trees scattered about. Patches of shade hung suspended in the air. The Indians had turned halfway around and were looking at him out of rheumy, alcohol-bleared eyes. Stashed in the bushes beyond the table was an assortment of empty foam cups and brown paper bags and cardboard boxes with shirtsleeves hanging over the tops. The hum of conversation came to an abrupt halt as he approached.

"Anybody know where I can find Joe?" he said.

A collective sense of relief ran through the group almost like an electrical jolt. One of the men sank onto the bench and ran a palm across his mouth, as if the relief that the Indian priest hadn't brought bad news for *him* had drained whatever energy he still had. The others were shaking their heads, except for the Indian at the end of the table. He cleared his throat—a succession of raspy, monotone notes that caused heads to swing in his direction, braids and ponytails swishing across the bony backs. He had a red, swollen nose and little red veins that popped in his cheeks, the alcoholic look, Father John thought. He felt a stab of pain for all of them. He might have had the look, he might have been in the park . . .

"Alley," the Indian said, giving a half nod toward the row of stores on the other side of the street.

Father John thanked the Indian and was about to head back across the park when one of the Indians said, "Joe got trouble?"

"I just want to talk to him," Father John said, the stab of pain still burning inside him.

He retraced his steps toward the pickup, crossed the street and started down the alley. Cardboard boxes were piled on both sides of a Dumpster next to a brick wall, and that was where he found the Indian, sleeping in the shade under a box. He could hear the sharp, intermittent snorts as if the man were trying to clear his throat and catch his breath at the same time. The smell of whiskey filled his nostrils when he reached down and shook the Indian's shoulder. His bones felt as thin as twigs. "Joe," he said.

On the other side of the Indian, the glass lip of a whiskey bottle poked out of a brown paper bag, the odor rising like smoke. He had to look away.

"Yeah, yeah," Joe said. He rubbed at his eyes and pulled up his knees to get his feet under him. "I'm movin', I'm movin'."

"Take it easy." He kept one hand on the man's shoulder. "It's Father John."

The Indian opened his eyes wide, blinked a couple of times, and hauled himself up until his head and shoulders were level with the cardboard box. He tilted his head, bracing it against the brick wall, and held very still in the deliberate way of a man trying to bring things into focus. "What you doin' here?" he said, the words slurred, cotton mouthed.

Father John got down on his haunches. "The girl's name was Liz Plenty Horses."

The Indian gave a series of blinks, as if this were some cloudy image out in the alley that he couldn't quite make out. "Liz, the dead girl," he said finally, reaching for the paper bag with the bottle. He took a long drink and, still gripping the bag, ran the edge of his hand over his lips. "They was mad at her."

"Look," Father John said, "I've found out that Liz went to see Ruth Yellow Bull that night after she left the meeting. She was looking for someplace to hide. Ruth didn't let her stay, so she drove to Lander and spent the night at Ardyth LeConte's place. She finally got ahold of Robert Running Wolf. He sent her to a safe house in Denver. Did you know any of them?"

Joe didn't move for a moment, then he began nodding, his head knocking the brick wall. "The one lady you're talking about, Ruth, I seen her and some other girls with some of the big shots."

"What about Liz? Did you see her with any of the big shots?"

"Tol' you. Only seen her that one time. She come to the meeting, scared like a deer." He stopped for another slug of whiskey. "I'm thinkin', you better haul your ass outta here, girl."

"Who were they, the big shots?"

Joe was shaking his head. The paper bag crackled in his hand. "Don't know. Didn't wanna know 'em. They was mean, that's what I heard. Didn't need to be mixed up with 'em. Got enough troubles of my own back then."

"What about Robert Running Wolf?"

Joe was still shaking his head, eyes closed against the question. "Tol' you . . ."

"Think, Joe. You might have heard something about him, knew somebody who knew him. I need to find him. He might know what happened to Liz."

"Never got mixed up with none of 'em. They left the rez, got outta here. I don't know what happened to 'em. Maybe they're all dead, how do I know?" The Indian tilted his head back and took a long drink. Lines of whiskey ran out the corners of his mouth and along his chin.

Father John held his breath a moment against the smell and the yearning. Then he said, "She wasn't the one who gave up Brave Bird. A man called in an anonymous tip."

"That's a good one." The Indian set an elbow on the edge of the cardboard box. He cradled the bottle in the paper bag to his chest and started to get to his feet. Father John took hold of his arm, steadying him as the box collapsed. He half lifted him up, holding on while the Indian planted his feet under him, swaying from side to side.

"What are you saying?"

"Brave Bird was one of 'em, a big shot. One of the other big shots might've wanted him dead. The girl got blamed." Joe steadied himself against the wall and tipped back the bottle. The last of the whiskey trickled onto his tongue. A couple of seconds passed before he listed sideways and sited the line between the bottle and the top of the Dumpster—locating the pitch's spot, Father John thought. He lifted his arm and threw. The bottle hit the edge of the Dumpster and crashed onto the alley, little pieces of brown glass jutting through the paper bag.

"Think, Joe," Father John said. "Who were the other big shots?"

"Look there." The Indian was staring at the bag and broken glass with so much sadness in his face that Father John had to glance away. "It's all gone," he said.

"I can get you help."

The Indian didn't take his eyes from the paper bag. "You got cash?"

"We can go to rehab right now. I'll take you."

"Five, six bucks? You got that on you?"

Father John waited a moment, giving the man a chance to change his mind. Then he dug the folded bills out of his jeans pocket and handed them to the Indian. Seven dollars. It was all he had.

"Jack," the Indian said, pushing the bills into his shirt pocket. "Somethin' like Jack or Jake. I heard of him. Mean sonofabitch. Got hit by a truck, I heard. Wasn't no accident, you ask me."

"What do you mean?"

"Heard he'd killed one of 'em . . ."

"Killed who?"

"Big shot back in D.C. when they was all on their big trail to get Indian rights. Heard he beat up some member in an alley and everybody thought the guy got mugged. I heard about Jake getting hit by that truck and I thought, payback time."

"How do you know he'd killed someone?" Jimmie Iron had been mugged in an alley, Father John was thinking.

Joe shrugged. He kept his arms at his sides, palms splayed against the brick wall, balancing himself. His gaze shifted back and forth from the broken bottle. "Just gossip," he said. "Made me start thinkin', they wanna kill each other—all them leaders fighting over nothin'—that's their business. I don't want no part of it. I figured she got herself mixed up in the fightin', so she snitched on Brave Bird. You're tellin' me it wasn't her that snitched?"

Father John glanced down the alley a moment, past the Dumpster and the pile of boxes to the long expanse of red-brick wall broken by rectangles of black doorways and the truck lumbering along the street. It was perfect, the way the pieces had started to fall into place, each one neatly fitting against the next. Jake Tallfeathers had killed Liz's boyfriend. Then he'd set up Brave Bird to be killed and put the blame on Liz. Two rivals for whatever place he wanted in AIM eliminated, along with the girl who must have also heard that Jake was responsible for her boyfriend's death. A girl who couldn't be trusted.

He pulled out the small notepad and pen from his shirt pocket, scribbled the number at the mission and handed it to the Indian. "When you're ready, call me," he said, nodding at the paper caught between Joe's fingers. Then he walked back down the alley, in and out of the slats of shade and sun, the Indian shouting behind him: "Hey, thanks, Father."

He drove south on 789, then turned right onto the reservation and drove toward the mission. Ahead, the billboard with St. Francis Mission in blue letters looked black against the sun flaring in the west. He kept turning the pieces over in his mind, examining each one separately, then fitting it back into place. The pieces fit tightly; he couldn't detect any gaps. It was Jake Tallfeathers who found Liz in the safe house and killed her.

And yet, Vicky had said that Jake was taking orders from somebody else. And whoever had given the orders was now trying to warn Vicky away from the truth.

He pulled into his usual space in front of the administration building. There were pickups parked along Circle Drive, and another vehicle had turned into the mission: he could see the chrome bumper glinting through the cottonwoods. Ian was taking the social committee meeting this evening; Father John had the AA group. It had probably started without him.

The building was quiet—no clacking of computer keys, no phone ringing. Elena would have put dinner on the table at six, and Ian would have been on time. After the AA meeting, he'd find his own dinner wrapped in aluminum in the warm oven. Why can't you be more like your brother, Mike, his mother would say when he got home late from baseball practice, supper over, and Mike grinning over the top of some textbook he was pretending to study.

He checked his messages; there were none. Ian must have taken all the calls. He picked up the receiver, then let it fall back into the cradle. He wanted to talk to Vicky about all of it, examine the pieces with her, but there wasn't time. He was already late for the AA meeting. He'd call her first thing tomorrow and see when she was free. He wanted to see her.

24

VICKY had reached the top of the stairs in her apartment building when the cell started ringing. She fumbled among the hard and soft surfaces in her bag and extracted the small, smooth object. *Adam* appeared in the readout. She hurried down the corridor, pressing the cell against her ear. "How are you?" she said.

"Look, sorry I couldn't talk earlier. The wake was about to start. Are you okay?"

She was fine, she told him, trying to inject the calmness into her voice that she wished she felt. She jiggled the key in her lock. The door behind her cracked open over the sound of Adam's voice talking about the wake, the relatives he hadn't seen in years, the feast the women had prepared.

Vicky glanced around. Mrs. Burton curled herself around the edge of the door across the hall. She glanced between Vicky and the elevator at the far end, her expression frozen in expectation, as if someone else might step past the elevator doors or emerge from the top of the stairway. Vicky gave the old woman a little wave and, still trying to follow what Adam was saying, pushed open her own door.

The strangeness hit her like a sharp gust of wind the instant she stepped inside. The apartment was shrouded in shadows. A thin beam of light from the corridor cast a tungsten glare over the small entry and the dining table. The wall beyond the table was in darkness with the cardboard tacked over the broken window. On the right, the darkened shapes of the sofa and chairs loomed against filmy light that filtered through the window blinds. She had an odd sense of *disturbance*, as if things had been looked at, pawed over, moved. As if another presence had inhabited her space.

"Vicky? What is it?" The tenseness in Adam's voice was like a beam of light shooting into the shadows. She tried to focus the jumble of thoughts in her mind.

"Hold on," she said, clamping the cell against her ear. She pushed the door against the wall to widen the column of light flowing inside, then flipped the light switch. The fluorescent lights in the kitchen staggered into life and swelled out over the dining area and into the living room. There was no one there, and yet she couldn't shake the feeling that someone had been there.

"What's going on?"

"I . . . I don't know." She left the door ajar and headed down the short hallway. "I just got to the apartment," she said, checking the utility room behind the kitchen, then the closet. "I have the feeling someone was here." She reached past the doorjamb and turned on the bedroom light. Everything was the same as this morning when she'd left, except for the strangeness—the sense that someone had moved through the apartment, rearranging the atmosphere.

"What are you talking about?" A rising note of anxiety sounded in Adam's voice.

She crossed the room and looked into the bathroom, then flung open the closet door. No one. No one. She was imagining things. It was the noise of the gunshot and shattering glass from last night, the shock of it—that was all. "It's okay," she said.

"You sure?"

"I've checked," she said. "There isn't anyone here." But someone had been here. She could sense the absence of the intruder.

"Lock the door," Adam said.

She was already down the hallway, closing the door. She turned the lock.

"I don't like it," Adam went on. "You should go to . . ." He paused, and she waited for him to say the mission. "Aunt Rose's," he said. "You should spend the night there. The apartment isn't safe with that psycho on the loose. I shouldn't have left you . . ."

She started to reassure him then, saying she'd be fine. She told him she was going to Denver tomorrow for an interview with the lawyers defending the man who assaulted the girl in the alley. She'd be gone two or three days, depending on how things went, and that should give Detective Coughlin and the police time to find the man in the silver sedan.

"I'll be back by then," he interrupted. "I won't leave you alone again."

Vicky took a moment before she said, "I found out she went to Denver."

"We're talking about the skeleton again." Adam exhaled a long breath that sounded as if he were blowing into his cell. "Haven't you accomplished what you set out to do, Vicky? Coughlin's investigating the murder. Sooner or later he'll find last night's shooter and wrap it up. Let it go."

"There was a safe house in Denver," Vicky said. "The people at the house must know what happened to her."

"For God's sake . . ."

"Adam, I need your help."

"Look, I told you I don't want to bring up AIM with my cousin."

"He might know about the safe houses that AIM had in Denver. He might know where they would have sent a girl in 1973."

"What? So you can go there while you're in Denver? It was over thirty years ago!"

"Please, Adam," she said. "I know she fled to Denver. Someone named Robert Running Wolf sent her there. She thought she'd be safe. I have to know what happened when she got there. Your cousin might know about the house. He might remember Robert Running Wolf. He might know where he is now."

"He might not know anything," Adam said. Vicky could hear the sharp edge in his breathing. A long moment passed before he said, "And then you'll be done with it?"

She'd be done with it, she told him. When she knew what had happened, she was thinking. She sank onto the stool at the kitchen counter and told him about meeting with Charlie Crow this morning and how he'd threatened Mammoth Oil during a phone call. They were going to have to file a complaint with the EEOC, she said. Roger could start interviewing the Indian employees while she and Adam were out of town. Adam agreed to all of it. Vicky could hear in his voice the way he was settling down, moving away from the past and a girl murdered so long ago that everyone had forgotten, focusing on what was important now. After a few more minutes, she told him good night and pressed the end key, feeling as if a distance had opened between them as vast as the plains rolling across Wyoming and South Dakota.

It was close to eleven when she crawled into bed, drained and exhausted. But the sense of strangeness had begun to lift, like the steam rising out of a lake. Just moving about the apartment, snapping on the television, listening to the voices of newscasters drone into the living room as she made herself a cup of tea and toasted a slice of bread—ordinary things—had brought back a sense of normality. Everything was fine. She was nervous, that was all. She had to get a grip on herself.

SHE sat up straight in bed and squinted at the neon numbers on the clock until they were no longer a red blur in the darkness: 1:29. She felt cold and clammy. She could feel her pajama top clinging to her back, like a second skin. The sense of danger had come again and awakened her like a clanging bell—*You must listen*, Grandmother had said. She shifted her legs off the bed, moving slowly, tentatively, as if the movements might be interrupted, until she felt her bare feet plant themselves on the carpet. Her heart had started pounding in her ears, the noise so loud it must fill the apartment, she thought. Anyone here would hear it.

She worked her way around the foot of the bed and past the dresser, then inched along the wall, the plaster catching at the thin fabric of her pajamas, until she was at the window frame. She glanced around the edge, still pressing against the wall, her muscles tense, waiting for the gunfire. The street below was empty, nothing but the flare of lights from the streetlamps over the gray asphalt and dark stalks of trees and clumps of bushes. Beyond the circles of light were the gloomy nighttime façades of the brick bungalows across the street. And in the place where the sedan had been parked last night—nothing.

Nothing. God, she had to get a grip.

She walked down the hall and across the living room to the wide window behind the sofa. The blinds were closed, strips of light outlining the rectangular shape. She approached sideways again, laced her fingers into the edge of the blinds, and peered through the tiny opening. The far side of the street was also vacant. The same dull yellow flare of the streetlamps over the quiet, motionless patches of grass and trees and sleeping houses. There was the faintest sound of an engine, and she held her breath and leaned closer to the opening. A dark sedan was coming along the street, but it was a steady, purposeful speed. The sedan crossed the intersection and drove past, red taillights flickering in the darkness.

The blinds rattled against the window frame when she dropped them. She started to make her way back through the dimness, then walked across the front of the sofa instead to the slit of window behind the lamp. She always left the blinds down to hide the view of the apartment building across the alley.

Now she inched the narrow blind to the side. The building loomed in front of her, a dark brick wall with vertical rows of windows from the sidewalk to the roof. Closed garage doors faced the alley. Parked in front of a garage was the silver sedan. She stared at it a moment, trying to make out a figure inside, then jerked her hand away. The blinds snapped back into place. The sedan was vacant. She stumbled over the coffee table, her heart thumping. Her mouth was as dry as dust. The man who wanted to kill her was on his way up. He'd been in the apartment earlier today, she was sure now. He knew how to get in.

She plunged through the dimness, cracking her thigh on the edge of the desk, barely aware of the pain spurting through her leg, her thoughts racing ahead. There had to be a weapon . . . where was a weapon? She didn't own a gun, but there was a knife in the kitchen. A knife! She clamped her hand over her mouth to hold back the hysteria building in her chest. What good was a knife? The man on his way to kill her had a gun. She spun sideways and lunged for the door, one thought hammering in her head. She had to get out of there.

She made herself look into the peephole. Empty corridor. Closed doors every ten or twelve feet marching toward the elevator and the top of the stairway that she'd climbed this evening. She opened the door, started for the stairway, and stopped. He could be coming up the stairs and she would meet him. God, on the landing between first and second floor, the explosion of a gunshot, and he would run back down and out to the sedan before anyone in the building registered what had happened.

Then she heard the whir of the elevator rising. She could feel the tremors running through the floor. It was too late. She'd never reach the stairway before he stepped out of the elevator. She swung around just as the door across from hers cracked open. Sleepy-eyed, hair mussed inside a net, Mrs. Burton peered out. "What is it?" she called. "I heard something." Hysteria was working into the old woman's voice.

For an instant, Vicky thought of slipping past the door into her apartment, but if Mrs. Burton panicked, if she started screaming—My God, he would come for both of them. The whirring was louder, and there were the bumping noises, the little gyrations before the elevator came to a full stop.

"Go back. Go back." Vicky darted past the old woman. The whirring had stopped, leaving the absence of sound, and in that absence, she realized Mrs. Burton's door hadn't closed. "Lock your door now!" she whispered. At the other end of the corridor, the elevator doors started to scrape open. She lunged for the door to the back stairs and gripped the knob. It slipped in her hand, and she had to grab it with both hands before it turned. She saw the elevator doors pulling apart as she stepped onto the cold concrete landing and slowly let the door move back into place. She could hear the muffled sound of his footsteps on the carpet as he came down the corridor.

There was a narrow window in the upper part of the door,

covered with mesh and cloudy. She moved to the far side and looked past the edge out into the corridor. He was down on one knee in front of her door, studying the contents of the small black case opened in his hands. A black knit face mask was pulled over his head. She could see the gun in the slit of his jacket pocket. She could see the glint of the metal handle in the pocket slit. Now he had what he was looking for—some kind of black object, like a nail, that he gripped between his thumb and forefinger as he turned his head toward the elevator, then toward the other end of the corridor. She pulled back from the window and waited, pressed against the wall, her palms stuck onto the plaster like suction cups, as if the wall might keep her legs from buckling beneath her.

She heard the crack of a door opening, and she inched closer to the side of the window in time to see him get to his feet and slip into her apartment. He was at least six feet tall, with wide, compact shoulders, and he looked clumsy in the way he balanced his weight on the balls of his feet, moving silently. The door closed behind him. She stood frozen in place, her heart banging against her ribs, trying to think. The stairs led down into the alley. When he saw that she wasn't there—God, she'd left her bag on the kitchen counter and her cell was next to the bag! She'd run out, he'd see that, and he'd come after her. She would run down the alley, run down the street, and the sedan would crawl alongside her.

Her door swung open. He stood in the opening a moment, narrowed eyes peering through the slits of the black mask, looking up and down the corridor, deciding . . .

Then he was staring at the service door.

She backed across the cement floor, took hold of the metal railing, and was about to fling herself down the stairs when she understood. That's what he would expect her to do—run down the stairs and out of the building. She pivoted about and started running up the stairs, bent forward, pulling herself along the railing. She swung around the landing and started up the next half flight. There was a sucking noise as the door opened below, a change in the atmosphere as if the oxygen had been pulled down the concrete steps. She could hear the sound of her own breathing—or was it his breathing, the quick ins and outs through the knit mask? His footsteps were on the steps below, the steady plodding of the hunter after a trapped animal. He was coming *up* the steps.

She reached the top landing, yanked open the door that led to the roof and stepped out onto the rough surface that grabbed and tore at her feet. Sirens were howling in the distance. She slammed the door and pressed herself against it. It made her want to laugh, the image of herself trying to hold the door against the weight of a six-foot man. She threw her gaze around the gray expanse of roof with little specks glinting in the moonlight. It was as clear as a frozen lake. There was nothing, nothing.

Then, stacked against the ledge that ran around the periphery, she saw the two-by-fours. She ran over, pulled one off the stack and dragged it back to the door. His footsteps thudded on the metal steps, taking his time—where was she to go?—checking his gun. She propped the end of the board under the door knob and pushed it into place until it was solid. The sirens were coming closer. Red, yellow, and blue lights flashed in the air like the residue of fireworks.

She heard the knob clicking as she darted back and dragged the next board from the stack. Below she could see the police cars racing along the street—her street!—the sirens swelling into a loud crescendo. She pulled the board toward the door, which was throbbing now with the blows of his weight. Her breath caught in her throat as the board propped under the knob started to give way. She stood the other board on end and held on tight, ready to slam it into him the minute the door opened. The noise of the sirens rose around her, engulfing the building, and then—nothing but the soft sound of the wind swirling over the roof. Below on the street and out over the town, there was only quiet, like the quiet at the end of the world.

The door had stopped throbbing. She leaned into it. Far away, receding like a nightmare, she could hear his boots clacking down the metal steps. She hurried across the roof toward the front of the building. Three police cars were drawn up at the curb, officers were running across the sidewalk toward the entrance. Mrs. Burton must have called the police. "In the alley," she shouted, but it was too late. The officers had disappeared from view, melted into the building.

She ran back toward the stack of two-by-fours and looked

down as the man emerged from the building and ran across the alley. He flung open the door and slid behind the wheel. The sedan had started moving even before his arm shot toward the door and pulled it closed.

Vicky went to the door, kicked the board free, and headed down the steps. The officers were coming down the corridor as she stepped onto her floor. "He's in the alley," she heard herself shouting, but through the panic in her voice, she knew that the man in the silver sedan was gone.

25

FATHER John swam upward toward the alarm, then realized the noise had stopped. He lifted himself out of bed. The digital clock showed 3:35. Too early by two hours for the alarm, but the clanging noise had started again, rising through the floor, he realized, from the front door below. He pulled on a pair of blue jeans and stuffed his arms through the sleeves of the shirt he'd tossed over the chair. Then he went into the hallway, flipped the light switch, and started for the stairs, fumbling with the buttons on his shirt.

Ian's door swung open. He leaned against the frame and blinked into the light, pajamas that looked a couple of sizes too big hanging off his shoulders. "I'll get it," Father John said, waving him back. Emergencies came at this hour, and he was wide awake now.

Halfway down the stairs, he caught sight of Vicky through the window next to the front door—standing on the stoop, arms crossed and head bent, small and alone. He yanked the door open and reached for her. She took hold of his hand and allowed him to bring her inside. It struck him that her hand was as cold as if she'd been lost in a blizzard.

"What's going on?" he said.

She stood in the entry, staring past him, still gripping his hand, as if she might fly away if she were to let go. "He came back," she said. Pinpoints of light flashed in her dark eyes, tiny explosions of panic and fear.

He led her into the living room, trying to swallow back the acrid taste of anger and fear—fear for her—rising in his throat. She sank onto the sofa, and he pulled a side chair around and perched at an angle next to her. "Tell me about it."

It started coming then, water rushing over a dam—not in any logical order. The silver sedan in the alley, the man crouched at her door, picking the lock, Mrs. Burton looking out and Vicky telling her to go back inside, the presence of someone in the apartment earlier, the sound of sirens crashing against the building and she, up on the roof, jamming the two-by-four under the doorknob. He had to supply the logic himself, trying to fit what she said into a chronological order.

"You're okay now." He took her hand again and held it between his own hands, feeling the warmth start to return. "You're safe here."

"I had to get out of the apartment." A strange calmness—resignation edged with fear—had settled into her voice. Still, she was beginning to sound more like herself, her voice closer to the one he heard sometimes in his head, like fragments of a song that came unexpectedly, background music to whatever else he might be thinking about. "There were half a dozen cops looking at everything, checking everything. What were they looking for? He was gone! I kept telling them he'd parked in the alley. One of the officers said, not to worry, he'd already radioed the dispatcher. They'd have him within minutes. But the thing is, they didn't get him. He got away. He's still out there!"

"He's not here." Father John kept his own voice soft and calm.

"The police think he must have hidden the car in a garage close to the apartment. Otherwise they would have spotted him. There aren't that many streets . . ." She was shaking her head, and in the brightness of her eyes, he could see her moving again toward panic. "The road to the rez is wide open. They'd pick him up, if he were still driving. He planned everything. He came to kill me. He wants to kill me! I don't know how I can hold on."

"You can hold on to me," Father John said, still striving for the calm note. It was harder and harder to hit. He was thinking that what he'd said wasn't the truth; that he'd probably be in Rome soon. He patted the top of her hand. "He can't hide forever." He made himself go on. "He's scared. He's taking risks. Sooner or later, he'll make a mistake and the police will have him." He waited a moment. "I can make some fresh coffee."

She nodded, and he let go of her hand, got to his feet and started for the kitchen, her footsteps behind him in the hall. She sat at the table while he rinsed out the glass container, poured water into the coffeemaker, fumbled with the filter, and finally managed to scoop in the coffee and flip on the switch. Then he sat down across from her. "The owner of the convenience store at the edge of town remembers her coming in," he said. The burbling noise of boiling water drifted over the table. "She bought gas and some baby formula."

"The baby's name was Luna."

Father John was quiet. It brought that night into sharper focus: A girl named Liz Plenty Horses fleeing for her life with her infant. A baby named Luna.

"My God, think how scared she must have been when they came for her at Ardyth's," Vicky said. There was a catch in her voice, and for a moment, Father John thought she might start to cry. "She kept trying to call Robert Running Wolf. She said he would straighten out everything. He was the only one she trusted." She stopped for a moment and the sound of liquid dripping into the container swelled into the quiet. Odors of fresh coffee wafted across the kitchen. "He sent her to the safe house in Denver."

"Robert Running Wolf," Father John said. "Who was he?"

"One of the leaders. Probably dead now, Ardyth thinks. He'd been hiding out on the rez, but she heard he left that summer, after Liz disappeared, and went to Minneapolis. There were a lot of AIM members there. A lot of the leaders are dead. They were boozing and drugging. Jake Tallfeathers stepped in front of a truck."

The dripping rhythm had stopped. Father John got up and

went over to the sink. He found two mugs among the dishes drying in the plastic rack, poured the coffee, and set the mugs on the table. Then he pulled a container of milk from the fridge and topped off his coffee, turning it milky brown. Vicky always took her coffee black; he remembered that about her.

"The leaders could have been killing one another," he said, dropping back onto his seat.

"What?"

He told her what he'd learned from Joe in the park this evening. How Jimmie Iron, Luna's father, had been mugged in Washington, D.C., and nobody had suspected anything else. Mugged in an alley. Could happen to anyone. "But Joe thinks one of the leaders had ordered the killing, and he thinks Jake was involved. It's the reason Joe got out of AIM and came back here. He heard that Jake got hit by a truck. He doesn't think it was an accident."

Vicky sipped at her coffee a moment before she got to her feet. She trailed the tips of her fingers over the table top, then broke free, carving out a half circle from the table to the window to the counter and back. She always paced when she was trying to sort out a tangle of thoughts. Father John took a long sip of his own coffee and waited.

"Why? What was going on?" She stopped pacing and stared out the window. Beyond the pane, he knew, was the darkness that swept across the backyard and the baseball field. "They'd gone to Washington to get the government to recognize Indian rights. Why turn on one another? It was the government they were fighting."

He'd been thinking about it. Tossing about in bed—for how long?—before he'd finally drifted into oblivion. Trying to make sense out of it. Indians trying to help other Indians, and turning on one another, just like in the Old Time, with the tribes fighting one another while the soldiers attacked the villages and helped the flood of outsiders carve off Indian lands.

"They must have had some kind of falling out." Vicky turned away from the window. "Maybe they were jockeying for position, fighting over who was going to make the decisions, call the shots. Maybe one of them wanted to be the top man; maybe he didn't want any interference, anybody else second-guessing him. He wanted to be chief."

She paused. "He might have wanted Brave Bird dead, too," she said. "He probably got rid of Robert Running Wolf. Anyone who challenged him was killed."

Father John nodded. It was the conclusion he'd reached last night, somewhere in the darkness when he was still aware of the minutes, then the clock clanging the hours and the dim strip of light from the streetlamps outlining the curtains. Jimmie Iron. Jake Tallfeathers. Brave Bird. And now, a man named Robert Running Wolf.

"Liz was set up." Vicky slid back onto her chair and took a quick drink of coffee, her thoughts now in the kind of order that allowed her to stop pacing. "Whoever wanted him dead called in the anonymous tip that Brave Bird was hiding in Ethete. He counted on the Feds coming in like gangbusters. He knew Brave Bird well enough to know he'd come out shooting. Death by police officer. But there's something I don't get . . ." She gripped the table and started to rise again.

Father John reached across and took her hand, holding her in place. "Why Liz?" he said, and she nodded. "He must have wanted her dead, too." Another conclusion that he'd pried out of the shadows in the bedroom. "He needed a reason to kill her, a reason that wouldn't turn the other members against him. He made her into a snitch."

Which only raised another question, he realized. What had she done? What had she really done that she had to die? And it wasn't until this moment that he knew the answer. "Liz *knew* too much. She wasn't the snitch, but Banner said there were snitches then—AIM members that talked to the Feds. Liz could have known who the snitch was on the rez. She might have known who had killed Jimmie Iron in Washington. She'd probably heard the same gossip that Joe had heard. At any moment, she could have brought the world crashing down on the man who killed her."

Vicky was nodding, and he understood that she'd reached the same conclusion. "The others—Jimmie, Brave Bird, even Jake—might have known who the snitch was. He had to keep them from talking." She took a moment before she said, "He's still here. He could be anyone. Lakota or Cheyenne or Crow or anyone of the people from a half dozen tribes who have blended into the background on the rez and put the past behind. Nobody remembers anymore why they're here or when they came. He was in hiding here in the seventies. There weren't a lot of people who knew him, and in any case, he's using another name now. Just another Indian, running a ranch, maybe, working for the highway department." She shook her head. "He has no intention of giving up whatever life he has now."

"He could be an Arapaho," Father John said.

Vicky's expression froze for an instant, and he saw that she knew the truth of it, that she hadn't wanted to believe. One of her own people breaking into her apartment this morning, planning to kill her. "He was the man in the truck when Jake came for Liz that night. He was the one. Somehow he must have found out where Robert Running Wolf had sent her, and he went to the safe house after her. I'm trying to find the address," she said. "I have to go to Denver tomorrow to give a deposition on the assault on the girl. While I'm there . . ."

Father John put up the palm of one hand. "Before you begin checking out safe houses, we'd better talk to Coughlin."

"And tell him what? That we have a theory about some anonymous AIM leader who killed three men who were crowding him? Then killed Liz Plenty Horses before she went to the Feds and told them what she knew about Jimmie Iron's death? Told them their snitch was a killer? Where's the evidence, John?" She leaned over the table, and this time, she took hold of his hand. "If I can find the house and track down somebody who was there when they came for Liz, I might be able to get a name. Then we'll have something concrete to take to Coughlin."

"Listen to me," he said. He turned her hand in his palm and held on tight, not wanting to let her go. "Whoever he is, he knows you're after him. He'll put two and two together and figure out that you know about the safe house. Anyone still in Denver who is willing to talk will be in danger."

"What other option do we have?" Vicky pulled her hand free and stood up. He could see the energy draining from her in the way she stood, the weariness moving across her shoulders. Yet there was something else—he knew it well—the determination flashing in her eyes.

He got to his feet. There was no dissuading her. He could only pray for her safety—God, keep her safe. "I'll take you to the guesthouse," he said. "You should try to get some sleep."

FATHER John struck out first, half running down the alley between the church and the administration building. The headlights of the Jeep flared behind him and swept ahead, casting a flickering yellow light over the bare dirt, the cottonwoods and the clumps of stunted, twisted brush. He had the guesthouse unlocked before Vicky had parked in front of the stoop. He open her door for her, then walked around, threw open the tailgate and lifted out a small piece of luggage. She went ahead into the little house—how many times had she been here? He'd lost track. The lamp next to the sofa switched on. So many other times when she hadn't had anywhere else to go. It was safe here, he'd told her. A safe house.

God, let it be so. They'd both been asking questions around the rez, talking to people, probing into the past. And yet, it was Vicky's apartment where the killer had gone. The windshield of her Jeep that he'd shattered with a bat.

Father John set the luggage next to the bed that took up most of the room attached like a shed at the rear, then walked back into the small living room. Vicky was standing next to the open door, arms hanging at her sides, and he was aware again of the determination and weariness, like alternating currents running through her. She should get some sleep, he told her again, and that was when she moved toward him and stepped into his arms.

"Thank you," she said. He could feel the warmth of her face against his chest. He ran one hand over the silk of her hair.

She pulled away then and stepped back. He felt an immense gratitude wash over him, because he wasn't sure he could have let her go. "I plan to get an early start tomorrow," she said, and he heard himself saying that breakfast was at seven. She might want to eat something before she set out. Banalities, he was thinking, normal, polite conversation, as if a moment ago, he hadn't been holding her.

He closed the door behind him as he left and started back down the alley, breaking into a run near the back of the church. He ran across Circle Drive and through the grass and brush in the center, past the pickup parked in front of the residence, up the sidewalk to the front door. There would be no going back to sleep tonight. He crossed the entry to his study, sank into the cracked leather chair at his desk, and turned on the hook-shaped lamp. Then he opened the old laptop computer Ian had lent him. It usually stuttered and spurted into life, balking at having to work, but now—thank God, he thought—it seemed willing. He tried to force his thoughts back into the logical, comfortable order of what he wanted to think about.

He typed in the name Robert Running Wolf and waited while the lines of black type assembled themselves across the screen. The first ten of hundreds of entries appeared. It was impossible. He typed quotation marks around the name, and this time five websites appeared, not even taking up the entire screen. He checked the first site, then made his way through all of them. Robert Running Wolf, who had lived ninety years in Georgia; Robert Running Wolf, born in 1913; Robert Running Wolf publishing house; a Blackfeet chief in the nineteenth century; the name of a book. None of the sites about a man who had belonged to AIM and would be in his sixties now.

He typed in Jake Tallfeathers. An article from the *Gazette* came up under the headline: "Man Killed on Highway." He read through the lines of black text: *The body of a man was found yesterday morning south of Rapid City. Police say the dead man was Jake Tallfeathers, 39, a Lakota who also went by the name of Jake Walker. Police believe Tallfeathers was the victim of a hit-and-run accident. Police are searching for any vehicle with a bashed-in bumper or headlight. They ask anyone who witnessed the accident to come forward.*

Father John sat back, staring at the words strung across the screen that related the story of Jake Tallfeathers's death, yet left out so much. He wondered how he'd actually been killed and where—before his body had been dumped on the highway.

ready for the moccasin telegraph, and Father John knew what it was about.

"How's Vicky?" Ian said.

Father John smiled. They both knew this was only the polite preliminary to what was really on Ian's mind. And yet, Ian had heard their voices; he knew who had rung the bell before dawn.

"Frightened," he said. "A man broke into her apartment last night. He would have killed her if she hadn't gotten out."

Ian stuffed his hands into the pockets of his khakis and stared absently across the room, as if he were trying to puzzle out a new thought. "Elena says you and Vicky have both been asking questions about the skeleton," he said finally, taking a longer detour around the real subject. "Looks like Vicky's put herself into real danger."

"She's going to Denver for a couple of days." Father John reached around, pushed away a stack of papers, and perched on the edge of the desk. "What are you suggesting?" he said. "That we should back off? Let a murderer continue on with his life, as if the girl he murdered didn't count?"

Ian was still tracking something, Father John realized, following the invisible target moving inside his head. "What would prevent the murderer from coming after you?" Ian said. "If he thinks you and Vicky are onto him . . ."

"We have no idea who he might be."

"But he doesn't know that, does he? He thinks you're getting close. That would explain why he wanted to kill Vicky before she could tell the authorities whatever she's learned. He'll think you know what she knows. You see where I'm going with this?"

Father John nodded. Ian was right. He should have realized it, but he'd been worried about Vicky, that she'd get off the reservation and go to Denver where she'd be safe. And then a new thought: the killer had found Liz Plenty Horses in Denver.

He pushed the thought away; it was more than thirty years ago.

"I'll watch my back," he said, but this new realization was taking hold of him. Whoever had shot out Vicky's window and broken into her apartment might come *here*. He was vaguely aware of Ian clearing his throat, shifting his thoughts, moving on to what he'd really wanted to talk about.

"Have you gotten back to the provincial?"

"I told him you'd like to take the sabbatical," Father John said. He'd finally spoken to Father Rutherford yesterday. "I said you were interested in spending time in Rome." There were other people at the mission, he was thinking. Father Ian, Elena, kids playing baseball, people coming for classes, volunteers, committee members. It was the people he had to protect. He'd have to cancel the classes and meetings for a while.

He was aware of Ian's voice droning on, background noise to his own thoughts, incessant and blurred. Reiterating about how he'd been giving Rome a lot of thought, how he could contribute to the dialogue on indigenous peoples . . .

St. Francis was their mission, their place; they wouldn't want everything canceled. They'd come anyway. He had to have an escape plan. Not by the road. He'd have to tell people not to run out onto Circle Drive. Not to run through the cottonwoods in the direction of Seventeen-Mile Road—the killer would expect them to go that way. Everyone should know to run through the brush and trees toward the river. They could hide in the willows, make their way along the riverbank . . .

"John!" The sharpness in Ian's voice made a clean slice through his thoughts.

"I'm sorry," he said.

"You're the one the provincial wants in Rome, right?" Ian was shaking his head. "I figured as much."

"Listen, if there's any trouble . . ."

"In Rome?"

"I'm talking about the mission. If the killer should come here looking for me," Father John said, "everyone should run for the river. That would be the safest route out of the mission." The escape route Father Leary had mapped out in 1973.

"What! What are you saying? Some madman could start shooting up the mission? My God, John. The cops have to stop him."

"We have to cancel everything for a few days, give Elena some time off."

"You're serious." The stunned look of incredulity flashed

in Ian's expression, as if the truth—the enormity of what he'd brought up—had hit him with full force.

A series of raps sounded on the door, followed by Elena's voice: "Breakfast!"

Father John stood up. "I don't want to alarm her."

"Alarm her? Tell her to go home because a crazy man might come around and shoot at the pastor and everybody else? Why would that alarm her?"

"I'll just say that I'd like her to take some time off." Father John walked past his assistant and pulled the door open. Warm, moist odors of oatmeal and fresh coffee floated down the hallway. He followed the odors into the kitchen where Elena stood over the table, dishing heaps of oatmeal into two bowls.

"Whatever you two are talkin' about, seems to me it can wait until after breakfast," she said, scraping the pan and dropping a last spoonful of oatmeal onto the top of a steaming heap.

"Looks good," Father John told her, as Ian walked around the table and sat down. She gave Father John an appreciative smile, then set the pan on the stove and opened the refrigerator. "I'd like you to take a little time off," he said.

She flung her arm around first, milk slopping out of the container in her hand, then brought herself about, finally facing him. "You worried about the shooting in Ethete last night?"

"What shooting?"

"Nothing to do with the mission. It was a drug deal, you ask me. That's why she got killed. Cops think so, too. Said so on the radio this morning."

"Elena, who was killed?"

"One of that Yellow Bull family. Never much good, that bunch. Don't surprise me they come to a bad end. Ruth Yellow Bull."

Father John shoved the chair against the table and headed back down the hall. He was running when he reached the sidewalk in front of the residence, Walks-On a blur that started alongside him, then fell back. Running full out across the grounds, past the church, and down the alley, the sound of his boots on the gravel thudding around him. He stopped on the other side of Eagle Hall. The guesthouse was vacant; he could sense the hollowness of it, like a false-fronted structure with nothing behind. Vicky's Jeep was gone.

VICKY pulled into the curb in front of the small café on Main Street in Rawlins and turned off the ignition. The sound of the engine died into the morning quiet. She took hold of the steering wheel again and gripped hard, trying to stop the trembling that threatened to take her over. She'd just reached Rawlins, tapping on the brake to ease the Jeep into the city's speed limit, when the news had come on the radio—all the news you need to know—the announcer, a man with a deep voice meant to be comforting, she supposed, while he related that a two-year-old had been run over in a Riverton driveway, and three cars had crashed on 287, and a sixty-eight-year-old Arapaho woman, grandmother of two boys that she looked after, had been found shot to death this morning when her daughter dropped off the boys. *Wind River Police say the victim was Ruth Yellow Bull, a long-time resident of Ethete. Mrs. Yellow Bull had a record of two arrests for possession of marijuana. Police believe her murder was drug related.*

Vicky had hit the off button. She hadn't wanted to hear any more. It wasn't a drug dealer or buyer who had come after Ruth Yellow Bull; it was the man who drove the silver sedan parked in the alley, the man with the black knit face mask pulled over his head who had knelt at her door, picked her lock, and let himself inside. The man with the gun handle jutting from the pocket of his dark jacket.

Now she stared at the window of the café, Breakfast All Day painted in white letters across the plate glass, and wondered how she'd gotten here. When had she turned off the highway that ran through town and detoured to the business district, as if the café were where she'd been heading all along, as if it were her usual stop? This was where they'd stopped for breakfast, she and Ben, at the oddest hours, she remembered, sometimes in the middle of the night or in the middle of the afternoon, on their way back to the rez from a rodeo in Cheyenne or the big powwow in Denver. They would stop here. And now, this was where she was, as if the little café were still a part of her life after all these years. It wasn't possible to jettison everything, she thought. Parts of the past just hung on.

Hung on for Ruth Yellow Bull who had talked to her—twice—and had paid with her life. And—here was what was ridiculous, when you thought about—she'd kept her secrets. She hadn't given up any of the leaders. If Ardyth LeConte hadn't called Diana, they never would have found her. They never would have found a woman now going by the name of Mary Hennings.

And yet the killer must have thought that Ruth was a snitch, and snitches had to die.

She glanced at her watch. Five minutes had passed since she'd nosed into the curb and turned off the engine, and the man in the white shirt behind the counter inside the café had been tossing glances outside at the Jeep. She got out, went into the café, and found a small, vacant table across from the counter. She sat down facing the door. It was absurd, this sense that the door might open and he would step inside. He had no way of knowing she was on her way to Denver. And yet, he intended to kill her. He would find her.

She felt her muscles tense against the fear kindling inside her like a flame that might consume everything, her ability to think, make decisions, save herself. When the man from behind the counter walked over, she told him she wanted a cup of black coffee. She'd planned to stop somewhere along the highway for something to eat, but the thought of food made her stomach lurch. She sipped at the coffee when it came, drawing down the warmth and the comfort. She left some change on the table.

Back in the Jeep, she flipped open her cell and pushed in the number for the mission. Across the empty stretches through which she'd driven, the golden-brown expanse of plains with arroyos running like faults in the earth and antelope leaping past clumps of dried brush, the phone in John O'Malley's office was ringing.

Then the familiar voice: "Father John."

"He killed Ruth Yellow Bull." She blurted out the fact.

"I know. Where are you?"

"Rawlins. I'm about to get back on the highway. God. Did he kill her before he came for me? After?"

"I don't think you should pursue the safe house in Denver. Someone there might let him know."

"We're close, John. We're so close to the truth that he's in a panic. He's desperate. We can't stop now."

The cell was quiet, vacant sounding, so that for a moment she thought the connection had dropped. Finally, he said, "It's too dangerous, Vicky. I'm going to call Coughlin. Tell him what Ruth told us. Let him put things together."

She said that was a good idea, then added: "Don't worry about me." She pressed the end key, then the menu key. She scrolled to Mary Hennings' number and pressed send. Another wait through the electronic buzzing noise, the man at the counter still looking through the plate glass window every couple of minutes, as if he would have liked to listen in on her conversations, as if there might be something different about them, something dangerous. Then the woman's voice, tentative and hurried: "Hello?"

"It's Vicky Holden," she said.

"I heard the news on the radio."

"Is there somewhere you can go for a while?"

"A friend's place in Bozeman. I'm about to leave now. When's it gonna stop, all that violence from back then?"

"He's bound to make a mistake," Vicky said. "Detective Coughlin will get him."

"When, Vicky? After he kills more women? After he kills you?"

"You've got my number," Vicky said. She was about to tell Mary Hennings to call if she heard anything, but she realized that the call had ended.

She turned the ignition and crawled back down the street to the highway. Once past the city limits, she pressed down on the gas and drove east on Highway 80, semis looming in the rearview mirror and swooshing past, the gradual hills rising and falling through the bare, open plains, finally dropping into Laramie. She kept going, climbing out of town, driving through the great expanse of nothingness until she was in Cheyenne.

She was heading south on I-25, traffic flowing toward her

and around her, when the cell started ringing. She kept one hand on the steering wheel and flipped up the lid. She caught Adam's name in the readout. "Hi," she said. Her voice sounded flat and dulled with exhaustion over the whir of the tires and the noise of a passing truck.

"I've got the address of the safe house," he said.

27

"WHAT can I do for you?" Detective Coughlin sat down behind the desk and waved Father John to the small chair with wooden armrests jammed between two filing cabinets.

"I'm here about Ruth Yellow Bull's murder."

"Wrong office." Coughlin picked up a pen, as if he was about to jot something on the white notepad squared in front of him. "Feds got that case. Not our jurisdiction, fortunately. We've got enough on our hands."

"Same man tried to kill Vicky last night. He's the one who shot out her window and shattered the windshield of her Jeep. He sent two warning messages."

"Last night's homicide was the result of a drug deal, Father. Feds are pretty sure of it. Victim's been on the radar of both the Feds and the Wind River police for some time. They suspect she was dealing marijuana. Somebody got real mad at her. Maybe she forgot to pay off her supplier, and he sent a collection agent. Woman was sixty-eight years old. You'd think she'd know better."

He shook his head, then stopped, folded his arms across

his chest, and leaned forward. He rested his arms along the edge of the desk. "What is it? What do you know?"

"We've been talking to people, trying to find out about the skeleton."

"I got that much from Vicky." Coughlin started leafing through a stack of folders at the side of the desk and extracted one from the center. He pulled it over and opened it. "Liz Plenty Horses. We verified the ID by some old dental records at the Indian Health Service," he said, fingering through the sheets of paper. "What's the victim got to do with her?"

"Ruth Yellow Bull and Liz Plenty Horses were friends. Vicky went to see Ruth a few days ago. We both talked to her yesterday."

"Why didn't you tell me this?"

"I'm telling you now," Father John said. "She wouldn't have talked to you or any other cops. You know that."

"Yeah? Suppose you tell me what she talked to you about."

"Liz Plenty Horses came to Ruth's house in the summer of 1973, looking for a place to hide. That means she was frightened."

"Yellow Bull tell you that? She was frightened?"

Father John shook his head. "She turned her away. She said Liz was a snitch, that she was responsible for one of the AIM leaders, a man named Brave Bird, getting shot to death in Ethete."

Coughlin was shuffling through the pages now. He pulled one out and set it on top. "Chief Banner sent over the report," he said, glancing down the page. "Lakota named Daryl Redman, aka Brave Bird, shot to death by Wind River police officer in altercation. Anonymous call . . ." He stopped and looked up. "Male voice called the local FBI agent and said that Brave Bird was hiding in Ethete, and Wind River officers were sent to check it out. Murdered girl didn't have anything to do with it."

Father John was quiet. "Somebody wanted both of them dead," he said after a moment. "Brave Bird and the girl. Ruth knew who it was."

"She tell you that?"

"It was what she didn't tell us. I think she was scared. She didn't want to be labeled a snitch. But she made the mistake of telling the man she was protecting that Vicky had come to see her. He couldn't be sure how much information she might have divulged, so he killed her to keep her from talking to anybody else, especially you. He tried to kill Vicky to make certain that whatever she'd learned didn't go any further."

Coughlin stared across the desk at Father John for a long moment. "Okay," he said finally, "I'll take your theory to the Feds. See if we can make sense out of who's behind this."

"Whoever it is was the actual FBI snitch."

The detective picked up the pen and flipped it across the desk in the direction of his gaze. "Thirty-how-many years ago? Some informer working for an FBI agent who hasn't been around in decades? There were a dozen FBI agents here then. Which one used the informer? Come on, Father. That's going to be a dead end, and you know it."

Father John started to get to his feet, then sat back down. "There's something else," he said.

"Something else?" Coughlin was still planted in his chair. He closed the file folder, reached for the pen and held it poised over the white pad. "You mean there's more you've picked up from Indians that aren't gonna talk to the cops, even if they end up shot to death?"

"Another connection between Ruth Yellow Bull and the murdered girl," he said.

"And that connection would be?" Coughlin's eyebrows rose into his forehead.

"Jake Tallfeathers. He was married to Ruth's sister, Loreen." Coughlin started writing something down, his pen making a scratching noise, like a mouse nibbling at the paper. "After Liz left Ruth's house, she went to a friend's in Lander, a woman named Ardyth LeConte."

"Ardyth LeConte?" Coughlin was scribbling on the pad.

"She goes by a different name now, but Vicky found her." He hurried on before the detective could interrupt. "Jake Tallfeathers came to her house looking for Liz. He wasn't alone. Someone else was in the pickup. Liz managed to evade them. The woman thinks Liz made it to a safe house in Denver."

"And her new name is?"

"She doesn't want to get involved."

"I'm going to need her name, Father. This is a murder investigation."

"She's scared to death. Now that Ruth's been killed, she'll probably leave the area." Father John stopped, waiting a moment for this to sink in. "Look, the point is that someone Liz trusted, a man named Robert Running Wolf, sent her to the safe house. All these years, the woman believed that Liz managed to escape and start a new life."

"Robert Running Wolf?"

"One of the AIM leaders. Nobody we've talked to knows what became of him. One more thing," Father John said, and the detective dropped the pen and began massaging the back of his neck. "Whoever killed Liz might have ordered the murder of Jimmie Iron in Washington, D.C. Jimmie was the father of Liz's baby."

Coughlin leaned toward the desk and picked up the pen again. "What you're saying is, we've got a kind of serial killer out there. Vicky should get away for a while."

"She's on her way to Denver."

"Denver? The safe house? She knows the location?"

Father John lifted his hands, then let them drop onto the top of his thighs. "Not as far as I know," he said, but he knew that, somehow, Vicky would find the house, if it was still standing, and trace whoever had lived there in the summer of 1973. He knew she wouldn't stop until she had the name of Liz Plenty Horses's killer.

"I'll check out this Running Wolf. You talk to Vicky, tell her to call me. I want the name of Liz Plenty Horses's friend." Coughlin lifted himself to his feet, a dismissive sign, Father John knew. He stood up. "You should both be careful," the detective said. He came around the desk and flung open the door. "I'm going to ask Banner to keep a car in the vicinity of the mission, keep an eye on things. If you hear anything else . . ."

"You'll hear from me," Father John said to Coughlin's back. He was already following the man back down the corridor toward the entry.

VICKY watched the brown sedan slide into the empty space at the curb across the street. She sipped at the iced tea she'd ordered. Lucas's image shimmered in the sunshine reflected in the café's plate glass windows as he got out of the sedan and started across the street, stopping to let a black truck swish past, then darting around another vehicle before he reached the sidewalk. The glass image evaporated, and he was inside, striding around the other tables toward her.

He was so much like his father, this tall, handsome warrior with black hair trimmed above his ears, brown skin and black eyes, muscular and strong looking in khakis and a yellow knit shirt. The first sight of Lucas, after a few days or weeks or even months, always made her heart take a little jump, as if she'd somehow stepped into the past and was eighteen again, and the man walking toward her was the one she'd watched riding the bronco bareback at the rodeo, gripping the edge of the bench, praying he wouldn't fall off. After the rodeo— walking toward her, smiling at her, holding out both hands as if there had never been any question but that she would run into the arms of Ben Holden. Later he'd told her how he'd seen her in the stands, how he'd ridden the bronco into the ground for her.

And this was their son.

She started to get up, but Lucas placed a hand on one shoulder, then leaned over and hugged her. "How's it going, Mom? Trip okay?"

She told him the drive had been fine. It wasn't exactly the truth. She'd stared through the windshield at the lines of traffic flowing like metal rivers as she drove toward Denver, so different from the open roads on the reservation, the vast spaces that melted into the horizons all around. It had taken a little time to adjust, refocus herself, concentrate on the lanes ahead, the merging cars and trucks, the semis looming in the rearview mirror.

Hovering at the back of her mind, beyond the traffic and the mechanics of driving, had been the image of the house. She had an address now; she wondered if the house were still there. She knew the neighborhood—the Indian neighborhood near the Denver Indian Center. Arapahos, Cheyennes, Lakotas, Ojibwas, Pawnees, Apaches, Crows, Blackfeet—crammed together in blocks of tiny houses with rusting pickups perched on jacks in the driveways and sofas with stuffing poking out of the cush-

ions jammed on the small porches. It wasn't where the so-
called successful Indians—the whiteized Indians—lived. Lucas
lived in a house in Highland, lights from downtown Denver visible from his kitchen window.

Of course the safe house would have been in the Indian
neighborhood. Anyone hiding there would have been safe.
None of the neighbors would have called the police to report
an Indian fugitive.

And yet, Liz Plenty Horses hadn't been safe.

Lucas settled across from her, picked up the menu, and
studied it for a moment. There was the usual polite exchange
of pleasantries. His job was going well; she was staying busy,
working on a discrimination case on behalf of Arapahos and
other Indians employed at Mammoth Oil. The only ones re-
quired to take regular drug tests, she told him. He shook his
head at this, light flashing in his brown eyes. There was no
sign of surprise.

The small restaurant was beginning to fill up. Only one
table left next to the window, in the flare of the setting sun, but
the couple waiting at the hostess desk would probably be
shown there. Memories crowded in on her; she'd spent a good
ten years in Denver, lived in a house a few blocks away. In the
Old Time, this had been Arapaho land, yet she could never
shake the sense that she didn't belong here. There were
restaurants she'd never gone into, shops she walked past,
movie theaters she ignored—as if there were invisible signs
propped in front: Indians Not Welcome.

And yet, Lucas had walked tall into the restaurant—college
degree, systems analyst job at a big company, unaware that the
signs had ever existed or that she still carried the image of
them in her mind, part of the collective memory of her people.
He would have walked just as tall into the office of Owens and
Lattimore today for his interview.

They had ordered plates of Italian spaghetti, and the waitress shook shredded parmesan over the top until the tomato
sauce disappeared under what looked like heaps of snow.
"How was the interview?" Vicky asked, after the waitress had
taken the hunk of cheese and the grater to the next table.

Lucas wound some pasta over his fork and shrugged. "You
know how all that legal stuff goes," he said.

"How does it go?" Vicky kept her tone light. There was always an edge to any discussion that inched toward her career. Lucas and Susan had been growing up on the reservation with her mother while she became a lawyer.

"The lawyer, Marshall Owens, kept asking questions. Was I sure I saw what I saw? Was it possible I'd been mistaken? How can I be sure? Was I willing to put his client in prison for a long time based on a shaky memory? Like he was trying to trip me up, make me doubt my own experience, start thinking that maybe I didn't see what I saw, I don't know what was real."

Vicky took a bite of her own spaghetti. After a moment, she said, "He's trying to build a defense."

"Want to know how he's building the defense? 'Isn't it true, Mr. Holden,'" Lucas dropped his voice a couple of notes, "'there were other people in the alley when you stopped your vehicle? Isn't it possible that another man was, in fact, beating the victim? Isn't it possible that, in the darkness and confusion, you failed to see Theo Gosman come to the defense of the victim? Isn't it possible that you confused him with the actual assailant, and that, thinking you were aiding the victim, you attacked the wrong man?'" Lucas worked on another bite of spaghetti, then he said, "He kept trying to shake my story. Better prepare yourself. He'll do the same to you tomorrow."

"And did he?"

"Did he what?"

"Shake your story?"

"Are you kidding?"

Vicky smiled. "If that bastard goes to trial, you can be sure Owens will try to shake your version of what happened." She knew the technique; she'd used it herself at times. Sometimes it worked, but those were the cases where the facts were blurred, where the truth could fall on either side.

"What about Susan?" she said. It wasn't her own interview tomorrow that she was worried about. But Susan . . . Vicky felt a prick of pain. Her daughter seemed to rummage through the past, select the memories she wanted, and discard the rest. It would be hard on Susan, the hammering: Are you sure? Can you be certain? Isn't it possible . . . ? *Did you select the truth this time?*

"They're flying a lawyer to L.A. to interview her," Lucas said. "We talked last night." He let a couple of seconds go by, apparently debating something with himself. "I told her what to expect," he said finally. "Stay calm. Tell them what happened. Don't let them make you believe otherwise. Don't let them make you doubt what we all saw and what we know to be true."

Vicky sipped at the ice water that the waitress had delivered. She needed a moment. Lucas *knew*, she realized. All those years with Ben—Lucas knew what was true. He knew that Susan still clung to what she wanted to remember. The good times, they were her reality; not the rest of it.

"What about the girl?" Vicky said, wanting to change the subject.

Lucas shook his head. "It'd probably help if she could testify. If she dies, that bastard's looking at a murder charge. He ought to be charged with murder anyway. Even if she lives, she's never going to be the same. I heard she has brain damage."

After the waitress had materialized next to the table, cleared the plates, and, smiling down at Lucas, set the brown leather envelope with the check inside next to his arm, Vicky said, "There's a house I'd like to see." What she didn't say was that she wanted to see if the house was still there.

"A house?" Lucas ran his eyes over the check, then leaned forward and extracted a wallet from his back pocket—and this, too, so like his father. How many restaurants where they'd sat across from each other, the waitress flirting a little, and Ben, leaning forward, gripping his wallet.

"You thinking about moving back?" Lucas inserted the credit card and handed the envelope to the waitress, looking up at her this time and smiling.

"It has to do with another case I'm working on," she said. "It will only take a little while. I'll see you later at home."

"You sure? You want me to come with you? Where's the house?"

"Lucas . . ." She reached over and laid her hand on top of her son's. "It's a house, that's all. I'll bet you've brought some work home tonight. I'll see you later."

28

VICKY took Sheridan Boulevard, the sun dropping over the mountains in the west, fracturing into a million pieces of light in the passenger window. Two lanes of cars and trucks lumbered ahead, belching noise and exhaust. A few blocks past Alameda, she turned onto a side street. In the Indian neighborhood now, driving through the shadows pressed against rows of small bungalows and oak trees with branches drooping from weeks of summer heat. She steered past the cars and pickups at the curbs, glanced at the address she'd scribbled onto a scrap of paper, then circled a block. She parked in front of a square-shaped house with yellowish siding, a front door in the center and vertical windows on either side. It had a vacant, run-down look, blue shadows washing across the front—like a Halloween house occupied by ghosts. She wondered how it had looked when Liz had come here.

Jammed into the patch of dried, brown grass was a sign: For Sale by Owner. The telephone number at the bottom might have been written with a black felt pen. Vicky switched off the engine, dug a pen out of her bag and copied it down. Then she got out and started up the sidewalk. Inch-wide cracks with tufts of grass ran through the concrete. A dog was barking in a nearby yard, and in the distance, she could hear the roar of traffic on Sheridan.

A narrow porch hung off the house with a white plastic chair smudged with dirt and twigs jammed into one corner. The screened door squealed on its hinges as Vicky pulled it open. She knocked on the inner door. There was always the chance someone might be around, she told herself, even though she could feel the vacancy leaking through the siding. She knocked again.

This was the house where Liz Plenty Horses thought she would be safe, she thought. Stood on the porch, knocked at the door, Luna in her arms. What time had it been? How late was it? A summer night, but it might still have been hot. How tired were they, she and the baby, after the long drive? *I gave her enough money for gas*, Mary Hennings had said. Was it enough? Had she made it all the way to Denver, to a house where she would be safe? Beginning to relax, maybe, thinking everything would work out. A misunderstanding, that was all, and someone named Robert Running Wolf would see that it was cleared up. And until he did, she and Luna would stay here.

There were no sounds inside, no footsteps pounding toward the door or TV noise suddenly turned down. But that night, the door had flown open—and then what? Come in, someone had said, pulling Liz and the baby inside where it was cool. The windows might have been open; there would have been the slightest stirring of air, the soft billowing of curtains. She could almost see her stepping into a small living room and glancing around. Everything had seemed normal and so far away from the reservation and the men who wanted to kill her, and she had started to weep, dipping her head over the baby, not wanting them to see—whoever was in the house—the mixture of fear and fatigue and relief spilling from her.

Vicky wiped at the wetness that blossomed on her own cheeks and moved toward the window on the right. She peered past the edge into the dimness inside: a small, bare room with a dark vinyl floor meant to look like wood abutting the walls. On the right were two doors and straight ahead, an opening into the kitchen in back. She could see the white enameled edge of a stove. She went back to the door and tried the knob, wanting to go inside, walk across the floor, see the kitchen and the bedrooms, see the place where Liz had spent her last days, as if the house itself might tell her what had happened. Places are changed by the things that happen there, Grandmother always said. Places remember.

The knob didn't turn. Vicky stepped off the porch, walked across the dried grass and down the side of the house. Windows were open in the house next door, and she could hear a baby crying over the noise of a TV and the sounds of a faucet running and dishes clanking. On the other side of the chain-link fence between the houses, a tricycle was tipped on its side in the dirt yard.

She walked over to the little stoop at the back door and reached for the knob. It was then that she realized the door wasn't tightly shut. It swung open when she pushed it, and she stepped into a small space with a stairway ahead that plunged downward into the dark of a basement and four steps on the left that led to what looked like a back porch with a row of windows on the outer wall, just below the ceiling. The air was hot and stuffy, as if the windows had been closed a long time.

She started up the four steps, conscious of her heels clicking into the quiet. A refrigerator stood against the wall, taking up most of the porch. She moved past it into the small kitchen with cabinets and a counter on the wall ahead and a white stove and sink on the right. The turquoise linoleum creaked as she crossed the kitchen and went into the long, narrow room that must have served as both dining area and living room. The dining area was next to the kitchen; she could see the fine black lines, like a spider's web, that the chairs had scratched on the floor.

They would have eaten at the table, the people who lived in the house and Liz—Liz cuddling the baby. There was probably a sofa, a couple of chairs near the front door, arranged around a TV against the wall, maybe, and she had been safe—until they came.

Vicky crossed the living room to the far door on the left and stepped into a bedroom. The same brown, fake-wood vinyl on the floor, with nicks and scratches where furniture had stood—the four legs of a bed, a chest of drawers below the window. Outside a blue sedan slowed past the house.

She went back into the living room and through the second

door into a tiny hallway with two more doors. One opened into the bathroom; the other led into another bedroom, smaller than the one in front, but the door in back went into a covered porch with windows under the ceiling, like the porch next to the kitchen. Almost too small for a bedroom, but she could see the marks on the floor left by the legs of a twin bed. There were other scratches, possibly from chairs that had been pulled about.

She closed her eyes and concentrated on the picture forming on the back of her eyelids. A twin bed and two chairs pushed together to hold the cardboard box where Luna had slept. The porch had been Liz's room, the safe place where she'd hidden.

A door creaked open somewhere in the house. Vicky opened her eyes and stood frozen in place, muscles tensed, listening. The house had gone quiet again, yet she could feel the change in the atmosphere, the presence of another person. The footsteps, when they started, sounded like the thuds of a drum. It wasn't possible, she told herself. How could he have known she'd come to the house? How could he have gotten here so quickly, unless . . .

Unless he'd followed her from the reservation, a silver sedan hanging back, staying in her wake, not drawing her attention. My God. Why hadn't she watched the traffic in the rearview mirror? She dug into her bag, extracted her keys, and jammed them between her fingers, making a tight fist. Then she moved slowly into the little hallway, walking on her toes, careful not to make a sound. She could see the living area— there was no one there—but the wall blocked her view of the dining area and kitchen.

The footsteps started again—tap, tap, tap—across the kitchen, into the dining area. Vicky squeezed her fingers around the keys and stepped out of the hallway.

The woman standing across the room whirled around and let out a strangled half scream. "Who are you?" she managed. She was pretty, with black hair that touched her shoulders, dark, almond eyes and the sculptured cheekbones and little bump in her nose of the Arapaho. Probably in her early thirties, Vicky guessed, about five foot seven and trim looking, dressed in a dark tee shirt, khaki capris, and sandals. A small purse dangled from her shoulder.

"Sorry to frighten you." Vicky felt her hand relax around her keys. "I was interested in seeing the house," she hurried on, "and the back door was open."

Tension began to drain from the woman's face and her entire body seemed to settle into what was probably her normal posture. "I was worried about that," she said. "I showed the house this morning and couldn't remember whether I'd locked the back door. Are you looking at the house for yourself or as an investment? It's a good neighborhood." She gave a little wave toward the front door. "Very friendly," she said. "Mostly native people."

"The sign said for sale by owner," Vicky said. "Are you the owner?"

"No. No." Another little wave, this time toward the space between them. "Just helping my mother sell the place. She lived here most of her life."

"Your mother?" Vicky said. She couldn't believe her luck. Standing before her was the daughter of the woman who had owned the house when Liz was here. Who could have opened the door, let Liz and the baby inside. "I came here to find your mother." She rushed on, aware of the flush of excitement coming over her. She was close, so close to the truth. "My name is Vicky Holden. I'm from the Wind River Reservation."

"Luna Norton." The woman held out a slim, brown hand.

Vicky wasn't aware of moving across the narrow room or of reaching for the outstretched hand, only that she was holding on to it, conscious of the warmth in the palm and the faint rhythm of Luna Norton's pulse.

"Luna," she heard herself say. Her voice seemed to come from far away.

"Do I know you?" The young woman withdrew her hand and took a step back, something new moving in her expression, questions and curiosity mingling with a hint of apprehension.

Vicky took a moment. She could feel her heart thudding. It sounded like the pounding of a drum, and she wondered if Luna could hear it. "I know your mother," she said finally. It wasn't exactly true, and yet, it seemed to be the truth.

"Who are you?" Luna said, still holding back.

"I'm a lawyer. I came here looking for your mother."

"My mother!" Apprehension fixed on the woman's face now. She took another step backward, clasped her hands, and held them in front of her. "I can't imagine why she would want to talk to a lawyer," she said. "My mother isn't well."

"I'm sorry. I didn't know."

"I don't think you know anything about us. My mother had a heart attack last month, so I moved her in with us—my husband and our baby girl. I couldn't stand the thought of her being alone. She doesn't want to sell this old place." She was glancing about the vacant room. "There are so many memories."

"Would it be possible to speak with her?" Vicky said quietly.

"About what?" A sharpness came into Luna's voice.

"About AIM and the summer of 1973." Vicky waited a moment before she added, "About Liz Plenty Horses."

Luna Norton squeezed her lips together and narrowed her eyes. An almost imperceptible moisture appeared at the corners and glistened on her cheeks. "There's no good that can come from stirring up all that trouble. What happened, happened. There's nothing we can do about it. I've had a good life. My mother made sure that I had a good life. What right do you have to come here and disturb her?"

"Listen to me, Luna," Vicky said. "Your mother . . ." Her mouth had gone dry. It tasted of dust. "Your mother could be in danger."

"Danger! What are you talking about?"

"Someone on the reservation might want to harm her." Vicky was aware of the keys still pressed against her left palm. She dropped them into her bag, took out the small leather container that held her business cards, and managed to pull out a card. Her hand was shaking as she held it out. "I have to see her right away," she said.

Luna hesitated, some kind of battle playing out behind the dark, narrowed eyes. Finally she stepped forward, took the card, and held it between her hands, flexing it back and forth, but not taking her eyes from it. "I have to talk to her first," she said. "I don't know if she's up to this." She held the card steady a moment, then slid it inside the thin envelope of her purse. "You'd better go."

"Will you tell me your mother's name?"

"I thought you said you knew her."

"I don't know her name."

"Inez. Inez Horn."

Vicky walked across the vacant room, took hold of the knob, and pulled at the door swollen in the frame. It gave in pieces—the top edge first, then the bottom. Still holding the knob, she looked back. "You should stay away from the house for a while," she said.

"Why are you telling me this?"

"Please, " Vicky said. "Don't come here for a while." She watched Luna take this in—fingers pinching the edge of her bag, lips pulled into a tight line—then she stepped outside and closed the door behind her.

THE phone started to ring, breaking through the afternoon quiet that had settled over the administration building. Father John reached across a pile of papers on his desk and picked up the receiver. "Father O'Malley," he said.

"Hey, Father." It was the voice of probably an eleven-year-old, and he matched the voice with the brown, smiling face and eager eyes of Mason Willow. "Hey, Mason," he said.

"When's practice?"

"Sorry, Mason. Not today." He'd spent the last couple of hours calling parishioners, canceling meetings and carry-in suppers—all the activities scheduled for the week. He'd called the homes of the kids on the Eagles team and left messages: no practice for a few days; he'd get back to them. He'd asked them to pass the word on to the kids who didn't have phones. Mason was one of those kids. "We have to take a short break."

"But we got the game with Riverton on Saturday." And there was something else, Father John knew. The kids looked forward to baseball practice; it filled a few hours of the hot, summer days; it let them forget about everything except baseball. He was going to miss practice, too, as much as the kids.

"We're better than Riverton," he said.

"Yeah, I guess. But . . ." The kid's voice crackled with disappointment.

"It's only for a little while." Father John hoped that would be true. Sooner or later, the killer was bound to make a mistake, and when that happened, Coughlin would have him in custody. Until then, whoever had shot Ruth Yellow Bull last night and had intended to kill Vicky was still walking around. There was no telling where he might strike next, and Father John couldn't risk having the parishioners at the mission. He told Mason that he'd make sure he knew when practice would start again, then he set the receiver into place against the disappointment still flowing through the line.

He went back to the work on his desk—making his way through a pile of papers, paying a few more bills, filling out the bank deposit slip for an anonymous donation that had floated out of a white envelope with no return address and a blurred postmark. Finally he switched off the desk lamp and headed for the front door. Strips of sunlight and shadow fell over the photographs of past Jesuits on the walls. Sunlight glistened on the wood floor that creaked under his boots. Father Ian had left sometime in the afternoon to make the rounds at Riverton Memorial. Six Arapahos hospitalized this week. He hadn't gotten back yet.

Father John let himself outside and was about to start down the steps of the concrete stoop when he turned back, fished the ring of keys out of his jeans pocket, and locked the door. He didn't usually lock the door until evening, after the meetings had ended, after the pickups and cars had carved their way around Circle Drive and out toward Seventeen-Mile Road. But there were no meetings tonight. If Father Ian wanted to go to his office, he had a key.

He started across the mission grounds, the great silence of the plains pressing around him, except for the almost-imperceptible sounds of the breeze in the dried grass, the far-away whir of tires on Seventeen-Mile Road, and his own footsteps on the earth. He tried to shake off the odd feeling that had come over him. He wasn't used to such quiet in the early evening; there were always people coming and going, pickups crunching the gravel, children shouting and laughing. The mission was alive! But now it seemed like a relic, a dead thing of the past. He pushed the thought away. The people would be gone only for a while; it was temporary. Besides, Elena was still here. It would be another thirty minutes before her grandson came to pick her up, and in the residence, there would be the odors of fried hamburger or chicken or tacos or whatever she had made for dinner tonight. Things were normal, he told himself, normal.

He was halfway up the sidewalk to the residence when he knew someone was watching. He stopped walking and glanced about. And that was stupid, he realized. Whoever was watching now knew that he knew someone was there. But where? The church glowed in the late afternoon sun, the alley running toward the guesthouse was deserted—a ribbon of gravel that disappeared behind the corner of the church—and the administration building looked quiet and vacant. There was the Arapaho Museum in the gray stone school building, but he'd sent the volunteers home and tacked a white piece of paper onto the door that said, "Temporarily Closed."

There was no one about.

Still, he couldn't shake the sense that he was being tracked, like a wild animal in the sights of a rifleman. The killer was here, somewhere.

He sprinted up the sidewalk, threw himself at the front door, and fumbled at the knob. It was like a piece of stone in his hand, and he remembered that he'd told Elena to keep the doors locked. He was extracting the keys from his pocket when, out of the corner of his eye, he saw the brown pickup bouncing past the cottonwoods, heading into the mission. The front bumper jiggled as the pickup started around Circle Drive. Jeffrey, Elena's grandson, coming to pick her up, now that he'd gone back on the wagon.

"Go back!" Father John shouted, waving at the dark head hunched over the steering wheel. But the pickup kept coming. The noise of spitting gravel burst through the quiet. The pickup slid to a stop in front of the residence, and the driver's door flew open.

"Don't get out!"

"What?" The young man pulled himself upright by the opened door.

"There's someone who could have a gun. Get back inside. Stay down."

In an instant, the young man had taken this in, thrown himself back inside, and pulled the door shut behind him.

Father John jammed his key into the lock and started to open the door. From somewhere behind the house, he heard an engine kick over and roar into life. He turned around, flung himself down the steps, and ran to the corner of the house where he had a view of the back road—scarcely a road, a two-track cut through the wild grass and brush—that ran past the baseball field and out toward Rendezvous Road. A silver sedan sped down the road, turning through the bends, back tires skidding sideways. In a moment, it was out of sight.

When he turned back, he saw Elena and her grandson standing on the stoop together, and in the set of the woman's face, Father John saw that she understood.

"He come here, didn't he?" she said.

Father John walked back along the front of the house and up the steps. "You'd better stay home for a few days," he said.

"Yeah, Grandma," Jeffrey said. "You got a shooter around here, it's no place you want to be."

"I tol' you, that killer's not runnin' me off."

Father John caught Jeffrey's eye. "Let's go on home, Grandma," the young man said. "We can talk about it later."

There were a few moments while Elena bustled about the house gathering her things and her grandson walked back and forth on the stoop, a sentinel watching for the enemy. The front door hung open, and the hot breeze swept through the house as Father John picked up the phone on the hall table and dialed Coughlin's office.

"The killer was here," he told the detective as soon as he'd made his way past the blond receptionist and listened to a line that seemed to have gone dead. "He drove out of here two minutes ago in the silver sedan, heading toward Rendezvous Road."

29

EXCEPT for the faint pull of the elevator on its downward plunge, Vicky felt as if she were in a small room with bodies jammed around her, briefcases and bags poking into her back and ribs. Her cell phone started vibrating through her bag, but it was impossible to dig it out. It had vibrated twice during the interview in the glass-enclosed conference room of Owens and Lattimore, and she'd ignored it while she told what had happened the night in the alley. Then she'd answered the questions Lucas had warned her about, all of which were meant to test her sense of reality, her grasp of her own life. Could she really be certain that she'd seen what she'd seen?

She was certain, she said over and over, holding fast to the image of the girl folding under the blows of Theo Gosman's fists, legs sprawled on the cement, jerking in spasms of violence. And that other image that hovered in the shadows of her mind, the girl in the Gas Hills.

The elevator bumped to a stop. Vicky was carried along with the crowd that spilled through the sliding doors out into the glass and marble lobby of the Seventeenth Street sky-scraper. There was a hush of conversation from groups standing about, and the clack, clack sound of heels on the hard floor. Vicky stepped out of the way of people coming and going and checked the readout on her cell. Three calls, all from Luna Norton. She hurried outside and pressed the callback key. People in dark suits and serious, dark dresses, briefcases swinging at their sides or hanging from their shoulders, hurried along the sidewalk. Familiar, she thought. A few years ago, she'd been one of them, hurrying to court hearings and interviews and depositions, marching along. The buzzing sound in her ear stopped.

"I've been trying to call you." Luna's voice sounded hurried and strained.

"I know. I was in a meeting. Will your mother see me?"

"If you still insist upon this, you'd better come right away." The words were rushed, notes of reluctance ringing through them. "She's better in the mornings." Then she gave Vicky the address.

THE house was in the Highland neighborhood, only a few blocks from where she and Lucas had eaten dinner last evening. She rolled to a stop at the curb, double-checked the address, and started up the sidewalk in front of a redbrick bungalow with gables and paned-glass windows and humps of trimmed evergreen bushes on either side of the door. Sloans Lake was a block away, and through the trees she caught glimpses of the blue water shimmering in the sunshine. The faintest hint of humidity hung in the air. She could hear a duck quacking in the distance.

She stepped onto a small porch with a black iron railing and a pot of red petunias pushed against the brick wall. The door opened just as she started to lift the iron knocker. Luna stood in the doorway, dressed much the same as yesterday, except that the tee shirt was white, the capris black. There was an anxious look in her eyes.

"You'd better come in," she said.

Vicky followed her into a living room that was all leather, chrome, and glass arranged around a polished wood floor that ran across the front of the house. Wallboard had been pulled from the side walls, exposing an expanse of brick behind large

framed posters of orange and red poppies and purple chrysan-
themums. In one corner were chrome shelves stacked with the
brightly colored rattles, toys, and padded books of a young
child. The hot, moist odor of chocolate chip cookies drifted
from the kitchen. There was no sign of anything Arapaho, no
prints of horses or buffaloes, no star quilts draped over the
brown leather sofa. It might have been the home of any young
couple in an old, trendy neighborhood. Except that Luna was
Arapaho, the same generation as Lucas and Susan, Indians
who knew they had rights and lived in gentrified neighbor-
hoods and worked in software and purchased leather and
chrome furniture.

"Mom'll be out in a minute," Luna said, but a woman who
looked about sixty, with short gray hair and deep lines cut into
her round, dark face, had already appeared in the kitchen doorway. Luna must have sensed her presence, because she swung
around. "Here's the lawyer I told you about," she said.

Without saying anything, Inez Horn walked into the room
and dropped onto the end cushion of the sofa. She wore a blue
blouse and a darker blue skirt with tiny smudges of what
might have been flour across the front.

Luna nudged a sling-back leather chair in Vicky's direction
before she started for the closed door to the right of the
kitchen doorway. "I'd better check on the baby." This was
thrown over one shoulder in the direction of the sofa.

Vicky sat down, conscious of Inez Horn watching her out
of narrowed eyes. Finally the woman said, "What took you so
long?"

"I'm sorry?"

"I've been waiting a long time." Inez sat very still, shoulders
slumped a little, hands clasped in her lap. "Every day, ever since
Luna was a baby, I've been expecting somebody to come or call
me. But nobody ever came. Nobody ever called. Oh, I called a
lot of people, everybody I could think of, and they told me the
same thing. Nobody'd seen her. Probably ran away, they said,
took off, left her baby girl. Maybe she was over on Colfax,
working the streets, drinkin' and druggin'. Did I ever think of
that? Maybe I should just forget her and go on. Luna was doing
okay with me, wasn't she? So don't worry about it. But I knew
that no way did Liz leave her baby. She loved Luna more than

anything. Now you've come here finally to tell me what became of her."

Vicky took her eyes away. She waited a couple of seconds before she looked at the woman again. "I'm sorry to tell you this," she said. "Liz is dead. She was murdered, and her . . ." She hesitated. ". . . body was discovered last month in a gulley east of the reservation. The man who killed her is still on the reservation. I want to see him charged with her murder. I want to see him convicted."

Inez was staring past Vicky now, seeing something beyond the living room and the interior of a tidy house on a tree-lined street. "I knew it was true, but I never wanted to believe it. I told Luna her Mommy had to go away for a while. I told her she'd be coming back just as soon as she could, because she loved her. 'Til she got back, I told her, I'd be her Mommy and I'd take good care of her. So that's what happened. I became her mother."

Vicky leaned forward. "Help me, Inez. Please. Tell me what happened after Liz came to your house."

"The house," Inez said, still staring at the point in space. "It was supposed to be a safe house. Nobody was supposed to know where it was. Well, that was funny. Turned out lots of people knew where my house was. Wasn't supposed to be that way. Nobody'd think a Cheyenne like me, twenty-three is all I was, working nights in a diner trying to pay the mortgage and keep some food in the fridge, was gonna run a house where AIM people running from the Feds could hide. That's what they told me, a couple of the leaders that used to come into the diner. 'You got the perfect place,' they said. They'd pay me a hundred bucks a month. It was a lot of money, and Fred was in Vietnam. I never told him what I was doing, 'cause I knew he wouldn't want me mixed up with AIM."

She took a moment, working through the memories. "Tell you the truth," she said finally, "I guess I was what they call a sympathizer. I saw how they were going to bat for Indians that got beat up by the police, thrown into jail just for being Indian, fired from their jobs. I almost got fired myself, 'cause the boss wanted to hire his girlfriend, so the AIM guys paid him a visit, asked him how he'd like a bunch of Indians protesting every day in front of the diner. Well, he backed down and kept me

on. Then, when Fred got killed, they took up a collection for
me. So I owed 'em, you know. I said, they could use my house.
It could be the safe house."

T H E streets were dark except for the light splashed under the
streetlamps here and there. Liz gripped the steering wheel and
drove around one block, then another. The safe house had to
be here somewhere, but she wasn't sure. It could be miles
away. She didn't know Denver. She'd been here only once before, and her mother was driving—driving and driving, looking for the guy she'd met at the bar in Riverton, some
salesman that had been coming through. He was gonna save
them. They'd gone around block after block then, too. They
never found the guy.

     She'd had to pull off I-25 when she got to Denver. The
stream of headlights coming at her, blinding her, and Luna crying in the backseat and the needle flicking on empty. She'd
found a 24-hour convenience store and used the rest of
Ardyth's money for a couple of cans of baby formula and six
gallons of gas. She'd asked the clerk—a white woman, and she
seemed nice, the way she smiled and cooed at Luna—how to
get to the address that Robert had given her. The woman had
started explaining, then had pulled a map out of the rack by the
cash register, opened it on the counter and traced the route with
a pencil. Highway south to Alameda. West on Alameda toward
Sheridan. Couple of blocks before Sheridan, turn here. She'd
tapped the pencil on two blue lines that intersected. Can't miss
it, she'd said, then she'd handed Liz the map.

     She'd fed Luna a bottle in front of the store, thinking about
what Robert had said when he'd finally answered the phone,
after she'd been calling most the night. "Best you go to Denver," he'd said.

     Denver? She'd been surprised. "You can fix it, Robert. Tell
Jake to back off. I'm not the snitch. Somebody else told the
cops." He'd ignored what she'd said, and that surprised her
again, but he'd insisted on the safe house in Denver. She
should stay there until he straightened everything out.

     She got back on the highway and followed the directions.
Now she was in a maze of houses that all looked the same,

white frame houses with flat fronts and dark windows, pick-ups in the dirt driveways, other pickups parked on the streets. She squinted at the numbers on the black mailboxes at the curbs.

Luna had started crying again by the time she had spotted the numbers she was looking for. She parked between two pickups, lifted Luna out of the cardboard box, and, struggling to hold on to the baby and fit the strap of the diaper bag over her shoulder, made her way up a sidewalk ragged with cracks. The night was warm, but she was shivering. She felt her legs shaking beneath her and she had to lean against the door frame to steady herself as she knocked. A cat was meowing in the bushes next to the house.

There was no sound from inside. She waited a moment, then knocked again. Luna whimpered in her arms and she tried to shush her. "It's okay," she said, "it's okay." But nothing was okay. She wondered if she was at the right house, on the right street. Had she copied down the right numbers?

Then, the sound of footsteps padding toward the door and a woman's voice: "Who's there?"

"It's Liz," she managed. She was afraid she might burst into tears.

The door opened. The woman wasn't a lot older than she was, only a few years maybe. She had long black hair and she was Indian. Cheyenne, she guessed. She had on a blue robe that she held closed with one hand. The other was waving her inside. "Been expecting you," she said. Then, "Robert didn't tell me you had a baby."

Liz stopped, one foot on the doorstep. "Her name's Luna."

"It's fine, it's fine. I'm Inez. Come on in."

And then she was showing her through the little house. Kitchen here, make yourself at home. Food's meant to be eaten. Liz followed her into a bedroom in back, then into what looked like a sleeping porch with a narrow bed, a chest of drawers, and a kitchen chair with chrome frame and a green plastic seat. "It's nice and cool here. You can open the windows," Inez said, glancing around the room. "Now, where'll we put the baby?"

"I have a cardboard box in the backseat," Liz said.

"Good. That'll work." Inez swept out of the porch and came back carrying a matching chair. She arranged the chairs facing each other. "You can put the box here." Then she turned, and Liz felt herself being scrutinized, examined the way she used to look at insects in the mud down by the creek when she was little. "What did you do," Inez said, "that you got the Feds after you?"

No, it wasn't like that. She tried to explain. It was a misunderstanding with some of the AIM people on the rez—but Robert would straighten it out. It might take a couple of weeks to convince . . .

"Well, never mind." Inez waved away the explanation. "You'll be safe here."

" I ran the house about two years," Inez said. "There was a lot of trouble. AIM was in the newspapers all the time. Protests in D.C. You know, they took over the BIA building! Imagine that! Then they took over Wounded Knee. A lot of them were wanted by the FBI. Mostly it was Lakotas that came to the house, but there were Cheyennes and Crows, a couple of Blackfeet. Liz was the last one that came. After that, I told them I couldn't do it anymore. Liz and the baby only stayed for four days, and we got on like sisters. She was like the sister I always wanted. She used to walk around the house singing her songs, singing to her baby all the time. 'Baby, baby, you're the sun rising in the sky, the moon riding high. Beautiful baby of mine.' Songs like that."

Inez dipped her head. She lifted one hand and ran her forefinger and thumb over her forehead, then squeezed the small of her nose for a moment. When she looked up again, Vicky saw the moisture shining in her eyes. "They broke down the door," she said. "They didn't even knock, just came bursting in here like they were some kind of SWAT team and we'd been holding hostages or some damn thing. Liz and I, we were sitting in the living room watching TV. I remember we were watching *Get Smart*. Funny what you remember. Liz jumped up and she clamped her hand over her mouth, 'cause she didn't want to scream, I could tell. She didn't want to wake Luna. The baby was sleeping on the porch. I think she knew they were going to drag her away and she didn't want them to take the baby. They must've forgotten about Luna, or most likely they would've taken her, too.

"I remember shouting: 'Get out of here!' I ran to the kitchen for the phone, and one of them came after me. Grabbed me from behind and hit me in the face. That's all I remember, his fist coming at me. Next thing I knew, I was on the floor and I heard a baby crying somewhere. There was blood everywhere, 'cause he broke my nose. I could taste the blood in my mouth. I had to hold on to the wall to get up, you know, sort of crawling up the wall, and I saw they were gone. Liz, too. I went into the kitchen, ducked my head under the faucet and tried to clean up some of the blood. My whole face felt like it was on fire with the pain. I went and picked up Luna and I knew, even then, that I was gonna have to take care of her. She was going to be my little baby."

"Did you call the police?"

Inez gave a snort of laughter and shook her head. "Oh, yes. I called. Took them two hours to get here. Indian neighborhood, another Indian fight, was how they looked at it. Let 'em go back to the reservation and settle their own troubles. Couple of officers wrote in their notepads, shoved the notepads back into their pockets, said they'd file a report. That was the last I heard. I wanted to call AIM, the guys I knew. But I didn't, 'cause they *were* AIM, you know."

She went quiet for a moment, kneading her fingers together. "Maybe you'd better tell me what they did with her."

"They shot her," Vicky said. "They beat her first . . ."

A sharp cry erupted behind them, and Vicky turned around. Luna was standing in the doorway to the bedrooms. In her arms was a baby girl, with brown, baby-fat arms and legs and black hair. A pink ribbon was tied around a snatch of hair that stood straight up from her head. She rubbed a chubby hand at sleepy eyes, then leaned back and stared at her mother, who was crying.

Vicky jumped to her feet. "I'm so sorry."

"No." Luna pressed a fist against her mouth a moment, then she said, "I want to know everything that happened to my mother."

Inez pushed herself out of the sofa and went over to Luna. She wrapped her arms around both the young woman and the baby and held them close. After a moment, she said, "Her body was found this summer near the reservation. We can see that she has a proper burial now, in the Arapaho Way." She led Luna and the baby back to the sofa and sat down beside them. The baby leaned against her mother and patted at her arm.

"Did you recognize the men?" Vicky said. "Can you identify them?"

A couple of seconds passed before Inez said, "One of them stayed at the house. Right after Wounded Knee, came and stayed a couple of weeks. Then he said he was going to Wind River with other AIM people. Lakota, went by the name of Jake Tallfeathers, but he told me once his real name was Walker."

And he's dead, Vicky was thinking. Struck by a truck probably driven by the other man—who was still alive. "Who was with him?" she said. Her voice was quiet; she realized she was holding her breath.

"I never saw him before," Inez said. She waited another moment. "All I know is, he had a funny name. I never forgot it. He was the one that hit me, and just before he grabbed me, I heard Jake yelling: 'Get her, Mister!'"

Vicky could hear the sound of her own breathing; it was like a bellows in the quiet house. "Do you remember what he looked like?" she managed. "Do you think you could still identify him?"

"I'll never forget their faces," Inez said. "I can close my eyes and see their faces."

30

"I know who the killer is!" Vicky shouted into the cell over the whir of the Jeep's engine. She'd tapped in the telephone number, hurrying down the sidewalk, then opened the door and crawled inside, the phone ringing in her ear. "Get me Coughlin," she'd told the high-pitched disembodied voice that had finally answered: "Fremont County Sheriff's Office." She'd turned on the ignition while she'd waited for the message to wind its way from the receptionist's desk down the corridors to Coughlin's office. Finally, the detective was on the line.

"Start over," he said.

"His name is Lyle Bennet. He goes by the name of Mister."

"We're talking about Ruth Yellow Bull's homicide?"

"And Liz Plenty Horses's." Vicky pressed herself against the seat and fought to keep her voice steady. My God, she and Adam had agreed to help the man. They were going to do everything they could to help him obtain his rights.

"Tell me what you've found."

Vicky told him what Inez Horn had said: that Liz Plenty Horses and her baby had stayed at her house—an AIM safe house—in Denver for four days, that Jake Tallfeathers and

Mister had broken into the house and forced Liz to accompany them, that she had never heard of Liz after that night, that she had raised Liz's daughter, Luna. "He's still on the reservation," Vicky said. "He's one of my clients, for godssake, and he wants to kill me. He killed Ruth, and he'll kill anyone who can connect him to Liz Plenty Horses's murder."

"It's a good lead, I give you that, and I'll definitely investigate . . ."

"A lead? You have to pick Mister up right away before he kills anybody else. I have his address." God, what was it? She fumbled in her bag, dragged out her Day-Timer and scrolled down to *M*. She had it then. Lyle Bennet/Mister, on Middle Fork Road. "He's desperate. He might come after Inez and Luna."

"Okay, take it easy."

"Inez can identify him, Coughlin. She's never forgotten what he looked like. She'll testify that Mister and Jake Tallfeathers dragged Liz out of her house. They were the last ones to be seen with her."

"It doesn't prove they killed her."

It came like a slap in the face. Vicky flinched at the truth of it. The heat of the sun bore through the windshield and burned into her forearm. They'd taken Liz from the house; yes, that was true. She could almost hear the rough, gravelly voice of Mister trying to explain his version of what had happened that night. They'd stopped for gas, and Liz said she had to use the john, and she never come back. That's the truth, so help him God. He'd swear it was true. He was no murderer, why would he murder her? Just bringing her back . . .

Bringing her back. The idea stalled in her head like a roadblock Vicky couldn't get past. Suppose it were true. Suppose Jake and Mister were the errand boys, dispatched to bring Liz Plenty Horses back to the reservation to answer for something she hadn't done. Suppose someone else—a man intent on remaining in charge, a man who had eliminated anyone he thought was competition: Jimmie Iron in Washington, D.C., Daryl Redman in Ethete—had given the order to bring Liz Plenty Horses back to the reservation. Then he had killed her to keep her quiet.

She could see Inez Horn looking out the window, the sadness outlined in the hunch of her shoulders. More than thirty-five years, and Liz's killer was still free. And now—where was the evidence that Jake Tallfeathers and Mister were the men who had beaten her and shot her to death? Where was the gun, the blood spatters in a truck that had been crunched into a scrap heap years ago, the bloody clothes and fingerprints and strands of hair, the DNA that might have been swabbed from under fingernails? There was nothing but a skeleton.

"He knows what happened to her," Vicky said, and she knew that was true. Mister knew who had killed Liz Plenty Horses. "You have to pick him up."

"We will, we will, Vicky. I want to talk to this Inez Horn."

"Hold on." Vicky checked the cell and gave him the number Luna had used this morning. Then she read off Luna's address.

"I'll see about sending a man . . ."

"There isn't time," Vicky said. "Pick him up now. Please," she added, and realized that was ridiculous. He would handle matters his own way. "Mister knows who the murderer is." And here was a new thought. She blurted it out, "He could be in danger."

This seemed to get his attention because the line went quiet for a long moment. "We'll pick him up, talk to him," he said. "Where are you now?"

She told him she was about to start for the reservation, and glanced at her watch. Two o'clock. She would have to retrieve her bag from Lucas's house, leave a note on the table: *Sorry, honey. Something came up. Had to return to the rez. We'll have a long visit soon—I promise. I promise.* So many broken promises. The house was near I-25 and she should be on the highway in thirty minutes. "I'll be on the rez by nine thirty."

"Look, Vicky. Until we find this guy and sort through things, maybe you shouldn't go to your apartment."

She told him she'd be at the mission.

HE thought he'd heard a car pulling into the mission a moment ago, and Father John had pushed back from his desk in the study and gone to the window. The last of the daylight had begun to fade. Darkness was crawling over the grounds, wrapping around the yellowish light of the streetlamps. No sign of any vehicle outside. The old house creaked around him, settling into evening, and from overhead came the faint clicking noise of Father Ian's laptop. Familiar sounds, and yet, he couldn't shake the sense of something different, some disturbance.

He'd been expecting Vicky at any moment; she'd called around three. Just leaving Cheyenne, I-80 flinging itself ahead through the sagebrush and wild grasses and blown dirt in a great expanse of nothingness. They'd talked a good ten minutes, Vicky's voice lost at times in the roar of semis barreling past her Jeep. Mister and Jake Tallfeathers had taken Liz from the safe house, she'd told him. They may have been involved in her death—the brutal beating, the gun fired into her skull. At the very least, Mister knew who the murderer was.

She asked if she could stay in the guesthouse. He'd hesitated at that. The silver sedan had been at the mission yesterday. "Just tonight," she'd said, a firmness in her voice that met his hesitation. She hurried on, explaining that Coughlin would have Mister in custody tonight, and tomorrow, Adam would be back.

"Yes, of course," he'd said. He didn't want to think of her alone in her apartment, a killer on the loose.

He peered across Circle Drive toward the road that tunneled through the cottonwoods, willing the headlights to appear, shimmering through the trees and lengthening across the grounds, but there were no headlights.

He was about to sit down at his desk when he heard a faint rumbling noise. This time, looking out the window, he watched the headlights gather and shoot across Circle Drive. Behind the headlights, he recognized Vicky's Jeep.

Father John went to the front door. He was halfway down the sidewalk when the Jeep slid into the curb and Vicky got out. She slammed the door behind her and came to meet him. The night was hot, probably only a few degrees cooler than the afternoon, but she was pulling the front of a sweater around her, as if she wanted to ward off whatever chill had come over her.

THE GIRL WITH BRAIDED HAIR 263

He placed an arm on her shoulders and ushered her into the residence. "Have you eaten?" he said.

THEY sat at the kitchen table. She took a few bites of the sandwich he'd made for her—bologna, mayonnaise, and a leaf of lettuce—and sipped at the fresh coffee he'd brewed. "It doesn't matter if Mister pulled the trigger," she said. "He and Jake Tallfeathers are accomplices in her murder. They went and got her, dragged her back to the rez so that some psychopath with a grandiose vision of himself could silence her forever, make certain she never told anyone about Jimmie Iron's murder in Washington, D.C., or who the real snitch was."

"You're saying someone else killed her," Father John said, and that meant, he was thinking, that even if Mister were arrested, the killer would still be on the loose.

Vicky nodded. "He couldn't trust her. She'd been picked up by the police, held in custody for twenty-four hours. No telling what she might spill if the police picked her up again. And chances were, they would pick her up. They knew who she was, a vulnerable girl with a baby and no one to protect her. No one to hire a lawyer for her. They would have held her as long as possible, putting pressure on her. Tell us what you know about AIM and we'll let you go. Whoever her killer was, he knew how it worked."

Father John got up, refilled her mug, and poured a little more coffee into his own. He set down the coffeepot and glanced out the window. The backyard, the baseball field, and the dirt road that the silver sedan had taken were lost in the darkness, but there was no sign of movement, nothing out of the ordinary. He took his chair again and thought of telling her about the silver sedan, then decided against it. He'd tell her tomorrow. She looked exhausted tonight, her eyes red rimmed with fatigue and strain.

Vicky set her mug down and pulled her bag off the back of the chair and around to her lap. She drew out her cell and began pressing the keys. Then she stared past his shoulder. "Put me through to Detective Coughlin," she said after a couple of seconds. "I know he's off duty. This is Vicky Holden and it's urgent. He knows what I'm calling about."

She threw Father John a half smile of exasperation and began tapping out a rhythm on the tabletop with her fingertips. A long moment passed before she said, "Do you have him yet?" She paused. "He couldn't have just disappeared, dropped off the face of the earth. He didn't know you were coming after him. Why would he run?" Another moment passed before she said, "I'll check back in the morning." She pressed a key, snapped the phone shut, and set it on the table.

"Mister's on the run," she said. "Coughlin thinks he got nervous after Ruth Yellow Bull's murder. He could be heading for Pine Ridge. He has relatives there. There's an alert out for him. The highway patrol will pick him up." There was little conviction in her voice, and Father John had to glance away from the tiredness in her eyes.

"You need to sleep," he told her. He'd decided that he'd stay awake tonight, watching, in case the sedan returned.

They walked back through the residence and out to the Jeep. The night was still warm, and a deep quiet had dropped over the mission. Across Circle Drive, the church and administration building loomed out of the darkness, washed in a mix of moonlight and the glow from the street lamps. "I know the way," Vicky said, giving him a little smile over the rim of the door as she got into the Jeep.

Well, that was true, he thought. Still he preferred to ride along with her tonight. He rapped his fingers on the hood as he walked around and got into the passenger seat, and—strange, this—despite her protest, Vicky waited until he'd pulled his door shut before she started the engine. How well they knew each other, he thought. He wondered if she'd sensed his worry about the mission, or even sensed that the killer had also come here. In any case, she knew he wouldn't let her go to the guesthouse alone, fumble with the key in the dark, search for the light inside.

The Jeep's headlights bounced over the gravel road, the edge of the lights catching the sides of the church and the administration building and throwing a column of light toward Eagle Hall. A few old cottonwoods lined the road, and here and there a stray branch dangled over the road. The guesthouse was ahead, a dark, blocklike shape against the pale moonlit sky.

Vicky parked in front and left on the headlights while Father John got out and, pulling the keys from his pocket, went to the front door. He kept to the side so as not to block the light, inserted the key and pushed the door open. He reached inside for the light switch, just as the headlights went off. There was a moment of darkness: the sound of Vicky's door slamming shut, her footsteps on the gravel. His fingers found the switch, and light burst out of the round glass fixture on the living room ceiling.

It was then that the sound of a gunshot crashed around them. "Get down!" Father John shouted. He hit the switch and turned off the light. God. They'd been sitting ducks in a shooting gallery, both of them, backlit by the light inside. He hunched over and ran toward Vicky, crouched against the front tire of the Jeep. Another gunshot then, blasting the air. Wood shattered in the front door where he'd been standing a half second ago. He felt the sharp pricks, like needles, driving into his back.

"You okay?" he said. She was so quiet, as quiet as death. He took hold of her shoulders. "Vicky! Are you hit?"

"No. No," she said. It was almost a whisper, a half-strangled noise in her throat. "I'm okay."

Another shot, then, slamming into the Jeep, rocking it sideways as if it might lift off the tires and collapse into a heap. There was the sound of glass shattering, and shards of glass rained over them. He was firing wildly, whoever he was, firing from the cottonwoods across the road. He knew he had them pinned down by the Jeep.

"We have to get out of here," Father John said. They had to get into the cottonwoods and scrubby pines on the right side of the house, then zigzag through the brush to the river. They could lose him there, he was certain. He knew where to cross the river—there was only the one place for a mile—and once they were on the other side, they could run for a house set back from Rendezvous Road. But first they had to run along the front of the guesthouse, he was thinking, and that would be dangerous—dark crouching figures moving against the white shingles. The killer would spot them in the moonlight.

The gunfire erupted again, and Father John realized that, this time, the bullet hit the passenger side of the Jeep. He could hear the window caving in, glass crashing over gravel. The killer was expecting them to make a run in that direction, he realized. They had only a moment before he grasped his mistake.

"Go left and run for the river. I know the place to cross." He nudged Vicky forward. She started running, bent over herself, arms swinging, propelling her forward. He took off after her just as another shot exploded against the right side. The killer hadn't seen them! They had another second of grace. He could hear his heart thumping.

"Run for the trees and keep going," he said, but she knew that. She was already darting crablike across the bare dirt and the scattering of sagebrush, and he was running after her. Another second was all they had. "I'm behind you," he said, not sure if she'd heard him.

The killer was onto them now, coming after them. The ground shook with a bullet that sprayed the dirt and brush. They lunged for the trees—he'd caught up to her now, close behind, shielding her—and they kept going, zigzagging around the trunks of cottonwoods that rose like black columns ahead. A broken branch caught at his shirtsleeve and swiped the nape of his neck. He felt the cool line of trickling blood. From behind them came the scuff of boots in the brush, hesitating, then advancing.

Vicky veered to the side, stumbling over a branch, and Father John reached out to steady her. Another explosion rent the air, and at that same instant—odd, he thought, as if they were one event—a sharp pain drove into his shoulder and lit his arm on fire and then his chest, a flame burning through his body, and he was aware of his right arm suddenly limp at his side, a heavy appendage that no longer belonged to him. His boot cracked against a fallen branch and he felt himself reeling sideways through the darkness and pain, Vicky a dark blur in the trees ahead. He tried to push on; he was still running, he thought, and yet why had his feet stopped moving? When had they turned into lead, barely lifting off the ground? He couldn't believe he was falling—he couldn't allow it to happen—and yet a clump of sagebrush was rising toward him and he felt himself sinking into it, all of his awareness now concentrated on the blinding light of pain.

31

VICKY plunged through the tangle of brush and fallen branches, the shadows of cottonwoods and the faint puddles of moonlight. Behind her, John's hard gasps of breath and the sounds of his footsteps mingled with her own. The Little Wind River was ahead; surely she was only imagining that she could hear it rushing over the boulders. And yet, they must be getting close, and *I know the place to cross*, he'd said. She tried to hold on to that thought, darting ahead, listening for him behind her. Then she realized she was alone.

She stopped and looked back, trying to make him out in the darkness, moving around the trees. *Keep zigzagging.* But the sense of being alone swelled into the darkness, and she knew, then—the realization squeezing her heart—that he must have been hit. She started back, a blind woman feeling her way. Which way had she come? Where had she left him behind?

"John!" she shouted. The gunshot followed, aimed in the direction of her voice, she realized. She felt the force of the bullet dislodge the air around her. She kept going, moving toward the killer, her eyes searching the shadows. Then she saw it: a disturbance that lasted only a moment and disappeared. She made her way toward what she'd seen. Her breath was stopped in her throat; her hands had turned to ice.

"John?" she said, softly this time, and in response came a moaning sound that cut through her like a serrated knife. She darted toward the sound and, in the corridor of moonlight, she saw him crumpled on the ground, branches of sagebrush bristling about him.

"Oh, God, no!" she said, throwing herself down beside him. In the dim light, she could see the blood pumping out of his arm, the black puddle growing on the ground.

"Go on," Father John said, the words coming in a rush of breath.

"Shhh." She laid a finger against his lips. "Save your strength." She grabbed his shirt with both hands and attempted to tear it. It was like steel. She bent close, took hold of the fabric with her teeth and pulled hard. The ripping noise burst through the quiet. She kept pulling and ripping until she had a strip, then another strip. She tied the strips together, willing her hands to stop shaking.

"Run," he said.

"I'm not going anywhere." She managed to loop the strips around his arm, feeling her way until she'd positioned them above the bleeding. He let out a groan of pain as she tightened the knot, but it wasn't tight enough. Blood was still pulsing from his arm. She twisted the knot with one hand and ran the other hand along the ground, searching for something— anything strong enough. Her fingers bumped against a cold, hard object. A rock, but oblong and flat, not like a rock at all. A piece of rock, sheared from something large and useless. And this she could use. She gripped it hard, not wanting to drop it into the darkness, and managed to tie it into the knot she'd already made. She started twisting again, using the rock for leverage, leaning close. The bleeding was stopping. God, let it stop.

She was barely aware of the beam of a flashlight washing over them, her thoughts on the bleeding. Yes! It had stopped. Then she understood that, behind the beam, stood the killer. She held the twisted knot in place and blinked into the light, trying to make out who he was, but there was only a black figure, absorbing the moonlight, like the trunks of the cottonwoods.

"Don't move." The voice from behind the beam was low and controlled and . . . familiar. She'd heard the voice before; this was someone she knew.

"How many more people do you intend to kill?" She was shouting into the darkness. "Haven't you killed enough?"

"Doesn't look like it, does it?" The voice again, cold and calculating. "You've forced me to do this, you and your priest friend, digging up the past, poking around in what isn't your business. What business was it of yours if some stupid girl got herself killed? Why should you care?"

She recognized the voice now. She could see him pushing back in his chair, fist tapping the edge of the desk. *Mister here's a good man. He's got the same rights as everybody else.* And she understood. There was only one man Liz had trusted. The man who had sent her to the safe house and knew where she was. The man who had sent Jake and Mister after her. And that man was still Mister's friend.

"Liz Plenty Horses was innocent," she said, "and you knew it. You set her up to be killed, didn't you, Robert? Robert Running Wolf, right? Wasn't that the name you used then? You convinced everyone else she was the snitch. But you were the one who was the snitch, isn't that right? You were working with the FBI in Washington, and Jimmie Iron found out. So you ordered Jake to kill him. Did Brave Bird find out, too? Is that why he had to die? Or did you just want to make sure nobody else took control? And what about Liz? She'd begun to figure things out, right? You saw the chance to eliminate Brave Bird and put the blame for being a snitch on her. She had nowhere to go. You sent her to Denver, so people would think she'd left the rez. Then you sent Jake and Mister to pick her up and bring her back. You wanted to kill her yourself. Why? To make sure the job was taken care of?"

"You don't know what you're talking about. We were at war, you understand? War! The hell with Vietnam. We were at war right here in Indian country. Things happen in war, get it? So sometimes you have to work with the enemy. A little give-and-take. You give 'em a little and you find out what they're up to. You gotta know what the hell you're doing. You can't have stupid people in charge. They'd bring the enemy right into the camp, with their stupid policies, so they have to be eliminated. Get it?"

"Why did you have to beat her to a pulp before you pulled the trigger?"

"All that bitch had to do was tell Mister and Jake that she was the one, she was the one ratted out Brave Bird, then everybody would've believed it. But would she say it? Would she? No. All she had to do was say it, for the good of the mission."

"And what mission was that?"

"Indian rights, you stupid bitch. AIM was fighting for Indian rights! That was our mission! You think they let you into law school 'cause you're so brilliant? They let you in 'cause they had to. They didn't have any choice, unless they wanted a big discrimination lawsuit. You think we weren't watching law schools, making sure they didn't discriminate against Indian applicants? You and your partner, you got AIM to thank for your fancy degrees and your fancy office. We made everybody sit up and take notice. We made 'em give us our rights. You think anybody wanted Indians to have rights before AIM came along? We went to the barricades for you and your kids and all the other Indians with fine jobs and houses. We protested and we demonstrated and we fought like hell, and we used the courts against 'em, made their own courts say that we had rights. You should've said thank you, that's what you should've done. Thank you and went on with your business. So some people got killed. People die in war."

Vicky saw the motion, the rent in the darkness as he lifted the rifle. "Now you're gonna die."

Then, brightness everywhere, flooding through the night, and the loud voice reverberating through a megaphone: "Drop the gun!"

Charlie Crow was illuminated in the floodlights: the flabby build and rounded shoulders, the black hair brushed back from the pockmarked face.

"Drop it!" The voice burst through the floodlights.

He took his time, bringing the rifle down alongside the pant leg of his jeans, still holding on.

"Now, Crow! Rifle on the ground!"

Vicky huddled close to Father John and kept her hand on the

stone tied inside the knot, holding it as tightly as she could. "Try to hang on," she whispered, but she saw that he was unconscious, his breathing slow and ragged. She bent over him and laid her face against his cheek, the cool dampness of his skin. "Don't leave me, John," she said. Her voice was choked and heavy. "Please don't leave me." In the dark that rimmed the perimeter of light, she could hear boots crunching the brush and undergrowth.

The rifle jerked upward, the barrel turned on them. She felt her breath stop—everything stopped—and she had the sense that she was floating overhead, looking down on a couple huddled together, waiting for the bullets to rip them apart. She was aware of her own hand gripping the stone, and that was what brought her back to herself. This was what she had to focus on; this was all she could do. She could keep the tourniquet tight around John's arm. She felt her pulse racing, her own blood coursing through her body, the screams strangled in her throat.

The gunshot, when it came, splintered the air. Vicky realized she had closed her eyes, and she snapped them open and lifted her head. Charlie Crow lay sprawled on the ground, the rifle at his side, the toes of his boots pointing toward the sky. She couldn't take her eyes away, and yet, at the periphery of her vision, she saw the men in dark uniforms walking into the floodlights, carrying rifles, some of them, others shoving handguns into the holsters on their hips. Some were walking toward her and John. And Father Ian, running toward them through the brush, dodging around the trees.

Then she understood what had happened. He'd heard the first gunfire and he'd called 911. There was a Wind River police car nearby—police were probably keeping an eye on the mission—and backup cars had arrived in minutes. Sheriff's officers, Riverton police officers, an array of uniforms tramping about.

"He's been shot," Vicky shouted to no one in particular, to all of them. "Get an ambulance." But somewhere out in the vast space beyond the lights, there was already the muffled noise of sirens.

She was still gripping the stone, keeping the tourniquet tight, she realized, when the ambulance rocked into the circle of light. Still holding on when one of the medics pried her fingers away.

VICKY stepped into the empty space at the rear of the crowd, Adam beside her, his hand firm against the small of her back, guiding her forward. From here she could see around the shoulders and the black heads of people standing close to the open grave. The little white crosses that erupted over the bare-dirt graves shone in the hot August sun beating down on the mission cemetery. Even the breeze was hot, sweeping up the hill across the flat bluff, plucking at her skirt and blowing her hair. The crowd was quiet, reverent, heads bowed. Almost everyone was holding a flower of some kind, little flashes of purple and yellow and red next to the plaid shirts, blue jeans, and cotton dresses. She breathed in the perfume of the yellow rose she was holding. Yellow, for life.

In front, the casket that held Liz Plenty Horses's skeleton stood poised over the grave on strips of thick, black plastic. Next to the casket were Father John and Father Ian, in the robes of priests—how natural John looked, except for the sling that held his right arm to his chest.

Father John dipped a sprinkler into the container that Father Ian held and started walking alongside the casket, sprinkling holy water over the top. She had to shift her position to keep him in sight, and each time she moved, she was aware of Adam moving with her, his hand firmly on her back.

"May the Lord receive your soul and hold you in his love . . ." Father John's voice drifted through the sound of the wind. Then both he and Father Ian stepped back into the crowd, making room for Thomas Whiteman and Hugh Bad Elk. The elders moved close to the casket and Thomas held up a pan filled with burning cedar. Oh, she knew the ritual: there had been so many funerals.

Hethaithe hadwanenaidethe Jevaneatha jethuajene. Vicky closed her eyes and let the prayers warm her, like the sun on her arms and face. She understood the meaning; the prayers of the elders were part of the memories lodged in her heart. *The good will go to live with God forever.*

The crowd remained quiet as the casket dropped into the

grave, the creaking of a motor punctuating the sounds of the wind. Then, almost in slow motion, people began filing toward the grave. Luna came first, head bowed, her black hair falling forward like a scarf. Behind her was a man probably in his thirties, dressed in a white shirt, leather vest, and dark slacks. His black hair was trimmed short around a narrow, Indian face. He held the baby in one arm—she fit comfortably on his hip—and he kept his other arm around Luna as they approached the casket. Maybe that was the way Jimmie Iron would have been with Liz, Vicky thought. It was possible. She watched Luna hold a clump of wild flowers over the grave a moment, before allowing them to float downward.

Inez Horn and Mary Hennings came next and tossed in little bouquets of flowers. The rest of the crowd had also begun moving forward, separating into makeshift lines, stepping back to allow room for an elder or a grandmother or a child, all of them letting the flowers drift downward over the casket. She spotted Diana Morningstar and the other women who had come to her office.

It had surprised her, the crowd that had jammed Blue Sky Hall last evening for Liz's wake and had come to St. Francis Mission this morning for the funeral. Traffic had backed up on Seventeen-Mile Road—lines of pickups and sedans—waiting to turn into the mission. Vehicles had parked everywhere. They had jammed Circle Drive and crowded into vacant spaces in the field in the center of the drive. The pews had been filled. She and Adam had managed to get seats in the back. People were standing in the side aisles and across the vestibule. So many people, she'd thought, for a girl murdered more than thirty-five years ago, a forgotten girl. Who cared? Charlie Crow had said.

Vicky followed the last of the crowd to the grave, Adam at her side, and tossed the yellow rose onto the pile of flowers. "Rest in peace," she whispered. "*Beni':i:ho.* We have found you."

THE cemetery was deserted now, the last pickups snaking out to the road, red taillights catching the sun. Vicky retraced her steps across the sun-baked ground, through the rows of graves to Liz's grave. The smell of the flowers wafted around her. She'd told Adam she needed a few more minutes and had headed back up the bluff.

"You have a beautiful daughter," she said. Now this is crazy, she was thinking, talking to a skeleton in a casket. And yet, she felt as if Liz Plenty Horses were an old friend, someone she'd known all of her life, a girl like herself at one time. "You have a granddaughter, too. Does that surprise you? And a son-in-law. He seems like a good husband and father. And Inez was a good mother."

Vicky looked past the grave at the brown plains running into the distance and the blue sky melting down. It would have been nice—appropriate somehow, she was thinking, if Liz's hair had been unbraided, all of her troubles released. And yet, Vicky had the feeling that it had been done.

When she turned around, she saw John O'Malley coming through the graves toward her, wearing blue jeans now and a light blue shirt, his arm strapped across the front.

"Thought I might find you here," he said when he reached her. "I haven't had the chance to thank you."

"Thank me?" she said. "I should thank you for helping me find Liz's killer. Robert Running Wolf had gotten away with murder for a long time. He would have always gotten away with it." Then she told him that she'd spoken with Coughlin yesterday. Mister had been arrested in South Dakota and brought back to the rez. He would be charged with kidnapping, aiding and abetting first-degree murder, and conspiracy to commit first-degree murder. Conviction on any one of the charges would put him in prison for life.

"You saved my life, Vicky," Father John said.

She smiled up at him. "Didn't you know," she said, "it was partly selfish. I couldn't stand the thought of your leaving." She glanced away for a moment. "When are you leaving, John?"

"In two weeks," he said. He turned his head in the direction of the mission grounds, the white steeple rising over the edge of the bluff. The movement seemed to cause a stab of pain in his wounded arm because he grimaced and drew in his lower lip a moment, and she realized that this—the subject of his leaving—was not something they should talk about. It was not negotiable. They'd both known this day would come.

Still, she pushed on. "I thought you didn't want to go to Rome."

"It's a sabbatical."

"That means you'll be back?"

"There are no guarantees." Father John moved the strapped arm forward about a quarter of an inch, then let it drop back into place, wincing a little, she could see. "No pitching for a while anyway," he said, and Vicky could feel the effort it had taken, that little joke.

They started walking back across the bluff, striking a zigzag path around the mounds of graves, right, left, then across the road. She reached out and slipped her arm around his good arm, wanting to hold him here for a while longer. The mission lay below, deserted now, except for Adam's pickup truck parked in Circle Drive. The administration building, the church and museum, the residence looked like an assembly of old buildings on a picture postcard. She could see Walks-On sprawled on the grass near the front door of the residence.

"I'll come back after the sabbatical for Walks-On," Father John said. "I don't want to leave him behind." Then he added, "With everything else."

"Yes," Vicky said. She let go of his arm then. "At least you can take Walks-On."

Turn the page for a preview
of the next mystery
from Margaret Coel . . .

BLOOD MEMORY

Available in hardcover
from Berkley Prime Crime!

THE August night was perfect. A full moon hanging low in a silver sky, just enough hint of a cool breeze to banish the day's heat. An automobile rumbling along a street somewhere and a squirrel scampering up a tree broke into the quiet. She watched her shadow fall around the golden retriever's as he plunged ahead, straining against the leash. They were alone, just her and the dog in the moon-filled night that wrapped around them.

They had reached an understanding, she and Rex, a kind of compromise. He would stay in the dog run at the side of the town house while she was at work. And she would take him on a mile-long walk around the neighborhood—good for both of them, she told herself—when she got home in the evenings. She'd gotten home later than usual tonight. It must be close to midnight. It was hard to get a look at her watch with the dog pulling her down the sidewalk.

Flattened behind the shadows on both sides of the street were townhomes that looked much like her own, fake adobe façades and red-tiled roofs reminiscent of Mexico or Italy, unlike the redbrick Denver bungalows that had occupied the neighborhood for the past hundred years. An enterprising developer, who happened to be her ex-husband, had bought up four blocks of bungalows and called out the wrecking crew before the historic preservationists could force a change in plans. Before anyone realized what was happening, a new neighborhood had been plunked down amid the old. Upscale is how the brochures termed the town houses, "green" for the young professionals who cared about such things, with minimal landscaping that consisted of a few strategically placed trees and bushes arranged around neat patches of groomed gravel.

They crossed the street and started down the next block, the dog still pulling ahead. She could feel the strength in his muscles transported along the rayon fibers of the leash. They had already made two swings around the periphery of the neighborhood, and she was beginning to relax, the tension of the day melting out of her muscles and sinews. Ahead, something moved in the shadows in front of one of the town houses. Her heart took a little jump. She gave a yank on the leash and closed the gap with the dog, not taking her eyes from the spot where she'd caught the movement, so slight it might have been her imagination. It wasn't there now.

A shadow adjusting itself in the moonlight, she told herself. Everything looked different at night, moved differently, even the spindlelike trees swaying in the breeze. Besides, the neighborhood was safe—perfectly safe, her ex-husband had assured her—the type of neighborhood a professional woman on her own, such as herself, could be comfortable in. She and her neighbors would have similar interests. And those interests would be—she gave the leash a little slack, watching the dog bolt ahead, shoulders rounded in the task—a total dedication to career, whatever the career might be, so total there was no space for anything else. Which explained the appeal of "green" gravelly yards, hardly the kind where children would be found playing.

A friendly neighborhood, he had said. That was funny, thinking about it now. Almost a year in the town house and she didn't know a single neighbor, probably wouldn't recognize a neighbor if she bumped into one at the deli. The sum of exchanges with the neighbors amounted to occasional eye contact across identical yards, nods and muted "mornings" as they backed their respective cars out of upscale garages and down upscale driveways. But that was her fault, she knew. She had preferred to bury herself in her work, staying late, working weekends. The neighborhood passed for okay, and it was close to the *Journal* building. And Rex helped. A friend waiting at home when she finally got there. Her life was her career now. A journalist at the daily newspaper read by everyone who cared about what was going on in Denver. Even if there weren't many newspapers left on the driveways, she suspected that her neighbors probably read her byline on the Internet in the mornings. The townhome was an interim place—a place to spend the night.

There was a scraping noise on the sidewalk behind her.

She pulled on the leash and wheeled around. Nothing except patches of shadow and moonlight. The sidewalk and street were empty, melting into the darkness down the block. She was imagining things in the night that weren't there. Still she felt jittery. Such a distinctive sound, the scrape of boots on concrete. She searched the shadows again, then turned and started walking fast toward the corner ahead, giving the leash a lot of slack. Her townhome was around the corner and halfway down the block. She was five minutes from home.

She heard the sound again. The footsteps tapped out a brisk rhythm that matched her own. Someone was following her. A jumble of thoughts clanged in her head. She felt her body tense, a thousand electrical impulses set to fire. Rex must have sensed the tension, because he was now walking beside her. She made herself keep the same pace—yes, that was what she must do. Not change her pace and tip him off that she *knew* he was there. It was a man, she was certain, the footsteps heavy and definite. She slipped her hand into her jeans pocket, pulled out her house key and closed her fist around the metal so that the sharp point protruded between her middle fingers.

She kept her head straight ahead, her eyes sweeping over the street and sidewalk and yards. Lights glowed in the upstairs windows of the town house at the corner. He wouldn't close on her there, grab her from behind, and try to pull her into the bushes. She tried to think the way he would think, a man planning to tackle and rape her, beat her. He would wait until she walked in front of a town house swallowed by the night. Until then, he had to think that she thought everything was normal. She was simply out enjoying a walk with her dog.

She reached the corner, turned past the thin slice of light on the sidewalk from the town house window and glanced around. She saw him then, a tall, large figure all in black, shoulders hunched inside a bulky jacket, hands jammed into the pockets, elbows sticking out like those of a wrestler strutting into the ring. He was close, not more than two houses behind, backlit by the moonlight. She thought about running to the door with the lights on upstairs, then dismissed the idea. By the time anyone came down the stairs and opened the door, he would be on her, and he would be strong. She could almost feel the clasp of a fleshy hand over her mouth, the arms dragging her off to the side while someone leaned outside, looking around, seeing nothing, except for a dog barking and growling near the bushes, frantic. *Go home! Go home! Damn people, why don't they keep their dogs locked up?* The door would slam shut, and she would be alone with him. At best, the person might call the police. The police would come, but it would be too late.

She was half a block from home.

She kept going at the same steady pace, keeping the dark figure in her peripheral vision. The instant she passed the corner of the town house, out of his sight, she broke into a full-out run, running as fast as she could, pulling Rex along. "Come on! Come on!" she managed to order in between gulps of air crashing into her lungs. Her heart was hammering. She glanced back as she turned up her own sidewalk. He had just rounded the corner, and in the way he hesitated, turning his head side to side, she knew that she had only a moment before he started running after her. She lunged for the door, jammed the key into the lock, and slipped inside, holding the dog by his collar now, bringing him with her. She closed the door quietly, not wanting to signal where she was, and pushed the bolt. She had to lean against the door a moment to catch her breath. Her lungs were on fire, her heart exploding in her chest. The dog rubbed against her legs and emitted little whimpering noises, as if he grasped that whatever was wrong, they were in it together.

She removed the leash, then flattened herself against the door and peered through the tiny view hole. He had passed her house, and now he stood on the sidewalk in front of the neighbor's, looking up and down the street. He had on a black ski hat, pulled low over his forehead. His face was distorted, filled with angry frustration, the face of a creature with a long nose and tight lips, half man, half monster. She watched until he moved down the sidewalk and into the shadows.

She'd left the light on upstairs, and a thin stream of light ran down the stairs and across the tile floor in front of the door. A Dave Brubeck CD was playing softly. She didn't turn on any other lights. There could be no changes, nothing to catch his attention and bring him to her town house. She went into the kitchen and threw the bolt on the back door. There were narrow alleys of gravel between the clusters of town-homes. The dog run was on the south side. But he might take one of the other alleys, come through the backyards. There were no fences, thanks to the homeowners' association, which had decreed that the tiny yards should flow like a dry gravel river along the back of the townhomes and create an illusion of space and privacy. It had practically taken an act of God to get the dog run approved, that and a phone call to the associa-tion president from her ex-husband.

She stared at the window. Moonlight winked in the black glass. She hadn't pulled the blinds—God, why hadn't she pulled the blinds? He could see her moving about in the faint light. She started to pull down the blind, then stopped. No changes. Her saliva tasted like acid.

She opened a cabinet, took out a bottle of Wild Turkey, and sloshed an inch or so into a juice glass next to the sink. She took a long drink, then backed across the kitchen, picked up the phone, and tapped out Maury's number. She cradled the phone against her ear, finished off the bourbon, and concen-trated on the buzzing noise of the ringing phone.

"Yeah? Who is it?" His voice was sleep clogged and tenta-tive, as if he were coming out of a dream and trying to adjust to a new reality.

"Maury, it's me," she said. "A man followed me home."

"What?" He was Maury now, a divorce attorney with a client he'd befriended after her divorce. "Where were you?"

"Out walking."

"Now? You know what time it is? You shouldn't be walking alone at this hour."

"Rex was with me."

"Yeah, right. Rex. You lock your doors?"

"Yes." She swallowed back the acid erupting in her throat and threw a glance across the kitchen. She'd intended to bolt the doors, but now she couldn't say for certain what she'd done. "He's still out there somewhere," she said.

"Jesus. Some pervert. I'm on my way over," Maury said. "Hang up and call the police."

Of course she should call the cops. She should have called the cops first thing. "Right," she said, but she was talking to a bleeping noise. The CD had ended. The house was quiet.

She pressed the Off key, then dialed 911, on automatic now, following directions as if she'd already done all she could to save herself and there was nothing else she had the presence of mind to do on her own.

"What is your emergency?" The woman on the line sounded as if she were at the end of a long shift. She told her that a man had followed her home.

"Did you get into your house?"

"Yes."

"Is the man still outside?"

"I think so." She could feel him outside, somewhere close. A pervert, Maury had called him. A pervert who had targeted a woman who happened to be walking her dog too late at night. He would still be looking for her. She tried to catch her breath, but it was like trying to breathe past a tightening noose.

"Where are you?"

She managed to spit out her address, then she heard the routine calmness washing through the woman's voice: A police car was on the way. She should lock her doors and not go outside.

She hung up and, feeling disembodied, floating somewhere above herself, went back into the living room and sank onto the tile floor in the corner away from the window. She pulled her knees to her chest and crossed her arms around her legs. She could feel her muscles twitching, as if they were twitching in someone else's body. God, she needed another drink. She pushed the idea away. She had to keep her mind clear; she had to think. She heard herself whispering, calling Rex. The dog skittered over, slid down beside her, and tried to fit his muzzle beneath her chin. She patted his head. "Good boy," she said. "Maury's coming."

She wasn't sure how long she sat there. A week, a month. Time had stopped. Probably no more than five minutes, she realized. Maury lived only a few blocks away in a Denver bungalow with a swing on the front porch and two strips of green lawn on either side of the walkway, all of it sloping down to the sidewalk under the shade of a big oak tree. He'd pull on a pair of jeans, stick his feet into the worn Docksiders, wake up Philip to say he'd be back soon, and drive over. Six, seven minutes at the most. She could picture him running up her walk, dark hair tousled, face puffy from sleep, the T-shirt he'd been sleeping in smashed against his chest.

Outside a car door slammed, followed by the scuff of footsteps.

She uncurled from the corner and threw herself at the door, barely aware of Rex barking and jumping about. Her hand grasped the bolt, but she stopped herself from slamming it back. She peered into the tiny circle of glass. Maury was coming up the walk, his face expanding as he got closer. He looked as she'd imagined, except for the determined look in his eyes and the rictus of resolve in the muscles of his jaw.

She pushed the bolt back and yanked open the door. "Thank God," she said in the instant before everything exploded. It happened so fast that, even later when she tried to place the events in the order in which they occurred, she couldn't be certain what had happened first. Maury had started to come inside, and she'd stepped back, pulling the door with her. Yes, that was how it went. Except that Maury had burst inside, as if he'd been shot from a cannon. Or had that happened first and then—with the shock of it—the door was slammed back? The man dressed in black blurred like a shadow flitting across her vision and threw himself against Maury. Maury toppled like an oak felled in a field. The sound of Rex barking came from far away, background noise as Maury rolled over, jumped to his feet and swung a thick arm against the figure dancing about, a grotesque marionette, swinging and dodging Maury's fists.

Then they were locked together, stumbling about the living room, breathing hard. The coffee table crashed onto its side; a chair toppled backward. She staggered toward them, looking for something to grab, some weapon. She spotted the lamp on the side table, but before she could reach it, they crashed into the table and the lamp fell, shattering into minuscule pieces of glass that spilled like marbles across the tile. Rex was circling about, barking and yelping. Finally Maury wrenched himself out of the man's grasp. He rocked backward before he threw a fist into the man's chest.

Then the man rocked backward. Yes, that was how it happened. There had been a moment when she'd thought that it was over, that the intruder would collapse. He staggered about, throwing his head around, and that must have been what she was watching because she hadn't seen him pull the gun out of the pocket of his bulky jacket. Yet he was pointing the black gun at Maury. Maury moved backward, both arms thrust out, as if he could have deflected the bullet that exploded in his chest. She blinked at the deadened report of the gunshot, when she had expected an explosion like an accumulation of all the noise in the world. Maury fell backward, head and shoulders hitting the floor in the doorway to the kitchen, blood blossoming across the front of his white T-shirt, running across the tile.

She pressed herself down behind the upturned table near the foot of the stairs and held her breath, terrified that the sound of her breathing would lead him to her. She could hear the small noise of Rex's whimpers coming from the corner where they'd waited for Maury. Her eyes were glued to the man standing over Maury, head cocked to one side, the knitted cap pushed up into a peak. At first she thought he was looking for her, then she heard the sirens and realized that he was listening. He glanced around, and she moved back into the shadows along the wall, still holding her breath. She felt as if a stone were crushing her chest.

A door slammed somewhere, followed by a cacophony of voices, neighbors yelling across the yards: "What's going on?" "You hear that?" And against the cacophony, the swelling noise of sirens.

The intruder swung about and ran through the front door.

She crawled around the table and across the cold tile to Maury. The black hole in his chest was like a crater sucking everything into it: T-shirt and blood and life, as if Maury himself would disappear into the crater. And yet it was his blood and life that were pouring out, turning the white T-shirt black.

She tried to find a pulse in his neck, her fingers as numb as dried twigs quivering against his warm skin. She was barely aware of Rex crouching next to her, or of the black boots and dark trousers of police officers moving toward them.

New in hardcover from
New York Times bestselling author
MARGARET COEL

BLOOD
MEMORY

"She's a master." —Tony Hillerman

Catherine McLeod is an investigative reporter for the
Journal, one of Denver's major newspapers. Her relent-
less pursuit of the truth in writing her stories has earned
her accolades—and enmity.

After narrowly escaping an assailant's bullet in her own
home, Catherine is convinced by her ex-husband to stay
at his family's ranch until the gunman is caught. When
she uncovers not only a conspiracy involving her ex's
wealthy family and state politicians, but also some startling facts about her own heritage, her would-be killer
becomes all the more desperate to find her.

DON'T MISS

THE
DROWNING MAN

"One of [Coel's] best."
—*The Denver Post*

By *NEW YORK TIMES* BESTSELLING AUTHOR
MARGARET COEL

———————————

Arapaho attorney Vicky Holden and
Father John O'Malley find themselves immersed
in the dark underbelly of the illegal market
for Indian relics.

———————————

"Spirits, stolen artifacts, soul searching—
this mystery has it all."
—*The Santa Fe New Mexican*

M273T0408

Penguin Group (USA) Online

What will you be reading tomorrow?

Tom Clancy, Patricia Cornwell, W.E.B. Griffin,
Nora Roberts, William Gibson, Robin Cook,
Brian Jacques, Catherine Coulter, Stephen King,
Dean Koontz, Ken Follett, Clive Cussler,
Eric Jerome Dickey, John Sandford,
Terry McMillan, Sue Monk Kidd, Amy Tan,
John Berendt…

You'll find them all at
penguin.com

*Read excerpts and newsletters,
find tour schedules and reading group guides,
and enter contests.*

Subscribe to Penguin Group (USA) newsletters
and get an exclusive inside look
at exciting new titles and the authors you love
long before everyone else does.

PENGUIN GROUP (USA)
us.penguingroup.com